Dear Jess
This boo_
about friends' and I
adore you and love our
friendship!

Lyrics Heart & Soul

By: Anne Marie Citro

Your never stop
amazing me your and
Old soul in a young
body. So wise!
I love you hear & Soul

Love alway & forever

16/16.

Editing by: C&D Editing
Cover created by: Ravenne Villanueva
ravennedesign@gmail.com

Table to Contents

Title Page

Copyright

Dedication

Dear Reader

Chapter 1 "Bad to the Bone" By George Thorogood

Chapter 2 "Animal I Have Become" by Three Days Grace

Chapter 3 "Glitter in the Air" by Pink

Chapter 4 "Money" by Pink Floyd

Chapter 5 "The Wind Beneath My Wings" by Bette Midler

Chapter 6 "Free Falling" by Tom Petty

Chapter 7 "Somewhere I Belong" by Linkin Park

Chapter 8 "Unsteady" by X Ambassadors

Chapter 9 "You Are Not Alone" by Lifehouse

Chapter 10 "The Sound of Silence" by Disturbed

Chapter 11 "Angels Among Us" by Alabama

Chapter 12 "Oh Darlin', What Have I Done" by The White Buffalo

Chapter 13 "Sorry" by Buckcherry

Chapter 14 "Believe" by Mumford & Sons

Chapter 15 "Secret Song" by Staind

Chapter 16 "Let It Go" by James Bay

Chapter 17 "Leather and Lace" by Stevie Nicks and Don Henley

Chapter 18 "In Your Eyes" by Peter Gabriel

Chapter 19 "Just Breathe" by Pearl Jam

Chapter 20 "Lost Boys" by Ruth B

Chapter 21 "With Arms Wide Open" by Creed

Chapter 22 "Everything I Do" by Bryan Adams

Chapter 23 "Time of My Life" by David Cook

Chapter 24 "Angel Eyes" by Jeff Healey

Chapter 25 "Heart & Soul" by Fornication

Chapter 26 "I Finally Found Someone" by Barbra Streisand and Bryan Adams

Epilogue "Home" by Blue October

Acknowledgments

Excerpt Thicker Than Blood

Dedication

This book is dedicated to all kids with special needs!
Getting to spend time with these incredible young people made me a
better person. I learned my greatest lessons in life from them. I
learned to see the world through their kind, sensitive, gentle eyes
that see the world, not how we think it should be, but how it really is.

The goodness is out there. We just have to open our hearts to the
people who can show us. You love unconditionally and your
contribution to the world, no matter how big or small, teaches more
lessons than any university. Live strong and proud!

This book is also dedicated to all the songwriters out there.
Your words bring us all to a place and time in our lives. You make
us laugh, cry, smile, and most importantly, you make us remember.
You write a whole book on one page, and expose your soul for the

world to enjoy.

Thank you!

Dear Reader,

First, I would like to thank you for reading my book. Without you, the reader, my words would have no voice.

The characters in this book haunted my thoughts and dreams for months. I love them and was so sad when I finished writing this book. I will miss them in my dreams. I am proud of all my characters.

Each chapter has a song that is important to the characters or their story. I encourage you to listen to them and read the lyrics to understand the depth of their meanings. We all have songs that bring us to a place and time in our lives. These songs are their strengths, weakness, fears, and hopes.

Enjoy!

Anne Marie Citro

Under Her Wings

Lyrics Heart & Soul

Please visit my website: annemariecitro.com

Or contact me at: annemariecitro@gmail.com

Chapter 1

"Bad to the Bone"

By George Thorogood

The bailiff asks everyone in the courtroom to stand. "The court of the Second Judicial Circuit Traffic/Criminal Division is now in session. The Honourable Judge Linda Belmore will preside."

The judge finished walking up to her podium and took her seat. "Thank you, bailiff. I assume all parties are present and ready to hear my sentence?"

"Yes, Your Honour," replied the Crown, Matthew Fairchild.

"Yes, Your Honour," replied the criminal defence lawyer, James Quinn.

"Then I will proceed. Let me start by saying I have closed this court to the public for obvious reasons. The accused would usually remain standing throughout sentencing, but I am going to ask all parties to sit. I have a few things I would like to say to Mr. Vaughn."

Ryder Vaughn looked at his lawyer in surprise as he sat. He

knew his fame wouldn't help in sentencing. He had a feeling it might work against him this time. What was the worst they could do to him? Throw him in jail for a year or two? At this point in his life, he didn't give a fuck if they locked him up and threw away the key.

"Mr. Vaughn, you have been charged a second time within a year with racing/stunt driving and dangerous driving. One is under the traffic code section 168 racing/stunt driving, and the other is under the criminal code offence 117 of dangerous driving.

"Sir, these are serious offences, and you obviously have not learned your lesson after just acquiring your licence back three months ago. Therefore, I had to think long and hard on what type of sentencing would make an impact on you. Mr. Quinn has argued that, because of your fame, it would be unadvisable to place you in the prison system, and regrettably, I agree. However, if you don't agree to my terms, you will in fact find yourself incarcerated."

She busied herself with looking over papers as she continued, "Your financial situation is so immense that a substantial fine under the laws I must abide will be no punishment. Taking away your licence has no bearing—you just hire drivers. So, sir, I have a very unconventional sentence to hand down to you." To this statement, she finally looked up at him.

"I have researched the letter of the law on this sentence, and consulted appellate court findings on the chance you could appeal my sentence. I believe, without a shadow of a doubt, that it would be impossible to overturn. If you choose to go the other route, that is a criminal charge of ten years. Of course, you might get parole after serving one-third of your sentence. But with a criminal conviction, you would be unable to enter the United States ever again, which would not be good for your career or fans.

"Please keep in mind, if you choose that, I would have to place you in protective confinement because of your fame. You would only have access to the outdoors for thirty minutes a day, and no access to the gym. A third of your sentence will feel like thirty years. Or, you will take the sentence I have been working on and hopefully gain some insight.

"Mr. Vaughn, you have a blatant disregard for your life, and lack of judgment which, in turn, makes you a danger to yourself and possibly others. I came about my decision after reading the letters submitted for your character reference. The one that impacted me the most was from Sick Kids Hospital." Now she flashed him a look that could only be described as regret or disappointment with a flicker of hope.

"I was shocked and instantly moved by the fact that you donated a million dollars a year for the last nine years of your career. Although that wasn't what touched me the most—anyone with any wealth can donate to a hospital, if for no other reason than to get a tax break. It wasn't until I read further and discovered that you donate your time—two weeks in the winter and summer—to teach sick children how to play the drums. I was also impressed you had a soundproof music room built for the hospital and furnished it with instruments.

"All of your donations of time, money, and equipment to the hospital has been strictly anonymous. I came to realize you have a deep connection with this hospital and its patients. I don't know the reason, but I do applaud it. You help children you have never met, but you still have no respect for the life you were given.

"Therefore, my sentence is as follows. You are to report to Reach Within Centre for individuals with special needs for a term of ten months where you will volunteer and shadow a CYW—a child and youth worker.

"I understand you have a police check from the volunteer work at the hospital. It will start in September and will continue until June. You will not be teaching music; you will be in the classroom, working under the direction of Frankie Moratti, assisting students with life skills.

"I am very familiar with this facility and the work they do with exceptional children and adults. It's a wonderful organization, and I believe they will teach you the value of life in every capacity.

"You will retain your anonymity since people don't know your real name. You will work eight-thirty to three-thirty, five days a week. If you renege on this agreement, you will be incarcerated with the time you have spent deducted from your sentence and a criminal record will be instated. I will give you fifteen minutes to make your decision. Choose wisely."

As the judge stood, the bailiff asked everyone to stand as the judge exited the courtroom.

Ryder was stunned into silence. When he regained his senses, he responded, "Can she do this to me? Can she force me to work with mental kids?"

His lawyer turned towards him. "This is very unconventional, but she has done her homework. And really, it's not as bad as I expected. You're the client, so the decision is yours, but I urge you to take this deal. Otherwise, you will never play another concert in the US, and you will never be able to volunteer again with a criminal charge."

"Fuck!" Ryder couldn't believe it. He wasn't sure what sentence was worse. He thought he was probably as retarded as the kids. What could he possibly learn from them? Honestly, if he ever became like them, he wished someone would just put him out of his misery. Not only that, but the judge was putting him with some little, greasy Italian pussy boy. Frankie Moratti. Fucking perfect.

"Watch what you say, or you're going to blow it before you have a chance to accept the deal," his lawyer rebuked his outcry "Does this mean you're going to accept it?"

"Like I have a choice." Ten months were going to feel like a life sentence. Nevertheless, his band had a tour set for next year, and he couldn't screw the guys out of their livelihood. "Yeah, I'll take the sentence."

***

Ryder left the courthouse and got his affairs in order. He had moved into the condo he purchased in Toronto, and had two of his cars and his favourite Harley transported to it. He might have to work in suburbia, but he sure as hell wasn't going to hang out there afterwards. He didn't sleep great at night and tended to hang out at strip clubs. He also didn't cook, so he needed access to lots of restaurants.

His condo had a gym, but he needed more than the building provided, so he joined a huge gym by the centre. He could go in the morning and probably after school hours. He would need some way to excise his demons after working with mental kids all day.

He went for the touring bike, figuring he would spend his weekend cruising. This was the last weekend he had left before reporting for duty at the centre, and he was going to party hard and hopefully dull a few brain cells. He sure as hell didn't need them.

***

Ryder arrived at the centre an hour early, unsure how long it would take to get to suburbia. He knew Mr. Fucking Frankie Moratti, the greasy, little Italian pussy, would be writing his hours in his bi-weekly reports for the judge until his sentence was completed. Dammit!

6

As he pulled up to the centre and parked in front of a room that was already occupied, he saw a flash of burgundy whip past the window. He slowly took off his helmet, leaving his sunglasses on, as he got off his bike, all while staring into the room.

There stood the most stunning little chick with gloriously long, thick burgundy hair and porcelain white skin. She was hot, and his dick acknowledged what he was seeing with a twitch. Damn, he hoped he got to see more of her around the centre. She must be the teacher in that room.

It was only seven-thirty. Christ, these nine to fivers were dedicated. With the band, he never woke up before noon.

He walked into the building, heading towards the main office. The door was locked and the lights were off, so he decided to sit on the bench outside of it and wait.

There was a window behind the bench with the blinds closed, but he knew it was part of the room that chick was in. He heard music blaring from the room, and she was singing. Well, not singing, per se. She sounded horrible. Thankfully, she was beautiful.

He could hear the female voice pounding out lyrics about not fitting in. He knew she couldn't really feel those lyrics, because she would fit in anywhere.

Ryder was a lyrics man. He wrote a lot of lyrics for the band's songs, and words were important to him. He didn't speak a lot. Instead, he chose to let the lyrics do his talking. That was why he hated pop music. They just slapped words together and people bought that shit.

Holy fuck, now she was playing Bryan Adams and Barbara Streisand, singing "I Finally Found Someone." He cringed then chuckled to himself when the beauty tried to hit the high notes. Jesus Christ, she had better keep her day job.

He was relieved when the song ended. His ears felt like they were bleeding.

He heard the door open around the corner as the beauty went barreling past him to the office door, completely oblivious to his presence, still mumbling the words to the song she had just decimated. She looked like she was on a mission as she tried to open the door, surprised when it didn't budge.

"Oh, David, you must be out of practice after the summer. You usually open up the office before I get here," she mumbled to herself as she turned then squealed at the sight of Ryder sitting there. "Holy moly, you scared me half to death!" She held her hand to her chest as she walked towards Ryder. "Are you waiting to get into the office? They won't be here for half an hour or so, and the custodian obviously hasn't opened the door yet."

Ryder moved his glasses down his nose as he looked her up and down, blown away. This beauty had it all: whiskey coloured eyes with a ring of black lashes; flawless, smooth skin; and a full bottom lip with a delicate, thinner upper lip coated in sable coloured lipstick.

He could envision them wrapped around his cock. *Twitch.*

She was wearing a feminine off-white jersey shirt with three quarter sleeves. Its scooped neck was tight on her bust with a satin ribbon woven tightly under her breasts. The shirt continued down and flared out to mid-thigh. Khaki green capris dressed her legs with dainty flat shoes on her feet. She also wore a chunky stone necklace in the shape of a dragonfly. She was captivating and delicate.

"Ah-hem."

As Ryder pushed his glasses back up, in a deep voice laced with undertones, he said, "Sorry. I was admiring your necklace."

"Yeah … okay. Well, the office will be opened soon," the beauty replied rather peevishly as she quickly turned and stomped back towards her classroom.

She switched the music to some man-bashing shit, and Ryder smirked. He couldn't think of the artist's name, but she was the truest form of ball buster ever born. She always wrote about her on-again, off-again hubby.

Ryder respected the singer to the ninth degree. She could write a song like no other pissed off broad. Plus, she was a tad psycho, and he admired that quality equally as much. Despite that, he couldn't help thinking he must have made the beauty angry. Not a great start to the next ten months.

"Hi, can I help you with something?" the administrator of the centre walked in after twenty minutes and greeted Ryder.

"Are you Mrs. Ramara? I'm Ryder Vaughn. You should be expecting me."

"Oh, yes. Sorry. Welcome to Reach Within." She stuck her hand out to shake Ryder's. "Please follow me into my office."

He entered her tastefully decorated office, where there was a big desk facing the door with two chairs in front of it. Off to the side, she had a smaller table with four comfortable looking chairs around it.

"Please take a seat, Mr. Vaughn. I am the administrator of the educational part of Reach Within. Today is the first day after the summer break, meaning it will be busy. I'm glad you're here early so I can give you the rundown and our expectations of you during your stay." She said "stay" like Ryder was on vacation, instead of the living hell that would be his existence for the next ten months.

"Mr. Vaughn, I don't mince words, so let's get right down to it." Mrs. Ramara put on her serious face. "I've had many conversations with Judge Belmore about your situation, and I'm going out on a limb by accepting you to work with the most vulnerable sector in society. She and I are both putting a lot of trust in you, and I advise you to take it seriously.

"This centre is highly regarded, and we have an impeccable reputation to uphold. The work we do here is important, and the students have a lot to deal with. I expect your behaviour to be professional always.

"I understand you will remain anonymous, and refuse any press interviews. I'm the only one who knows your true identity and will keep your secret. But in return, you will not discuss any students outside of this facility. Confidentiality is a must, as I am sure you can understand.

"To be in this facility, the students all have to have a minimum of three disabilities, one being developmentally delayed. Most of the students are in this facility because they have severe behavioural issues, or are medically fragile and need specialized equipment. Our staff is trained in behaviour management and crisis intervention, and are very good at what they do. In fact, the teaching staff is top notch and work their tails off with very little recognition or rewards. I am telling you this because they deserve respect. They work in an extreme environment and are unfathomably dedicated to their students.

"Judge Belmore and I both decided to have you shadow and support Frankie Moratti. Frankie is dedicated, kind, and compassionate. The students love and trust her, and for good reason. I'll let you discover that on your own.

"I spoke to Frankie last week about your situation. However, she is unaware of who you are. Frankie was more than willing to take you on and made the preparations needed. I do not want you to have any physical contact with any of the students—leave that to Frankie. You are not allowed to intervene under any circumstances.

Do you understand?"

"Yes," he replied, knowing he wouldn't intervene if he could. He would leave that to Frankie boy.

"Good, then without further delay, I will call Frankie and introduce you. Then I'll touch base with you later. Do you have any questions?"

"No."

"Okay, then, Mr. Vaughn. I understand this will be daunting and will be overwhelming to begin with, but I believe that, in one month, you will have a totally different outlook on this centre than you have this week."

Mariana picked up the phone and dialed an extension. "Good morning, Frankie, and welcome back ... I was wondering if you could come to my office and meet Mr. Vaughn ... Great. Thank you."

Not two minutes later, a knock came to the door.

"Frankie, I would like you to meet Mr. Vaughn."

Ryder was still facing the desk and didn't turn until Mariana finished her introduction. Then he stood and turned, hoping his height and size would intimidate the little pussy boy.

He nearly toppled over the chair when he came face-to-face with the beauty he had just pissed off. He must have looked like a moron with the shock on his face as he stuck out his hand.

"Ryder. Ryder Vaughn. Pleasure to meet you, Frankie ...?"

She extended her hand with a chuckle, and his engulfed hers.

She could read his face. He thought he would be working with a man, one he hoped to intimidate with his bulk. He had met his match, because she might be small, but she could kick ass with the best of them. She had two brothers and could hold her own.

"It's actually Francesca. One of my students overheard my brother call me Frankie, and it kinda stuck. Pleasure to meet you. Follow me, and I'll get you settled."

Ryder followed the beauty back to her classroom, feeling like he was in deep shit. He couldn't take his eyes off the sway of her beautiful, curvy hips and ass. *Twitch.* He had extreme control, but she had splintered his reserve. How was he ever going to work with this beauty? Jail might have been a much better choice.

She could feel his glare on her back, thinking he wasn't happy having to follow a woman around.

"This will be yours," she said as she stopped at a locker. "You have a one-digit lock. The combination is thirteen. If you can't remember it, let me know, and I will remind you." She raised an arched brow.

The way her eyebrows curved over her eyes made them look like angel wings. *Shit.* Francesca was going to make him pay for giving her the once over. *Well, game on, sweetheart. Give it your best.*

He lifted a corner of his mouth into a semi-lopsided grin, not a smile. He never smiled. "Got it."

Wow, a man of many words. Not. Perfect, she could deal with that. Her focus was for the kids, not this beast.

Francesca's smile grew as the nickname she had just branded him with settled into her bones.

He was a very imposing man, standing closer to heaven than anyone she had ever met. He had to be six and half feet easily, and he was freaking massive. Her mom would have said he was built like a brick shit house.

His arms were huge, probably the size of her thighs. He had longish, brown, curly hair with natural gorgeous auburn highlights. His thick eyebrows were arched in way that made him look malicious, the right one having a scar through it. She was sure there was a story there.

His eyes were so dark brown they looked almost black, and they were extremely intense. His skin tone was a dark olive tone, with tattoos peeking under the sleeve of his shirt and one crawling up his neck. He had a goatee that was light brown, and a shadow of whiskers from his goatee along his jaw. Holy smokes, he was good-looking in a rough sort of way.

He reminded her of that actor, Jason Momoa, eyebrows and all. Sweet, now that would screw with her mind.

She looked up, way up, to see him with that lopsided semi-grin. He knew she was giving him the once over.

She blushed from her chest to the edge of her hairline.

"Payback?"

"Just thinking it would probably take me a few more seconds than I originally thought to take you out at the knees," she answered quickly and without much thought, knowing she was being equally as rude as he had been.

The intense moment was broken by his cackle.

"Give it your best shot."

Goddamn, she had balls bigger than most guys he knew, and a sense of humour to boot.

"Follow me into our class so I can give you the rundown on the teachers and students." She buzzed them in then went to the computer to turn down the man-bashing music. Then she grabbed some papers and sat down at a round table before the door even closed. She moved around like a bee on crack.

She got right down to business, looking at her papers. "Okay, Mr. Vaughn, Mariana and I formulated a cover to explain your presence at the centre. We decided to tell people you're here from California because you've been asked to create a similar facility in your city."

"Ryder."

She lifted her eyes to his, then quickly moved them back to her papers. "Excuse me?"

"My name is Ryder, not Mr. Vaughn."

"Okay, good. Because, unlike other places, we don't insist on the students calling us by our surnames. We are much more relaxed than the school boards.

"Julianna Kerr is the teacher in this room," she continued. "She's responsible for the curriculum, while we, the CYWs—a child and youth workers—and teaching assistants, adapt it to the students' individual needs. She is fabulous; you'll like her. We have five students."

She then went on to tell him about the other two CYWs and explained all about the students and their different diagnoses. She reiterated that, regardless of what the kids did, he was not to step in. He started getting uncomfortable with all the talk of this "hands-off policy." Really, how much damage could a head case do?

The three remaining staff members eventually entered the room. Francesca greeted them all with hugs, and then introduced Ryder to Julianna first. She was friendly, average height, a bubbly woman with strawberry blonde hair. Layla was a tall, attractive black woman with a beautiful big smile and welcoming personality. Amanda was Southern European with olive skin. She made no bones about telling Ryder how delicious he looked.

He hated forward woman like her. She thought she was all that and more—cocky and blatant. After all the lectures he had received in the last hour, he was surprised by her unprofessionalism.

"Okay, people, the busses are here," Julianna announced. "Let's

16

get this party started. Francesca, you get Mason. And just to warn you, his group home emailed and said he went off the rails on Saturday. They figure it's anxiety about a new year starting."

"Understood. Anyone hurt?" Francesca asked.

"Nope, but about seven thousand in damages. Feel out his demeanour and let me know."

" 'Kay, will do. Let's roll." Francesca gave Ryder a wave to follow her. "Just follow my lead, and I'll introduce you once I know his anxiety level." She buzzed to the busses just as quickly as before. Even with his long legs, he had trouble keeping up, meandering around all the staff and students.

He watched the seventeen-year-old kid who looked normal to him step off a bus, looking totally pissed off at the world until he spotted Francesca.

Mason was lanky, about five-nine; four-inches taller than Francesca. He had long, straight black hair with long bangs that he had to keep throwing his head back to move from his eyes..

"Hey, Mason. What's shaken, my friend?" Francesca greeted him like a long-lost friend, giving him a high-five.

"Lookin' smokin' hot, Frankie. Did you miss me?" He smiled at her with worship in his eyes.

"Always miss you, buddy. But let's not start with the inappropriate comments already, okay?" She gave him a big smile so it would seem like she wasn't reprimanding him. Smart girl.

However, her remark had instantly pissed him off.

"Whatever," he retorted.

She didn't let him withdraw as she linked her arm with his. "Did you have a good summer?"

"Yeah, same shit as always … like being in prison," the kid answered as they walked into the centre with many of the staff welcoming him back, which he ignored.

The kid didn't look like he had any issues, except a bad attitude, which Francesca had warned Ryder about, saying his behaviour was unpredictable. She had also told Ryder that he had been a crack baby and had Shaken Baby Syndrome. Thus, he was developmentally delayed and had a seizure disorder.

Francesca got Mason into the classroom where he grunted his hello to the teacher, then took his handheld game console out of his knapsack and started to play, ignoring everyone around him.

Francesca turned to Julianna and flashed eight fingers. Julianna nodded and headed out to warn the rest of the team that he could blow this morning.

"Frankie, who's the wrestler? New staff or a bodyguard? If you think he scares me, you're fucked," Mason said without lifting his head.

Ryder couldn't control his reaction, growling at the disrespect Mason was dishing out, "Her name is Francesca."

Francesca's eyes flew to Ryder's with a scowl of her own as she shook her head no then gave him a chin lift to indicate he should move away.

"Mason, language, buddy. And yes, he is a staff member, but he isn't teaching. He wants to build a centre like this in California, so he is here to learn from us."

Mason still didn't lift his head as he ground out, "They don't have any school for crazy freaks like us in California?"

She ignored his dig. "Mason, this is Ryder. Please put your game down for minute and say hello."

He ignored her, not acknowledging the comment about his game. Then, after about three minutes, he said, "What kind of stupid name is that, *Ryder*? Your mom must have been a junkie like mine."

Ryder's spine stiffened. This kid was a punk who was jealous of any male in Frankie's vicinity.

"Come on, Mason; let's turn this around. Don't ruin our first day back together. I missed you, and I want to hear all about your summer. Now say hi to Ryder, and let's start over, okay?" She moved over and rubbed her hand up and down his back in comfort.

When he lifted his eyes to hers, that worshipping look was back. He looked starved for her attention.

He turned to Ryder. "Hey."

"Hey," Ryder responded, figuring if Mason could move on, then so could he.

Francesca had said at least a dozen times this morning not to take anything personally. Therefore, he wouldn't. Still, he didn't like this kid, not at all. Francesca had said she loved him. He wasn't sure how she could, or why.

Julianna looked at Francesca, and Francesca smiled. Their silent language inferred that Mason had been defused.

The door opened, and four more students walked in with the rest of the staff. They definitely looked challenged to Ryder.

A blond, curly-haired kid ran in the room and threw his arms around Francesca. "Give me some tongue, Frankie." He tried with all his might to get his tongue near Francesca's mouth.

Frankie laughed as she pulled him off. "Theo, let me look at you. How are you? How was your summer?"

"Give me some tongue, and I'll tell you."

"No. Nice try. How many other people did you try to tongue on your way in?"

Theo grinned from ear-to-ear. "Everyone. But I like your mouth the best." He licked his lips.

"I bet you say that to all the girls." She turned towards Ryder. "Theo, this is Ryder. Say hello and shake his hand."

Ryder backed away, nervous the scrawny, little boy would try to tongue him. *Gross.*

"Fornication with elation, Ry Herr!" Theo said as he held out his fist for a bump.

Ryder was dumbstruck. The fucking kid knew his band's name

was Fornication, and his stage name was Ry Herr? *Fuck!*

He fist-pumped the kid and waited for the backlash. But Theo just turned away like he didn't have a clue, on to better things, like trying to tongue every chick in the room.

"Sorry, Ryder. He says random stuff like that all the time," Julianna told him.

Ryder just nodded, relief sweeping through him. They didn't know the kid had him pegged.

He was introduced to the other three kids. Veeta was an Indian girl who walked with canes due to a severe limp, and she had a slurred language he couldn't understand, yet everyone else seemed to. Katrina was a pretty, little redheaded thing, who didn't even acknowledge his existence. And lastly, Taz, who walked in holding his ears, humming loudly.

Fuck. If he wasn't crazy now, he sure as hell would be by the end of his sentence.

At the end of the day, Ryder was so mentally exhausted he couldn't even go to the gym. First thing he did when he got home was grab a beer and turn on his music. "Bad to the Bone" by George Thorogood blared out of his speakers.

Since the day he heard the song, he thought it best described him. Great lyrics. But those kids gave it new meaning.

Chapter 2

"Animal I Have Become"

By Three Days Grace

The first month had passed, and Mariana Ramara had been right; Ryder did have a different point of view on the centre. His respect for most of the staff had increased tenfold. It took a special person to work with special needs kids. They were extremely patient and kind, each one having a sense of humour. He swore it was because, if they didn't laugh, they would cry. Better to laugh.

His coworkers were not paid a lot of money, which was a crime. People were willing to pay millions to hear his music or see him in person, yet the people who looked after the neediest children in the world were paid peanuts. How was it that society placed so much value in what he did, yet the people who nurtured and cared for the medical misfits of the world weren't even given safety gear to protect themselves from the people they were caring for? There was no justice in the world.

The students had slowly wormed their way into his heart ... what little heart he had. Ryder was mostly drawn to Mason. The kid had an anger management issue he could relate to.

Mason hated his mother with every fibre of his being, and that was something Ryder could also relate to. He hated his father with as much passion as Mason hated his mother. Both he and Mason were blamed as children for being the way they were, yet they were a product of the people they blamed the most.

Mason and Ryder also both totally and completely worshipped Francesca. They competed for her attention. Good or bad, they would take what they could get.

Ryder wasn't a talker. He preferred to listen and observe, having been told since an early age that he would never say anything people wanted to hear. So, he didn't. Most of his discussions happened in his mind. He had never found anyone he wanted to share his thoughts with, anyway. Until the day he met Beauty.

He came to the centre early every morning just so he could be alone with Francesca. But before he went in, he stood outside their classroom, listening as she bastardized every song she sang, judging her moods by those songs. They didn't talk a lot, but when they did, he cherished the thoughts she shared with him. She was so pure and good, he felt like a better person simply by being in her presence. It empowered him; made him want to be someone she would be friends with.

She was a puzzle he couldn't figure out. Like a Rubik's cube, colourful, yet complex. Or a book with beautiful pictures but invisible writing on the pages.

Francesca was so loving and freely shared her emotions with the students, yet she was incredibly self-conscious outside the classroom. She loved to ask people about their lives, yet she rarely shared details of her own. Many would seek her out for advice, but she never asked anyone for help.

Ryder had watched her closely, noticing how she never looked a coworker in the eye, averting questions they asked about her personal life. Then she would redirect the conversation back to them, almost like she wasn't deserving, or that maybe they might learn something about her that she wasn't comfortable sharing. She also never ate in the staff room, always eating alone on the benches outside, and she never spoke at assemblies.

Francesca did have a close-knit group of girlfriends who worked in different areas of Reach Within. They called each other The Sistas of the United Nations, and they drank their beloved Caesars every "Caesar Friday." Other than the core group of five women, though, she didn't appear to have any other friends.

At the same time, everyone at the school would say they were Francesca's friend. Bus drivers, secretaries, custodians—they all made a point to seek her out. She just made you feel that special.

He observed jealousy from female coworkers. Those who

smiled to her face couldn't wait to put her down when her back was turned. Ryder knew the women were vying for his attention, intending to use Francesca to get to him. Those broads were pretty faces; fake, puffed up lips; nice tits; tight asses; and too soulless to understand the true meaning of friendship.

The disadvantaged kids at school understood the real Francesca. She knew every student by name and high-fived them or hugged them as they passed her in the halls. And she stood patiently while students with very little vocabulary spoke, never rushing them, and then responded patiently.

Most of the students weren't capable of waiting in line, yet they all did when it came to gaining her attention. Even the most despondent, medically fragile students would smile, giggle, or track her with their eyes when she was around. Everybody wanted a piece of Francesca, yet she shared so little and hid herself so well.

The greatest gift she gave them was her laughter. Ryder would hear her laugh and knew Francesca had just made some kid's day.

Ryder wanted just a little bit of what she gave the kids. He would do anything if she would just look at him with her big, beautiful smile. He would be in Heaven if she wanted to spend time with him.

He couldn't believe he was jealous of the students, but he knew it was true. He wanted some of the sweetness directed solely on him. Though she was too good for him, he would take any scrap she was willing to throw his way. Something had to change.

He spent all weekend at the gym, working his muscles while trying to figure out how to get closer to her. He was getting calluses on his hands from the amount of times he jacked-off to visions of her. He was going to break down the wall she had erected around herself gently, by removing one brick at a time, slowly and quietly so she didn't notice. Today's goal was to find out what she did after work, how she enjoyed her time off.

Ryder walked into the room like he did every day and turned down the speakers on the computer. Francesca turned at the interruption.

"Hey."

She smiled. "Good morning, Ryder. How was your weekend?"

"Uneventful, yet still tired," he responded. "Yours?"

"Good, thank you. I want to warn you about today."

He slightly smirked. She had answered his question, then diverted any discussion regarding herself by changing subject, all in the matter of one breath.

"In a minute," he interrupted. "First, tell me one detail about your Sunday."

She quirked her head to the side and drew her eyebrows together in confusion. "What do you mean by *one detail*? I'm not sure what you're asking?"

Damn, she could try the patience of a saint.

"What *specifically* did you do yesterday?"

Ryder had taken her for a loop. He had strung more words together in this conversation than he had since he had started at Reach Within. She wasn't sure why he was asking this of her suddenly or where his verboseness was coming from. He had never seemed that interested before.

He was a methodical man. Most people couldn't see through his rough, good-looking exterior, but Francesca knew quite a bit lurked under all that muscle. She had watched and learned a lot from him, and he never missed a beat. He had the pulse of the school under his fingertips.

"I really need you to pay attention to my warning about today, and then we can talk about my Sunday."

"No." He folded his arms in front of him, looking determined and intimidating. "First, tell me what you did yesterday. Then I will listen to your warning."

"Ryder," she said on a sigh of frustration. "I don't mean to be rude, but I don't take direction from you. You take it from me."

"I do take direction from you ... during work hours. Work hasn't begun, Beauty. Have the decency to answer my question like I am worthy of an answer," he growled out, not allowing her to push him away.

Ever so slowly, her look of bewilderment was replaced by anger. "Are you kidding me? You start out with a fake compliment,

27

and then make it seem like I am better than you?" That was bullshit, and he knew it. "Are these your true colours coming out?"

Man, she looked hot when she was pissed. He could feel the anger rolling off her, and it was making him hard. *Twitch.*

"Don't say things I don't mean." He held his hands out to the side in apology. "You're beautiful. Part of your beauty is that you don't have a fucking clue. You share yourself with everyone else, yet freak when I want an answer to one simple question? Is it too much to ask? I have no life here, Francesca." With that admission, he shrugged and slipped his hands in his pockets, feeling vulnerable. "No friends, no family, no activities outside of this centre."

She deflated, all the wind knocked out of her sails.

He was right; she had never asked him about his life or what he did outside of the centre. The truth was, she knew he was doing community service hours, and she had unintentionally judged him for that. Not once had she tried to get to know the man.

She knew firsthand that not everyone who had trouble with the law was bad. Sometimes they were in the wrong place, at the wrong time.

Jeez. She really was self-centred and insensitive.

"I'm so sorry. I have been totally insensitive and ignorant to you. I was so caught up in my own life that—"

Ryder took three giant steps towards her, tipped her chin up with his finger, and pushed her hair out of her face with his other hand. He saw shame and hurt in her eyes. He liked her angry, but he didn't want this.

"Not your job to look after my feelings. You have enough people depending on you. I should never have said that." He cleared his throat, uncomfortable with his next words. "I guess I'm just lonely and took it out on you.

"I've watched you for a month. You have passion." He chuckled, thinking how Mason and him had a lot in common. "Just wanted your attention and tried to get it any way I could." He shrugged.

Still embarrassed, Francesca pulled out of his grip and turned so she could regroup. When she turned back, she said, "Let's start again. Good morning, Ryder. How was your weekend?" She smiled the smile he had been waiting for all month, but she kept her eyes averted.

She was hiding shit; he knew it. However, he decided he had pushed enough for one day.

"Morning, Francesca. Mine was quiet. Tell me about yours. Eyes on me," he demanded.

Her eyes sprang open, realizing she was still being rude. "Sorry. It won't happen again." She gave him her eyes, and what beautiful eyes they were. "I had a busy weekend. *Yesterday*"—she emphasized—"I went for a drive up north to visit my dad and was back to start my other job by noon."

He was surprised she had another job. He knew CYWs didn't make great money, but he had assumed it would be enough to survive on.

"Another job? What is it?"

"Well, it's kind of complicated. Are you sure you want to hear?"

"I don't ask things I don't want to know."

"Okay, then. The community living part of the centre posts extra positions when parents request it. A year and a half ago, there was a posting for a live-in healthcare worker who could cook and do laundry. I applied for it, and now I help three young men live independently. I live over their garage in an apartment, and I cook and do laundry for them so they can all live independently together. Their parents share the expenses and pay me.

"They have a cleaning lady come in once a week. If they have any troubles, they call me, and I go over and solve them. Scotty, Shawn, and William all have menial jobs and are graduates of this school.

"I love to cook, and I also cook for my brothers, so I split the grocery bill in half. I pay for my family, and the parents pay for the boys. It works out great, and the money comes in real handy." She winced at letting the last part out.

"How do you do it? I'm exhausted after a day here."

"Sometimes, you do what you must to survive." She dropped her eyes again. The action made him aware that she had slipped up;

said something she didn't want him knowing.

He had his secrets, too; so who was he to question hers? Eventually, she would trust him enough to share all her secrets. He would make damn sure of it.

"So, you love to cook. I love to eat ... takeout. Can't make toast if my life depended on it." He smirked.

That was the closest to a smile she had ever seen from him, except for the day Theo almost got his tongue in Ryder's mouth. Theo had tricked him into bending down by whispering. Then, when Ryder had bent over to ask him to repeat his question, *wham*! Any closer and Ryder might have tasted Theo's lunch. She didn't think a beast that big could move so fast. She had laughed so hard she nearly peed herself, and that had just encouraged Theo to try more often.

Ryder loved watching Francesca laugh, but he had scowled when it was at his expense. Lesson learned: these kids were way smarter than him.

Francesca knew he was giving her a free pass by not asking about her comment. She had made a mistake not being nicer to this man.

"I can't imagine eating takeout all the time. How are you in such great shape?"

"You think I look chiselled?"

She rolled her eyes on a huff. "We are back to day one, I see."

"No, only pulling that little leg of yours."

31

She put her hands on her hips. "There is nothing little about me. Maybe if I laid off the pasta and cannoli—"

"You shittin' me?" He looked incredulous. "You're tiny and delicate."

She lowered her eyes again, whispering, "In my dreams."

"Francesca, eyes up here."

She slowly lifted her eyes. He could clearly read she didn't believe one word he had said, which was weird because she saw beauty in every kid in this school.

He wished she could see herself through his eyes.

"What's this about warning me?" He quickly changed the topic.

Twice now he had given her a free pass and didn't push. She had never met anyone like him.

"Well, we are in for a bad couple of days with the students, so I wanted to forewarn you."

"You got a crystal ball I should know about?" He reverted back to the Ryder she had been mentoring.

"No. Tomorrow is a full moon, and it really affects the kids."

"I call bullshit." Ryder rubbed his hand along his goatee, questioning her sanity.

"Seriously, full moons affect a lot of people. Ask any maternity nurse. She'll tell you more babies are born on or around a full moon. It's a known fact that even emergency rooms are busier during that time. I'll bet you five bucks we have an incident by lunchtime."

"I'll do you one better. Loser buys lunch," Ryder suggested, hoping to get to spend more time with her.

"Uh ... I only have five bucks on me, but I brought lunch for today and tomorrow. You can have one of those. Shake on it." She held out her hand, and Ryder took it, not releasing her hand for a minute or so due to the sparks he felt flying between them, something he had never experienced before.

Finally, he let go when he realized she was trying to tug her hand out of his.

Just as he went to apologize, Amanda walked in, noticing the tension.

"What's going on in here?" she asked like she had walked in on her best friend cheating with her boyfriend.

Francesca blushed, embarrassed. For what? A hand shake?

Ryder saw red.

"Nothin'. Doesn't involve you." He was back to clip responses. He couldn't stand the girl. She was loud, intrusive, and believed she was a star at her job, which she wasn't.

"Whatever. If you can't tell me, then it's not appropriate at the centre," she bit back, but with a smile so she appeared to be joking. They both knew she wasn't.

Amanda was the biggest gossip at the centre. By lunch, everyone would assume Francesca had been inappropriate with him.

Just as Ryder was about to tell Amanda to back off, Julianna stepped through the door.

"I have a feeling it's going to get wild in here today, so put your war paint on and get ready for battle. Busses are here. Let's do this."

Ryder and Francesca silently made their way out to the busses.

"Hey, Mason, what's shaking, besides my big backend?" Francesca joked, trying desperately to set the tone for the day at her own expense.

"Fuck off, Frankie. It's not funny," Mason said as he pushed past her, knocking her off balance.

Christ, the women were right; the kids coming off the busses were crazier than usual.

Ryder stepped into Mason's path. "Not cool, dude. Her name is Francesca. And she deserves better."

Mason threw his bag down on the ground and got into Ryder's space. "What are you going to do? Clothesline me, macho man? Fuck you, too!"

Francesca, seeing three male CYWs approaching, jumped into action.

"I got it. One of you go tell Julianna to clear the room. Ryder, step back!" She calmed her voice and stepped between Mason and Ryder. "Mason, look at me. You and I are okay. We don't want to start our day like this. Come on, buddy; let's go in and start fresh. Take my hand and calmly walk into school. Please, Mason."

Mason was breathing heavily, wanting a fight. But the pleading look on Frankie's face and her softly spoken words made him stop for a minute.

He kicked his knapsack, grabbed Frankie's hand, and walked into the school, kicking a locker along his way and denting it, as Francesca tried to talk him down.

Ryder was close on their heels. He wasn't comfortable with this little slip of a woman trying to control a postal kid.

Julianna had the classroom door open. She gave Francesca a look, and Francesca nodded her head.

In the classroom, Mason walked over to his desk and flipped it, causing Ryder to take a defensive pose, ready to take on the little punk.

Julianna motioned for Ryder to leave, but he shook his head, negating that idea. When she did it again, he again shook his head.

Was she crazy? He wasn't leaving two women in there with an out of control kid.

When Mason walked to the next desk and flipped it, Francesca started talking to the kid.

"Mason, come on. I get it. You're pissed. But talk to me. Let me help."

"Fuck off, Frankie! I don't want to hurt you. *Get out!*"

Francesca got her cue from Julianna to leave the room when Mason went back to destroying the classroom, and Ryder followed.

Mason was in a blind rage by the time they had cleared the

room. Everything in his path was thrown as they watched from the windows by the door.

"What set him off this time?" Mrs. Ramara asked as she joined their little pow-wow.

"Came off the bus bent," Francesca answered. "You could see it in his eyes. He was gearing for a fight. It's a full moon."

Mariana huffed. "I forgot. I guess I'm going to have a busy day. We got lucky last month since it fell over the long weekend before school started."

They stood there, watching for twenty minutes. Ryder was blown away. The kid was destroying everything in his path, and they were blaming the moon cycle? The kid needed a good beating to put him in his place.

Eventually, Mason started to slow down, tired now that he had done a lot of damage.

"I'm going in," Francesca declared.

Ryder grabbed her arm. "Like hell you are."

Mariana scowled at his hand on Frankie's arm. "She's doing her job, Mr. Vaughn. If you can't handle it, then go to the library with the other students and staff."

"I'm not leaving her after everything that kid just did."

Francesca could see the feral look in his eyes. He was terrified for her. He just didn't understand how these kids could lose it on a dime, and then once it was done, it was done and they moved on.

Francesca knew one month had not exposed him to enough, but if he made it through this first major blow out, he would learn. She also didn't want to jeopardize his sentence with Judge Belmore.

"Ryder, I'm okay, I promise. Mason is okay now. I have to reach him in the downwards spiral to see if I can prevent it from happening again. If he starts to lose it, I'll get out. Promise." When she saw she wasn't reaching him, she said, "Look, you can't blame him. It's the result of the brain damage done to him as a baby. This isn't his fault. It's not that he is a bad kid; he's just the product of a bad life. Trust me to do what's right for him and me."

Ryder let go of her arm. Her words had hit him in the gut. He almost thought for a second she was referring to him. Furthermore, funny enough, he did trust her, probably more than anyone he had ever met.

As she entered the classroom, Ryder's heart rate soared. He clenched his fists, praying he had made the right decision to let her go in there.

"You done, buddy? You want to talk? Or how about a hug?" He heard Francesca ask through the cracked open door.

Was she fucking nuts? Hugging that kid right now would be like trying to hug a lion after its kill.

He broke out in a sweat, positioning his body so he was ready to get to her if she needed him.

"Mason, I'm going to join you on the floor. Is that okay?"

Mason nodded, and she sat down beside him, rubbing his leg. "Better?"

Mason threw himself into her arms and started to sob. "Sorry, Frankie. I didn't mean to hurt you."

Ryder felt like he had a baseball lodged in his throat as he watched Mason fall to pieces.

"You didn't hurt me," Francesca assured him. "You kept it under control until you got in the classroom. I'm proud of you for that. And I understand how it feels to be so angry—you don't know what to do with it—but we should figure out a better way to get your aggression out. What happened to set you off?"

"You know Trevor at my group home?" He waited until Francesca nodded. "Well, he stole the prize out of the cereal that was supposed to be mine. I hate that fucking goof. I hate having to go to bed when they tell me. I hate eating that shit food. I hate that they don't leave me alone for a second. Frankie, I just want to be left alone. Why can't anyone understand that?"

"I get it, buddy. I swear I do. What do you think if we find a quiet space at the centre, and if you feel that way when you come in, you tell me or Julianna, and we will get you there? We will give you the space you need."

"Okay, Frankie. I'm sorry I fucked up." He sobbed again, knowing he had disappointed her.

"I know you are, but there are consequences for your actions, so you need to clean up this mess. I'll help you, but we have to write a personal reflection, and you have to apologize to Ryder, okay?"

"Yeah, Frankie, but will you stay with me?"

"Sure. Let's get started so your classmates can come back in."

They stood up and started to right all the toppled furniture. Francesca knew he needed time to mull over his actions so they didn't talk.

Ryder was blown away. She was a vision, fixing all the damage Mason had done, asking for his help when something was too heavy. He saw the worship in Mason's eyes, and damn if he didn't respect her even more than he did an hour ago. She was a master at her job.

Ryder didn't say anything to her when they brought the other kids in and started fresh. He couldn't even look at her when she urged Mason to come over for his apology.

Mason's hair was in front of his eyes as he walked over to Ryder. "Sorry, man."

"Accepted. But listen, Mason; not cool with me when you swear and disrespect Francesca—she doesn't deserve it. But I also understand uncontrollable rage. You ever want to work out your frustration, I'll have some equipment brought to the gym, and I'll teach you how to work out your frustration without destroying everything."

Mason raised his head in astonishment. "Really? You'll teach me to lift weights, so I can get as big as you? Cool!"

"Two conditions." Ryder held up two fingers. "Only take your aggression out in the gym, and you commit to an exercise plan I make up for you."

"Thanks, Ryder! You rock! I can't wait to tell the guys at the group home." Mason lifted his fist to bump against Ryder's.

***

At noon, Ryder and Francesca headed out to the benches to eat. Although he had lost the bet, he would rather have her lunch today and take her out tomorrow. That way, he got to have her all to himself two days in a row.

"Doesn't look like spaghetti," he grumbled as she opened the containers full of ear-shaped pasta and a ton of vegetables.

"I didn't say it was spaghetti. This pasta recipe is my zia Concettina's. She taught me how to make it, and I love it. Not only that, Scotty and the boys love it, and I get their vegetables into them. Don't turn your nose up until you try it."

It did smell delicious, so he took a small bite.

His eyebrows shot up. "Fuckin' amazing."

She laughed as she dug in. "Well, that was a backhanded compliment if I ever heard one." Then she got serious. "Listen, Ryder, I really appreciate what you said to Mason—he's a good kid who is dealing with the backlash of really bad parents—but how are you going to get gym equipment? That will cost a fortune."

"A buddy of mine owns a gym. I'll beg him for donations," he lied, shrugging like it was no big deal, which it wasn't.

Ryder inhaled the rest of his pasta, disappointed when it ran out. He eyed Francesca's lunch, and she laughed again.

"Would you like some of mine? I won't be able to eat it all."

"If you insist."

Chapter 3

"Glitter in the Air" By Pink

Ryder had a bit of hangover after hitting up the strip club the night before, knowing he only had to get through today before the long weekend. If he felt like crap for eight hours, so what? He would deal with it. Everyone had ways of dealing with their shit, and his was to drink and hang out with loose broads.

He had never had a serious girlfriend, nor did he ever want one. He had nothing to offer a woman, and he sure as hell didn't want to be intimate. He liked to fuck hard and always from the back. He didn't even need a bed. He liked them against a wall, where their hands were away from his body. No human contact, no touching, no kissing, no cuddling. Just sweet release.

He didn't even care if the bitch got off. He needed control, and he didn't want to see their face or the look of disappointment in their eyes because he couldn't give more. He didn't even like to be sucked off unless the bitch had her hands tied. He just wanted to get his rocks off fast and furiously.

Last night, he'd had every intention of getting laid when he had entered the club, and many overzealous chicks had tried to hit on him, but they hadn't excited him. His mind had been screwing with him, so he drank more than usual, thinking how Francesca was the only person lately who could stir the monster in his pants. He hadn't screwed anyone in over a month. Good thing he had a good, strong grip and a vivid imagination.

The next morning, he took a taxi to work, still feeling the effects of the previous night.

Francesca had seen the cab pull up and wondered if Ryder's Harley had broken down. He rode that bike rain or shine, yet she knew he would use a car soon since it was getting colder.

Ryder walked up to the room and heard the same song she had been playing all week blaring from the speakers. "Glitter in the Air" by Pink. She played it nonstop, yet it made her melancholy. What was it about that song? Why was she obsessing over it?

He walked into their classroom, and she turned it down as soon as she saw him, almost like she didn't want him to hear it.

"Good morning. What happened to your bike?"

"Morning. Nothing happened to the bike." Plain and simple. No extra information given and none asked.

She looked him over, noticing how rough he looked. "Did you get an early start to the long weekend? I can give you a ride home tonight if you want?"

"What about your famous Caesar Fridays?" he asked, and then could have kicked himself in the ass. He could have had her all to himself for one whole hour, trapped, alone in the car, her scent enveloping him. That might have been enough to get him through the three days until he saw her again.

"Not tonight because of Thanksgiving. The girls are all going to spend time with their families. I met them last night after the boys were fed for a quick one so we could start the weekend off right. Now I'm free after school, and I really don't mind. Besides, I have to drive into Little Italy on St. Clair Street in Toronto to grab some freshly made ricotta cheese for my Thanksgiving lasagna."

"Only if I can go with you. We could grab a pizza or something. Payback for all the lunches you shared."

"Ryder, you never have to feel like you have to repay me. I already cook for six; what's one more? Besides, it makes me happy that not everything you eat is takeout." Then, suddenly her face changed. Her smile fell, and she bit the corner of her full, luscious bottom lip like she had just remembered something.

The monster in Ryder's pants would have gone to full-mast if he hadn't seen the overwhelming pain in her eyes.

"I have to give you a heads-up, though," she continued almost reluctantly. "I have to make a stop at the cemetery before heading downtown. It will only take a few minutes, but it has to be today."

She put on an easy smile, like a carefully constructed mask, not wanting anyone to notice her pain.

Ryder quickly realized Francesca was still hurting from the loss of someone close to her. He assumed her mother since she had only spoken of her father and brothers.

For the first time in his life, he wished he could offer more of himself. He wished he could wrap her up in his arms and hold her close. He had never comforted another soul.

"No problem. Got no other plans." He walked to the other side of the room to give her privacy with her thoughts.

She turned the music back up, sat down in front of the computer, and started to type when Ryder interrupted her.

"I have to drop off my hours. Be right back."

He just got out the door when she yelled, "Ryder, I just printed something. Will you grab it?"

He re-opened the door that had just closed on her last word and replied, "Sure."

He walked into the office and put his hours in an envelope, wrote Mariana's name on it, and dropped it in her mail slot. Then he went to the printer and picked up the only sheet in the tray. He saw the title, "Glitter in the Air." It was the lyrics to the song she had been playing all week.

He read them, wondering: Why would she want the song printed when she knew the words by heart? How did these words relate to school? His bandmates would have a field day if they knew he was analyzing pop lyrics.

She had changed the standard font to a whimsical one, and that just struck one more chord within him. What do they mean to Francesca? As much as he wanted to ask, it was none of his business.

He gave her the page and watched as she drew hearts on it then laminated it. She then took it out of the room, and when she came back, it was no longer in her possession.

The staff rolled in, and the laminated page was forgotten. The ladies were all busy exchanging stories of how they were spending Thanksgiving, when Layla turned and asked Ryder what he was doing.

"Going out with a friend tonight. Haven't made plans for the rest of the weekend," he replied, quickly realizing they would question why he wasn't with family. "I live in California. We don't celebrate Thanksgiving until November," he excused.

"That sucks to be stuck here," Amanda piped in. "If I were you, I'd be missing the parties, the heat, the ocean. If I could get my green card, I would be out of here in a second."

"You're not me," Ryder mumbled as he left the room to head out to the busses, annoyed by the woman.

The team had decided to let him get Mason off the bus. Having a male influence in his life seemed to have a positive influence over

Mason. Ryder still encouraged him to work his frustration out with an exercise program, and Mason ate up the attention.

Theo was wired when he came in with Francesca, trying desperately to get his tongue anywhere near her mouth. He saw Ryder and started singing, *"Whacked up, bitch. I got you gagged and tied. Just how I want ya ... on your knees—"*

"Theo! Not appropriate. I swear, I don't know where you come up with this stuff," Francesca chided as she tried not to laugh at the adorable kid with a mouth most sailors would blush at.

"Fornication with elation. Theo funny. I make Frankie laugh." He hugged her while giving Ryder the horn symbol, just like a rocker.

Ryder stilled. That little joker knew exactly who he was, and he had just repeated lyrics from one of the songs he had written. The kid, was going to blow Ryder's cover.

He was saved once again when their student, Katrina, came into the room screaming. Layla and Amanda were trying to calm her, but it wasn't working.

"What happened?" Julianna asked.

Layla answer quietly as she walked towards Julianna, "Bus driver said her dad's back in the picture, and her mom was frantic to get rid of her this morning. Can't be good."

Julianna nodded as she walked up to Katrina. "Katrina, honey, talk to me. What's wrong?"

Just as Julianna approached, Katrina grabbed the microwave off the counter and threw it at Julianna, the door flying open, smashing into the floor and hitting Julianna's leg. Julianna screamed as she fell to the floor.

Ryder jumped up and ran to Julianna. Francesca ran to help Amanda with restraining Katrina, and Layla ran to the phone and requested support. Within twenty seconds, two teaching assistants and a CYW rushed into the room with Mariana hot on their heels.

"Ted, help us get Katrina to the safety room," Francesca started barking orders. "Becky and Carl, help Layla get the other kids to the library. Mariana, call for an ambulance and stay with Julianna and Ryder."

Mariana called the secretary to phone for an ambulance and to clear the halls. They announced the rest of the school was on lockdown until the situation was under control.

Ryder was freaked. He picked up Julianna and carried her to one of the comfortable reading chairs, stopping to grab a cloth from the sink to hold against the gash on her leg. His heart was pounding. How the fuck did these people do this every day? All hell had broken loose in less than two minutes, and nobody could have predicted it.

Ryder was panic-stricken for Francesca. He could hear Katrina screaming, and he couldn't help her. He felt as useless as two tits on a bull.

"You okay? I need to help Francesca," he told Julianna.

"No, Ryder, you stay here," Mariana answered. "Frankie is trained for this. She and Julianna are the leaders on the behaviour plan in a crisis situation for this room. Get control of yourself. She'll be fine."

Ryder growled in frustration as he raised his eyes from Julianna's leg to the administrator's face. "Her name is Francesca. And have you seen the size of her? That out of control kid could hurt her, too. Let me help her."

Mariana crossed her arms in a defiance pose. "You can't help her; you're not allowed to touch a child in crisis. Neither am I, for that matter. I get you feeling helpless, but if you go out there and can't help yourself from getting involved, it will put Francesca in a dangerous position. Knowing your restrictions, she will feel the need to protect you as well. So, if you really want to help, go to the library and look after Mason—take one burden off her shoulders. Mason will be just as upset as you are, and we have already had one kid blow up today. I'll stay with Julianna until the ambulance gets here. Now go." Mariana took over holding the cloth against Julianna's leg.

Ryder got up and went to the library, though it went against everything he was feeling. He felt like his skin was too tight for his bunched-up muscles. He could still hear Katrina screaming. Her sobs were killing him.

She had always been so sweet and quiet. He had often asked

Francesca why she was in their room. She was autistic and socially withdrawn, but the only thing that he could see wrong with her was her fascination with animals. She always carried around two plastic toy animals and knew everything about them, from their mating habits to what continent they lived on. She was cute. What the hell could have triggered her outburst of violence?

These kids fought as good as any street fighter he had ever witnessed.

Ryder walked in and saw the fear on Mason's face. He was pale, and it just about broke Ryder.

He pulled a chair out and sat down beside him as Mason put his head onto his folded arms on the table and breathed deeply.

Squeezing his shoulder, Ryder said, "She's good, bud. She's got this."

He felt Mason's body shudder. Ryder knew he was crying and why. He felt the same way.

He let the kid keep his dignity and said nothing.

***

Three hours later, Francesca walked back into their classroom, going to the students first.

"Hey, how you guys doing?" She spoke softly and with a gentle smile to ensure they knew it was going to be okay. "Katrina is going to be fine. Her grandparents just picked her up and told her how much fun they were going to have this Thanksgiving. Julianna is good, but she needs some time off. She'll be back next month. Maybe we can make her a card to make her feel better." She stood up and clapped her hands together once. "Let's move on with our day and set up for lunch. We'll use the microwave in the next room until we get a new one."

After the kids started on their lunch, Francesca motioned for the staff to come together. She quietly explained that Julianna had gotten fourteen stitches and wouldn't be back for a few weeks. Then she went on to explain that Katrina's father was indeed back in the picture and had decided that morning that Katrina was too old to be carrying around little plastic toy animals. He had thrown her whole collection into the garbage, which was what had set Katrina off.

Ryder's whole body tightened with fury. He could feel the anger rising as Francesca spoke. His asshole father had been just like Katrina's.

Francesca picked up on his body language and quirked her head towards him in a questioning gesture.

"I need to walk. Is it okay if I take my lunch now?" He needed to get the hell out of the school now.

She wasn't sure what was going on, but she nodded.

He was out of there in five seconds flat. He went to the centre's track and walked laps as fast as his legs would take him, telling himself this wasn't about his father. It was about Katrina's.

Forty-five minutes later, he came back in and was somewhat

more composed.

When school ended, and they were driving away, Francesca turned to him. "I just have to stop and grab some flowers. Do you mind?"

"Told you, no schedule, Beauty."

She winced at his nickname for her but didn't say anything, too lost in the sorrow of her next task.

No words were spoken as they headed to the cemetery, not even when they stopped and Francesca ran into the florist to buy two bunches of lilies.

Once they got there, she finally said, "I hope you don't mind waiting for me. I just need a few minutes alone." Her voice broke at the end of her sentence.

He nodded then watched as she grabbed her phone, the flowers, and the laminated piece of paper from her school bag. She then got out of the car and walked up and over a hill, disappearing from sight. He got out, too, just wanting some fresh air after the day they'd had.

She had been gone fifteen minutes when Ryder decided to take a peek and make sure Francesca was all right. He quietly walked up the road, where he saw her over to the left and just down the hill.

The sun was low in the sky and shining through the trees that lined the cemetery. A few rays settled upon her as she knelt over the grave. She had placed the lilies against two different headstones.

He could hear faint words as she spoke to each of the

headstones while running her hands along the names. By the shaking of her body, he could tell she was crying.

He struggled past the lump in his throat, feeling guilty for intruding. Not enough, though, to leave his beauty alone in her sorrow.

Then he watched as she placed the lyrics against the headstone on the right, stood up, and turned her phone on. He could hear "Glitter in the Air" playing as she started to turn in slow circles.

He was mesmerized as he watched her dig deep into her pockets and pull something out. Then she lifted her hands up and threw handfuls of sparkling little dust into the wind as she turned.

The sun caught the magical fragments, making her look like an angel in a snow globe. Her long, burgundy hair and the edges of her thigh-length sweater were flying around her body. She sang loud, in a broken voice, as she continued to pull out more sparkling dust and toss it up into the air over and over until the song ended. Then she was on her knees again, sobbing, her head on the grass.

He couldn't take it another second. He had to hold her and comfort her.

He cautiously walked up to her as he heard her gut-wrenching sobs. When he placed a gentle hand on her shoulder and she quickly lifted her head in surprise, he gathered her up into his strong arms. Then he awkwardly sat down on the grave with her sobbing in his lap. He didn't say a word, just rocked her back and forth.

After about five minutes, she calmed and wiped her tearstained face, nestling a little closer as she said, "I'm sorry you had to see that. I don't know why it was so hard today. I just miss them so much."

"No need to explain. Who are they?"

She pointed to the grave on the left. "This is my mom, Cassidy Murphy-Moratti. Everyone called her Cassy. She was a beautiful woman, who loved her family more than life itself. She was the perfect mom and wife. She was my rock and always made everything okay.

"I miss her so much. Some days, I just wish I could crawl back into her lap and let her take all my problems away. If you had the chance to meet her, she would have welcomed you in with open arms, treated you like a long-lost son, and smothered you with love."

"I've never known a woman like her," Ryder said quietly. "Until I met you. How did she pass?"

"Bladder cancer," she answered, ignoring his compliment. "She spent so much time looking after all of us that she neglected herself until it was too late. She's been gone for eight years."

She sniffed as she indicated towards the other gravestone. "The other grave belongs to my little brother, Tommaso, or Tommy, as everyone called him. Tommy had Down Syndrome. He died three years ago. He was diagnosed with leukaemia and died a year later."

The lump in his throat got larger. "I'm sorry. Life can be a bitch." He pointed at the laminated page against Tommy's headstone. "Why the song?"

Francesca smiled. "He loved that song. One day, when he was struggling with missing our mom, I took him outside and showed him the sky and told him Mom was watching us from Heaven and wanted us to be happy. I heard the song playing in the house, and it gave me an idea. The next day, I brought some glitter home. I took his hand and led him outside, brought out my phone, put the song on, and turned it up loud. We threw handfuls of sparkling glitter up into the sky. I told him she could see us having fun, and that it made her happy. He laughed and insisted we do it every week.

"Today is Tommy's birthday. Every year, I come here and throw glitter into the sky, hoping they can see me and are laughing up in Heaven," she said with the saddest voice he had ever heard.

Ryder unconsciously kissed the top of her head. "He was lucky to have you. I didn't mean to butt into your business. I just felt like I needed to check on you."

She thought for a moment, and then lifted her eyes to meet his worrisome ones. "I was the lucky one to have Tommy in my life. And I am glad you didn't listen to me. I do feel better now that I shared a little bit about them. I don't feel so alone ..." She cleared her throat and started to get out of his lap. "Let's get going. I want to get the ricotta cheese before the store closes, and we still have to get downtown."

Ryder struggled to get up from his position, thankful she had already turned to face the gravestones.

Francesca kissed her hand and rubbed it over her mom's name on the stone. "Love you, Mom." Then she turned towards her brother's headstone and did the same thing. "Love you, little Tommy."

When they got back in the car, she turned the heat on, chilled from the whole experience. Ryder, on the other hand, was so hot he was sweating. He didn't complain, though. She seemed to need it.

He glanced over at her, watching the amazing little creature who had so much love to give yet asked for nothing in return. She had cried for a while, yet she still looked hauntingly beautiful.

He liked silence, but he needed to speak to lift her sprits.

"I like using lyrics to speak for me, as well."

She jumped, startled out of her thoughts. "What do you mean?" She turned quickly to look at him with furrowed eyebrows.

"You use lyrics to express your emotions. Every morning, you listen to music and read the lyrics, like you need the writer's words to reach out and touch you. I do the same." He looked away, facing the windshield and trying to give her time to process his comment.

"Really? Now that you mention it, I guess I do. I like when the words make me remember something or someone, and listening to a song that makes me want the same things the artist is singing about. What kind of music do you like?"

Tread carefully, Ryder reminded himself.

"Classic rock, grunge, metal."

She laughed. "I should have known by looking at you. You totally look like you could be a rock star—tattoos and all."

Ryder tensed, thinking, *If she only knew how right she was.*

"Can you guess what type of music I like?" she asked

He grunted with a sound of frustration. "You're kidding me, right?"

She glanced at his rugged face that held the hint of a smile. He was ridiculously good-looking, but it was his voice that made her feel things. It reminded her of shards of glass—cutting deep and raspy, edgy. It sent chills down her spine.

"What?"

"Beauty, I'm with you every morning when you play all the shit you like. No offence, but most days, you kill me."

Shock crossed her face. "I take offence to that. You just said the words from my songs caress my soul, yet you don't like them? Really? You're obviously not listening to the words."

"Never said 'caress your soul.' And I can't get past how the melodies all sound the same. Can't even hear the words wrapped around that shit."

She narrowed her eyes at him, taking her focus off the road. "You so did not say that. At least my music has words. With your music, you have to get through ten freakin' minutes of guitar and drum solos just to get a few words."

He loved to rile her up, but now she was treading on sensitive territory, and his bristles were rising.

"You're an intelligent woman; you can't honestly believe that."

"Oh, dis my music, then my intelligence? Have I hit a sore spot, Beast?"

Not a minute later, he bellowed in laughter, shocking the shit out of them both. The man never smiled, and now he was uncontrollably laughing. Francesca couldn't hold back; she started to laugh, too.

"Fucking Christ, you just called me beast, and I call you beauty. Those two characters have their own lyrics." He started to laugh again.

He had a great laugh, and he looked even more handsome when he did.

"I'm blown away that a guy like you knows the story of *Beauty and the Beast*."

"Your intelligence is in tack, but your memory sucks. Veeta made us watch that movie every Friday afternoon in September. Damn thing haunts me," he said with disdain.

"Hey, that's a great movie. An incredible love story," she said with indignation.

"Stop pushing your luck. You think two cartoon character make a cute couple? That shit isn't real, Francesca. That's why it's called a fairy tale."

"That's it! I am done with you. I am turning up my music now so I can't hear you." She waited for a red light, then hit Bluetooth to connect her phone, chose the song "Die A Happy Man" by Thomas Rhett, and cranked the volume.

"Bad enough you make me listen to pop. Now you're punishing me with country?" He talked over the music.

She turned the radio down. "I'm going to start the song again, and I want you to forget what genre it is and just listen to the words. I pray one day someone will feel that way about me. I know I'm being unrealistic, because the girl in the video is beautiful." She shrugged. "But a girl can dream."

Before he could reply, she cranked the volume, letting the words tickle her fantasy.

He did as she asked and listened. He hated to admit it, but she might be right. The words were captivating to anyone who had a pussy. He was sure it was written for all chicks, not about one in particular; hence, why singers made so much money writing love songs.

"Well?" she asked when she turned down the music.

"Let's just not talk about music." He was happy she was so naive.

She huffed. He just made her want to scream with frustration.

She decided she would torture him by playing all her music

while they made their way downtown. He should be ready to gnaw off an arm by the time they got to the cheese store.

Chapter 4

"Money" By Pink Floyd

Ryder followed Francesca around the European meat and cheese store as she picked up ingredients he had never heard of, let alone eaten. He was dumbfounded when she started to speak Italian to the old lady behind the counter. Her appearance was the polar opposite of how typical Italians were portrayed on T.V. and in movies. He stereotypically thought most Italians were olive-skinned, with long noses, were loud, and used hand gestures all the time. She was quiet, skin white as snow, and had a cute button nose. He had assumed her only claim to Italy was her last name. When would he learn not to draw conclusions about this woman?

He struggled not to beat the shit out of all the men who ogled her as she floated through the aisles. His height worked to his advantage as he tried to intimidate every man who stopped in their tracks and stared at her.

She was stunning, but these men didn't know the half of it. The exquisiteness on the inside far outshone her outside beauty. She was totally oblivious to her magnetism.

Relieved when they were done, he watched her cautiously and carefully count her cash out and hand it over to the cashier. Francesca had mentally tallied all her purchases so she would have enough money.

When he insisted on carrying her bags out to the car, she struggled with him, trying to wrestle them away from him, used to doing things for herself. She finally relented when he growled at her, drawing the attention of those around them.

She felt the blush move up her chest and across her face, and he watched it, instantly getting hard. Thankfully, all the grocery bags would hide it, but he did lick his lips, and that she didn't miss.

Francesca had an old car, so she had to turn it on before popping the trunk. As she leaned in, she noticed her gas tank was almost empty.

Damn, how had she missed that? She only had ten dollars and thirty-seven cents left on her; how was she going to pay for her slice of pizza and a drink and still have enough for gas?

"Ryder, why don't we go to your place, and I can cook something instead of going out?" She knew she could stretch the items she bought to make a meal.

"Won't work. No kitchen stuff, and fridge is for beer."

"Well, then I will just drop you off at your place and head home.

I have a busy day tomorrow."

He couldn't understand why she was getting flustered. What was her deal?

"You dumping me for something better? Or are you embarrassed to be seen with me in public?" He was full-out pissed off now, reverting to the insecurities he had developed throughout childhood.

"What in God's name makes you say that?" Damn the beast.

"What else am I supposed to think after we agreed to go out and get something to eat?" Angry, his tone hadn't changed.

She sat in the car, trying to figure out how to explain that she was strapped for cash.

She was looking at her lap, chewing her lip again, when he sat beside her, seeing her internal struggle, which further pissed him off.

"Just fucking say it. I get it. People don't like to be around me."

She lifted her head and turned towards him, her eyes filled to the brim with tears. "I can't afford it, okay? Are you happy? I only have ten dollars and thirty-seven cents left to my name until I get paid from the boys' family. And that money is already spoken for. Ten dollars has to last me until next Friday." She started to really cry as she blubbered out, "I'm an idiot. I don't know how I forgot about gas. I just noticed." She dropped her face into her hands so he couldn't see her distress.

With a soft, gentle voice she didn't think he was capable of, he breathed out, "Francesca."

He was dying to touch her again, but he knew he wouldn't be able to hold back. His intensity would probably scare her.

She didn't take her hands away, not wanting to see the pity in his eyes. She had seen that enough from people. He had no conception of just how pathetic she was. She had come from a proud, loving family that had fallen from grace. She would never allow anyone to judge her family ever again, or to criticize the sacrifices she had made to keep them together. Her brothers were sacrificing, as well. They all knew you did what you had to for your family.

"Francesca, look at me. I want to look you in the eyes when I apologize."

"Please don't look at me with pity," she said as she removed her hands and wiped the tears from her cheeks.

She hesitantly turned, not seeing pity, but surprisingly, guilt.

"Sorry, Beauty. I judged you before accusing you of judging me. I don't have a lot of friends, and the ones I do have don't talk about their feelings. This is all new to me. It's none of my business where your money goes—and I won't ask—but I did invite you to dinner, so I'm paying. I'll take care of your gas, too, since you're driving me home."

With a heartbroken look, she said, "No, Ryder. I had to drive to St. Clair, anyway, so I can't take your money for gas."

Ryder blew out a very frustrated breath, mentally reminding himself to be patient with this headstrong female. "Francesca Moratti, we're going to dinner, and then I'm filling your gas tank. Otherwise, I'll be going back to your house right now and taking a cab. Two choices. You decide."

Francesca gently smiled. "Has anyone ever told you that you're a stubborn ass?"

"Let's go eat. I'm starving."

They set off to a very popular Italian eatery, where they had to wait twenty minutes for a seat.

While they were waiting, Ryder looked down at Francesca and told her, "You are a tiny, little thing."

"I'm short, not tiny," she retorted. "And I am not a thing. Has anyone ever told you that you're ginormous?"

He semi-grinned at her smart mouth. "Only when my pants are down."

"Ryder!"

He laughed out loud for the second time in his life when her mouth gaped open, and she blushed from head to toe.

"Sorry. Couldn't help myself. You're tiny, but you don't come across as small. Your personality is over seven fucking feet tall."

The waiter took them to their table before she had a chance to rebuttal. He handed them menus before walking away to give them a few minutes to browse it. When he came back and asked if they wanted a drink, she said, "No," and he said, "Yes, we will have a beer and a Caesar to start."

When the waiter left, Francesca reprimanded him again. "If I wanted a drink, I would have ordered it."

He watched her closely as she looked over the menu. He knew what she was doing.

"Bullshit. What's good to eat here?"

She let it go for now and rambled off all her favourites.

"What are you getting?" he asked as he raised his eyes from the menu and saw her shift uncomfortably with a light blush as she continued to look at the menu. He knew she was looking for the cheapest shit they had. It fucking killed him that she was struggling with money, while he had so much money he couldn't spend it all in ten lifetimes.

"I think I'm having a child's sized cheese pizza. I'm not that hungry," she answered, not looking at him as she closed the menu and took a sip of her water.

The waiter returned with their drinks, asking if they were ready to order. Ryder was quick to respond.

"Yes, we will be sharing everything, so bring extra plates."

Her mouth dropped open as he ordered all her favourites. Then he told the waiter to leave one menu because they would be ordering dessert.

She narrowed her eyes, but before she could lambaste him, he held his finger up.

"Play nice and indulge me, Francesca. I always eat dinner alone. I'm excited to try Italian food, in an Italian restaurant, recommended by an Italian girl, okay?"

This frustrating man had manipulated her again, and now she was feeling sorry for him instead of being affronted.

She raised her glass. "Salute. Happy Caesar Friday, Ryder, and Happy Thanksgiving. Thank you for dinner."

"Cheers."

They clinked glasses and took a well-earned sip of their drinks.

"What do you have planned this weekend in the big city? Where are you spending Thanksgiving?" she asked.

"Wasn't kidding when I said I have no family or friends here. Just bumming around all weekend." He shrugged.

She instantly felt like crap again. She forgot his family was in California.

"Oh, no, you're not. You're going to join my brothers and me at my place. Dinner's at two, and you'll be there. I'm not taking no for an answer." She glared at him, daring him to challenge her.

"Who's stubborn now?" He sighed as he looked away. "You know I'm not good with people. I might make your brothers uncomfortable. Besides, aren't you visiting your father up north?"

"Yes, I will drive up at eight and be back by one." She glanced away then brought her eyes back to him. "You don't make me uncomfortable, and my brothers are great guys. A little overprotective, but good hearts, nonetheless."

"Don't say I didn't warn you." With another sigh, he extended his hand towards her. "Give me your phone. I'll put my number in. Text me your address."

While Ryder entered his number, the food was delivered. It was a good thing the table was meant for four people, because every inch was covered with food. People were staring. However, one scowling look from Ryder and they turned back to their own conversations.

They ate a ton of food while they talked for hours. Well, she talked for hours while he absorbed it all. She told him how she was drawn to her job after experiencing all the good things the centre did for her brother. She wanted to be a part of that, to make a difference in other kids' lives. She thought it gave her a unique ability in understanding her students' family lives, so she went to school for it.

She knew she shocked him when she said, "I like my students more than I like most 'normal' people. This isn't a job I do for money—the money is crap. I love these kids unconditionally. They are so cool, and they teach me way more than I could ever teach them.

"Wait until you go to one of our dances. It will blow you away. They have no inhibition. Everyone dances with everyone. Able-bodied students dance with wheelchair bound students. Boys with boys, or girls with girls. Even staff with students. They don't care how it looks. They just love how the music makes them feel.

"They smile and laugh when you dance with them. It's like you've given them the best gift in the world. There is no feeling that compares to it. They just want to fit in and not be judged for who they are. And really, Ryder, doesn't everyone want that? The centre gives them a place to safely experience life for themselves; what society refuses to give them because they are different."

What Francesca had said struck a chord so deep in his heart that it seared his soul. If she believed that, then maybe she could look past all of his defects. She was the first person in his thirty years who he wanted to share all his fucked-up-ness with.

He didn't know what love was, but if it felt anything like what he was experiencing in this moment, he now understood why people killed for it.

He was such a selfish prick. He should walk away from her, but he wasn't going to. He was going to do everything in his power to spend as much time with her as he could.

"You have the purest soul of any human I've ever met. And I've met a lot in my lifetime." He sat there, staring at her in awe.

She blushed again and decided to change the subject. "I … thank you. Um … what do you do in California?"

He smirked. "I work in the entertainment business. I have three really good guys who are my only friends, but beyond them, everyone always wants a piece of me, and not in a good way." He ran his hands through his overly long hair and yanked at the roots in frustration. "Most of the time, people just want to use me to further their own gain. My career has jaded me. I make good money, but I wish I could just do my job. I always aspired to be in the business, but hate all the bullshit that comes with it. Basically, I just want to be left alone to do what I do best, and fuck the rest of the world." Now it was his turn to look away.

She was a master at reading body language. Her safety at school depended on it. She knew he was uncomfortable discussing his job. Therefore, it was time to move on to a safer subject.

"And what about your parents and siblings?" she asked, hoping this was a more pleasurable topic.

Ryder shut down completely and reverted back to his beast mentality. "No siblings. Parents are in Brazil half the year, and half here in Toronto. I haven't spoken to the sperm donator in over twelve years. He's a real piece of work, and so is his wife, the woman who gave birth to me. The dudes I work with, I consider brothers. They are my only family." He was so private, and his confession had cost him.

She reached over and grabbed his hand, stunned and saddened by his omission. She had never heard anyone describe their parents like that.

A total of three in his circle of friends and surrogate family. Meanwhile, her Caesar buddies were larger than that. And her family

… Well, between here and Italy, there were too many to count.

"I didn't mean to upset you. I shouldn't have asked," Francesca apologized quietly.

He looked at her delicate hand over his. It hit him deeply. She was such a compassionate woman. He would tarnish that goodness, fuck up like his sperm donor had always said.

"We live with the cards we are dealt, whether it's a winning hand or not. It's my life. I accept it." He started to get up. "Let's get going. Take this food and give it to the boys; save yourself one night of cooking."

"No, Ryder, you take it. The boys are all with their families for Thanksgiving. Besides, you just said you don't have any food in your fridge, and you paid for it."

"Don't fucking say that again," he growled. "You give easily, but suck at receiving."

When he took the bag of leftovers and walked to the car, he was shocked when she squealed, thinking something was wrong.

"What?" he bellowed, spinning around and ready to do battle.

"Look at what's parked beside my car. It's a two thousand BMW Z3, and it's red! Here, take my phone; I want a picture with it." She stood and smiled from ear-to-ear as he took her picture. Then she looked over the car like she was a dude at a strip joint, assessing the goods. "This is my dream car. One day, I'm going to own one." She followed the lines of the car from the front to the back where she stopped to admire the backend. Smiling, she then made her way over to look inside.

He loved watching her examine the car. It was sexy.

Francesca peeked at the interior and made another noise. He couldn't decipher if it was good or bad, so he asked, "Like the interior?"

"No, it ruins the car," she complained. "It's white, and the roof is black. It should be black on black, or a black roof with red interior."

He chuckled. "Why a Z3 and not the Z4? It's newer and has an amazing ass end."

"No, no, no. You don't understand. The Z4 doesn't have the shark gills. I love the shark gills. You know James Bond drove this car in one of those movies? Although he's cool, I really think it's a chick mobile."

He lifted one eyebrow. "Gills?"

She rode her hand over the chrome side grilles. "These little puppies just make this car so hot!"

Holy fuck. He was watching her caress the car, envisioning her hands running along his dick. He was going to full-mast right in front of her. And at six and a half feet, there was no hiding the monster. Thankfully, her attention was diverted.

He let her indulge in her little fantasy while he talked his dick down.

"Well, enough dreaming for now," she sighed out longingly. "We should get going. I have to get up early so I can prepare for Sunday." She turned without looking at him and went to the driver's side.

They didn't talk much on the drive to his place, and when she pulled up to his condo, she looked up and up and up.

"Wow, pretty cool building. What floor are you on?"

"Wanna come in?" he asked hopefully.

"I would love to, but another time. I have to get up early." She smiled. "Thank you so much for dinner and for the gas, which I will be paying you back for next week."

She was making him bristle again.

"Not a chance. But you could cook for me sometime."

Blunt and to the point; that was this gorgeous man. She had to admit that it was refreshing.

"Sounds like a plan. I expect you at two on Sunday. Don't disappoint me."

"Never intentionally." He started to get out then paused. "I'm worried about you driving home in the dark and unloading your groceries. I could follow you."

She smiled. "That defeats the purpose of me driving you home. I'll be fine." She waved him off. "Good night, Ryder."

He unfolded his overly large body out of the car then leaned in. "Text me when you get home." He locked and closed the door before heading past the doorman and straight to the front desk, where he told them to phone down to the garage and quickly bring up his 1969 Camaro.

Francesca was busy on her phone, so she didn't see him exit the other side of the building. When his car arrived, he quickly got in and pulled up behind her as he watched her make a phone call. In California, they allowed heavy tinting on the windows, so he knew she wouldn't see him.

She hung up then drove away, and he pulled out two cars behind her.

He followed her all the way home and parked across the street, watching as she grabbed half the bags then climbed the stairs on the outside of the house to her apartment over a garage.

A light went on, then she trudged back down for the rest of the groceries and her school bag. When she was in, he watched as more lights were turned on in the apartment.

His phone beeped with an incoming text after five minutes.

LMAO. Almost didn't find your number after looking for Ryder & Vaughn until I scrolled up and saw Beast. Great night, thanks!

See you Sunday, Beauty.

Ryder drove home with Pink Floyd's "Money" blasting the speakers.

Chapter 5

"The Wind Beneath My Wings"

By Bette Midler

Driving up north to see her papa always gave Francesca time to think. She hooked her phone up and played "The Wind Beneath My Wings" by Bette Midler. It was the song that always reminded her of her papa. No words were ever truer. He was her champion.

After the song was over, she thought about Ryder and what he had said about his parents. She couldn't understand how someone could hate their parents so much, yet she knew that some parents weren't worthy and should never have had children. Mason reminded her of that all the time.

Then her thoughts drifted back to her papa. He only allowed his children to visit him once a month, and they were never allowed to visit during religious holidays like Christmas and Easter. This would be the second Thanksgiving he missed, and they had three more to endure. She would never get used to traveling up to the penitentiary every third week to visit him.

Francesca had been named after her papa, Francesco, because, unlike most Italian men, he had always wanted a daughter. Cassy had assumed he would name their daughter after his mother, Lena, whom he cherished. To the surprise of everyone, he had named his precious little girl after himself. He always said it was because, if his wife gifted him with a daughter as fair and beautiful as she was, and if she looked like her mama, he wanted his daughter to have something of him.

Frank adored all his children, but his little Francesca was a gift from the angels. He swore on his life, the minute the nurse had placed his little girl in his arms, she had smiled at him and never stopped. His wife had told him it was probably gas, but he had disagreed.

Francesca could sweet talk her papa out of any punishment her and her brothers had earned. He was so lenient when it came to his little girl, everyone told him she would grow up spoiled. Frank knew differently, and he had been right.

Her stomach clenched when Francesca arrived at the penitentiary. She took deep breaths, trying to calm her nerves.

She hated going in there. She always arrived half an hour early because, if she was late, they deducted time off her visit. Once she had encountered a snow storm, and by the time she had arrived, there'd been only ten minutes left. Then, by the time she had made it through security and walked to the area he was held in, they had only gotten three minutes before they had cut off the phone.

She entered the waiting area and signed in. The prison guards checked her name off the visitors' list then asked if she was depositing money into his commissary account.

She handed over four hundred dollars, which was the maximum she could afford for the month. She despised the fact that the food portions were small and bland. The inmates' protein intake was very minimal. Her papa had lost so much weight, so she constantly encouraged him to buy protein bars or cans of tuna to keep his muscle mass.

The prison supplied the barest of essentials, and the commissary allowed inmates to purchase stationary, stamps, hygiene products, and snacks.

The male guard looked her over from head to toe creepily, while the female guard just glared. She hated this female guard. The woman tried to make Francesca feel shameful every chance she got.

She had to leave her driver's license to get a key for the locker to store her purse and sweater. Then she sat in the waiting area with other families and girlfriends.

It was an eclectic group. Some of the people looked like they belonged there. Others looked like they were the all-American family.

She learned early on not to judge. Most inmates belonged

behind bars, but they still had mothers, fathers, wives, and children who were paying just as high a price as the men who sat behind the locked bars.

When they called her name, she lined up with the five other visitors, and then they entered the first locked room where they removed wallets, belts, jewelry, hair clips, and then went through the metal detectors. Each family member then went through a body scan machine to ensure they were not concealing weapons.

Francesca knew she would get a body pat down. They singled her out each time she visited to set an example for the rest of the families.

"Arms up. Back to me," the female guard snarled. "Turn around."

As she scanned Francesca, something beeped on the wand. The guard placed her hand in Francesca's top and pulled out her Saint Gregory, the patron saint of teachers, students, and musicians, necklace out of her shirt.

"Are you trying to get denied visitations?" the guard snapped.

Francesca's face heated with a blush. *No, please don't deny me,* she thought.

"Sorry. I forgot to take it off. Please, I am sorry."

The male guard walked up. "Is there a problem?"

"She was trying to sneak in with jewelry on," the female guard said in the same bitchy tone.

The male guard lifted the medallion from her chest and brushed his thumb over the warm metal. "Come on, Sue; being a little bit tough here. She forgot and apologized. What's she going to do? Hold it up and curse us all? Let her go. She never gives us a bit of trouble," he responded with an even tone, looking at the religious symbol.

"Rules are rules, Pete." The female guard was furious.

"Let it go. You've embarrassed her enough. It won't happen again, will it, Miss Moratti?"

"No, I am sorry. I don't want to cause any problems. I just want to visit my papa." Francesca could feel tears welling up in her eyes.

"Make sure it doesn't happen again, or you'll be denied access. Now get out of here," the female guard snarled.

Francesca walked with the other five people to the elevators, seconds away from falling apart. She had to pull herself together before she saw her papa; otherwise, she would upset him.

Inside the elevator, she faced the back door, knowing she would be exiting from the rear. The door closed, and she took a deep breath.

One of the other male visitors whispered, "Ignore the bitch. Some people are just power hungry."

Francesca nodded, afraid to answer for fear they would revoke her visit.

The elevator opened, and the long, daunting walk to the area her father was kept in awaited her.

As she walked to the farthest door from the elevator, the ten other footsteps behind her disappeared through the various doors to each cell block. After her first visit, she had learned not to wear shoes that made loud pounding sounds that echoed off the walls and made her feel like she was attending her own execution.

She approached the last locked door and pressed the button, both nervous and excited to see her papa.

"Name of inmate?" echoed through the speaker.

"Moratti."

The door buzzed, and she opened it before approaching the second door. When she looked at the camera, another *click* sounded as the door opened. Then she finally walked over to the glass wall separating her from her papa.

Each partitioned cubicle had a phone under the ledge and a cement stool. She sat down and looked down into the cell block her father lived in. She could see inmates walking around and the guards at their station.

A guard looked up, and then picked up his phone and paged Moratti. She watched her papa walk around a corner, look up, and searched each cubicle until he saw her and smiled.

He walked towards the metal stairs that would bring him up to the visitors' area. He was wearing an orange jumpsuit, sneakers without laces, and looked so much older than his fifty-two years. Her father had always looked and dressed so immaculate before prison. Now his hair was unkempt, and he looked pale.

She picked up her phone as did he. "Ciao, Papa."

"Ciao, mia bella. How is my little ray of sunshine?"

"Good, Papa. How are you?"

"Always better when I see my sweet bambolina"

"If you would let me come more, then you could be better more often, Papa."

"This is no place for my girl. I hate that you come as much as you do."

Francesca kissed the palm of her hand and placed it on the glass. Frank did exactly the same thing, and tears formed in both their eyes.

"I miss you, Papa."

"I know, mia bella. I miss you, too. But time is passing, and before you know it, I'll be home." He could see that was no comfort, so he changed the subject. "How is school? And the man who is doing his community service hours in your class; how is he managing?" She had told her papa all about Ryder and why he was at the centre.

Her mood instantly lifted, and she giggled as she told him about Theo finally managing to get his tongue into her friend.

"Papa, it was so funny. Ryder was bent down, spotting Mason while he was lifting some weights, while us girls were having spa day in our classroom. A male CYW was in the gym, but didn't see

Theo approach.

"Theo was out of control that day, bouncing off the walls. He surprised Ryder when he bent down and stuck his tongue right into Ryder's ear. I had just walked up and saw the whole thing. I heard Ryder bellow for Theo to back off. Theo saw me coming in and ran with all his might to me. He jumped into my arms like a monkey wrapped around its mother. I nearly fell over from the impact as Ryder stalked towards us, wiping spit out of his ear.

"I told Theo that's disgusting, and he owed Ryder an apology." She laughed. "Ryder responded 'Listen, you little …' I cut him off before he could call Theo a little shit." She giggled now as she thought back to that day. "I begged Theo to apologize right away, trying to defuse the situation as I pulled him from my body. Theo said sorry and started talking about fornicating, and I think that scared Ryder even more. Then Theo started to pretend to play the drums. I swear, Papa, I don't know where he comes up with this stuff.

"I took him back to class and encouraged him to stay away from the big man." Francesca was nearly in tears from laughing as she told her papa that Ryder had told her she had to do something with the sick, little bastard and that he couldn't go around tonguing people. "I reprimanded Ryder by saying he was buying right into the reaction Theo wanted. I told him we aren't going to change Theo; we have to change how we react to him.

"Papa, I'm telling you, he is just the most adorable little boy. He's just figured out how to get people's attention." She shrugged. "I have to keep reminding Ryder that he's the adult. He doesn't respond. He just glares at me like I'm the problem, 'perpetuating the little shit head,' his words not mine."

Her father belly laughed as he listened and imagined this six and half foot man ready to pommel the little kid, and Francesca's response leaving him speechless.

She talked non-stop for forty-five minutes about school before she got the five-minute warning beep. Instantly, her happy disposition changed to one of sadness.

"Don't do that, bambolina. Let me remember your laughter instead of your tears for the next three weeks."

"Sorry, Papa." She looked down, dejected.

"Don't be sorry. Just give me one more story before you leave." Frank tried to lift her spirits.

She honoured his request, and soon they were laughing again. They missed the final beep before the phone disconnected. She looked at the phone, surprised.

When her dad knocked on the glass, she looked up, and he looked right into her eyes and mouthed, *"I love you, bambolina."* She smiled and mouthed, *"I love you, too, Papa."* Then she kissed her fingertips and placed them on the glass. He did the same thing, and then he got up and headed for the stairs. She knew he wouldn't look back, knowing she was probably crying and couldn't bear that.

She stood as he descended the stairs and disappeared into the cell area. Then she wiped her tears and stood to leave, glancing over once more and hoping to see him. She didn't.

She went out the two doors, hearing them click as the locks engaged behind her. Then she stared down the endless hallway to the elevator. This was the worst part about coming here. She was all alone in her sorrow as she walked away from her papa for another month with tears streaming down.

She glanced at the cameras every ten feet, knowing the guards were watching. She had no dignity, because she wasn't even allowed a tissue to wipe her eyes.

It destroyed her to think she had to cook a huge meal and they were celebrating Thanksgiving without her papa. She couldn't do anything for him while he was incarcerated. She wasn't even allowed to send books because some assholes had laced the pages with drugs. Her only gift this Thanksgiving had been the money she had left for the commissary, hoping he could buy products to ease his comfort during the holiday.

She had sent pictures of their family the first month he had been there, hoping he would never feel alone with them. But he had sent them back in his first letter, explaining how it was dangerous for him to keep them because other inmates were making rude comments about her and her mother, and he had nearly gotten into a fist fight over them. As sad as it made her, she respected his wishes. It was most important that no harm came to her papa.

She grabbed her belongings from the locker, returned the key, collected her license, and then took a few tissues from the box on the desk. She walked out the door and was at her car when she heard a guard yell out to her.

"Miss Moratti, wait!"

She turned and saw the male guard from earlier approaching her. Her heart pounded, afraid something had just happened to her papa.

"What's wrong? Is my papa okay?"

"Yes, he's fine. I just wanted to apologize for my partner's rudeness earlier. It was uncalled for. You and your brothers are always very respectful to all us guards and, believe it or not, we do appreciate it. She's just jealous of how we like it when you visit. We all fight for this shift. She knows you're hot, and that makes her pissy."

Relief swept through her, and then her spine stiffened. That wasn't an appropriate comment. Nevertheless, she couldn't mention it. They held all the power over her visits.

"Thank you. I understand. Good-bye, and have a happy Thanksgiving." She turned quickly to get into her car.

As she eased herself in, he quickly added, "Miss Moratti, listen. I was wondering if you would like to grab a drink with me next time you're up here?"

Ew. Her skin crawled. Was he kidding? There had to be rules against this.

"I'm sorry, but I can't. My son is waiting for me at home." She was lying through her teeth, but mentioning a child should squash any interest he might have with her.

"Didn't know you had a kid. I see you're not married." He gestured towards her ring finger as he drew his eyes up to her breasts. "You know … I can make it easier on your father."

Was he trying to blackmail her into going out with him?

"I have to go."

"Sure. See you next time." He stood there, watching her close the door and start the car before pulling away.

Damn him. How was she going to avoid this creep?

A shiver ran down her spine. She hated this place and couldn't wait for her papa to be released.

***

Ryder pulled up to Francesca's home just as she was pulling in, even though he had mixed emotions about it. He desperately wanted to spend time with her. Her brothers were another story.

"What's wrong, Beauty?" He could see she wasn't her happy-go-lucky self. She looked like a scared rabbit.

"Nothing. I'm okay. How are you?"

"Tell me why you aren't yourself. Did your father upset you?"

"God no. I love seeing him. It makes me sad when I have to leave him; that's all."

Ryder knew she was bullshitting him. He grabbed her arm to halt her, and she flinched like she was afraid of him. *What the fuck!*

"Francesca, I know your moods like they are my own. That reaction wasn't one of sadness, but fear. Not gonna ask again. What happened?"

She couldn't look him in the eyes as she said, "Someone spooked me; that's all. Nothing major. Just me overreacting, as usual."

He lifted her chin and looked into her eyes, seeing indecision. "Tell me."

She shrugged out of his grip. "Have you ever wished you could run and not stop until you exorcised all your demons?"

That was deep, meaning she was freaked about something.

"Yeah, Beauty. See that bike over there?" He pointed at his beloved Harley. "I jump on that little lady and drive her as fast as I can until all my problems are left in the wind."

She blew out a breath. "I wish I had a release like that. I cook or paint when I'm upset, but even that sometimes can't help me from over thinking things."

A piece of hair fell in front of her face, and it took all his willpower not to gently tuck it behind her ear.

"After your brothers leave, we're gonna chase your demons

away with a ride."

Feeling how skittish she was, he stepped back while she rolled the idea around in that beautiful head of hers.

After a couple of minutes, she said, "I'm scared. I've never been on a bike, and I don't have a helmet."

His heart skipped a beat. If he could arrange it, Francesca would be wrapped around his body by the end of this day. "I'll get a guy I know to drop off another helmet. You go in. I'll be right behind you."

Ryder called his manager Ted and told him he had to find a woman's helmet and a unique leather jacket in a medium, and have it delivered to the address he texted him.

"Impossible," his manager replied. It was Thanksgiving, and he would have to drive to Buffalo and back in under three hours.

Ryder was pissed. "Buffalo is an hour and a half away. If you want me to play the Christmas break concerts, it better be here." He hung up then texted Francesca's address to him. Ryder wasn't worried; his manager did all kinds of shit for his bandmates, and Ryder had never asked for a thing. They were paying their manager a shit load of money, so he could do Ryder's bidding for once.

Francesca was busy in the kitchen when he walked in. He felt calmness come over his body when he saw her, the likes he had never felt before. She was so good for his soul, the soul he didn't know he possessed until he had met Beauty.

Her apartment had one main room that held the kitchen and living room. There were two other doors he assumed were her bedroom and bathroom. Her furniture was old and worn, but the paintings hanging on the walls blew his mind. They were all famous monuments from all over the world, but they were in the background, like the artist was trying to tell you whatever was featured in the front was just as important.

He saw a cafe in Paris with the Eiffel Tower in the background. One with the Coliseum peeking out behind a big pink oleander tree. Ayers Rock in Australia with a rainbow shining in front. The coolest by far was the storm clouds surrounding Stonehenge in England. The focus was definitely the mystery of the storm, and not the rocks.

"Where did you get these?" Ryder asked, indicating the paintings.

"They're mine," she remarked like they were nothing.

He huffed. How could she be so smart and so dense at the same time?

"I know they're yours. Where did you get them?"

She stopped what she was doing and looked at him like the simpleton he sometimes was. "They are mine. I painted them."

She had to be shitting him. They were amazing.

She must have seen his thoughts on his face because she shrugged and said, "They're okay. Nothing special. I like to dabble."

He was emanating frustration. Could she really be that naive?

89

"Damn, Beauty, they're awe-inspiring."

A bright red blush covered her face and chest. She hated being the centre of attention.

"Thank you. Which one speaks to you?"

"One hundred percent Stonehenge, without a doubt," he was quick to respond as he walked closer to it. He looked over his shoulder at her. "The storm clouds seem to speak for the mysterious of the rock formations. I've been there, and this painting captures everything I felt that day. Do you sell your work?"

"God no. I'm not that good." She glared at him. "Don't look at me like that. It's true. Anyway, I only do it for fun. It's one way I work through my emotions, besides cooking."

"A dark time in your life?" He nodded towards the painting.

She lowered her head in embarrassment. "Yes. I questioned my faith in God for a while and all the mysterious things in our universe, and this painting was the result."

"Everyone questions what they believe in from time to time." Ryder felt like he was invading her privacy, so he demanded, "Now tell me what smells so amazing."

Francesca rambled off all that she had cooked. Thankfully, turkey was not on the list. Ryder wasn't a fan. He was sure it was because turkey was meant to be shared with a loving family, and he didn't have that. It left a sour taste in his mouth.

She got him a beer and a glass of wine for herself. Just after their first sip, he heard some jackass yelling, "Frank the Tank, open the damn door."

"Brothers," was all Francesca said as she jumped up from her little card table that was beautifully decorated for dinner and rushed to let them in. "Lucky, Sal … Oh, my gosh, you didn't have to bring me flowers. You two are the best."

The three walked in, arm in arm. She was holding a beautiful arrangement of sunflowers and greenery. Ryder's displeasure at their nickname for her melted away as he watched her beam at them.

"Ryder Vaughn, I would like to introduce you to my big brothers. This idiot on my right is Luciano, or better known as Lucky, although Lady Luck is never on his side. To my left is Salvador, better known as Sal."

They both stood stock-still and glowered at the man who had invaded their baby sister's kitchen. Ryder, not to be intimidated by anyone, stood up to his full-height, dwarfing the two men who were both around five-eleven. Their eyes just about popped out of their heads, and he was pleased with their response.

"Gesù Cristo, egli è un fottuto mostro!" Sal mumbled.

"Salvador Benito Moratti, don't be rude. Speak English. Shake his hand. Sorry, Ryder."

The two brothers jumped to do this little slip of woman's bidding.

Ryder made sure to squeeze their hands a little tighter than usual to show his dominance. The guys instantly picked up on his message and went back to scowling.

Lucky pulled him in for a man hug, whispering into Ryder's ear, "You might be big, but our hunting rifles don't give a fuck about your size."

"Respect that, man," Ryder said, relaxing. He respected that the two little pricks were willing to put her safety in front of their lives. Maybe these greasy little Italians weren't so bad, after all. And both brothers did look Italian—dark hair and dark skin with almost black eyes.

"So, we hear you work with Frank the Tank," Lucky said as he walked to the fridge to grab a beer. He grabbed three and handed one to his brother before offering one to Ryder.

Ryder shook his head. "You want to keep my respect, call her by her given name."

The brothers laughed. Maybe they weren't as smart as he had assumed.

"We don't know how long you've known our little bruiser, but trust me; she is like a tank when she wants something. There's no hiding from her. She's been a force to be reckoned with since she was in diapers."

Ryder gave his semi-smile. "Learned that twenty minutes after meeting her. But her name is as beautiful as she is, so it's disrespectful. True?"

"Listen, Satan's children, I am in the room, so stop talking about me like I'm not here." Francesca took away the centre piece she had on the table and replaced it with the flowers.

"Of course. Sorry, *Francesca*," Sal said as he sat his ass in a chair that he would remain in for the next four hours.

Over dinner, they talked about school, their family business, and how their dad was. The guys listened and laughed hysterically as Ryder told them stories about the students.

"Couldn't pay me enough to be in your shoes, bro," Sal commented.

"No choice. Placement for community service hours. It was the nut house or jail," Ryder didn't hesitate to answer.

"Ryder! That's not nice. It's not the nut house. I love those kids."

"And they love you, Beauty, but not my brand of beer; that's for sure."

Lucky turned towards Ryder. "What are you serving community hours for?"

"Lucky, that's none of our business. Sorry, Ryder. Don't answer that." Francesca was mortified by her brothers. They had left their manners at the door.

"Don't mind answering. Got caught stunt driving on my motorcycle when I was in town. Second offence."

Her brothers both winced.

"Sucks, bro," Lucky said. "But you're still driving. I saw that sweet ride outside."

"Yeah, lost my license once already. Judge figured I need my license to get to the centre. She's trying to teach me the value of life."

"Is it working?" Sal asked.

"Unbelievably. Respecting what I was given a lot more." Ryder nodded with his beer at his lips.

Francesca had never asked why Ryder was serving community service hours, so his answer definitely surprised her. He wasn't a criminal at all.

As they continued their conversation, she got up to clear the table and saw someone pulling into her driveway.

"Someone just drove in." She panicked a bit after her encounter this afternoon with the guard.

Ryder noticed her stance, and that worried him.

When he looked out the window, he told her. "That's the delivery I was waiting for."

He jogged out the door and down the stairs to the guy from some dealership in Buffalo.

The delivery boy handed him the package. "Dude, you must be someone special. I've never seen my boss bow to anyone like this before. It's all paid for."

Ryder ignored his comment, peeling a hundred out and handing it to the kid. "Leave all the packages and price tags in your car."

"It's the most expensive jacket we carry and was specifically requested. The best rated helmet we sell, too. Thanks, man." The kid tucked the money into his pocket, got into his car, and drove away as Ryder ascended the staircase.

He walked in and announced, "My buddy dropped the jacket and helmet off. Try it on and see if it fits." He helped her put on the jacket, pleased when it fit perfectly. It also didn't hurt that she looked fucking sexy in it.

She caressed the leather down the front, looking at every small detail. Then she removed it. "Wow, it's so beautiful. Are you sure your friend won't mind me borrowing it?" It had a dream catcher woven into the leather on the back, and the bead work on the front was stunning.

Sal stood, red-faced with fury. "Don't even think about it, Frankie! You're not getting your ass on the back of that bike. This guy has been charged twice with stunt driving, and those are only the times he got caught."

"Her name is Francesca," Ryder rumbled with a deadly, evenly toned voice. "And I would never put her in danger. Ever. Don't question my integrity when it comes to your sister. I respect her more than anyone else and will keep her safe. I swear my life on it."

Francesca was thrilled down to her panties, but the three of them were discussing her again like she wasn't in the room.

"Stop! All of you! I am a grown woman, and I can make my own decisions. Sal, Lucky, you both had motorcycles, so don't you dare tell me I can't ride one. Now, we all enjoyed Thanksgiving dinner, and you both have to leave because we are going for a ride."

"Francesca ..."

She lifted a finger, pointing it back and forth between them. "Not a word from either of you, or I swear, no dinners next week."

That hit the mark. They both pursed their lips, mad as hell.

"I love you both, but I need this for me. I went to the cemetery Friday for Tommy's birthday and visited Dad today. I just want to forget for an hour. Is that too much to ask?"

Both boys looked ashamed.

"Sorry, sweetheart. We weren't thinking. It's just ... we love you and worry. We can't lose you, too. We wouldn't survive that," Lucky told her.

"You are the centre of our world. With Dad not here, it's up to us to protect you," Sal added.

She walked into both of their arms for a hug.

"I trust Ryder, not just with my life, but also your piece of mind. I'm good; I swear."

Ryder had never been so humbled in his life.

Chapter 6

"Free Falling" By Tom Petty

Francesca could not believe how conflicted she felt. She was so excited she could hardly contain herself, yet she was also jittery about getting on Ryder's motorcycle. She was questioning her sanity. Her brothers were right; it was dangerous, but she wanted to try it so badly.

She had always been the responsible one, not that she minded. She always thought it was her calling. She loved to look after everyone. She stayed by her mother's side during her illness and took over the care of her little brother at the tender age of fourteen. When her mother passed, she took over all the household duties, cooking and cleaning. Her father and teenage brothers had also been working hard to pay the bills for her mother's treatments.

Then, when Tommy got sick, she took him to all his doctor appointments, nursed him while he threw up for hours, rocked him when he sobbed in pain, and read to him when he was well enough to listen. She had been the one to make all the arrangements when he died, while her Caesar buddies were instrumental in keeping her head above water after all the sorrow she had suffered.

At his funeral, she organized the children at the centre to sing, "This Little Light of Mine." Francesca painstakingly wrote Tommy's eulogy and read it at the funeral because she needed the world to know he was such a special kid. She stumbled a few times while reading it, stopping to pull herself together. She spoke about what a gift his life had been.

She wondered who would look after her remaining family if anything happened to her.

Her mom had always encouraged her to take the bull by the horns and try new things, even if she was uncomfortable. Therefore, she was going to get on Ryder's bike and relinquish all control for the first time in her life.

"Stay still, Beauty," Ryder reprimanded her fidgeting as he tried to tighten her helmet. "You have to listen to my instructions. Get me?"

"Yeah, yeah, hurry up before I lose my nerve," she said as she shifted from foot to foot.

He stepped back and pulled the zipper of her jacket right up to the top so no wind could get in.

"Ryder, I'm not a child. I can zip up my own jacket, and I don't want it zipped up to the top." She lowered it again to mid-chest.

He pulled his eyebrows together in annoyance. "Trust me; leave it. You're not in charge here." He batted her hand away from the zipper and pulled it back up to the top. Then he took her sunglasses out of her hands and placed them on her face.

She blew out a frustrated breath. "Beast." Then Francesca stomped as she followed him to the bike.

"We are going to mount from the left side." He showed her the foot peg as he pulled it down, and then moved to the other side to do the same before coming back to the side she was standing. "This is where you're going to put your left foot while you swing your right leg over the bike. I'll get on first, turn the bike on, and stabilize it. Once I'm in position, I'll signal you. Hold on to my shoulders and pull your leg over. Keep your feet on the pegs and away from the heat of the pipes. I want you to put your arms around me to hold on. Next time we ride, I'll put a back rest on for you. So far so good?"

When she said *yes*, he continued, "I installed a suicide shifter here." He pointed at the extension of chrome wrapped in leather. "Don't hit this at anytime, or this leg. Got me?"

She nodded.

"Finally, when we go into a turn, don't lean in. Just keep your body normal and let me shift the weight of the bike." Ryder was being extra careful, because this was the first time he was taking a passenger. "Ready to feel a freedom you've never experienced before?"

"Yes, please," she said with a huge smile.

He started the bike, and she jumped from the loud noise. He lifted one side of his mouth in a hint of a smile, signalled to her, and she jumped on like a pro, wrapping her arms as tightly as she could around his chest and squeezing his ribs.

He turned his head and spoke loudly over the sound of the pipes. "I need to breathe."

"Sorry!" she screamed unnecessarily. She lessened her grip as he revved the motor, released the clutch, and shifted. She screeched and tightened her grip again as they started to move.

He chuckled, not saying anything. He knew she would settle down once they got going.

Francesca was so nervous she couldn't open her eyes for a few moments. As time progressed, she cautiously opened first one eye, and then the other. Then she unconsciously loosened her grip as she got more comfortable.

She peeled her front off his back as she looked down at the pavement. Looking at the ground was screwing with her equilibrium, so she looked up and saw the trees whizzing by her. When they turned onto a four-lane road, she panicked when a car pulled up in the lane beside them and tightened her thighs around Ryder's hips.

He removed his left hand from the suicide shifter and leaned slightly back to rest his elbow on her leg as he wrapped his arm around her calf and rubbed softly along her muscles, soothing her fears. He removed it every time he had to shift it, and then immediately placed it back.

After about a half an hour, she settled down completely and started to really enjoy the ride.

Francesca could smell the unique scent that was all Ryder. She inhaled deeply every few minutes, not wanting to lose his scent in the wind. She found it comforting.

She was just becoming aware of what she was feeling underneath her hands. The guy was definitely built like a brick shit house. She couldn't feel one ounce of fat anywhere on his waist.

She wished for the first time that he would hang around after his community service hours were served. She knew he would go back to his old life, his job, and all the gorgeous California women. She couldn't compete with all those tanned, blonde bombshells. It made her sad, because he was becoming such an important part of her world. It killed her not knowing how she would survive yet another loss.

Now is not the time to think of sad things, she scolded herself. She needed to concentrate only on the ride. She couldn't even get over the fact that she was riding on a road without a seatbelt, or without the metal that surrounded her in a car, for that matter.

Look at me, Francesca Maria Moratti, taking a walk on the wild side. Yup, Ryder was right; this was a freedom she had never felt before, and her courage was growing by the second.

She leaned forwards and asked, "Can we go on the highway?"

"You sure?" he questioned. They had already been on the bike for an hour.

"Yes, please!" she responded as he watched her from the rear-view mirror. She had a smile that was so filled with anticipation that it sent palpitations to his heart.

Her wish was his command.

At the last traffic light, he turned his phone on and connected it to the radio.

Ryder felt her tighten her thighs against his hips as they ascended onto the highway ramp. He cranked the tunes as the wind picked up to help loosen her up. They were cruising at the speed limit, but he knew it felt so much faster on the bike. He wouldn't increase the speed past the limit. Her safety was of the utmost importance to him.

They had been driving for a couple of hours now, and he could feel her moving slightly to the tunes. When "Free Falling" by Tom Petty started to play, he heard her burst out in laughter.

The bike shifted slightly, so he glanced quickly to the side mirror, just as he felt her release her grip from around his waist. She tightened her thighs as she opened her arms out into the night sky while she tipped her head back and sang the lyrics loudly.

For once, he was thrilled that she bastardized the tune while she sang the words with all her heart. He would never forget the vision of her finally letting go.

He squeezed her calf muscle to acknowledge her abandonment of all that troubled her. This had turned out to be one of the best days of his life. It was like watching a caterpillar morph into a butterfly.

He wondered when he had started to think metaphorically and knew instantly it was when he had first laid eyes on Francesca.

They headed back to her place after another half an hour. He was cold, so he knew she must be freezing.

He pulled up into her driveway and, just as he turned off the motor, she jumped off, knocking him in the back with her foot, not even aware of it. He watched her happily struggle to get her helmet off as he got off the bike. Then he nearly fell over when she threw herself into his unstable body.

"Thank you so much! Thank you, thank you! That was, by far, the most exhilarating thing I have ever done." She locked her arms around his back as she gushed, looking up at him from his chest.

He wrapped his arms tightly around her in a hug. Then he pushed her back and placed his hands under her arms, lifting her so they were eye level. "Anytime you want to be free, you call me, Beauty. Got it?"

She smiled from ear-to-ear and nodded as her feet dangled about a foot off the ground.

He placed her back on her feet and wrapped his arm around her shoulder, leading her to the stairs of her apartment.

"Are you cold?" he asked as he placed a cold hand to her frozen cheek.

"Only my skin. My insides are bursting with warmth. Ryder, that was the best therapy for my state of mind. Thanks again."

As Ryder began to reply, he was interrupted by the ringing of Francesca's phone inside the apartment.

She rushed up the last few steps and quickly unlocked the door, grabbing her phone off the table the second she was inside.

"Hello? Holy crap, is that you, Gabriella …? I'm great. How are you?" He knew Gabriella was one of her Caesar buddies who now lived in Scotland.

He watched as she motioned with one finger that she would just be a minute. He nodded as he watched her wander into the living room and sit down on the couch.

He jumped when she screamed, "*What?* You're getting married …"

Ryder felt like Taz was in the room. That kid would quietly saddle himself beside Ryder then scream. Ryder knew if he didn't end up with a heart attack, it would be a miracle. The ladies in the room thought it was hilarious to see him jump in fright, so they never warned him like they did each other.

He decided to clean the kitchen as he half-listened to Francesca's giddy responses. He internally smiled when she said, "Get out! Prince Edward is hosting your wedding at Balmoral Castle?"

He started to scrape the plates she had loaded on the counters before they had left for their ride. He heard, listening as the pitch in her voice lowered, thinking he couldn't hear her.

"Gabriella, I can't afford to come … Gabby, I can't let him do that … I should pay my own way … Really? Okay, well, let me think about it …"

Francesca continued to talk for half an hour more, and just finished saying good-bye when she turned and saw her spotless kitchen. Her eyes bugged out of her head as she placed the phone on a box she used for a coffee table.

"Wow, you didn't have to do that. Sorry I was on the phone so long."

"Don't apologize. You cooked, so it's only fair," Ryder replied as he hung the tea towel on the handle of the stove.

She softened as she said, "No one has ever done that for me."

"Your brothers don't help you clean after you spend half the day cooking for them? That just pisses me right the fuck off."

"Don't get mad. That's just how my family works. And really, I don't mind. I like to do things for them. They do things for me, too."

Not believing the chauvinistic pricks reciprocated, he asked, "Like what?"

"They fix my car whenever I tell them something is wrong."

He knew it. "And?"

She got flustered. "They do a lot. I just can't think right now."

He let it go. It wasn't like he knew the dynamics of a family. He also didn't want her to feel he was judging the only family she had left. Internally, though, he thought they were fuckers.

"So, is your friend Gabriella okay?"

Francesca beamed. "Yeah, great news. She's getting remarried, and I couldn't be happier for her. Let me make us a cappuccino, and I'll tell you all about it."

He wasn't into funky fucking coffees, but if it bought him another hour of her time, he was in.

They sat in her living room, and she told him all about Gabriella and how her family had been murdered in front of her after her husband had been falsely charged with vehicular manslaughter. She said Gabriella had barely survived, and then she had disappeared for months. When she had finally resurfaced, she had met Liam, her future husband.

Francesca was very animated when she told Ryder that Liam was the personal bodyguard to Prince Edward, the third son of the King of England. She still couldn't fathom the fact that Prince Edward was hosting Gabriella's wedding and flying all her friends and family to Scotland to attend.

"You going?" he asked curiously.

"I'm not sure. I've been planning a trip to Italy in the summer to visit my nonna. I've been banking a hundred dollars bi-weekly for a year and a half. I arranged it so I can't stop the withdrawals and I can't touch the money until June fifteenth next year. I wasn't thinking at the time that my situation could change on a dime. I have some other financial obligations that popped up, so I have to be very careful with my money."

"Yeah, but if the prince is paying, then what are you worried about?"

"Well, I know I can get the two weeks off, but it would have to be unpaid. Then, even though he is paying for my flight and accommodations, I still have to pay for food and drinks, and I would have to buy a gift. I just don't know if I can swing it." Insecurity played across her face.

Ryder wanted to help. Fuck, he could give her the money; it was pocket change to him. However, she would never take it, and he didn't want to insult her dignity by offering. He had to think fast.

When he raised his head and looked at her paintings, it hit him.

"You could paint them a picture of Scotland for a wedding gift. Not only that, I have a proposal I wanted to ask you but was too embarrassed."

Her mouth dropped open. "You, embarrassed about anything? I find that hard to believe. But it's a great idea to give them a painting for a wedding gift, even if they never hang it up. What's this proposal?"

He wanted to remark on her lack of self-worth, but refrained. He had something bigger to say.

107

"Don't say no until I finish, okay?"

She nodded but didn't speak, racking her brain and trying to figure out what this proposal was all about.

Ryder needed to play this right to get her to believe him, so he positioned himself like he was lacking in self-confidence. He folded both hands between his legs and dropped his head to look at the floor.

"I know you have a lot on your plate already, but after experiencing your cooking, I'm starved for more. The takeout food is killing my stomach, and I was going to hire a service to deliver more nutritious meals to my condo." He lifted his head and looked directly into her eyes so she could see his sincerity. "I could hire you to do it for me. You would make the money, and I would reap all the health benefits. Do you think you could manage one more man on your list?"

Her smile brightened the whole room. "I could *so* do that. I would give you your cut of the grocery bill, and I could charge you, like, five dollars an hour for prepared meals you could microwave."

"Are you fucking nuts?" Ryder was stunned. She had no clue. "I was quoted seven hundred dollars for five days a week, breakfast, lunch, and dinner, Sunday through Thursday. I won't pay you any less."

She stood up from the couch, hands on her hips. Oh, fuck, he knew he was in shit now.

"Ryder Vaughn, how dare you call me nuts? If anyone is nuts, it's you. I feed six adults a week on five hundred dollars, so who's the dummy now?" Her face was red, but it wasn't from embarrassment. "Who quoted you that? Because that's highway robbery."

"I got three different quotes, and they were all within forty dollars of one another. It's not highway robbery. They have to shop, prep, cook, package, and deliver it. That's a lot of labour, apart from the price of the food." He wasn't sure he was getting through to her.

Damn, if only she knew he paid a chef fifteen hundred dollars a week, and that was part-time, and groceries were extra.

"Well, it should bloody well be served with champagne at that price." She exaggerated with a hand gesture.

He burst out laughing.

"Not funny, asshole."

Fuck, this was the angriest he had ever seen her, and it was making him hard. He bet she was a spitfire in the bedroom. Not that he would ever know, but a guy could dream.

When he regained his composure, he said, "Two swear words in two different sentences. You're coming along, Beauty."

She bent down and punched him in the arm. Hard, too. Then she backed away quickly like a true fighter, just in case he wanted to retaliate.

"Swear to Christ! You got bigger balls than most men I know. I get why your brothers nicknamed you Frank the Tank."

She rolled her eyes at him, and then threatened him by shaking her fist. Then she kissed her own bicep.

He choked on his chuckle.

"Compromise," he finally said. "I'll pay you five hundred dollars a week, and not a penny less. But you have to promise to make me dessert once a week and some of those hard, Italian cookies."

"They're called biscotti, dumbass." She shook her head. "You really do bring out the worst in me. I never swear. Anyway, I accept your offer. At least I can save you two hundred dollars a week."

Tonight, after the palm sisters helped to give him some relief, he would sleep easy, knowing he had won.

Chapter 7

"Somewhere I Belong"

By Linkin Park

Ryder walked into the classroom early, carrying a large bag. He tossed it on a desk before throwing his jacket on a chair.

Francesca heard him come in and turned down the music. Turning from the computer, she asked with a quizzical expression, "What's in the bag?"

"Just a few things I picked up for the kids on Saturday when I was out. It's nothing really."

She was really curious now. "Can I see? Or is it a secret?"

"Not a secret," Ryder mumbled, knowing he had quite a few secrets, but this wasn't one of them.

She stood and walked over to the bag, melting when she saw what was inside.

"This is the largest collection of plastic animals I have ever seen. And there are two identical bags!"

He walked over beside her and took out the other bag of animals. "I wanted to make sure, if Katrina's father threw these ones away, she would know she had more at school."

She looked up at him with adoration in her eyes. He had finally made a personal connection with the kids. The man could intimidate most people, and he didn't talk much, but he sure paid attention.

She picked up the next item. "A video game for Mason's handheld gaming console, right?"

He nodded as he took it out of her hand and turned it over. "Yeah. Couldn't get something for Katrina, and not the rest. They told me this is the most popular game right now."

She took out a huge package of plastic animated characters from all the movies Veeta watched. "Oh, Ryder, Veeta is going to love these." She placed it on the table then dug back into the bag, pulling out a big stuffed sloth. She quirked an eyebrow.

"Watch this." Ryder took the sloth from her, wrapped it around her neck, and fastened it. Then he wrapped the legs around her waist and fastened them. "Press its belly."

Francesca did, and the stuffed animal said, "*Give me a hug.*"

She laughed. "I guess that is better than 'give me some tongue.' What a perfect gift for Theo."

"Last but not least, I got Taz seven new belts, because we all know he's obsessed with them. One for each day of the week. But there is a means to my madness," he said as he lifted each belt out.

Each one was adorned with bells or dangly things. "The little bastard will never be able to sneak up on me again and scare the shit out of me when he screams."

She full-out belly laughed. "Well, now you're taking all my fun away." Holding her hands up, she said, "Only kidding. Seriously"—she beamed at him—"this is the most thoughtful thing anyone has ever done for our kids. Thank you. You really are a sweet man under the unapproachable biker façade."

"Not done yet. Got you a little something." He pulled out a wrapped package with a bow. "This is for Thanksgiving dinner. A small token to say thanks. Don't look at me like that. Just open it."

She tore into the package and laughed out loud again. "*Beauty and the Beast* dolls. How appropriate. Thank you. I will cherish them. But I'm warning you now, if you piss me off again, I'm using yours as a pin cushion. I'll do some crazy Italian curse like 'malocchio' and instead of the evil eye, you will be feeling each and every one of the beast's pins. So be nice!" She walked up and hugged him.

The rest of the staff shuffled in at different intervals. There was a supply teacher assigned to their room, but the administration thought it would be better to place the supply in another room and move an experienced teacher who knew the students' histories into their room. Therefore, Daniel was relocated into their room for the next few weeks.

They decided to have a team meeting to discuss how the students were going to react to the changes.

Daniel started the meeting. "Okay, what are your concerns regarding the transition of me into your room? Let's go around the table. Amanda, do you want to start?"

Amanda started off on the wrong foot with a giggle. "I'm all for having another man in the room with big muscles, right, girls?"

Her lack of professionalism irked Ryder, and he couldn't let the comment pass.

"Yeah, lady, 'cause we're here for your entertainment."

"Hopefully Daniel's muscles won't impede his ability to string together more than two sentences when he speaks," she fired back.

Francesca was shocked by her rudeness. If the tables had been turned, and a man had made a similar comment, there would have been a sexual harassment suit.

"Ryder doesn't deserve that. You owe him an apology."

Now Amanda was spitting mad. "Says the princess about her slave."

"People, can we stay on task?" Daniel waded in before things got out of control. "The kids will be arriving in fifteen minutes. Frankie, what do you think?"

Francesca quickly answered before Ryder could correct Daniel. "I think Mason and Veeta are going to struggle the most. Mason doesn't respond well to people he doesn't know. Veeta's diagnoses are autism and obsessive-compulsive disorder, but we deal with the OCD first. In her world, everything and everyone must be *exactly* the same, so we have to defuse that. Truth be told, change will be difficult for all of them. Let's introduce the change of teachers, and then jump into something positive that will occupy their minds while they unknowingly adjust to Daniel's presence in the room. Ryder gave us the perfect solution. He bought the kids some toys after Katrina's meltdown on Friday."

"Good idea." Layla was right on board with the suggestion. "It will give Veeta a visual cue, as well as a tangible one. I'll put her change card on her desk. That way, she'll know instantly a change is coming. As soon as she comes in, I will show her the card, introduce Daniel as our teacher, then take her to the calendar and show her when Julianna will be back in. Ryder can give her the gift, and I will play with her. Then Daniel can join us. I will phase myself out, giving them a chance to bond."

Daniel smiled. "Great plan. I'll try to interact with each student while they play, and hopefully, they will be more receptive to my presence. Let's play the rest of the day by ear. Thanks, team. Let's have a great day."

When they all stood up to leave, Daniel intercepted Ryder, shaking his hand. Daniel had heard about him but hadn't been formally introduced.

"Nice to meet you, Ryder. Heard you're considering opening a facility like ours in California. You couldn't have picked a better place to learn from. I look forward to working with you."

"Good to meet you, too. And just so you know, her name is Francesca, not Frankie." As he pulled away his hand, Ryder tapped Daniel's upper shoulder blade, downplaying his words. "Too smart and sweet to be a Frankie." Ryder quirked an eyebrow and walked away.

Daniel got the message, realizing this was definitely going to be an interesting month.

Each of the CYWs brought a student in, and the introductions went better than anyone expected. Mason was miserable when he first walked in, but he turned a corner as soon as Ryder gifted him with the newest and greatest game.

He looked at Ryder with mistrust. "Why'd you do it? 'Cause if you're going to take it away when I'm bad, I'd rather not have it." He thrust it towards Ryder, the light that had shone in Mason's eyes a minute ago filtering out. He had trouble with the concept of a gift that held no strings.

That statement was a total punch to the gut for Ryder. He knew better than anyone how a kid learns not to trust adults. They said one thing, then did another.

Ryder didn't take the game. He pushed it back towards the kid.

"Free and clear, Mason, it's yours. You can play it, give it away, or toss it in the garbage. You make the decision." Ryder meant that one hundred percent. If it took Mason smashing it and Ryder allowing it, so be it. He wanted the kid to trust him.

Ryder watched as Mason painstakingly opened the box and tried to remove the Styrofoam casement. A corner of the Styrofoam snapped and broke off, and Mason panicked, waiting for Ryder to take it from him.

"*Fuckin' bitch!*" Mason screamed as he pounded his fist down on the desk.

Daniel started to approach as the rest of the team readied themselves to move the other students safely out. Ryder motioned with his hands for them to wait.

Not understanding why Mason was freaking out, Ryder bent down and placed a hand on his shoulder to ground him from losing his cool or jumping up and tearing the room apart. Using a deep, commanding voice to get the kid's attention, he told him, "Words, Mason. Look at me and use your words."

Mason's eyes went from anger to defeat. "Fuck, Ryder, I broke the packaging. You can never return it now. I know you say it's mine, but I know I'll piss you off and you'll return it. Believe me; I know."

Ryder was so goddamn angry at this kid's mom and anyone else who had treated him so horribly. The kid's brains had been scrambled; what didn't they get? If any one of them were in the room right now, he would have caved their skulls in.

Words obviously weren't going to work, so Ryder took the half-opened box, removed the game, the Styrofoam, and the plastic, and tore the packaging to pieces. Then he walked to the teacher's desk, got a sharpie, and wrote Mason's name on every surface of the game.

Walking back, he said, "It's yours. End of story. I won't touch it. No one touches it. And if anyone does, they answer to me."

A strange look crossed Mason's face. Ryder couldn't decipher it. It wasn't a smile nor a smirk. Then Ryder realized it was the pride. Pride in ownership.

These kids deserved so much more than what they were used to getting.

Chapter 8

"Unsteady" By X Ambassadors

Ryder had been at the centre for three months now. His friendship with Francesca had blossomed, and it seemed to soothe the demons within him. He was learning to view the world through her innocent, loving eyes, and he was definitely a better person in her presence.

He wondered if she had been born so carefree, or if it had been taught. Had her parents showered her with so much love and respect that she didn't see the evil in the world? It was something he often pondered.

Ryder was still a very solitary man who kept most of his thoughts to himself, or he waited until they were alone before sharing them with Francesca. He had also formed a silent bond with some of the men in the centre.

Daniel had asked him to shoot hoops after school one day, and a few of the guys had joined them. They had asked him to play hockey with them, figuring his size would help their team—the perfect defenseman, no one would get through that monster. However, Ryder had turned them down with no explanations. They simply assumed he couldn't skate because he was from California.

The guys had tried to learn more about the centre that Ryder was opening in the States, but he wouldn't offer any information. Eventually, they stopped asking. He did join them at a local pub once a week for beer and wings and to watch the Toronto Maple Leafs play. Ryder liked hanging out with a normal bunch of guys. No egos, no drugs, and no fighting over or the sharing of some groupies. He didn't offer a lot to their conversations, but they didn't seem to mind in the least.

Ryder was shocked to learn the guys gossiped about the women at the centre as much as the women did. The difference was, they didn't expand on the gossip; they just stated facts and moved on.

They told Ryder about the ranking system they had for the women at the centre. They each had a list, numbering the women they would sleep with if they could. Francesca's name was in the top three of every list. It pissed him off, but he knew even "normal" guys were pigs.

Ryder had no claim over Francesca, so he kept his mouth shut. If they had been disrespectful at all, he would mess them up, and they knew it. The instant they referred to her as Frankie, he growled, correcting them. With the scary-ass vibe he sent out, the guys finally learned to call her Francesca.

Ryder's life was anything but average. However, he was starting to understand why everyone strived for the American dream. He liked waking up every morning and going to a job where he felt he made a small difference. He liked the camaraderie of the guys and the goodness he got from Francesca. He loved the home cooking he paid her to make each week. Fuck, he was eating stuff he couldn't name, but it was damn good.

It was Thursday morning, and Ryder was curious why Francesca's phone was burning up today. She seemed to be getting dozens of text messages. It started early in the morning, and at break time, she read them, smiling and replying. It kept beeping, and her fingers were flying over the keyboard.

The next text beeped in, and she giggled, responded, and put down the phone. He hoped she smiled like that when she read his texts. If only she could be his. But he knew his black heart would never allow him to give her what she deserved. She also had an important job and people relied on her.

Ryder was jealous and couldn't take it anymore when her phoned beeped once again.

"Popular today?"

She smiled when she looked at him. "Yeah, Dakota's birthday is this weekend, so we're going clubbing tomorrow night, as well as Caesar Friday."

He didn't like the sound of that. When she was with her sistas, they were a wild bunch.

Francesca had invited him to a Caesar Friday a couple weeks ago and introduced him to Dakota, Taya, Zara, Jocelyn, and they had Skyped Gabriella. They were a gorgeous group of women and out of fucking control when they were together.

"You clubbing in Toronto?" he asked, wanting the name of the place so he could go and keep an eye on these loose cannons.

"Yeah, we're going to Cream. We are all getting ready at Jocelyn's, having a couple of Caesars, and then uber it downtown." She sounded excited.

He wasn't happy with her answer, having trolled many of the clubs and knowing that one.

"That club is a fucking meat market. Why the hell are you girls going there? Are you looking to hook up?" He sounded bent.

"Ryder Vaughn, just because we are going clubbing, that doesn't mean we are looking to hook up," she said with an outraged attitude, hands on her hips, and that seven-foot personality rearing its ugly head.

"It's not safe," he grunted out.

She was having trouble whispering because she was seeing red. "First, you're not my father or my brothers. Second, there are five of us. Third, we go there occasionally, and it's perfectly safe. Lastly, I don't answer to you!"

She questioned why she was even explaining herself. Maybe, if he was her boyfriend, she would allow it, but he wasn't. He was her friend, and that's all he would ever be. She might have entertained more if they lived in the same city, but they didn't.

"Got it," he growled as he stomped out of the classroom.

Francesca didn't care if he was pissed off. It was none of his business.

They didn't speak the rest of that day or early the next morning. Francesca figured, if he was going to be a pissy jackass, she was going to make him pay for it. She wasn't sure how, but then the perfect revenge presented itself.

Mason was sick that day, and Theo was with a therapist in another part of the centre, working on speech and language. It was Julianna's first week back, and they were organizing a spa day when Francesca's idea started to form.

"Seeing as Mason and Theo aren't here, I think it would be a good day for Ryder to learn how spas work," she said with sweetness.

Julianna was surprised. "How do you want Ryder to participate?"

"Well, the only way to get the full experience is to dive right in," Francesca responded professionally, even though her intentions were anything but. "We won't put him with any of the girls from the other classes. I think he should pair up with Katrina today. He can paint her nails and brush her hair the same as we do. It doesn't matter that he is a man. Daniel did it, and Ryder will be running a centre and should know every facet of how we run ours. Hands-on experience is the best."

Ryder's eyes just about bugged out of his head. Was she kidding?

He crossed his arms over his broad chest. "Don't think I'm suited for that."

She loved his discomfort and continued to push the issue.

"You already have a bond with Katrina. You can't be afraid of her. When you run a centre like this one, sometimes you have to do things you aren't comfortable with. I'm not asking you to do her personal care, but I think this one time, you should join in. If it's beyond your capability, I'll take over." She smiled and thought, *Take that, Beast.*

He could see the manipulative little witch was trying to chastise him over their fight. Capability? Yeah, he knew he was totally incapable, but he would be damned if he let her win this battle. Little Miss Sweet and Innocent was being a conniving witch, knowing he wasn't opening a centre.

This was a side of her that he had never seen. It didn't piss him off as much as it should have. If anything, he was proud she could fight dirty. He would love to get down and dirty with her. He would take the challenge. Then maybe she would realize she couldn't paint him into a corner.

"I'll do it. Where do you keep the spa stuff?" he asked smugly.

Francesca was shocked, along with every other woman in the room.

"Well, good, then. Let's set up," she said when she regained her composure.

Katrina was thrilled Ryder was her spa partner. He had proved his worthiness to her. Every morning, she shared information with him about the two animals she had chosen for that day. He was a good listener, and she loved to talk endlessly about her animals.

Katrina chose three colours of nail polish and let him choose the final colour. He didn't say a word, just picked the neon pink because the brown was the colour of shit and the green reminded him of fungus. He started to open the bottle, but she stopped him and told him that he couldn't paint right away. He had to remove the old polish. Then she had to soak her hands in soapy water. Next, he had to massage her hands. And finally, he could paint.

She told him what cream she wanted for the hand massage, and then he started.

Her hands were so goddamn tiny and fragile that Ryder was afraid he might break them during her massage.

Francesca and the other women snickered as they listened to Katrina boss the giant around. He had been putty in her hands since the day she'd had her meltdown, doing anything she requested. It was sweet that he just wanted her to be happy. He had a big heart under all that muscle and rough exterior.

Now it came time for the painting. She told him he had to shake the bottle, and then paint each nail, starting with the pinky.

She laughed out loud when the first blob fell onto her pinky and had no bones about telling him how she wanted it done.

"No, Ryder, wipe the brush first, then paint. Now wipe it off, and do it again."

Damn, another bossy, little female to add to his list today.

He did as commanded, and Katrina giggled when he whispered something to her. She whispered back, and he countered with a look of pain. More whispering, and then he nodded his head.

Layla turned and asked the little girl, "What did Ryder whisper?"

Katrina looked at Ryder for affirmation before answering, "Can't tell you. It's our secret. But look how pretty my nails are." She lifted the first hand he had painted and everyone gasped.

There was paint on the nails and the surrounding skin.

"Don't judge. Her nails are too tiny. You like it, don't you, Katrina?" Ryder smugly defended himself. He was going to beat Francesca at her game, no matter the cost.

"I love it. It looks good, Ryder. Now continue so we can go on to hair," Katrina commanded as she fidgeted in her seat. She moved around so much the wet nail polish ended up everywhere. It didn't matter, though, because she couldn't make them any worse than they already were.

Francesca was stunned. She couldn't believe Katrina liked it. She only allowed Amanda or herself to paint her nails because she was so particular—part of her OCD. That was one of the reasons Francesca had paired them up together. She wanted Katrina to give him a hard time.

This wasn't making sense. Something was definitely up. He had probably bribed her with more plastic animals.

While Katrina's nails and fingers dried, Ryder brushed her shoulder-length hair. It was a task he didn't mind. It was calming, and she seemed to enjoy it. He had already told her that he couldn't do anything but brush it, and she had accepted that due to the deal they had made.

Francesca had to go to the office to submit some paperwork and ended up talking to the secretaries for about ten minutes while the students' nails dried. When she walked back into the room, she lost her mind, bursting out in laughter to the point of tears.

When she pulled herself together, she ran for her phone and asked them to smile for a picture. Katrina beamed a vibrant smile. Ryder … not so much.

"Don't. You. Dare," Ryder threatened with a rumbling, menacing voice.

"You know it's important to capture all the good things the kids do for their memory books," she replied sweetly and winked, which travelled straight to his dick.

She showed him the picture and burst out laughing again.

Ryder looked at the picture of himself with thirty fucking little ponytails sticking out of his head and a hair barrette with a flower clipped to his goatee.

Katrina stood behind him with a smile as big as her little face could hold.

"If that's the face of victory, you win hands down," Francesca conceded as she laughed again, along with everyone else in the room.

After seeing Katrina's smile in the picture and hearing Francesca's laugh, he got a strange, warm feeling in his chest and mellowed out. Not only that, it had broken the tension between him and Francesca, so it had been worth his humility.

The rest of the day went by quickly, and the kids had all just left on the busses.

Francesca gathered her stuff and said good-bye to the girls. Then Ryder and her walked out to their cars.

"Well, goodnight, Ryder. Have a good weekend."

He swallowed his pride and asked, "I know you're busy tonight, but how about a movie tomorrow night?"

She looked pleased they were still going to do something, even though he was ticked she was clubbing with her sistas tonight.

"How about if I cook, and we stay in and watch a movie? I sorta figure I'll be in recovery mode tomorrow."

"No cooking. I'll grab some Thai food and a movie."

That sounded perfect to her. "Sure. How about six? That way, we have time to watch two movies, and one better be a chick flick," she suggested strongly with a smirk.

He groaned but nodded. "Be safe. See you tomorrow."

"Always am."

Yeah, well, he was going to make damn sure of that, because he was going to that club to keep watch over her and the psycho bunch she hung out with. Not only that, he was following her to her father's on Sunday morning. He knew someone had upset her the last time she had visited, and it was eating him alive that she wouldn't talk about it.

He knew she was becoming his obsession, but she had no one to look after her.

***

Ryder arrived at the club at ten o'clock, having no idea what time they planned to arrive. He staked out a dark corner, ordered a beer, and waited. At eleven thirty, the girls stumbled in.

Two Caesars, my ass. These chicks are loaded.

He had to pick his jaw off the floor when he spotted Francesca amongst her girls.

She had on a little black dress with a black mesh V-cut down the front of her dress to below her ribs. There were some serious hints of cleavage showing, and it was too fucking short. What the fuck? She said she wasn't hooking up, but it sure didn't look like it to him.

She had sky-high, fire engine red fucking heels on, too, that made his spine stiffen. Her hair was curled and wild looking. Her eyes were made up smoky, and her full lips matched her red shoes. She looked stunning. His dick was more than twitching; it was goddamn pounding to get out.

Every bastard in the club stared at the group of gorgeous women. If anyone touched her, he was going to lose his shit.

He instantly saw two guys walk up to them, trying to stake their claim. However, the girls shook their heads and moved to the dance floor where they threw their arms in the air and danced for an hour, laughing and smiling. Any guy who tried to muscle his way into their group was pushed out, or they turned and danced in a different direction. They were there to enjoy each other's company and dance, plain and simple.

He smirked as he watched her sing, knowing that, if anyone could hear her, they would be running for the hills.

Then, all five of them went to the bathroom together and stayed in there forever. He considered going in when they came out and got a drink before moving back to the dance floor. That went on more times than he could count.

A couple of barely twenty-something skanks kept trying to get his attention, but he just pushed them aside so he wouldn't lose sight of Francesca.

They did a round of shots when last call was announced. Then he followed them as they stumbled into their uber. Not one of them hooked up with anyone.

When the door closed and they were off, he finally took a deep breath, settled down, and went home.

The next night, he went to Francesca's, and they shared some food and talked about her night at the club. Francesca teased Ryder and told him she met a big, burly guy. He laughed, knowing she was just goading him.

When he saw her rubbing her sore feet, he took over after a small argument. Then they watched a couple of shitty movies, and he left. He still had visions of her in the outfit from the night before, which made his dick throb.

The next morning, he was waiting up the street at seven forty-five. She pulled out of the driveway at eight, and he followed in the sixty-nine Camaro, not the Mustang GT he had started taking to the centre every day since the weather had turned cold.

He followed at a safe distance so she wouldn't get suspicious. After an hour and a half, he saw her pull into a driveway on the right. He was four cars behind her, so he didn't know where he was until all four cars pulled in and he read the sign.

Ryder was bowled over as he realized she was heading into the penitentiary. He had assumed he was following her to a retirement home. Jesus, her old man was in prison? He had not expected that from everything she had said about him.

She had told him many times that her parents had been very active in the church. Her father had even been an usher for the ten o'clock mass. She had said they used to attend mass every week, and then had a big family lunch at two. What could the man have possibly done?

His mind wandered, wondering if Mr. Moratti was involved in the Italian mafia. He was stereotyping, he knew, but he couldn't fathom anything else the man could have done.

He pulled up kitty corner to Francesca's car after she got out and walked into the building. He left the passenger window slightly open. Then he settled in, playing some games on his phone. After an hour, he decided to read the paper he brought to hide himself from Francesca.

Her burgundy hair got his attention when she bee-lined out of the building and towards her car.

He held the paper lower so he could watch her and still stay hidden with the assistance of the car's dark tinting.

She had been crying, but that wasn't what freaked him out. She looked scared.

She was almost to the car when he heard a man yell, "Miss Moratti, wait up."

She stiffened.

"I'm sorry, but I am in a rush. I'm meeting someone," Francesca responded with a quiver in her voice.

As the man got closer, Ryder could see he was a guard.

"If you care about your father, you'll listen."

Ryder knew instantly this was the fucker tormenting Francesca. He didn't know why, but his instincts were screaming at him to turn his phone on so he could videotape this conversation. He was thankful he did.

"Miss Moratti, I did a little research on you, and I was disappointed to learn that you lied to me. You don't have a child. You too uppity to have a drink with a lowly guard?" he spat at her.

She looked at his name tag. "Listen, Mr. Carson, I don't want any trouble, please," she begged, and that nearly made Ryder jump out of the car and punch the living shit out of the bastard.

"I warned you about your father's well-being last time. You didn't take me seriously. Did you know he happened to get into a fight and spent three days in solitary? It will be a little harder to get parole now." He grinned, which made him look even more evil.

"Oh, my God, no!" The tears started to fall as her frame shook.

"You underestimated my power," he said as he licked his lips and puffed up with the control he held over her.

"Please don't hurt my papa," she begged as all colour drained from her face.

How was she going to get out of this? She was panicked beyond belief. Visions of every TV show she had seen of an inmate getting knifed ran through her head.

Ryder was like a caged tiger, dying to get out and rip the man apart. He was crawling out of his skin. He could kill the little punk with one punch to the head, but then it would land him in prison, and Francesca would be visiting him, too. Therefore, he didn't move an inch, knowing he had to be smart and get it on tape.

Keep recording. Get what you need, he kept repeating in his mind.

"Why me? What did I do?" she asked, hoping he would see she just wanted to be left alone.

"I was kind to you, and you shoved it in my face. I tried to help you with the female guard, and what did you do? Nothing. Not even so much as a thank you. You think you're better than me, yet I hold all the power, not you. All I wanted to begin with was to get to know you and for you to acknowledge me, but no, you're too stuck up for that. Then you lied to me about having a kid. You think you can use that face and that body to get what you want? Bitches like you sail through life, using your looks to get everything you want."

"What do you want from me?" Francesca whispered, afraid to ask, but more afraid of the consequences her papa would suffer. This man had to be mentally deranged.

"I want to use you like you do others. I want you to show me it's worth my while to keep your father safe. You're going to pay to keep Daddy in one piece. And don't even think of telling anyone, because if anything happens to me, a price will be placed on your father's head," he replied with a holier than thou attitude. "We're going to have some fun, Miss Moratti. I'm off next Saturday, and you're going to meet me. Don't worry; you might even enjoy yourself." He winked then licked his lips again.

She tried to stall him, trying to think of something. "I can't come Saturday. I have a job and responsibilities." She was grasping at straws; she knew it, and by the look on his face, he knew it, too.

"You think I'm an idiot? I did my research. You work for Reach Within with fucking retards, and your hours are eight to three-thirty, Monday through Friday. You have two brothers, Luciano and Salvador, and no boyfriend. I have your cell number and your address. You went to club Cream on Friday with a bunch of sluts." He looked her up and down salaciously. "I didn't realize until I saw you in action what a slut you are. I think I'll start you on your knees, like the whore you are. Then you can satisfy all the rest of my needs any way I want."

Ryder was seething. He was about to lose his shit, consequences be damned. His knuckles were white from the pressure of his fingers around the phone. If that fucker touched one hair on her head, all bets were off. Ryder wouldn't be responsible for his actions.

Her eyes widened in sick fear, and she shivered. He had followed her? More frightening was the fact that he had some way of

135

finding information about her life. She was terrified.

She didn't have any choice. She would have to do as he said, or she was going to get her papa beaten, or worse … killed.

Could she sell her body for her papa's safety? She was a freaking virgin and didn't know the first thing about how to give a blowjob, much less anything else.

She lowered her head and nodded in defeat.

The guard smiled, his lips curling up with the knowledge he had her. "Be at the Coffee Express up the street at eight a.m. Don't make me wait. Now lift your head and smile, so if anyone is watching through the cameras, they will think I'm consoling you, and that you are thankful."

She lifted her head in one last ditch attempt to look at him and prove she wasn't the person he accused her of. She smiled as best she could, looked into his eyes, and saw the ugly soul of a heartless man. She knew her fate was sealed. There was no going back.

"See you Saturday, Miss Moratti." He turned and strutted through the front door of the penitentiary.

Ryder wanted to go to her instantly, but he knew the guard could be watching the parking lot.

Francesca struggled with getting her keys into the lock because she was shaking so badly. She finally got into her car and managed to get her keys into the ignition. She knew she was going to lose it, but she had to get away from the cameras first.

Ryder, knowing how important the video was, watched it for few minutes to make sure the sound was good before emailing a copy to himself and his high-priced lawyer. Then he followed Francesca for about half an hour until she pulled off the highway and into one those fast food chain restaurants. She parked behind the restaurant, threw the car door open, and ran behind the dumpster where she threw up the contents of her stomach.

Ryder watched her puke twice before he could get to her. Between the puke and her gut-wrenching sobs, he was afraid she was choking.

"Francesca?"

She screamed before she turned and saw Ryder.

He opened his arms, and she flew into them without any hesitation, like he was her lifeline. He held her tight and rubbed her back with one hand. The other he ran repeatedly down her hair in a soothing motion. She was so unsteady and shaking as she sobbed hard into his chest that he had to loosen his grip a bit so she could draw each deep breath.

"It's okay, Beauty. You're safe now. I won't let anyone hurt you again. I promise."

"Why is God punishing me? What did I do?" She sobbed harder. "I don't know what to do. How do I survive this?"

He was beside himself with rage. His black heart was torn to shreds by her comments. Ryder couldn't believe she was blaming herself. This was the guard's fault. She had to see that.

He didn't believe in God, but no God would believe she did anything wrong. She was too sweet and giving.

He pulled her head back, keeping her body close to his in a protective stance. "You did nothing!"

She tried to lower her head in shame, but he wasn't allowing that. He wanted to see that seven-foot personality that fought for everyone else.

"Don't hide from me. Talk. Let me help."

He wasn't prepared when she tore her body away from his. Now she was mad. He wanted her to be angry, just not with him.

"You can't help. You don't get it. I must have done something horrible, because God made my mother sick, and then took her from me." She flung her hands out, yelling, "Then Tommy! What the hell did that beautiful child ever do to anyone? He didn't just kill him, He made him suffer first! Then my papa—paying a debt he doesn't owe!" She lowered her voice, the fight leaving her as she spoke with a scratchy voice from screaming. "And now I have to put my papa in jeopardy by being stupid and inconsiderate. What is the common denominator here, Ryder? Let me tell you. *Me!*"

"God isn't punishing you, sweetheart. Sometimes bad things happen, and we can't control it. We need to blame someone, so we blame ourselves or God. None of this was your fault. I believe, in this life, we all suffer, either when we were young or when we are older. You can't go through life without suffering. Otherwise, you won't recognize the good."

"I try so hard to be a good person," Francesca continued. "I really do. I believe you reap what you sow. But nothing I do works. At every corner, I get knocked down."

"Being a good person doesn't exempt you, Francesca. It only makes you feel it more deeply than most."

She weakened with his response and lowered her head. "So how do I change? I don't want to feel deeply anymore. I want to numb myself from the pain."

Ryder gently lifted her chin. "You can't change, Beauty. It's who you are. You feel more than most because your soul is extraordinarily pure. Don't try to change that. You won't like the person you become; believe me. Let me help you. Let someone else carry the burden."

"I can't, Ryder." She wanted that more than anything in the world, but she knew the consequences and couldn't risk it.

"Do you trust me?" he asked.

"Yes, but not with this. I can't risk you, too."

Ryder was getting irate again. "The question was: Do you trust me?"

She stomped her foot in frustration. "Yes, but—"

"Leave out the but and it's a good answer." He slightly smirked.

"Ryder, how—"

"Get in my car, and let me deal with it." He looked at the indecision on her face. "Now!" he barked.

Ryder continued to smirk as he watched her jump at his command and stomp off in the wrong direction. In two strides, he was beside her and wrapping his arm around her shoulder, guiding her towards the Mustang.

She pulled to a quick stop. "This isn't your car. And what about mine?"

"You're not listening very well, Francesca. I said I would take care of everything. Now get in."

Chapter 9

"You Are Not Alone"

By Lifehouse

Ryder glanced over at Francesca as he drove away. She looked haunted and frightened. He wasn't happy that she was still white as a ghost. At least she had stopped crying, though. And she had been so wrapped up in her head that she hadn't asked how he had found her.

Ryder reached over, laying his hand on her thigh, giving it a squeeze to reassure her. She turned and looked at him, tried to smile, but failed.

Ryder was going to make sure that bastard paid for abusing his girl.

Jesus, when did he start thinking of Francesca as his girl?

"I will take care of it, I promise. Please just trust me."

"You don't understand, Ryder. He will hurt my papa. I can't allow that to happen."

Ryder kept turning away from the road to watch her as she

chewed on her bottom lip, deep in thought. Then Francesca whipped her head around to face him. She was shaking again.

"How d-did you even know I was in that parking lot?"

"Not going to lie. I need you to trust me. I was worried. You wouldn't tell me what scared the shit out of you last time you visited your dad, so I listened to my gut and followed you. You're too proud to ask for help."

He waited for the fireworks. She was such a strong, independent woman, so he knew she would be offended.

"So you know where I went?" she asked quietly, wringing her hands in her lap.

Relief swept over him. He hoped she might have missed the part about him following her.

"Yeah, Francesca, I figured it out when I pulled up to the prison."

She looked at his profile. "My papa is a good man. Please don't judge him."

"Not my place to judge your old man. He raised you; I know he's good." He faced forwards, looking at the road.

Her tone changed. "He's not old! He is my papa, not my old man. My brothers call him that, and I hate it. It's so disrespectful," she spewed with anger.

Ryder was shocked by her venom but understood she was raw. "Meant no disrespect."

She instantly felt guilty. "Sorry."

"Francesca, you need help. I'm calling my lawyer."

"I can't afford a lawyer," Francesca was embarrassed to admit.

"Can you afford to get attacked?" Ryder snapped. "After he gets what he wants, can you guarantee he won't still hurt your father? Put your pride away for ten minutes and think this through logically. That man is a predator."

She wrapped her arms around her stomach, the thought of it all was making her want to puke again.

Ryder was comfortable knowing he had scared her. He needed Francesca to know this was beyond them both. He would get advice from his lawyer and let the legal system deal with that bag of shit.

He handed his phone to Francesca. "Password is three-seven-eight-six. Go under contacts and look up James Quinn. Push speaker."

Lost in thought, she did as he requested without thinking.

"Hello?"

"James, Ryder Vaughn calling. Need some advice. You got a minute?"

"Uh, sure, Ryder. Give me a second … Okay, I can hear you better. What's wrong? Did you get in trouble again? You know you have to stay at Reach Within for your full-term, except for the prearranged dates we set with Judge Belmore."

Annoyed, Ryder answered, "James, I'm driving, and you're on

speaker phone. I have a friend in the car."

"I apologize, Ryder. What can I do for you?"

"I have a good friend who is in some trouble and needs some guidance and protection for herself and a family member who's in prison. I need to know how to proceed."

"I need more information. Sum it up with specifics," the lawyer responded, piqued with interest.

"Her name is Francesca, and her father is in prison. A guard just threatened her with her father's life if she doesn't give up her body to the fucker. I recorded the whole conversation and sent you the video through email about an hour ago."

This was news to Francesca. Her eyebrows shot up, and her mouth gaped open as she looked over at him.

"Jesus," James exclaimed. "Head to my office now. I'll meet you there. In the meantime, I'll make a few calls."

"Will do. About forty minutes away. And, James, I don't need to tell you discretion is a must. I don't want this asshole seeing us coming."

"Without question, Ryder. See you soon."

Ryder hung up on his lawyer. Now he had to deal with his beauty.

"I need you to fill me in on your father. Why is he in prison?"

"You recorded our conversation? How? Why?"

"Francesca, we don't have time for this now. I need the

background information on your father."

Francesca knew in her heart, if Ryder was going to help her, she needed to tell him the whole story.

"You know about my mother and Tommy. What I didn't tell you was that my mom's medicine and treatments were expensive. The government pays for the treatments, but a lot of the medications are extra. My family owns a small cabinet-making business that my papa and brothers run. It's successful, but my mother's medications were too much.

"My papa never told us kids that he drained my parents' accounts, and then borrowed money from his family, hoping some unconventional treatments would cure her. When she died, he mortgaged the house to pay for her funeral and most of his debt. He could have recovered from that, but then Tommy got sick. He didn't have the money to pay for the medications, and it was months of treatments and pain management.

"He didn't tell us, but he got a second job at night. Then, one of his long-time customers asked if he could store a couple of pallets in their unit and pay rent for the space. Papa said yes because we could use the money. The pallets kept increasing, and so did the money he paid. Just after Tommy died, the police showed up and seized the goods.

"My father was charged with possession of bootlegged alcohol. He had no idea the wine was bootlegged and got five years. We sold the house, but it was mortgaged to the hilt, so we got a huge loan from one of Papa's best friends to pay for the lawyer and Tommy's funeral. My brothers and I pay a monthly fee for the loan. My brothers now live in an illegal loft above the shop that has no kitchen. That's why I cook for them."

Francesca sat quietly while he absorbed all she had told him.

"I don't know what to say." The anger building inside of him was ready to burst, but Ryder didn't want to frighten her.

Everything she had tried to hide came rushing back into his head—the gas for the car, the dinner, the second job, her furnishings. He was sick for all the struggling Francesca and her siblings had endured for the love of their family. Meanwhile, he could pay all their debts without it making a dent in his portfolio.

"If you've changed your mind about helping me, I totally understand." She straightened her shoulders. "Just drive me back to my car. I'll deal with everything else."

Ryder slammed his hand against the steering wheel, making Francesca jump. She moved closer to the door and farther from him.

"I haven't changed my mind, okay! Just give me a minute to process all this shit. It makes me sick … all the burden you have to carry."

She softened and relaxed. "We all have crosses to bear. I accepted mine and moved on. I just need to figure out a way out of this without incurring more debt."

"Don't push me over the edge. I said I'll take care of this. Get me?"

Ever so softly, she tried to calm the beast. "Ryder ..."

"Don't do that. Don't *Ryder* me. We are doing this my way. The right way. And if you mention money again, I'm really going to lose it." He took a calming breath. "Let's just stop talking until we hear what James has to say."

They drove the rest of the way to the lawyer's in silence, each battling their own demons.

When they arrived and introductions were made, Francesca followed James into a boardroom, Ryder right behind them. There was another man sitting at the conference table. James introduced him as Carl Brady, an RCMP—Royal Canadian Mounted Police—officer.

Francesca panicked and backed up into Ryder, afraid.

Ryder grabbed her hips gently from behind and whispered into her ear, "It's okay, Beauty. He's here to help."

She relaxed marginally, and Ryder grabbed her hand, guiding her to the seats across from the officer. He didn't let go of Francesca's freezing cold hand, offering whatever support he could.

"Miss Moratti, Mr. Vaughn, I realize this is an uncomfortable situation, but I'll do everything in my power to make this as easy as possible," Officer Brady stated. "James and I are old friends, and right now, I am here under no other pretence than to lend an ear and listen to your story. I will advise whether it warrants an investigation. If I need to get officially involved, I will. This is totally confidential. Anything you tell me will not leave this room unless a law has been broken.

"First, I need to speak to Miss Moratti alone, and then Mr. Vaughn. James, will you take Mr. Vaughn to your office? I'll let you know when I need to speak to him."

"I'm staying." Ryder was not comfortable leaving Francesca alone.

"I get you wanting to support Miss Moratti, but if this is as serious as I am led to believe, I have to handle it to the letter of the law. She'll be fine with me, I promise."

Francesca was torn, scared. She wanted Ryder with her, but she knew he needed to calm down. He was strung tighter than a rope; ready to snap at any minute.

With pleading eyes, she said, "Ryder, I'm okay. Please go with James so we can get this over with."

"You need me, you call," Ryder conceded. He would do anything for her. Then he looked at the officer. "Be gentle; she's gone through enough today."

"Of course," Carl replied with a professional smile.

Ryder followed James to his office and threw himself into a chair across from his lawyer, running his hands through his long, unruly hair. "This is fucked up. I want that bastard destroyed." He rubbed his hands across his face and down to his goatee as he looked up for James's response.

"We'll get him, Ryder. Let the legal system deal with it. Tell me your version of everything that happened today."

Ryder explained the whole incident to his lawyer and everything he had learned about Francesca's family. "I want you to look into Mr. Moratti's case. I know they didn't have a lot of money, so his representation was probably shoddy at best. I want you to arrange for me to meet him after this situation is taken care of. I want to know when he is up for parole, and I want you to make it happen. I'll cover the cost. I want this to become your number one priority, and I don't want Francesca to know."

"I can certainly do that. You must realize, though, that I have other clients and cases coming up. I'll need help from my junior partners."

A knock came to the door, and Carl stuck his head inside. "I'm calling in a team. We're taking over your conference room for the day. I need to talk to you alone," he directed at Ryder.

Ryder was on his feet. "Need to make sure Francesca is okay first."

Carl nodded. "Just don't discuss the case."

Ryder charged into the conference room, frightening Francesca from her thoughts.

"You scared me!" she exclaimed with her hand held to her

149

chest.

"Sorry. You know they're going to bring him down, right?"

"Oh, God. What if something happens to my papa in the process? I can't lose anymore of my family." Tears filled her whiskey coloured eyes and began to fall.

Ryder walked over and pulled her out of her seat, wrapping her up in his powerfully large arms. He kissed the top of her head, smelling the green apple scent of her hair.

How much can one little person go through without breaking? he wondered for the thousandth time.

"Beauty, nothing is going to happen to your father. I promise." He grabbed her shoulders and pushed her back a bit so she could see the sincerity in his eyes.

Right now, she was his top priority. He needed to get her through this.

"I trust you," she told him as she stepped into his comforting arms and smell. She took three deep breaths of the scent that was all Ryder, closing her eyes and drawing strength from him. "Thank you," she whispered into his chest.

***

The day progressed slowly as plans were made to catch the twisted guard. James started finding everything he could about Mr. Moratti's case, while Carl arranged to have Francesca followed by undercover officers to insure her safety.

"I want Francesca at my place until this is over," Ryder stated firmly, not leaving room for argument. He should have known it wouldn't be that easy. The one who fought him was the one he needed to protect.

Francesca shook her head. "I can't, Ryder. I have the boys. In fact, I still have to cook tonight when I get home."

"I'm not arguing with you over this. You're coming to my place. The fucker knows your address."

She pulled her shoulders back and unleashed a tirade of her own. "If he knows my address, then the boys are in jeopardy, and I won't leave them alone." She stomped her foot as she often did when she was frustrated. "The undercover officers will watch my place, and protect me and the boys. I put them in this situation, and I'm not leaving them to fend for themselves. Sorry, but you're not the boss of me. I appreciate everything you've done, but I can't have my life turned upside down anymore than it already is. What if my brothers stop by and I'm not there? What do I tell them? No, it has to be this way."

All the men in the room tried not to smirk, knowing she was winning this fight, hands down, no matter how much he tried to intimidate her with his deep, lethal voice.

Ryder threw his hands in the air. "Fine! Then I'm staying at your place. No arguments, or I swear, Beauty, I'll lose my shit!" He walked out of the conference room, mumbling something about seven fucking feet of personality.

"Thank you," she huffed out, needing control over something when everything else was spiralling out of control.

After they left the lawyer's office, they stopped by Ryder's condo to pick up the essentials he would need for the week.

Ryder introduced her to Carlton, the building's concierge. He was a friendly man who seemed pleased to meet Ryder's guest. Ryder informed Carlton that, if Francesca ever needed anything, he was not to hesitate in assisting her. He also told Carlton that, if she needed access to his condo, he was to let her in, no questions asked.

Francesca wasn't sure why she would ever need anything from this man, but it was nice to meet him.

As they walked through the lobby, she was overwhelmed by the opulence of the building and the security it offered. Francesca assumed Ryder must do very well for himself to live in a building like this. She felt like she was in a five-star hotel until they stepped off the elevator and into Ryder's place.

Francesca walked through the condo while Ryder went to collect his things, saddened by the appearance of his home.

It was on the fifty-fourth floor, and it was huge, but it held no life. There were no pictures anywhere, the walls were stark white, and the floors were a cold grey veined marble. One black leather couch and a ginormous TV, and floor to ceiling windows with no window coverings.

She looked out the window at a stunning view of the city. Then she wandered into the kitchen where all the appliances were stainless steel and there was a huge marble island. The kitchen would have been gorgeous with some furniture and decor pieces. Still, it was a cook's dream.

She opened the fridge, finding only beer and one dinner she had made, with a couple pieces of fruit and one of her muffins.

She continued her tour, wandering up to the second floor where she found his bedroom. Ryder was throwing things in a small duffle bag from a larger one. He hadn't even unpacked yet, and he had been in Toronto for well over three months.

She felt sorry for his lonely existence in this big, empty apartment. He had come such a long way at school, but other than that, he seemed to have no one in his life, except her. She knew it must have been for lack of wanting, or maybe he already had someone in California.

She knew it wasn't lack of women wanting him. The ladies at school fell over backwards trying to get his attention. Everywhere they went, women tried to push her out of the way to get closer to him. He was intimidating, but that added to his allure.

Francesca loved to stare at him. When he walked, it was with an uneven swagger. Maybe it was hard to walk carrying all that muscle? He was confident, strong, and hot, but obviously very lonely.

"Ryder?"

He looked up from his packing and saw her leaning against the doorframe, still looking sad and lost.

"Yeah, Beauty?"

"Why does it look like you don't really live here?" She moved closer to the ginormous bed with its crumbled black duvet.

"I don't really. Just doing time."

She guessed this was his self-appointed prison.

"So, your place in California … it's your home?"

He stopped what he was doing and sat down on the bed, looking her straight in the eyes. "Never had a home. I have a place where I throw my shit and sleep, but no home. Never needed or wanted one."

Her heart fractured a little for him. No family, no home, a handful of friends, and his job that he wanted to love, but couldn't because people were making it difficult for him.

"I don't understand that," she said, sincerely hoping to gain some insight about her friend.

"I was taught at an early age that a home represents family. The sperm donor and incubator weren't family. The first place I ever felt like I was in a true home was in your place."

Francesca's eyes welled up. "You would have loved my parents' place, then. My mom made our home beautiful. She filled it with colourful things—photos, paintings, candles, different art pieces she made. Everywhere you looked, there was something. Our fridge was covered in her collection of magnets from places all over Italy she wanted to visit. She was Irish, but she fell in love with my papa's hometown in Italy and wanted to discover more places like it when my papa and her retired."

While Francesca spoke, she rubbed the medallion attached to a chain around her neck. "The trip I'm planning in the summer with Taya is to all the places she wanted to visit. I'm going to take pictures and bring them to the cemetery to show her."

Ryder looked at her in awe. She was the most selfless person he had ever met.

"What's with the necklace?"

She smiled from ear-to-ear. "This was the last thing my mother gave me. See? It's a St. Gregory medallion. He is the patron saint of teachers, students, and musicians. Not sure where the musicians fit in because I can't play any instruments, but the student and teacher, I get. My mother gave me the necklace to guide me as I followed my dream."

"Sorry I'll never get to meet her."

Her smile dropped. "I hope I can be half the woman she was." Francesca got up and walked towards the door, wiping away a stray tear. "We better get going. I still have to cook, and it's getting late." She walked out of his room and back downstairs to find her purse and phone.

Ryder shook his head, knowing she had probably surpassed her mother's greatness years ago.

***

Francesca was in her element as she cooked, looking adorable. All her apprehension seemed to have melted away in the kitchen. She had her hair tied back in a messy ponytail with a bandana wrapped just behind her bangs and tied on the left side of her head with a little bow.

Ryder didn't think she could ever look anything but perfect. It didn't matter how she styled her hair or dressed. She could wear a brown paper bag, and she would still be alluring.

"You're staring at me, and it's making me uncomfortable. You don't have to worry about me. I'm okay now that you're here. Now find something to do before you make me crazy. Dinner will be ready in half an hour."

He smirked. She thought he was worried about her, which he was, but that wasn't why he was staring at her. She was just that beautiful.

He wanted desperately to make a move on her, but he knew his empty heart would somehow taint all her goodness. He had spent many nights dreaming about sinking himself to the root in all the pureness that was Francesca, something that could never happen.

She needed someone with a stable job. Someone who would always be around to help her and love her the way she deserved. She needed someone whole, kind, and who could lovingly show affection. A man who could give her children and a white picket fence. He was none of those things.

He stopped staring and looked around her home, entirely comfortable in her tiny apartment. He again looked at the paintings she had done, full of emotion, drawing you in. He was still beyond impressed and hoped to commission her to paint him one. Although, his favourite would always be Stonehenge. The mystery and darkness spoke to him. The girl was full of talent and didn't have a fucking clue.

He picked up her sketchbook from off the crate she used for a coffee table and started flipping through the drawings. He assumed they were all of Italy by the names of the sketches. The Amalfi coast; Castello Gradara, Tropea, San Marino; and one that intrigued him the most was labeled, Civita di Bagnoregio.

"Is this place real?" Ryder asked as he walked into the kitchen with the sketchbook.

She smiled. "Yes. Isn't it spectacular? This is one of the places my mom dreamed of seeing. It's a town in Tuscany that eroded over hundreds of years ago, and only the core of the city is left. In the research I did, they said the morning fog makes it look like a castle out of a fairy tale. Cool, eh?

"They built a walking bridge to the town, and they say it has one of the oldest working olive presses left in the country. Can you imagine how good the olive oil must taste?" She licked her lips, and all thought of the town disappeared for Ryder.

Thankfully, she packed up the boys' dinner and said she would be right back.

Francesca delivered the boys' dinner and made sure they were settled before she left. When she got back, she sat down with Ryder and ate a delicious meal.

"Francesca, we need to talk about today."

Ryder saw the blood drain from her face. She had been happily pushing all thoughts of the guard away until now.

"I know. I guess I'm just not ready—"

"Listen, I'll be with you every step of the way. Promise. The RCMP are going to come to the centre on Thursday and Friday to brief us on the takedown. Carl told me they'll be wiring you and recording the whole conversation. There will be a large team in place, and I'll be there. Don't be frightened."

"I'm not scared for myself. I'm worried about my papa."

Ryder took her little hands in his, noting the size difference. Turning them over a few times, he was mesmerized by the strength that came from the tiny appendages.

"He'll be fine. They are considering transferring him to ensure his safety, but they won't do that until the fucking guard is locked down. James is gonna be your father's contact to the outside world. Carl said he'll keep him in the loop, and James will keep you in the loop. Trust me, Francesca."

"I do, but I can't talk about this anymore. Just let me live in my little bubble until I have to face it." She looked away, trying not to cry again. "Thank you for rescuing me today. I don't know what made you follow me, but whatever divine intervention brought you to me, I am so grateful. You're a good man, Ryder Vaughn. You're my hero."

"I'm nobody's hero."

Chapter 10

"The Sound of Silence"

By Disturbed

It was five a.m. on Saturday, and Ryder knew Francesca hadn't slept a wink. She baked when she was upset. After her three-hour baking session last night, they talked until two a.m. Ryder listened attentively while she told him all about her family and friends. Then, from two until four-thirty, he'd heard her pacing in her bedroom.

Ryder had spent the week sleeping on her couch, watching over her as promised and being a shoulder for her to lean on. He loved the fact that she was depending on him for emotional support.

Their work week had been difficult because Francesca wore her emotions on her sleeve. Even the kids picked up on it. He learned that kids were very intuitive, something he was convinced was instinctual.

Mason had asked Ryder twice if Francesca was all right, and he had lied to the kid, telling him Francesca just wasn't feeling well.

That said, the kids rallied around her, trying to get her to laugh or hugging her just a little longer than normal, giving her a little of what she gave them daily.

Now Carl was busy talking to her, while a female officer knelt behind Francesca, taping a device to the small of her back. Ryder was irritated, watching how embarrassed Francesca was becoming as the officer lifted her clothes, exposing her to everyone in the room.

"Carl, give her the lowdown after she's wired. Leave her be for five minutes." He gestured towards the living room, and Carl followed him out.

"Sorry, I'm used to working with agents," Carl apologized.

Ryder mellowed a bit at his comment. "Francesca's scared, she hasn't slept, and she's worried sick about her father."

Carl could plainly see the man was totally infatuated with Francesca. He himself was impressed by her strength and determination.

"It will all be over today. We'll get this prick, and then move Mr. Moratti to safety."

Ryder ran his hands through his hair. He was still unsettled with the thought of Francesca going anywhere near that fucker. He swore to himself, if that bastard laid a finger on her, he was going to rip him apart with his bare hands. Police be damned.

"I want to be right there with you. As soon as you have that fucker in your hands, I want Francesca in mine. Get me?"

161

"Mr. Vaughn, you're too emotionally involved. We don't need you losing your temper and screwing this up. You'll wait up the road with our secondary team. We don't allow civilians anywhere near a takedown."

Ryder tensed, crossing his arms and ready to fight. "Either I'm with you, or I'm there on my own. You choose."

Carl was not used to anyone challenging him or his authority. Regardless, it wasn't worth the fight. Besides, Ryder had earned the right to be in the van. He had watched over and protected Francesca, and convinced her to help nail the crooked guard.

"Here's the deal. You must give me your word that you will follow my instructions to the letter. If I don't believe you can, I will lock your ass up until this operation is over."

"If I'm there, I'm cool, man. And she rides back to the city with me. You get some lackey to drive her car back."

"You can drive her back, but I have to debrief her. I arranged a visit with her father. You drive her to the new facility. I'll put your name on the visitors' registration."

Ryder was silent while he absorbed the gift he had just been handed. He had wanted to visit Mr. Moratti without Francesca knowing. Being on the visitors' list allowed him that opportunity.

Francesca and the female officer came out of the bedroom, Carl gave his final instructions, and then they all left in separate cars.

Francesca was a nervous wreck as she drove in silence to The

Coffee Express, arriving half an hour early, full of apprehension and dread. Carl had wanted her there early so she could settle in by the window. That way, they could keep an eye on her. Hopefully the guard would sit with her and state his intentions. Otherwise, they would have to follow her to whatever location he demanded.

Francesca was terrified they would lose her if he drove her to another location. Her skin crawled at that thought of being trapped in his vehicle, or that he would discover the wire.

She tried to bring the coffee cup to her mouth, but her hands were shaking so badly she spilled it on her hand.

"Jesus Christ, that's hot. Calm down, you stupid idiot," she mumbled to herself, forgetting everyone could hear her.

Ryder's heart dropped at hearing her. He was breathing deeply, ready to explode.

Carl watched the giant's leg bounce up and down. He was starting to second-guess his decision to allow Ryder to be at the scene.

"Calm down. It's only going to get worse. Are you sure you can handle it?"

"Fuck you," Ryder spat.

Carl needed to defuse the monster, so he tried another approach.

"I know it's hard, but be the man she needs you to be. Put your feelings aside."

Ryder turned his fierce expression towards Carl, realizing the man was only trying to help.

He blew out a long breath. "I'll lock it down."

Ryder turned towards the monitor and watched Francesca in silence. Fifteen minutes passed before he saw the guard get out of his car and approach the coffee shop.

"That's him," Ryder said as his body went rigid with awareness.

"Suspect's approaching now. Black jacket, jeans. Everyone in position," Carl spoke into the headset.

An evil smile appeared on the guard's face when he saw Francesca sitting by the window. He looked around the parking lot, not noticing the decoy electrical van. Carl had two undercover officers dressed as electricians sitting beside Francesca, and two cars with undercover officers in the adjacent parking lot.

The guard watched the fear spread over Francesca's face as she saw him approach.

"Nice to see you could make it this morning, Miss Moratti," he said as he smoothly sat in the chair across from her with a smile on his evil face.

"I said I would. How is my papa?" she asked as she fidgeted with her hands, glancing at him through her bangs.

The guard's smile faded as he leaned forward over the table, whispering so no one around them could hear, "You have little faith, Miss Moratti. You act as though you're going to an execution. Change the attitude, because we are going to have a lot of fun today.

If you do all that you're told, he'll be fine." He placed a hand over her trembling ones and gave her a sinister smile, getting off on her fear.

She recoiled a bit, but didn't remove her hands, whispering back in an unsteady voice, "What do you want from me?"

He stood and offered his hand. The guard wasn't stating his intentions in the middle of the coffee shop. "Make it look good, Miss Moratti. Remember what's at stake."

Francesca stood on shaky legs, placing her hand in his. He pulled her close to his side, and then removed his hand from hers, casually throwing his arm over her shoulders and yanking her tighter into his side.

He guided her to the door, and when they stepped outside and away from anyone who could hear, he said, "You, my uppity little whore, are going to start on your knees and suck me off good. Maybe I won't even wait until we get to the motel. Maybe I'll have you do it while I'm driving. Then, I am going to fuck you in the rest of your holes. You are going to worship me all day long, seeing as I am spending thirty-nine dollars on a motel room for you. I've been fantasizing all week about this, and you're going to make it good."

Francesca didn't reply right away. His words had stolen her response.

Ryder whipped his head towards Carl. "He said it. Now get him the fuck away from her."

165

"We need more," Carl snapped at Ryder, his patience gone.

Francesca stopped at the passenger door the guard had opened with tears in her eyes. "Please, I am begging you not to do this to me. I didn't do anything to you. I just wanted to visit my papa." Her voice crumbled on her last sentence.

"Come on, Francesca; get him to say it," Carl coaxed, though she wouldn't hear. "Get ready, people. Vehicles, pull out and get ready to block."

Ryder grabbed the ledge the monitor sat on so tightly his knuckles were white, but he kept his mouth shut, knowing it was a critical moment. He chanted in his head, *"Come on; you can do this. Don't cry."*

"Get in the fucking car and shut your mouth. Otherwise, I'll stuff something in it." He roughly pushed her in and slammed the door.

Francesca was terrified. She tried to breathe through her crying as she desperately looked around, hoping they were watching her and could hear. Their silence was breaking her.

She tried again when he got in the car. "Please, please, don't hurt my papa!"

"Listen to me, you little cock tease!" he exploded. "You are going to do exactly as I say, or I will make one phone call and your precious father will have an unfortunate accident today." He put the car in gear and started to move.

Carl screamed into the microphone, "Got it! Stop the fucking car!" He threw his headset off and took his gun out while ripping the sliding door open with his other hand. Ryder was right on his heels.

The two cars in the parking lot screeched out and into the road, blocking the guard from exiting the parking lot.

"What the fuck? *You set me up, you fucking bitch!*" the guard screamed as he rammed into the car in front of him before he could slam on the brakes.

Francesca fell forwards with a jolt, and the guard grabbed her hair and yanked hard.

"He's dead!" the guard managed to say as six officers pointed guns at him, yelling at him to let go and get out of the car.

Francesca screamed, "*No!*" as the doors ripped open from both sides.

"Let go of her before I shoot you," Carl warned in a lethal voice

The guard yanked a little more to bring her closer before releasing her hair and whispering, "Fucking dead."

"*No*. He's going to kill my papa!" she screamed as Ryder pulled her out of the car and into his arms.

The officer beside Carl yanked the guard out and pinned him facedown on the pavement as he took his handcuffs out of their case.

Carl was on his phone. "Get Moratti out now. We got him." Carl then moved to the other side of the car where Ryder was trying to calm the frantic woman down who was chanting, "They're going to kill him. Oh, my God, they're going to kill him. What have I done?"

"Francesca, stop!" Carl spoke louder than he'd intended, but he needed to get through to her. "They are moving your father as we speak. He's okay. He is surrounded by six RCMP officers, as well as the warden. Nothing is going to happen to him, I swear."

When she collapsed into Ryder's arms, sobbing, he swept his arm under her legs and her shoulders as he lifted her up. He tucked her closely to him, whispering close to her ear, "It's over, Beauty. He's okay. Shh ... Baby. Shh ... It's over." He looked at Carl and gestured towards his car.

"Take her over to my car," Carl said before Ryder got two feet away. "I'll drive you. Look after her in the back. I'll have officers take her car home and yours to my office."

Ryder nodded and headed to the car. There were bystanders gathered around with cell phones out, recording the takedown.

Ryder turned back as the secondary team arrived on scene. "Carl?"

The officer turned, and Ryder threw his chin out to indicate the bystanders. Carl turned to the secondary team and spoke to them. Then they fanned out, confiscating the cell phones and deleting the videos before returning the phones to their owners. The last thing Ryder wanted was Francesca's face plastered on every news channel in North America.

An officer opened the rear car door as Ryder approached. He

placed Francesca on her feet and steadied her before he climbed in and pulled her into his lap.

Now safely behind tinted windows, he cradled her and pushed the hair from her face. "Shh … Baby. Your father's fine. They are moving him now. After we leave Carl's office, I am taking you to see him. I got you, Beauty. It's over. You did good. Really good. I'm so proud of you."

She calmed down, snuggling into his warm, comforting arms. They didn't speak as they waited for Carl; Ryder just continued to run his hand up and down her back, offering her all the strength he could muster.

Carl got in the car ten minutes later and turned to face them. "Francesca, your father is out of the prison and on his way to the new institution. After the debriefing, we'll take you there."

She nodded and closed her eyes, exhaustion setting in. The adrenaline rush had drained from her body, and the security of being wrapped in Ryder's arms allowed her to finally sleep.

Ryder felt the moment her body relaxed and her breathing levelled out. Carl looked at him in the rear-view mirror with quirked eyebrows. Ryder nodded and continued to rub his hand up and down her back, not as much for her now, but for himself. He had been wound tighter than a drum, and his actions were easing his own tension.

***

Ryder pulled up to the new prison with Francesca in the passenger seat, looking anxious. Carl had explained this facility was a minimum-security institution, and that her father would have more freedom here.

They got out of the car and headed through the entrance where they were met by James and the warden. Introductions were made, and then they were guided to the rooms where lawyers met with their clients.

When they opened the door, Francesca saw her papa and ran to him, sobbing. She hugged him for the first time in a year and a half.

Frank Moratti had tears in his eyes as he cradled his daughter in his arms. He pulled her back a fraction so he could look into her eyes. Wiping her tears before he kissed her on both cheeks, he held his face next to hers.

"Bambolina, I'm so sorry. They told me what happened. Please don't cry. You're making your papa cry."

She looked up at him with adoring eyes, so thankful he was okay. She had missed him so much, and she just wanted to stay locked in his arms forever. She wrapped her arms tighter around him and continued to softly sob.

"Please, bambolina, you're breaking my heart. Talk to me. Tell me you're okay. I knew I should never have allowed you to come to the prison. It's no place for my figlia dolce. You won't come again."

Francesca stepped back with a look of shock. "Papa, prego, no!"

Her father became stern. "Mia piccola amore, I cannot allow it. You will honour your papa and respect what I say. I don't want you coming here anymore. I will worry needlessly every time. Ascoltarmi, bambolina!"

"Non, Papa!" Francesca was panicked.

Ryder had to intervene. He couldn't stand by and watch Francesca be denied one more thing.

"Excuse me, sir, but what if I promise to come with her and make sure she is safe?"

Francesca was stunned into silence.

"And you are who?" Frank asked, not intimidated by the muscular man walking towards him.

Ryder stuck his hand out. "Ryder Vaughn, a friend of Francesca's. We work together, sir."

"Ah ... Yes, the one doing community service," Frank said.

"Papa, please!" Francesca yelped, embarrassed her papa had spoken to Ryder like that.

Ryder wasn't the least bit offended. He respected the fact that the man was protective of his daughter.

"Sir, I respect you having concerns about me, but I care about your daughter, and I will protect her at any cost. Don't take away any more of her family. She needs you." Ryder wanted Mr. Moratti to know that Francesca had trusted him enough to share the loss of her mother and brother with him.

Frank looked away from Ryder to Francesca. "You trust this man?"

"Si, Papa, with my life. If it wasn't for him, we wouldn't be standing here. He's a good man."

Frank nodded. "Okay, I'll allow you to visit with him, but bambolina, never ever alone again. Si?"

"Si, Papa. Grazie!" She wrapped her arms around him and hugged him tightly as she kissed his cheek.

After Francesca had a moment with her father, they all sat and told Frank their version of the events that had unfolded. James had explained earlier in the day why Frank had been moved. Unbeknownst to Francesca, James had also explained that Ryder hired his firm to look into Frank's case and future parole hearings.

Frank also knew Ryder wanted to visit him alone, and he had granted the lawyer's request, wanting to understand why Ryder was doing all this. He wanted to know the man's intentions.

After leaving the group to talk for an hour, the warden entered. "Sorry, folks, but we need to get Mr. Moratti settled in before I leave. Again, I apologize for the unfortunate circumstances that brought you to this institution. I can assure you that Mr. Moratti is safe here. I will personally guarantee it. You have five minutes to say your good-byes."

"Thank you. I will give you no trouble," Frank replied. "I just want to do my time, so I can go home to my family."

The warden nodded and walked out.

Frank looked at his daughter. "No tears, bambolina. I love you and will see you next time … with Ryder. You must go now, mi amore." He took her in his arms and hugged her before pulling back and slowly kissing each cheek, lingering for a minute. Then he walked to the door and knocked.

The guard opened the door and escorted Mr. Moratti away.

"Ciao, Papa. Ti amo." Francesca turned away from the door in case her papa turned around and saw her tears falling.

Ryder walked over to her, watching her shoulders shake in silence, and James left the room to give them a minute of privacy.

Ryder turned her around and wrapped his arms around her while she silently cried. When she calmed down, he led her out of the prison.

It was six o'clock when he started his car. He picked up his phone and placed an order for pickup from the Chinese restaurant by Francesca's house.

After they got the food, he carried it while assisting Francesca up the stairs. She was dead on her feet. He just wanted to get her fed and tucked into bed.

They never said a word until he made plates for them and told her to eat the whole thing. She ate half of it before falling asleep with the plate still in her lap.

He removed the plate then ever so gently picked her up put her to bed. He should have taken her clothes off to make her more comfortable, but he knew he couldn't resist her if he did. Therefore, he just pulled the blanket over her and tucked her in.

He stood for a minute and watched her as she rolled over and tucked her hands under her cheek as she sighed in her sleep. Then he gently moved a length of hair that impeded his view of her angelic face.

He knew while he stood there watching her that he was falling in love with her. In that moment, he realized love wasn't just a good feeling. Love also brought out another emotion, one he had never experienced before. Fear.

Fear for her safety and her delicate feelings. Fear she would not feel the same way. Fear he wouldn't be the man she needed or deserved. Fear he would never be enough and was as useless as his father had always told him he was. Mostly, he feared she couldn't see past the gimp.

He walked out and left the bedroom door open in case she needed him in the night.

***

Ryder was dragged from his sleep when he heard pounding at the front door. He removed the blanket from his body and jumped up to answer it. He was glad he had stayed, worried someone would fuck with her over the guard's arrest.

In three strides, he was at the door and nearly ripping it off its hinges as he threw it open. Sal and Lucky were at the door, danger written all over their faces.

"Where the hell is Frankie?" Sal demanded.

"Keep your voices down," Ryder barked back just above a whisper. "*Francesca* is sleeping." He waved them inside. "You wake her, or upset her, I'll throw you out."

The men recoiled at the venom behind his threat. However, their loyalty to their sister brought them right back into Ryder's personal space.

"Why did I have to find out *after* driving up to the prison that our old man had been moved and our names aren't on the list? The warden at the new facility suggested I should talk to my sister. What the hell happened? And why are you in her apartment at eight a.m.?" Lucky asked.

"Calm the fuck down," Ryder growled, looking towards Francesca's room to make sure she hadn't woken. "Are you able to whisper? If not, see your way out." Ryder filled the doorframe they had yet to pass through, challenging them.

The intimidation didn't change the men's attitude. They needed to make sure their sister was all right, and they had to get by the monster to do it.

Sal looked at Lucky, and they had a silent conversation. He nodded at Lucky then turned to Ryder. "We'll be quiet if you show us Francesca is okay. Then we want to discuss our father's situation."

Ryder nodded as he turned and walked towards Francesca's room. Both brothers stuck their heads through the doorway to confirm she was sleeping and with clothing on. Then Ryder silently closed her bedroom door before leading the men into the kitchen table.

Still not saying a word, he started to make a pot of coffee. The brothers waited until the coffees were placed on the table. Then Ryder sat down and started to talk.

"This is going to make you furious. You need to keep a lid on it. If you raise your voices, or wake her up, I will forcibly remove you. She's gone through enough and needs sleep." Ryder could see the men were tightly coiled, concern written on their faces.

"Last month, when Francesca went to visit your father, a guard made inappropriate advances. She lied, hoping to deter him. However, he hacked into the prison computer, which is linked to government files, and found out all her personal information and that she had lied. Enraged, he threatened her and demanded sexual favours when she went to visit your father last week. If she refused, he told her your father would be harmed and possibly killed."

Sal jumped up from the table and started to pace the room, whispering in a disheartened voice, "Why the hell didn't she come to us? We would've helped her. We would've killed the son of a bitch!"

Ryder understood his frustration. Francesca *never* asked for help.

"That's why she didn't."

Sal was pissed, pointing accusingly at Ryder. "So she goes to you instead of her family?"

Ryder wished that was the case. "No, she didn't come to me. I knew something was off after her last visit. I asked her, and she wouldn't tell me, so I followed her." He went on to explain the incident he encountered and what followed. "Your names not being on the visitors' list was merely an oversight. Francesca can call the warden today and fix it."

Both brothers were looking down at the table, struggling to keep their composure. Lucky lifted his head first and looked at Ryder.

"Thanks, man. I don't know if I could've kept my shit together and done the right thing."

"Hardest thing I ever did. Your sister's been teaching me to do things differently. Did you know she's been dumping four hundred bucks a month into your father's commissary account? How 'bout the fact she has three jobs?"

Sal looked embarrassed. "Fuck, didn't know she had three. We have some debt we are all trying to pay off. All three of us work our asses off, but we don't begrudge a second of it. It's for family."

Ryder was starting to understand what it meant to have a real family, unconditional love.

"Not saying it to make you feel guilty or embarrassed." Ryder scratched the day-old growth on his chin. "I know a way for her to earn more money and not work so hard, but I need your help."

"That sounds too good to be true." Sal looked at him apprehensively.

"I took pictures of your sister's paintings and sent them to a gallery owner in California. He thinks he has buyers for them. Francesca doesn't believe her work is good enough, even to give as a gift for her friend's wedding, so I want to bring it up in front of you guys, and I want you to push her to let him sell them."

Lucky's eyes lit up. "Yeah, I have four she gave me. I want to keep one, but I'll sacrifice the other three."

"I have a few packed away, too," Sal jumped in.

Ryder slightly smirked. "Good, then you'll help me convince her."

"Convince me of what?" Francesca asked, startling all three men who turned to look at her.

"Why are you up?" Ryder growled, walking towards her. He tried to turn her around and put her back to bed.

"Stop!" She slapped his hands away. "It's nine o'clock. I'm fine, honestly. What I really need is a coffee, and then you are all going to tell me what you want to convince me to do." She walked into the kitchen to grab a mug.

Ryder watched her. She still looked tried, but she also looked less fractured and more like her old self. She must be letting go of everything that had happened yesterday.

"What are you guys doing here, anyway? Do you all want breakfast?" It was unexpected, but she was happy they were there.

"I'm running to the bakery for bagels and pastries. Visit with your brothers. I'll be back in fifteen." Ryder grabbed his keys and threw on his jacket.

Francesca started after him, grabbing her purse. "Here, let me give you some money."

"Don't insult me, Francesca," he growled.

She put her hands on her hips and stomped her foot. "You're not feeding my family. Besides, you paid for dinner last night."

Ryder bent down so he was nose-to-nose with her. "Really?"

She clenched her jaw and stared back. "Yes, really!"

"Too fucking bad."

Francesca threw her arms in the air then gestured to her groin. "Basta! Mi stai proprio rompere le palle!"

Her brothers cracked up laughing, Lucky spitting out his coffee in a fit of giggles.

"Now you did it. She's slamming you in Italian!"

He raised his eyebrows and looked at her brothers. "What'd she say?"

They continued to laugh, along with Francesca.

"Holy shit! She sounds just like Zia Concettina!" Sal finally managed to get out. "She said, enough, you're breaking my balls!"

Ryder was confused. "She doesn't have balls."

"That's the point. She doesn't have any, and you're still breaking them."

Chapter 11

"Angels Among Us" By Alabama

Ryder would be heading back to California in five days for the Christmas break. His band, Fornication, had a two-week mini-tour scheduled. They were playing in San Francisco, Reno, and then Las Vegas on New Year's Eve. Then it was off to San Diego, and finally Los Angeles. The only two days they would have off would be Christmas Eve and Christmas.

Back in September, Ryder honestly thought he would be counting down the days until he could leave Toronto. Now that it was almost time for him to go, he was dreading it.

Ryder and Francesca had become extremely close. She loved to refer to him as her BMFF—Best Male Friend Forever. As much as he loved being her confidant and friend, he wanted more. In the last four months, he hadn't discussed his childhood, but he was beginning to open up about how he felt about the centre and all the students.

He told her how impressed he was with the skills the students were mastering. Ryder was proud of himself, too, and his accomplishments with the kids in their room. The work they all did was important. Not only that, but if anyone had told him four months ago that five special needs children would worm their way into his heart, he would have told them that they were out of their fucking minds.

The centre was a flurry of activity with only one week before the break. The teaching staff and students were all hyped up, getting ready for the Christmas concert they were hosting on Friday. They had invited parents and caregivers to the morning performance, and the staff and clients from the adult programs for the afternoon performance.

Ryder had been working on a surprise for everyone for the final performance, and had asked Mariana to help him. She had agreed, and they conspired.

Francesca was busy working with their students on the props for the concert when Ryder approached her. "I'll be leaving in half an hour. I have a meeting with James Quinn."

He had requested the afternoon off, explaining to Mariana he had an appointment with his lawyer, and she had granted his request.

Francesca stopped what she was doing and raised an eyebrow, looking around to make sure nobody was listening. "Is everything okay?"

"Yeah, just have to fill out some legal papers before I head back to California."

"Oh, right. You know I'm going to miss my BMFF over the break. I can't wait for our Christmas dinner celebration on Saturday night. We're still on, right?"

"Wouldn't miss it, Beauty." Ryder believed that, if everything turned out as he hoped, she would have a Christmas to remember.

From the depths of her heart, Francesca wanted more from Ryder, but she was terrified to get too attached only to let him go in six months. He had a job and a life in California, and she didn't fit into that, nor would she ever leave her family and friends. Her friendship with Ryder was something she could hold on to and cherish. She knew it would stand the test of time and distance.

She watched Ryder get ready to leave, disappointed they couldn't spend the rest of the day together. He had become a constant in her life. Her heart beat faster every morning when she saw him come in. He was not classically handsome, but to her, he was gorgeous and made her feel things she had never experienced before.

Meeting Ryder had been a blessing. She had gone to church every Sunday over the last month and thanked God for bringing him into her life. She would never have survived the incident with the guard if he hadn't helped her.

Francesca knew he would support her through the trial, when he also would have to testify. As if that wasn't enough, he had also found a buyer in California for her paintings. Incredibly, she had sold eleven paintings at five thousand dollars apiece and had made fifty-five thousand dollars. More money than she would make in a year. She paid forty-five thousand towards the family debt and kept ten thousand in the bank for a cushion.

The gallery had said they would take as many as she could produce, so Francesca planned to paint over the holidays. She would also paint one for Gabriella's wedding present, and if all went well, two to sell. At this rate, she would pay off the debt in no time.

***

Ryder left the centre and headed to the prison to meet James and Sal for Frank Moratti's parole hearing. Ryder arranged to have James help with the proceedings, and Lucky agreed to run the business while Sal attended.

Sal, Lucky, Frank, and Ryder had decided not to tell Francesca about it, in case her father was denied parole. He hated to keep her in the dark, but she had gone through enough. They were all afraid to see her disappointment if things didn't go their way.

Ryder saw Sal and James when he walked through the front doors of the prison. They waited silently until the guards gave them the fifteen-minute warning that Frank's case would be heard at one-thirty. James had ten minutes to prep Mr. Moratti.

Sal and Ryder sat in the waiting room. Ryder had his arms crossed over his broad chest, his right leg shaking a mile a minute, which was unnerving Sal.

He turned towards Ryder. "Why are you doing all this? What do you get out of it?"

Ryder turned towards Sal with the scowl he had been sporting since arriving at the prison. He didn't lift his sunglasses off as he stared at him. "I get to see Francesca happy, plain and simple."

"Are you sleeping with my sister?"

Ryder balked, taken aback by his bluntness. Then he became livid. "Not your fucking business."

Sal, not to be swayed, retorted, "Always my business if it includes Frankie."

Ryder assumed he was trying to push his buttons. He hoped it was because Sal was nervous about the hearing. It still didn't excuse his rudeness.

"*Francesca*," he corrected. "And what happens between Francesca and I is none of your business. You tell her when you're banging tail?"

Sal's outrage increased. "She's not some goddamn piece of tail, asshole. She's my little sister, and I won't let you disrespect her." Sal jumped to his feet and started to pace to prevent himself from punching Ryder in the fucking face. He could give two shits if the monster was double his size; nobody talked about his sister like that.

Ryder liked Sal's loyalty towards his sister, and instantly chilled as he responded, "Meant no disrespect. I like that you're protective of her. Know that I would never betray her privacy by telling you if I was sleeping with her. She deserves better than me. If there is anything she needs, and I can give it to her, I would sell what little of a soul I have to make sure it happened. She deserves more than she's been dealt. You want to know personal information about Francesca, you need to ask her."

"You better not be fucking around with my sister. She deserves a man who's going to be there for her, not some long-distance relationship. If you think you can string her along, and then go months without seeing her, banging—your words, not mine—some other chick in California, I won't stand for it."

Ryder tensed. The bastard didn't know the first thing about him. If he was lucky enough to have Francesca, he sure as hell wouldn't bang anyone else. Why eat Spam when you could have steak?

Ryder got up and went nose-to-nose with Sal, losing his cool again. "You're crossing a line. Think long and hard about how you choose your next words."

A guard interrupted their argument, telling them the parole hearing was about to begin. He explained that they would not be able to speak during the hearing; they were there for moral support only. If they interfered in the hearing, the hearing would be forfeited, and Frank would have to reapply in a year. They were also told not to touch the inmate under any circumstances.

Once they agreed to the rules, they were led into a room and shown their seats beside James.

There was a three-man panel and two guards present. The conviction was read out loud, as well as the sentence. Then each of the panel members questioned Frank on why he was convicted and how he felt about the sentence. Next, his conduct since he had been incarcerated was evaluated. They also brought up the fight the guard had set up, his transfer, and what his plans were if he was granted parole. After half an hour of questioning, the panel said they had all the information they needed and would call them back in when the decision was made.

Frank was led back into a holding cell, while the rest of their group went back to the waiting room.

"Ryder, I owe you an apology, man." Sal's nerves were frayed, but he also realized he had overstepped with Ryder. "I'm sorry. I was totally out of line. I have no excuse, except to say that I love my sister and worry about her. You have already done so much for our family. I struggle, because I don't know how we are ever going to repay you." Sal held out his hand, hoping Ryder would accept his apology. Otherwise, he was going to have to deal with the wrath of a very pissed off "Frank the Tank."

Ryder willing took the man's hand and shook it. He was happy Francesca's brother was willing to go fisticuffs with the likes of him to protect his girl. "No problem. If she was my sister, I would react the same way. Only thanks I want is to see the look on Francesca's face when she has her father back. Your old man was wrongly convicted. His only crime was trying to do everything in his power to look after his family."

The guard interrupted again, saying the panel had made their decision and to follow him back into the hearing room. Once everyone was seated, the head of the panel told everyone in the room that, as soon as the decision was read, no one was to speak.

Sal's heart dropped, thinking the man was bracing them for more bad news. He steeled himself. His family had overcome many things, and they would survive this, too.

Once the panel had everyone's assurance, the head of the panel declared parole granted.

Both Sal and Frank lowered their heads as the tears flowed. Sal, trying to be discreet, breathed in deeply. Ryder lifted the corners of his mouth in a smug grin, knowing how happy Francesca was going to react. He reached over and grabbed Sal's shoulder, squeezing in a comforting gesture.

The head of the panel then went on to explain that the paperwork would take about a week and half. The date of release would be eleven a.m. on December twenty-fourth.

No one congratulated Frank until the panel left.

"Papa, you're coming home!" Sal sobbed. Against all the rules, the guards allowed father and son a moment to hug before they led him back to his cell.

Frank turned before he walked away and looked up at Ryder. "Angels come in many forms, son. You have to be the biggest, ugliest, scariest angel of all. Thank you, Ryder." He turned before Ryder could form a thought and walked away.

Ryder stood there, absorbing the kindest words that had ever been spoken to him. He often wondered what a real father's words would sound like, and for the first time in his thirty years, he finally knew the pride in hearing a father's praise.

When Sal grabbed Ryder in man hug and kissed both his cheeks, Ryder pushed him away, backing up in embarrassment.

Sal bellowed in laughter. "Sorry. Italians are really touchy feely." He cleared his throat and lost his laughter. "I got one more favour to ask you, and it's a big one. Do you think you could fly back Christmas Eve and bring my old man to Francesca's for dinner?"

Ryder shifted from one leg to the other. "I don't know. Christmas is about family. I don't want to be a fifth wheel."

"Are you fucking kidding me? You said the only payment you want is to see Francesca's face. It's the only gift we can give you."

Ryder turned to James. "Can you make it happen?"

James was still smiling over Ryder's embarrassment when he replied, "Let me speak to Mrs. Belmore and see what I can do."

Ryder was thankful for his discretion in using Mrs. instead of Judge. "That's all I can ask."

Sal slapped his shoulder, tempted to give him another hug just for shits and giggles. "Thanks, man."

***

School had been flying by, and it was now time for the last performance of the day before the Christmas break. Francesca had worked tirelessly over the last week to make sure every class had amazing props.

She had been pleasantly surprised by Ryder's mood after the meeting with his lawyer. He seemed happy. He very rarely smiled, but he had been grinning as much as he seemed capable of. She assumed he must be excited about heading home for the holidays.

Her class had just preformed the song "You're A Mean One, Mr. Grinch," featuring Ryder as the Grinch and Mason as his trusty dog. The rest of the students and staff in their class were the characters in Whoville. Their set was cool, and the costumes were phenomenal.

The audience was laughing before they even started. They got their biggest laugh when Theo managed to once again get his tongue in Ryder's ear after the song ended. Ryder couldn't react immediately since Katrina and Veeta were leaning against him, pinning him to the makeshift sleigh.

Ryder gently moved the girls aside, grabbed the little hellion, and placed him in the big cloth toy bag. He tied it and placed him in the sleigh before pulling it off stage while Theo screamed,

"Fornication for the nation!"

Mariana stepped up onto the stage and asked for all the performers to come out front and take their seats. That made Francesca curious, because the morning performance hadn't had a special act.

Francesca gathered most of the students and took them to their seats just as Mariana began to speak.

"I want to thank all the staff and students for all their hard work on this year's concert. It was the best we've ever seen, by far. Give yourselves a round of applause." When the clapping stopped, she continued, "To the staff, you are a remarkable group of people. Your devotion to our students far exceeds any other facility anywhere in the world. Your remarkable hard work often comes with very little praise, so I want to take this opportunity to thank you for your dedication and commitment. Each and every one of you has often been referred to as angels. This next act is a gift to honour all of you. Ryder and Mason, take it away."

The curtain opened, and Francesca gaped in astonishment. Her heart started pounding as she saw Ryder and Mason sitting side by side. Ryder had a guitar in his hands, and Mason sat in front of a small drum set.

Ryder tapped the mic as he looked out over the crowd. He found Francesca and said, "This is for you." Then he caught himself and said, "All of you."

The lights dimmed and a soft spotlight highlighted the two performers. Ryder and Mason began to play softly while a slide presentation began on the big screen beside Ryder, featuring pictures of all the staff with their students.

Ryder began to sing the most beautiful rendition any of them had ever heard of "Angels Among Us" by Alabama. His voice was deep and raspy, perfect for the song.

Francesca got chills all over her body as he stared at her. Her heart filled with so much admiration for this beast of a man. She hadn't known he could play a guitar, let alone sing so beautifully.

He never took his eyes off her as he caressed her soul with the lyrics. She silently prayed the moment would never end.

Who was this man who was so easily misunderstood?

Although Francesca couldn't tear herself away from Ryder's piercing eyes, she could hear Mason playing the drums, and she was as proud as any mother could be.

Just before the song ended, the crowd were on their feet, giving the two performers a standing ovation.

As many concerts as Ryder had played in, no standing ovation had ever made him feel as proud as this one.

Theo was screaming and clapping. Then he made a horn symbol with both hands and screamed, "Fornication singing at Reach Within! Take a bow!" He then stood on a chair and bowed.

Ryder quickly deflected his comment by standing. Instead of

bowing, he lifted Mason high in front of him, giving the boy all the accolades. Once Ryder placed him down, the two descended the steps to receive congratulations.

Francesca stood back, waiting for everyone to give their praise. After a few minutes, she spotted Mason and walked up to him, hugging him from behind.

"I couldn't be prouder of you. When did you learn to play the drums?"

Mason turned, sucking up all the praise Francesca was bestowing on him as he glanced up at her with adoring eyes. "For the last month, instead of working out in the gym, Ryder has been teaching me the drums. He's really good, Frankie!"

"Yeah, I sorta figured that out when I heard you guys play. That was such a cool surprise."

Mason was still riding the adrenaline rush. "Did you see the picture of you, me, and Ryder?"

"No, sorry, buddy. I was so busy watching you two play that I didn't see any of the pictures. But as soon as I see Mrs. Ramara, I'll ask her to post it on the website. That way, I can look at the pictures before I leave today."

" 'Kay, Frankie. Gotta go make sure Theo's not pissing Ryder off."

Francesca giggled. "Good call. I'm sure Ryder has probably stuffed him back in the bag. You know how he hates when Theo screams fornication."

Francesca stood back and watched all the staff vying for Ryder's attention. She couldn't help the little butterflies fluttering in her lower region. The man defined the term "hotter than hell." He was smokin' hot.

Every few minutes, he would seek her out and look straight into her soul. The man had learned to speak volumes with a quick glance. She felt her cheeks heat with awkwardness.

Someone touched her arm, and she whirled around.

"Judge Belmore, what an incredible surprise." And just the reprieve she needed before she did something stupid, like run into Ryder's arms and kiss him senseless. "I didn't know you were coming."

"Ryder's lawyer told me about the concert. I remembered all the concerts Derrick was in. The case I was hearing got pushed ahead to the new year, and I knew nothing would put me in the Christmas spirit like a concert at Reach Within. So here I am. Great job. I laughed, and of course cried."

"Thank you, Linda. That means so much. How is Derrick?"

"Good." She nodded with a happy smile. "They're all coming home for Christmas. My daughter said Derrick is finally settling in Arizona. I miss them all, but I especially miss Derrick." She nodded towards Ryder. "Mr. Vaughn seems to have adapted well."

"Yes, he was a force to be reckoned with when he first got here.

The uncertainty and fear of the kids took him a couple of months to overcome, but he has grown incredibly and is making such a difference, especially with Mason. Not that Mason doesn't still lash out a few times a week, but at least now he is learning to redirect some of his uncontrollable rage.

"Ryder is teaching him to work some of his anger out with exercise. We were all blown away today, surprised he had taught Mason how to play the drums for this song. No one knew Ryder could play an instrument, or that he could sing."

"I am sure there's a lot that would surprise you about that man," Linda replied. "But I'm glad it's working out. If ever I wanted to teach someone the value of their own life, it's to that man. I knew it would take more than just a few months."

Ryder excused himself from the crowd when he saw Judge Belmore speaking to Francesca. He had to make sure she wasn't giving away their surprise.

"Judge Belmore, pleasure to see you. What brings you here? Is there some trouble with my paperwork?"

Linda saw the questioning look in his eyes. "No, no, Mr. Vaughn. I told you I had an affiliation with the centre. My oldest grandson, Derrick, graduated from here last June. When Mr. Quinn told me about the Christmas concert, I knew I couldn't miss it. By the way, congratulations on your performance. It was quite a tribute to the staff."

Ryder felt himself relax. "So that's how you know Francesca."

"Yes, she worked miracles with my grandson. Frankie opened a whole new world to him when she introduced him to the arts. He is autistic and nonverbal, but now he expresses his emotions through drawings. I owe her a debt I can never repay."

Ryder ground his back teeth at the use of her nickname, while Francesca burned up with embarrassment at the compliment.

"Linda, you don't owe me anything. Derrick taught me far more than I ever taught him. I miss having him around here."

Ryder turned to look at the blush crawling up Francesca's face. It still astounded him that she was so humble.

Without thought, she fought for the underdog. If she heard a coworker complaining about a student's behaviour, she was the first one to defend them and point out their strengths. If anyone complained about a student's hygiene or lack of nutritional lunches, she was the first to explain how difficult the families had it. He often heard her say, "You have no idea what the families are dealing with. They work all day, then do our jobs at night. We get to go home after eight hours, and we can tag off when it becomes overwhelming. But the parents have a lifetime to contend with."

He wondered if her perspective was different because she had raised her brother, or if she was just born with insight most people would never gain.

Society was so fucked up. As a famous entertainer, Ryder was held up to a different standard than ninety-nine percent of the population, and for what? A talent in playing an instrument and singing? He hadn't earned that position. People like Francesca, nurses, doctors, volunteers, caregivers—they were the true heroes in the world.

"Ryder?"

"Hm?"

"Linda was just saying good-bye."

"Mr. Vaughn, I hope your Christmas holiday is memorable. Frankie, Merry Christmas, and I hope you get everything you desire. See you soon."

"Judge, no disrespect, but her name is Francesca." He just couldn't help himself.

"Ryd—"

"No, Frankie, don't interfere. I'm the one person in this world he can't intimidate. Mr. Vaughn, I knew Frankie long before you, and I will continue to associate with her long after. Merry Christmas." She smiled.

Ryder growled as the obstinate woman walked away laughing.

***

"Dinner was fabulous. I knew you would love my godfather's restaurant, Pulcinella," Francesca bragged as she watched Ryder wipe his mouth after eating his dinner and half of hers.

"It was good, but not half as good as your cooking."

Francesca's godfather and her father's best friend, Maurizio, approached to check on them and heard the comment.

"Ah, Ryder, you've been spoiled. I have to agree with you, though, mia bella Francesca is only superseded by her nonna."

Ryder lifted an eyebrow at her godfather. "I don't know who this nonna is, but after travelling the world and eating food served by the best chefs, no one compares to Francesca."

Maurizio bellowed a laugh. "Your loyalty is admirable, although dangerous. Her nonna—her grandmother—would have you face down in the dirt, smashing your head with her marble rolling pin for a comment like that."

"Being crazy doesn't make her right," Ryder challenged.

"Ryder! That's not nice. You're talking about my nonna." Francesca said with a mixture of pride and indignation.

Maurizio, still laughing, responded, "Please, bella, promise me an invite when Zia Lena gets a hold of this one. My money is on your nonna!" He started laughing hysterically again, as was his nature.

"It's a deal." She winked at him.

They both laughed at Ryder's expense.

"I will get you some espresso and dessert," Maurizio said as he chuckled to himself, walking away and shaking his head.

Francesca quickly changed the subject. "Time for presents." She beamed. "I want to go first."

"Sorry, Beauty, but I've been waiting weeks to give you this."

"Not fair—"

He handed her a small white bag, effectively cutting her off. "Open it."

Resigned, Francesca took the bag that she recognized was from their family friend's store, Cullinan Jewellers. She pulled out the beautifully embossed tissue paper, finding a long, velvet box. She took it out and slowly opened it. Inside was a beautiful platinum necklace with her name written in diamonds.

"Oh, Ryder, it's beautiful. Thank you. Will you put it on me?"

Ryder got up and walked behind her. He brushed her hair to the side, sending a rush of chills down her spine. Then he gently clasped the necklace to her throat.

Maurizio walked up with the dessert and coffee as Ryder retook his seat.

"How does it look?" she asked Ryder.

"You look beautiful." *And now everyone will know your name,* he thought to himself.

She smiled widely as she turned to her godfather. "Zio, what do you think of my necklace?"

"It's gorgeous, bella. Nice taste, Ryder." Her godfather gave Ryder a scrutinising look, all humour gone.

"She should always be draped in diamonds," Ryder commented.

"*What!*" she screeched, jumping up and knocking the tray out of

Maurizio's hands, causing everything to crash to the floor.

Ryder jumped up to make sure the hot coffee hadn't landed on Francesca. "Are you okay?"

Her hands were shaking, having no awareness of where she was and what she had done. "Diamonds? Are you freaking kidding me? This had better be a joke!"

Ryder didn't respond, helping Maurizio clean up the mess.

"I'm so sorry, Zio," she said when she finally realized what she had done. "And he thinks we're crazy. Ryder, this better be a joke." She narrowed her eyes at him.

Once the mess was cleaned up and apologies were given and accepted, Maurizio decided to get a ringside seat before going to get more espresso. "I personally think she looks good in diamonds."

Francesca winced as she put her hand to her head. "Dio mio, has everyone lost their minds? I can't accept a diamond necklace. It's too much. Ci pazzo!"

Ryder, now fully seated, turned calmly towards Maurizio. "What'd she say?"

"She said 'My God, has everyone lost their minds? I can't accept a diamond necklace. It's too much. You're crazy!'" Maurizio was loving this. He would have a fine story to tell.

Ryder rolled his eyes, knowing her godfather was fuelling the fire. "I got the English part." Turning to Francesca, he asked, "What did you think it was?"

The blush rose faster than her words as she whispered, "I thought it was silver with Cubic Zirconia."

Ryder bellowed out a rare laugh. "Really, Beauty?"

"Yes, really. I mean, who buys their BWFF diamonds? And he thinks we're crazy." She rolled her eyes, debating taking the necklace off.

Maurizio was now confused and turned towards Ryder. "What did she say?"

Knowing he was referring to the acronym, he muttered, "Best Woman Friend Forever."

Maurizio laughed.

Francesca turned towards her godfather, her face beet red. "I don't mean to be rude, Zio, but, do you mind?"

"Aw, just when it was getting good. Fine, take my fun away. I'll go get more dessert and espresso." He pouted as he walked away.

Francesca turned towards Ryder, fiddling with shaky hands to try to undo the clasp. "Please try to understand that it's too much. I can't accept it."

"No refunds or exchanges. I had it made for you." He reached over to calm her hands. "Let's move on. I want my present now."

Her face fell. "I can't possibly give you my gift now. It's not worth anything." She looked down at their entwined hands.

"Look at me." When she met his eyes, he told her, "Don't you dare compare gifts."

No sooner had he made the comment that Maurizio came out of the kitchen carrying a big, wrapped box.

"No, no, Zio. Not now, please. I can't!"

Maurizio's cool snapped. "Don't you dare, bella. Be proud. It's beautiful." He dropped the box beside Ryder and walked away in a huff.

Ryder slowly removed the beautiful paper from the box as Francesca fidgeted in her seat, wishing the floor would open up so she didn't have to see his face when he opened her worthless gift.

Ryder opened the box and pulled the Stonehenge painting halfway out before he stopped, sitting there silently for two to three minutes.

She couldn't see his face, so she could only assume he was disappointed.

After she swallowed the lump in her throat, she said, "Ryder, I'm sorry. It's okay. You don't have to take it. I'll get you something else."

He slowly turned towards her with what looked like unshed tears. Stunned into silence, she couldn't believe what she was seeing.

After another few moments of him staring into her eyes, he spoke with a hoarse voice. "I have never received anything as precious as this. You have no idea how much this means to me. Thank you."

Chapter 12

"Oh Darlin', What Have I Done"
By The White Buffalo

Francesca had been cooking for two days straight, wanting everything to be perfect for her Christmas Eve celebration. Sal had called yesterday, asking to invite two of his friends who had nowhere to go for the holidays, so Francesca honoured her mother's tradition of welcoming anyone.

Lucky had brought a large folding table that spanned the length of her kitchen and living room. It was tight, but with all her decorations, it still looked festive.

Last week, she had conned Ryder into stringing popcorn and cranberries with her for the little Christmas tree she had by the apartment's entrance. He had grumbled the whole time, but she knew he had secretly enjoyed it, especially because he had made her pop another batch, claiming there wasn't enough perfectly puffed kernels.

Ryder had confessed he had never decorated a tree, and had

thanked her for the experience. He told her his sperm donor traveled during the holidays for work, and he had been left in the care of his nanny.

She wondered what Ryder was doing right this minute, hoping he was with friends and enjoying all the season had to offer.

Keeping somewhat with Italian tradition, her meal would be served at two p.m. She expected her family to arrive at one.

With a few minutes to spare until her guests arrived, she lit the candles on the table and restarted her Christmas playlist. Right on cue, she heard Lucky and Sal before they reached the stairway, laughing and evidently pushing each other out of the way to get up to her apartment first

She savoured the sound of their laughter after years of sorrow. Only three more years, and they would all be together and truly happy again. Her papa had finally agreed to let Francesca and Lucky visit tomorrow. She was thankful he was in a better place.

Her brothers came tearing into the apartment, Lucky winning the race.

"Buon Natale, Frankie. Damn, it smells great in here," Lucky said as hugged her, giving her a kiss on both cheeks.

"Buon Natale, Lucky." She left his embrace and walked into Sal's arms for kisses and to wish him a Merry Christmas Eve, as well.

Sal walked over to the shellfish tomato sauce to taste it. "Mm ...

Delizioso! Holy shit, Frankie, this is the best sauce you've ever made."

"Grazie. This year, with my extra income, I could afford king crab and lobster, along with the usual mussels, clams, and shrimp, so it does taste better." She turned to Lucky and jumped up and down. "I am so excited we get to visit Papa tomorrow. Remember, dinner will be at four, okay?"

Her brothers looked at one another and smirked, knowing she would be serving dinner at two.

Lucky continued to dip some bread into the sauce, answering with a full mouth, "Sure, whatever works."

They all heard a car pull up, and the brothers' hearts sped up a little, hoping it was Zio Maurizio and his girlfriend, and not their special guests.

Lucky yelled with a full mouth, "I'll get the door!"

"No need to yell. Jeez. You guys sure are acting weird today."

"Just happy to have two days off and some of our baby sister's famous seafood pasta," Sal claimed.

Lucky let Maurizio and Paula in, and more hugs and kisses were given.

Maurizio had brought two bottles of Amarone wine for dinner. Francesca was pleased since it was her papa's favourite.

"Thanks, Zio. This is quite extravagant. We will savour it. Will you do the honours?" She held one of the bottles out to him.

He opened it, and then they decided to have a glass while they waited for Sal's friends.

Francesca got up to put the water on for the pasta, chatting away with Maurizio at the stove, when a knock sounded from the door. Sal said he would get it.

"Merry Christmas. Come on in and meet my sister," Sal greeted his guests.

Francesca, standing behind Maurizio, couldn't see who was at the door.

Maurizio turned and said, "I didn't know you were coming."

She peeked around Maurizio and just about fell over, screeching, "Ryder! I dropped you off at the airport last Sunday. What are you doing here?"

"Merry Christmas, Beauty. I brought a friend. I hope you don't mind." Ryder grinned from ear-to-ear, his six-foot-five frame encompassing the entire doorway.

"Of course not. I'm just thrilled you could make it. For God's sake, don't leave him in the cold. Invite him in."

He moved out of the way, and Frank walked in.

"Buon Natale, bambolina!"

Francesca couldn't believe her eyes. She froze in place, all the blood draining from her face. Paula had to quickly snatch Francesca's wine glass as it began to fall.

"Impossible …" She rubbed her eyes twice before whispering,

"Papa?" She then closed her eyes and started to tremble. "This is not possible. Oh, God, please don't let this be a dream. Please don't let me wake up," she said on a sob.

Everyone stood with tears in their eyes, looking back and forth from Francesca to Frank, waiting for one of them to make a move.

Frank's strained voice choked out, "Bambolina, come and give your papa a kiss." He opened his arms, willing his daughter to come to him.

Francesca took off on a short sprint and threw herself into Frank's arms, knocking them both into Ryder. She grabbed his face and kissed him repeatedly as she sobbed out, "Oh, Papa! Papa! How is this possible?"

Frank couldn't answer as he quietly wept into his daughter's hair. He tightened his grip on his beloved daughter and continued to hug her, overwhelmed with feelings he hadn't had since the day the nurse had passed him his little pink bundle of joy. Her goodness was the reason he was standing here.

Sal couldn't wait another second. He wiped his tears with one hand and dragged Lucky into the fold of their family with the other hand.

Ryder looked on with emotions he didn't know he was capable of feeling. His throat was closed tightly, making it difficult to breathe. His eyes misted over as his heart felt like it was going to explode. Her sobs were gut-wrenching.

He heaved in a deep breath. Witnessing their love was a gift that money couldn't buy. This was what it meant to have a family. Everything he had done came to this one glorious moment. He would never forget this moment for as long as he lived.

Merry Christmas to me, Ryder thought.

Maurizio broke up the emotional reunion by demanding, "Will someone please tell me how the hell this happened? And let me give my best friend a hug."

The family broke apart, and Francesca turned, unable to focus on Ryder because of her tears. She instinctively walked the two steps towards him and leaned against his chest, hugging him as tightly as she possibly could.

Ryder enveloped her against his body, running one of his big hands up and down her back, and with the other, he petted her hair. She was shaking like a leaf, and her body convulsed with sobs. He knew it wasn't due to sadness, but overwhelming happiness.

When she regained her composure, she lifted her head. "You did this, didn't you?"

He nodded, muttering, "Merry Christmas, Francesca." He couldn't say more around the tightness in his throat.

She looked up at him with wonderment and whispered back, "I love you, Ryder Vaughn, and I always will." Francesca reached up and grabbed the edges of his hair, yanking his face down to hers.

His eyes widened in astonishment at her bold move as she

closed her eyes and kissed him. With the soft texture of her full lips pressed against his, he closed his eyes with a soft groan.

She poked her tongue between his lips, and he opened. She tasted him for the first time, stroking his tongue, inviting him to play.

He didn't need another invitation. He delved deeply and consumed her, tasting the wine she had been drinking and cinnamon.

She hummed, totally absorbed by his sensual touch.

Their moment was ruined when Frank spoke up.

"Angel?"

Francesca and Ryder broke apart in embarrassment at having had their first kiss in front of her family. They turned to Frank, Francesca blushing.

"Not the big ugly angel; the angelic one." Frank laughed.

"Papa, don't you dare call Ryder big and ugly. He's beautiful!" she defended the man who had come to mean so much to her.

Sal and Lucky burst out laughing.

Sal couldn't help saying, "hey, beautiful, come and give us a kiss." He made kissing sounds and held his arms open to Ryder.

Ryder growled as he attempted to move around Francesca to get to the boys, but she stepped in front of him.

Putting her hands on her hips in disgust, she used her Frank the Tank voice. "Enough! You all should be down on your knees, kissing his feet for what he has done for this family. Now apologize.

You, too, Papa!"

"Si, bambolina, I'm sorry I offended you. Ryder and I got to know one another quite well. He knows I have the utmost respect for him. I'll treat him like my own son, bad form or not. And I won't apologize for that," Frank finished to the astonishment of even her brothers.

"What do you mean you got to know him?" his daughter inquired.

"First, we eat, and then I'll explain everything to you. Francesca, your sauce smells heavenly," Frank replied, his stomach growling loudly.

"Here, my friend, some long-awaited vino. Ryder, here, have a glass." Maurizio handed a wine glass to Ryder.

"I don't drink wine. I'll take a beer." Ryder gave it back to Maurizio.

Frank took the glass from Maurizio and handed it back to Ryder. "You are family now, and family drinks vino whether they like it or not, son. Bambolina, please, I'm starving."

Jumping at her father's request, Francesca moved on autopilot to put the pasta into the boiling water, still in a daze.

A stunned Ryder took the glass and sampled the wine. He grimaced as he swallowed it, but he would drink anything this man asked of him.

After Francesca got the pasta cooking, she happily rearranged the table so her father and Maurizio would sit at the important positions at the heads of the table.

Frank guided everyone to their seats after rearranging back the seating so that there were no heads of the table. Everyone here had earned the same respect. He left the seat between him and Ryder empty for Francesca.

When she had all the food on the table, they all joined hands. All except Ryder lowered their heads and closed their eyes as Frank began the prayer.

He thanked God for the love of his family, and of course the people he missed every day—his deceased wife and innocent son. He thanked God for providing the meal and his daughter for her exquisite talent in cooking. Then Frank lifted his head to see Ryder staring at him. He thanked Ryder for his freedom. Then Frank lowered his head again and thanked God for their health and happiness. After he said "Amen," they all raised their heads and made the sign of the cross and recited, "Nel nome del Padre, del Figlio, e lo Spirito Santo."

The family dug into a feast that could have easily fed thirty. Frank shared the story of how Ryder had orchestrated his release, and that Ryder had visited him three times a week since they had moved him to the new faculty. He teared up again when he looked at each of his children and thanked them for the incredible sacrifices they had made on his behalf.

Francesca was blown away that Ryder had shared so much with her father, and astonished at the lengths he had gone to protect her feelings.

She placed a hand on Ryder's thigh and squeezed, needing a physical connection with the man she had fallen in love with. He acknowledged the gesture by lowering his hand, interlacing their fingers.

After looking at their interlaced fingers, Francesca raised her eyes and gifted him with a beautiful, heartfelt smile.

***

Francesca hugged her papa as she said her fourth and final good-bye to him. She was afraid to let him go after just getting him back, but she knew in her heart he would be back tomorrow. Frank was going to the new apartment her brothers had rented last week when they had found out their father was coming home.

Her heart was at peace for the first time in years as the door closed.

She turned to Ryder with fresh tears swimming in her eyes. "How can I ever thank you? No one has ever given me so much. How did I ever get so lucky to fall in love with a man like you?"

Shocked by her comment, he replied, "I'm the lucky one, Beauty. You never stop giving." Ryder gently brushed the side of her face with his hand as he drew her closer. "It's nice to be able to give back a little of what you give to everyone around you." Bending down, he brought her face to his and tenderly kissed her lips.

She sighed ever so softly, inciting his passion.

He ran his tongue along the seam of her lips, and she opened. He knew, when she had said she loved him, she meant it as a form of gratitude. He, on the other hand, was head-over-heels in love with her.

However, Ryder knew his love would tarnish her. His sperm donor had always said he was a monster and brought the worst out in people. He shouldn't be encouraging her further when she was meant for better.

Even after that thought, the passion he felt for Francesca brought out the animal in him, and he lost what little reserve he had.

Francesca purred into his mouth. It vibrated down his body and straight to his dick.

He deepened the kiss as he slipped his hand up to her breast.

"Please, Ryder," she begged against his lips.

He lost all common sense as he guided her to the table and started to jack up her dress. In the deep recesses of his mind, he knew she deserved better than the fucking he was going to give her, but lust had taken over, and nothing else mattered.

Simply thinking about consuming her had Ryder shoving her harder against the table. He couldn't wait to sink into the pure, clean soul of a woman. Maybe some of her goodness would remain on him as he connected with this little slice of heaven.

Francesca was lost in a wave of excitement when he turned her to face the table. She quickly placed her hands down so she didn't topple over as he finished hiking her dress up.

He was rotating his hips against her ass as he reached into his back pocket and grabbed a condom from his wallet. She moaned at the exquisite feeling of his hard-on pressed against her ass.

When she reached back to hold his hips, he growled, "No."

She froze. His voice had been deep, panicked.

The minute she tensed up, he said, "Please, Beauty, don't touch me. Let me take the lead."

Confused but lost in her love for this man, she obeyed.

She ground her backside against his erection, and he growled again, unzipping his pants and pulling out his erection.

Once he was sheathed, he grabbed the white lacy, tanga underwear that melded to her luscious curves and pushed it aside. He gathered both of her hands in one of his and held them tightly so she couldn't touch him. He only knew one way to have sex, and this was it.

He caged her body against the table, pushing a foot between her high heels and gently tapping them apart. She struggled for balance until she felt his hand at her most imitate place. She was dripping wet.

Ryder groaned with satisfaction.

"I need you, Ryder … Please!" Francesca pleaded.

It was too much for Ryder. The beast within him moved her cream around. Then he removed his hand and placed his cock at the core of her body and thrust in.

She screamed in pain at the large invasion.

He knew he was extra-large, but he was so caught up in the feeling of her muscles squeezing the life out of him that he neglected to hear her scream as one of pain, and not passion.

Francesca raised her head in agony and tried to move away until she stopped dead in her tracks when she saw their reflection in the mirror over the couch. She *was* in excruciating pain, but nothing compared to the vision in front of her.

His face was a mask of pain and hurt. What was wrong? Was he not attracted to her? She was inexperienced, but she couldn't be that bad, could she?

Everything in her screamed at the invasion that she wanted so badly. It was ripping her apart. She would take what he gave, but she was embarrassed and scared. She knew she loved him, and that he had feelings for her, but something was terribly wrong with Ryder. She had never done this before, so she couldn't help. She had no experience to understand it.

He continued to thrust into her ravished body while she watched in horror at the torment on his face. His final thrust made her scream out again with the deeper penetration.

She dropped her head to the table, breathing deeply and trying to recover. *What the hell just happened?*

Not conscious of his movements, Ryder pulled out and quickly walked to the bathroom, oblivious to the world around him. He turned on the light and glanced down at his penis, staring at the blood covering the condom.

Fucking hell, she must have been on her period. Why didn't she stop him or tell him she was on the rag?

He trembled as he stripped the condom off and flushed it down the toilet. Then he washed his hands, and when he looked up into the mirror, he saw the monster.

This was the beast he kept buried down deep in his black soul. He hated him, this creation of his father's, who would pay one day for that.

How could he have been so cruel as to let the monster anywhere near Francesca?

Instantly sickened, he leaned over the toilet and heaved.

Francesca's heart broke when she heard the retching. Could he be that disgusted with her, that it made him physically sick? Or had her dinner made him sick, and that's why he looked like he had been in so much pain?

He probably only had sex with her because she had begged him like a slut. What had she done? Would he forgive her? Had she ruined the best thing in her life?

She walked towards the bathroom and opened the door, finding

Ryder kneeling over the toilet, throwing up, with his penis still hanging out. Resting his head on the seat. She watched him gasp for breath.

She cautiously walked closer and whispered, "Ryder?"

Without lifting his head, he asked, "Why didn't you tell me you were on your period?"

Not thinking, she nervously responded, "I'm not on my period."

It took a minute before her words sank in. When it did, his head snapped up with a haunted look on his face. "But the blood ..." His eyes expanded in revulsion. "No, please, Beauty ... Please tell me I didn't just take your virginity!"

She lowered her eyes to the floor in embarrassment and insecurity, she couldn't respond.

"Francesca!" he snapped in a low, haunted voice. "Fuck! Fuck! What the fuck have I done?" He unsteadily jumped to his feet, tucking himself back into his pants.

She kept her eyes cast down as her tears dropped onto the floor. She was such a loser. Of course he wouldn't expect a woman of twenty-five to be a virgin.

She had only dated a few times before all the turmoil her family had endured. She hadn't had time to invest in a relationship. Loser, plain and simple.

"I hate that I did this to you!" he roared as he moved her out of his way. He quickly stalked across the room, snagging his jacket, and then opened the door to leave.

Hearing the door open spurred her into action.

"Ryder, don't blame yourself. This is my fault."

He turned, wearing a mask of vengeance, before he stepped out into the cold. "Did you ask to have your fucking virginity ripped from your body?" he yelled, angry at himself, not her. Then he was flying down the stairs at an uneven pace.

She ran to the door and out onto the landing, begging him to stop. "Please, Ryder, I'm so sorry. Please don't leave me ... I love you!"

As he reached his car door and flung it open, he looked up at the woman who held his shattered heart in her hands. "I'm sorry, Beauty." He wiped a stray tear that had escaped from his seared soul, got in the car, and then peeled away like the Devil himself was chasing him.

Francesca fell to her knees as she had done so many times at the cemetery and sobbed her eyes out. She then lifted her eyes to the night sky and cried, "Mama, what have I done? I love him. What do I do, Mama?"

In the form of a thought, the advice she was seeking came to her. "*He needs you. Go after him.*"

She took her mother's advice, brushed her tears away, and decided to fight for Ryder and the love she felt for him.

She ran inside and got the keys to her car, so absorbed in her thoughts she forgot her jacket. She ran to the car, thankful she only had one glass of wine. She had been afraid that, if she had consumed more, there would be a chance she would forget a small detail of this monumental day.

Twenty-five minutes later, she parked in the front of his building and ran as fast as she could in her high heels to the front desk. Carlton greeted her with a surprised smile and wished her a Merry Christmas.

"Carlton, I need to see Ryder," she declared.

"Miss … I'm sorry I forget your name. I haven't seen Mr. Vaughn since he left this morning."

"It's Francesca, and please, Carlton, I need to know he's okay. Can I wait here till he gets back?" She waved at the lounge area.

"Of course, Francesca. I'll call down and see if he snuck by my monitors. The garage will know if he has parked and already gone up."

Carlton phoned down while an anxious Francesca paced. He broke her frantic pacing when he addressed her again.

"Sorry, Francesca, he hasn't come back. But he did say I could let you into his apartment whenever you requested it. If you want, you can wait for him up there."

"I would really appreciate that. Thank you."

"Is there anything else I can do for you?" Carlton asked as he led her up to Ryder's condo, sensing her distress.

"No, thank you. I just really need to see Ryder."

They rode the rest of the way in silence. Then Carlton led her to Ryder's door and unlocked it.

"If you need anything at all, please call down, and I will assist any way I can."

"Thank you again," Francesca said as she closed the door behind her.

She placed her hand on the dark wall, searching for the light switch. Once she found it, she advanced towards the living room. She spied the next light switch and flicked it on.

When she glanced up, she gasped, dropping her purse as she brought her hands to her mouth. "Holy shit," she mumbled through her fingers.

She walked slowly into the room, amazed at what she was looking at. She walked towards the beautiful, cream coloured, extremely large, kid leather chair facing the wall. She stroked the soft velvety chair as she glanced at the Stonehenge painting she had given Ryder a week and a half ago on the centre of the wall.

A professional art light had been installed above the painting, shining directly onto it and hitting it at the perfect angle. Around the painting were photos of different parts of her painting printed on canvas, each one exemplifying a different part, giving credence to every element of the painting. There had to be fifteen canvas photos surrounding the original. It looked incredible.

A flash of light caught her attention, and she walked in a daze towards the shining object.

Her breath escaped her lungs again as she read the plaque and the title he had given the painting. *"Beauty's Mystical Depth."* Underneath the title, engraved in the same soft scrolled font, read, *"Painted by Francesca Moratti. Gifted from her soul to Ryder Vaughn. Christmas 2016."*

Her heart skipped a beat. She was trembling.

She walked backwards, taking in the spectacular view, until the back of her knees hit the chair and she fell unceremoniously into it. She shuffled back and curled her feet under her bottom as the impact of the words on the plaque hit her.

He was in love with her.

She started to play back all the things he had said and done over the last four months. He had cherished her, respected her, been kind to her. She would even go so far as to think he worshipped her. She had not seen all the signs along the way, too caught up in her own drama.

She had labeled him her BMFF. How insulting that must have been to the love he felt? How could she have been so insensitive? He had been her knight in shining armour, and she had been too freaking dense to see it. And now he was crushed, thinking he had stolen her virginity.

Where could he be? He had left before her and at a faster speed.

He should have been here by now.

She pulled out her phone and texted him.

Ryder, please call me. I'm sorry!

After five minutes of staring at the wall with her phone in her hands, mentally urging it to vibrate his response, she tried again, hoping her plea would reach him.

Ryder, I need you. Please call me.

Still nothing. Well, damn him. She would sit here until he came home for his passport and his plane ticket.

She got up and decided to look around and see if his passport was in his condo. She traveled through the big kitchen, not spotting it anywhere. Then she headed towards his bedroom. When she opened the door, she saw the extra-large bed was unmade, but that wasn't what stopped her in her tracks. What laid on the two night tables brought her to her knees again.

There on his night table was a beautiful frame with a picture of herself, Ryder, and Mason. It was one of the photos from the slideshow presentation at the Christmas concert. The other night table held a close-up picture of Francesca laughing.

Stupid didn't even begin to describe her.

She slowly got up and walked towards the bed, lifting the picture of the three of them. She placed a kiss to her fingers then laid them against Ryder's smirking lips. Then she sat down, gazing at the picture.

After a while, she slowly got up as she hugged the frame to her chest and turned to examine the other photo. She dropped the frame to the soft, carpeted ground when she noticed the wall across from the bed.

It held more pictures of them and the students. They were beautiful photos, each one capturing the essence of each child. This man wasn't just in love with her. He was obviously out of his mind in love with each of the kids, too.

There were four more pictures of her and him with each of the kids, as well as individual photos of the kids. She smiled at the picture of Ryder and Katrina with ponytails. It was apparent to Francesca that the kids and herself were the closest thing he had to a family. This man felt way more than he ever led on. Why couldn't he express his feelings?

She picked up the picture she had dropped and hugged it closely to her chest again. Then she got into his bed and surrounded herself with his scent. She started to cry as she thought about the things he had told her about the "sperm donor" and the "incubator." They were responsible for destroying the little boy he had once been.

It was inconceivable to Francesca that any parent could treat a child like that. He had distanced himself from almost everyone he had met, except a handful of friends he worked with. Why? She needed answers, but she was going to have to wait for them. And wait she would.

Francesca knew with every fibre of her being she would never love anyone the way she loved Ryder.

She laid in his bed, determined to teach him how to share the feelings he kept bottled up inside. He had saved her, and now it was time to repay the favour.

Chapter 13

"Sorry" By Buckcherry

Ryder had destroyed the trust of the one person he treasured most in the world, just because he couldn't allow anyone to touch him.

He didn't know how to caress another person in a gentle manner. He could hold hands and hug Francesca, but beyond that, the thought of anyone running their hands over his disgusting body made him cringe.

Why had his parents never taught him how to give and receive affection? He didn't care anymore that his parents never loved him; he just needed to know why. Why had his father accused him of being Satan's spawn? Why did his father think he was so repulsive?

Ryder recently realized that he was capable of love. He felt love for Francesca and the kids in his class. He learned it was all encompassing to love another person. Yet he didn't know how to show it.

He always assumed his father hated him because he was a gimp.

After working at the centre for over four months, though, he realized he didn't see the kids' disabilities anymore. He only saw the beauty behind the disability.

Frank had adored his son who'd had Down Syndrome. Judge Belmore felt blessed for her grandson. What terrible crime had he committed to deserve his parents' hatred? Why was he so unlovable to his sperm donor? He needed answers. He wasn't even sure they would be there, but he had to try.

Ryder drove to the address he hadn't been to in over twelve years, finding the outside was beautifully decorated for Christmas, as it had been when he had been a child.

Nothing had changed. They always made sure the outside world thought they had the picture-perfect life. His incubator always made sure she came home to Toronto to visit her parents during the holidays, which was ironic to Ryder, seeing as she had no loyalty to the only child she bore.

He walked up and pounded on the door. He heard voices approach, and a moment later, the door opened and there stood Salina and Diego Vargas.

His parents had aged. His father was mostly grey, and had lost most of his muscle mass. His mother obviously dyed her hair, and her face was lined with age. She was still a weak woman, and it showed. Nothing like the strength Francesca had.

"Yes? Can we help you?" his sperm donor asked.

Salina stared at the familiar face, moving to get a closer look, before gasping in realization. "Rolando!"

Disgusted by the reference, he said, "My name is Ryder. Ryder Vaughn. Rolando stopped existing nineteen years ago."

Shocked by her son's venomous statement, the incubator stepped back, but caught herself, donning the fake mask of sincerity he was familiar with. "We have missed you, Ro—Ryder. Please come in."

Ryder gave a snort of disbelief.

His father still hadn't said a word as he examined every inch of his son, ending at his left leg. Diego couldn't believe how big his son had grown. He was huge, and looked powerful and strong. Diego was six feet, but he had to look way up at Ryder.

Slightly intimidated, he moved aside when Ryder entered their home. There would be no hugs from those two.

"Come. We will have coffee and talk," the incubator said.

Ryder waited for them to go ahead of him, knowing his position had always been behind them. He was amazed he was still conditioned after all these years to accept his lack of status in his family.

Anger seeped from his pours as he looked around the house while they headed into the kitchen. Not much had changed. There were still pictures everywhere of his father when he played soccer for Brazil, but not one picture showed their dirty, little secret. Their gimp.

His mother started to make espresso, while his father sat and indicated for Ryder to join him. Ryder ignored the gesture and leaned against the counter in a defensive stance. These people made him uncomfortable. He remembered never to be within striking range. Some lessons were ingrained.

His mother broke the silence when the coffee pot was placed on the stove. "It's a nice surprise to see you on Christmas. I tried to find you over the years, but to no avail."

He tensed at her remark. Was she for fucking real? Ryder was full of fury at her disclosure, doing everything in his power to keep it in check. He wanted answers.

"Why?"

"Rolando, you are our son. A mother wants to see her son."

That was just too much to take.

"You never wanted me around before. Why now?"

"Do not disrespect your mother, boy!" his father snarled.

Boy? Really? Did the asshole not see he wasn't a boy anymore?

Frank's kind words and the title of son came back to him. His father had never called him son; he had always been simply *boy* or *gimp.*

Ryder had been waiting for his father to show his true colours towards his "boy," and this was the opening he needed.

"She is not my mother, and you aren't my father." He pointed at her. "Incubator." Then pointed at Diego. "Sperm donor."

Diego had a short fuse. The uncontrollable rage Ryder associated with him exploded.

Standing, Diego's face turned a molten red, and veins protruded from his neck. "You fucking bastard! Who the hell do you think you are, *boy*?" Diego said "boy" like a master to his slave, and it cut deeply, even after all this time.

"I wish I was a bastard. I am not your boy. I'm the *gimp*, remember? Your fucking punching bag. Your dirty little secret. *Boy* was the derogatory term you used so you didn't have to call me son, old man."

His mother, forever protecting her husband, stepped in front of the enraged man. "Why did you come here, Rolando?"

He felt no sympathy for this weak woman. "My name is Ryder. Rolando died. The *boy* was killed by his sperm donor and incubator. Not here for some pathetic reunion. I want answers! Why …? Why did you two hate me so much? What did I ever do to you?"

"We gave you a healthy body. We trained you to become the greatest soccer player Brazil has ever seen. We hired trainers, coaches, nutritionists, massage therapists. We gave you everything money could buy! And you fucked that up with your fear and weakness," his father spat with the rage Ryder associated with the man.

"I was eleven years old! A small child, and I was hurt. You

blame me for what happened?" Ryder clenched his hands into fists, hating these people down to the deepest parts of his soul.

"You were feeble and an embarrassment to your mother and I. We deserved better than a puny, useless, decrepit boy! My one chance at a legacy, and you were the fastest sperm? Unbelievable. You're an abomination who brings the worst out of people. I deserved better than a cripple."

Ryder had heard those words a million times over the years. It was nothing new. Regardless, he still wasn't getting what he came here for.

"*He* was still the same child on the inside. Did *he* mean nothing to you?" He was speaking in third person, truly believing they had killed the innocent child he had been.

"I was meant to teach and mentor a star, not a weak, little mutant!" his father responded with the same selfish attitude he'd had all of Ryder's life.

Ryder knew at that moment he had gotten what he came for. It had never been about him. It had always been about his father's ego.

He was born and bred to fulfill a dream his father had never attained. He was bred to be the best of the best, and nothing else would do. Yes, Diego had been a famous soccer player, but he hadn't been the star. Second best was never good enough for Diego.

"Here is the irony, old man. I *am* a star. In ten years, I've made more money and achieved more fame than any soccer player in the world could make in five lifetimes. Thousands of people pay good money to hear me play all over the world. So, you see, old man, I superseded your fame in the first year of my career." Ryder turned to leave. He had gotten the answer he was seeking.

Then he turned back and looked at his mother. "You are almost worse than him. You carried me and nurtured me for nine months. But your priority was never to the life you created. Your priority was assuring you could keep the devil in your bed. He was never faithful to you, even I knew that, yet you stayed by his side and allowed him to demean the both of us. You disgust me. I hope you both rot in hell and live the rest of your lives in misery."

His parents were so shocked at his claim that they didn't reply or follow him to the door.

Ryder slammed the door shut when he left. He got in his car and drove, no destination in mind. He just needed to get away from all the madness and those heartless cows.

He couldn't stop thinking about Francesca and her family. They had treated him more like family in the short time he had known them than his own parents had his entire life. His heart clenched when he realized he had betrayed their kindness.

His phone beeped, and he read the text while he drove. Francesca wanted to speak to him. He couldn't respond. He was afraid she would banish him from her life.

When the next beep came, he couldn't even look at it.

Parking, he eventually looked at his surroundings, surprised at his location. He was at Mason's group home.

They were kindred spirits, and he hoped the kid could ground him tonight.

He picked up the presents for Mason he had already stored in his trunk, knowing he was going to drop by and see him on Christmas Day before going back to California. Then he headed to the door.

A man answered. "Hi, can I help you?"

"Yes, I'm Ryder Vaughn. I'm here to see Mason. I don't know if you remember me, but I work with him at the centre. I drove him home on a few occasions."

"I remember you." His expression turned downcast. "Mason isn't having a good day. His birth mother came by, and they had a fight. He's been out of control ever since."

"Please, I need this as much as he does." Maybe something good could come out of the last few hours.

"Okay, but I warn you, if he goes off the rails again, you're outta here."

Ryder nodded his understanding, and then the man led him to Mason's bedroom and knocked on the door.

"Fuck off, Ryan. I hate you!" Mason screamed from behind the closed door.

"Mason, it's Ryder."

"Ryder?"

"Yeah. Can I come in?"

"I'm not in a very good mood. My bitch of a mother was here. I hate her. I don't understand why the courts say she gets to visit."

"I get it. I just saw my own parents, and I know exactly how you feel."

"Really?"

"Yeah. You gonna let me in?"

"Okay."

Ryder put the presents down outside the door then opened the door, seeing the mess Mason had made of his room. He was sitting on the floor by his overturned bed, and all of his clothes were tossed all over.

"Hey. Mind if I sit?"

"I don't know why. No one else can stand me. Not even my own mother." He dropped his head to his knees. He knew no one loved him, not really; his mother had said so. The people at the home and the centre were paid to look after him. "Why are you here? Did someone call you? Guess they needed someone with some muscle to keep me in my place. I thought you went to California?"

The kid was smart. It always amazed Ryder how Mason couldn't read or write, and still played with toy cars and action figures, yet he was insightful. He got things most people missed. He memorized song lyrics, could recite most movies word for word, and he was damn good at video games.

Ryder had read a lot about Shaken Baby Syndrome and the various degrees of the infliction. It was impossible to treat, because the damage to the brain was permanent, and the degree of damage varied from victim to victim.

Mason looked like any other teenager, but his temper was uncontrollable and his academic level was measured in months, not years. He would never be anything more than he was now, just his body would mature. At the centre, they were teaching him life skills so he could live more independently and function in a small way out in society.

"I came back to see a friend, and I wanted to see you, of course. You know you are loved. Francesca loves you. I love you."

"My mom says you are paid to love me. And Francesca … Well, she loves everybody so she doesn't count." The kid looked up at him. "Ryder, why am I this way? Why can't I change? I want to. I try hard, but nothing works." His voice dropped in shame. "My mom says I'm retarded like all the kids at the centre. Do you think that's true?"

Fucking bitch, Ryder thought. She caused her son's disability, and he's the retard? What a bitch.

Ryder moved the kid's bangs from in front of his face and tilted his chin up. Mason looked up with apprehension.

"No, Mason, you're not retarded, and don't say that about

yourself or the other kids. I love you, and I'm not paid by the centre. You have special needs—that makes you special. It doesn't make you retarded. You have behaviour issues. I'm thirty, and I still have behaviour issues. I just hurt the person who means the most to me in the world, and I ran away so I wouldn't have to face it. I get it, kid. I know how you feel. We aren't that different, you and me."

"Yeah, sure. How would you know how it feels to be made fun of? You're big and strong; nobody would pick on you. They think because I'm 'special' that I can't hear their comments or see their looks of disgust. They treat me like I'm invisible and like I don't matter. Well, fuck my mother, and fuck everyone else. One day, I'm going to run away, and no one will be able to find me. I'm going to find somewhere to fit in like the lost boys in *Peter Pan*."

Ryder sighed. "I've lived your life. My parents didn't like me, either. My father used to beat me and call me all kinds of names."

"Why would anyone make fun of you? I wish I was just like you. You're perfect."

Ryder knew actions spoke louder than words, so he did something he hadn't done in eighteen years. He slowly lifted his left pant leg and showed Mason his prosthetic.

"No fucking way! You're like a transformer. That's so cool! Can I touch it?"

Ryder laughed. It wasn't the response he had expected. That was part of the charm with these kids. They didn't judge. They didn't see your flaws. They only saw the good. They had no expectations. They knew who treated them right and who didn't.

"Of course."

"What's your foot look like? What's it made from?"

"Hold on." Ryder took his boot off. "3-D printed titanium leg and foot."

"Were you born that way?"

"No. I lost my leg when I was eleven. I got a prosthetic, but not this one. This is the newest in technology. But trust me; I got picked on a lot when I was a kid. I spent six months in the hospital. That's where I learned to play the guitar, and then the drums. They had classes for kids who didn't leave the hospital very often. It took four months of physical therapy before I could walk with the prosthetic."

"You really do understand, don't you?"

Ryder ruffled his hair. "Yeah, buddy, I know what it's like to fight the world and feel like you don't fit in. My father used to beat me because I lost my leg. He was embarrassed that I wasn't his perfect son."

Mason looked up at him, full of sincerity, and replied, "Sorry, Ryder, but even if your dad was an asshole, your leg is still cool!"

"Thanks, Mason." He looked around at the mess, telling him, "Let's straighten this room up. I have some gifts for you."

"Really? Can I open them tonight, or do I have to wait for Christmas morning?"

"We get this room put together, you can open them tonight."

"Can you help me lift the bed? It's easy to flip when I'm pissed, but a bitch to put back when I'm not."

Ryder laughed, which felt good.

They spent forty-five minutes righting the room. The kid babbled nonstop about how cool Ryder's leg was, and asked if Ryder thought transformers were real. All the anger Ryder had felt slowly seeped away.

He started thinking about Francesca and what an asshole he had been. He needed to put his faith in her and explain his torment, the same way she had trusted him. He didn't know if she would ever forgive him since he had treated her like a whore.

Much like Mason, Ryder didn't trust easily, he still lost his shit when he got frustrated, exploded when he was faced with situations he didn't know how to deal with, had been abused by his father, and he didn't know how to show affection. He had learned right alongside Mason at the centre that there were good people in the world, and he had to start believing in them.

When he was ready to leave, he stood outside the door. Mason surprised him by jumping into his arms and hugging him.

"I love you. Thanks, Ryder, for all my gifts!" He leaned in close and whispered in Ryder's ear, "I know you had a fight with Frankie, but whatever you did, she'll forgive you. She always forgives me." With that, the kid jumped down and slammed the door in Ryder's face.

Ryder was blown away by the kid. He was right; she probably would forgive him, but he needed to fix himself first.

He had to see one more person before he left, so he got into his cold car and texted Francesca. Then he headed to his next destination.

Frank received a call on the new cell phone Ryder had given him earlier, explaining how it would give Francesca peace of mind if she could reach him whenever she wanted.

"Hello?"

"Frank, it's Ryder. Sorry to bug you on your first night home, but I need to talk. Can you meet me outside?"

"Sure. I'll be right out."

Frank didn't know what Ryder wanted, but he understood this talk was personal. He told his sons he just wanted to grab some fresh air and to walk alone. Then went outside to find Ryder waiting at the curb. Frank jumped into the car.

"Is everything okay?" He could see that Ryder was nervous, and wondered why he wasn't with Francesca.

"No, Frank, I fucked up."

"Talk to me, son. How did you fuck up? Does this involve Francesca?"

Ryder heaved out a deep sigh. "I … I'm a monster. I'm not good enough for her. She was meant for someone better than me. I'm a prick, and she is so loving and beautiful. I'll destroy that. You have to encourage her to stay away from me."

"What makes you believe that? I've met a kind man, not a monster."

Ryder slammed the steering wheel with so much force it should have shattered. "Fuck, Frank, you're not listening. I hurt Francesca tonight! You should be beating the shit out of me, not trying to make me feel better. Ask her. She'll tell you. I destroyed her tonight. She should never forgive me, but even Mason believes she will, and that's not right.

"Save her, Frank. Show her what I truly am. She thinks she loves me, but she doesn't know the real me. I'll never be able to reciprocate her love the way she deserves. I'm a broken man she can't put back together. Anyone who knew me never could love the real me. Do your job and protect your daughter; convince her it's just hero worship. She doesn't love me. She can't. I won't allow it." Ryder lowered his face into his hands, rubbing it roughly. He needed to get through to this man, and he wasn't listening.

Frank looked at the tortured soul beside him. "Do you love her, Ryder?"

The question deflated him. He didn't want to reveal his crime without embarrassing and betraying Francesca's trust.

"Yes, I've loved her since the first day I saw her. But she can't love me. She'll only get hurt. I came to you for help. I need you to be there for her and protect her from me. Italian fathers are supposed to be ruthless when it comes to their daughters. Do your job! Stop the madness, Frank. Please, I'm begging you!"

"You may love my daughter, but you don't think very highly of her."

Ryder growled as he snapped his head towards the man, appalled and instantly pissed off by Frank's words. Before he could rebut, though, Frank continued.

"Don't assume she's not smart enough to know what's in her mind and heart. She's a very smart girl. You can't control someone else's feelings, or tell them how to feel. They are her feelings, and you have no right to them.

"I've watched many young men bend over backwards for her attention, yet she was unaffected by them all. I knew it would have to be someone special to win her heart. You might not like yourself, but she loves you. Don't discredit that because, if you do, you discredit everything she loves: her family, her friends, the children under her care, the paintings she creates, the food she makes. Don't belittle her choices. Whatever happens is between you and Francesca. If she is hurting, I'll be there to help her, but I won't bad mouth you to my bambolina."

Frank laid his hand on Ryder's shoulder. "Don't be angry at her for not seeing clearly. Maybe it's you who isn't seeing clearly. Look inside your heart and try to see what she does, not what you've been taught to see. It might surprise you.

"When Francesca chooses to love, she does it unconditionally. You of all people should know that. Go home to California and take the time to think. We all make mistakes. God knows I've made my fair share. In a loving relationship, you will make many mistakes, but without forgiveness, you cannot have true and lasting love. Learn to love yourself, son."

With that, Frank opened the door and exited. He walked away, knowing there was a reason God chose this moment to release him from prison. His family needed him, and he would step up to the plate and see right by his daughter.

He went back into the apartment and made Luciano show him how to text. Then he slowly typed his baby girl a text, waiting until it said "delivered," and then waited for her reply.

Nothing tonight had gone as Ryder thought after the initial reunion. The world's axel must have slipped, because he felt like he was in the twilight zone.

He was confused. He stole Francesca's virginity, yet she screamed her love for him. He went to Mason's to feel grounded, but the kid threw him for a loop when he summed up the answer to Ryder's problem in one sentence. He went to her father to incite his anger and protectiveness, hoping Frank would forbid Francesca from seeing him, yet Frank didn't try to kill him. Instead, he tried to show Ryder the goodness inside of him. Had everyone gone crazy?

He would take Frank's advice and go back to California. The three people he cared the most about had given him something to think about, and now he had to honour their words. But first, he needed to drive by Francesca's place, just to make sure she had gone back inside.

Ryder drove into her driveway and looked up at her apartment. All the lights were still on. He would bet his last dollar she was up there crying. He had caused that and would carry that guilt for the rest of his life. His heart broke a little more for the sweet soul of the woman he had crushed tonight.

He glanced down from the apartment and noticed her car wasn't in the driveway. Where the hell was she? Was she okay?

He grabbed his phone and looked at the texts she had sent. Damn, she had said she needed him, and he had ignored the text because it was too hard for him to face. What a coward.

He texted her back.

Beauty, I'm sorry. Where are you?

He pushed the send button and waited for a reply. She wasn't picking up the message. If something had happened to her, he would never forgive himself. Where could she have gone? He had been at her father's, so he knew she wasn't there. Frank would have said something. She must have gone to one of her girlfriends.

He texted Taya, knowing her the best out of all the Caesar buddies. He had given each of the girls his number so they would call him to drive them all home on Caesar Fridays.

Have you talked to Francesca today?

No. Is everything okay?

She might need you. I fucked up. I can't find her.

I'll try the other girls and get back to you.

Thanks.

There was somewhere he knew she might go, so he drove away and headed towards the cemetery where he walked around her mother's grave.

When his phone beeped, he rushed to retrieve the message. It was Taya.

No one has heard from her. Should I be worried?

He didn't want to panic everyone. Francesca would be devastated if he disclosed too much.

No. Tell her to text me if you hear from her.

Will do. But if you hurt her and she needs me, you better tell me!

He didn't reply, not knowing what to say.

He drove back to her apartment and sat in her driveway, waiting for her to return. He fell asleep in the cold car and was awoken at five a.m. by the ringing of his cell phone.

"Francesca?" he answered in a groggy, sleep-deprived voice.

"No, son, it's Frank. I just received a text from Francesca. She's fine. She's going home to prepare for Christmas dinner. I'm heading there now for a father/daughter talk."

"Thanks, Frank." He was relieved she was okay.

"She wanted to call you, but I asked her not to. I think it's best if you have time to figure things out alone. She's worried about you, but I assured her you're all right and that I spoke to you. I won't tell her the context of our conversation, but I will let her know you care for her."

"I'm sorry I hurt her, Frank. I love her."

"I know, Ryder. Spend your time wisely, my friend."

Ryder arrived home and learned that Francesca had come to his condo and that Carlton had let her in before his shift had ended, as per Ryder's instructions. Carlton was worried about her, telling him she had left half an hour ago. Ryder thanked him and told Carlton that, if she ever showed up upset again, he was to be notified immediately. Carlton nodded and wished Ryder a Merry Christmas.

He walked into his condo, instantly smelling her perfume. It was such a comforting smell.

He walked to his bedroom and saw the picture laying on the bed with mascara smeared on his pillow. He was such an asshole. He had ripped out her heart and destroyed the first Christmas her family had back together. He desperately needed her forgiveness. He was as selfish as his father had always accused him of. He needed to tell her now, but he couldn't come up with the right words. He sent her a text.

I'm sorry. You deserved better than what I did to you. I wish I could find the words right now to tell you what is in my heart, but I can't. Forever, Ryder

Then he sent her the link to a song that could convey what he couldn't put into words. "Sorry" by Buckcherry.

Chapter 14

"Believe" By Mumford & Sons

Francesca drove to her apartment and quickly changed, throwing on a pair of jeans and a big, warm sweater. She couldn't get warm, and she wasn't sure if that was due to her not having a jacket last night, or the sadness that had seeped into her bones.

When her phone beeped that she had a message, she quickly retrieved it, hoping it was from Ryder. Relief swept through her when she saw his name.

She read his message twice to make sure she didn't rush through and miss anything. Then Francesca clicked on the link and listened to the song as she read the lyrics. Tears formed in her eyes as the melody and words curled around her heart.

Ryder presented himself as such a tough guy with his size and intimidating presence, but the truth was, he was just a big marshmallow. He said he had a black soul, but he was dead wrong. He was kind and compassionate, and his most endearing quality was his sensitivity. He was quiet and used that time to listen to people, absorbing and reflecting on their thoughts, so when he answered, it was profound.

He might not know it yet, but he was her forever. She knew it was going to be an uphill battle, but she would fight tooth and nail for the love she felt.

Francesca never envisioned losing her virginity that way. She had read so many romance novels that she believed it was going to be awe-inspiring. Angels were going to break out into song, and stars would fall just for her. Reality was a slap in the face. Nevertheless, she couldn't totally regret it, because Ryder had shown her the broken little boy who lived inside the thirty-year-old man. She knew now that he was vulnerable and simply human.

She resolved herself to nurture his shattered self-confidence and teach him that touching was as essential as breathing.

She was startled from her thoughts when she heard a knock at her door. Her heart sped up, hoping it was Ryder. Maybe he had changed his mind and wanted to see her.

She flung open the door, surprised to see her papa.

"Buon Natale, sweetheart."

"Buon Natale, Papa. What are you doing here so early?"

Frank didn't release his daughter after he kissed her. He searched her face, looking for answers. This wasn't the carefree girl he had left last night. There was real sadness in her eyes.

"After our conversation this morning, I thought you might need me."

She dropped her head with an overload of emotions. "How did you know?"

"Ryder called and asked me to meet him last night. He was upset."

There was silence for a minute while each contemplated their thoughts and how to start. Frank instinctively knew Francesca had an intimate encounter with Ryder, and that it had gone wrong. Experience had given him wisdom, and he promised himself not to go into depth about it. He had to have an answer to one question, though.

"Bambolina, did he force you?"

"No, he would never do that. You should know better." Francesca was beside herself with shock and disappointment that her father would suggest such a thing.

She turned away from him, heading towards the coffee machine.

Frank exhaled a breath of relief. His mind had wandered last night after his conversation with Ryder. He didn't believe Ryder was capable of forcing Francesca, yet he'd had to know for sure.

"Sorry, but I had to ask. He was so agitated when we spoke. I know it would be easier for a girl to speak to her mother about these things. Your mother would have been so good at this. I want you to know you can tell me anything, and I won't judge. As your father, it's my duty to look after you. He is a friend, but nothing comes before my daughter. I will be respectful of him because he has earned that from me, unless you tell me otherwise."

Francesca listened intently and contemplated how much to reveal without betraying Ryder.

"I love him, Papa, and I'm going to do everything in my power to get him to accept my love. I want him in my life, and I won't let anyone change my mind. If you came here to tell me not to see him, you're wasting your time. I appreciate you trying to protect me, but I don't need protection from Ryder."

"I know Ryder loves you equally as much, if not more. But he is fighting demons and hates the man he thinks he is. He feels unworthy. What you feel for him might not be enough to save him from himself." Frank sighed, trying to find the words to explain Ryder's behaviour. "He opened up to me and asked many questions. He is baffled by the dynamics of a family and unconditional love. He is damaged and frightened, like a wounded animal. He will strike out to protect you from the man he thinks he is. He trusts no one, especially himself. You have to dig deep and question whether you are strong enough to take that on."

"Why does it have to be so hard? Why can't he just accept what I offer and relish it?"

"You grew up in a family who loved you before you were even born. You were taught to express and receive love. We encouraged you to blossom and become anyone you wanted to be, to try new things and find your inner self. When you failed, we picked you up and dusted you off, pushed you to try again. We allowed you to express anger, hurt, and frustration, and you were taught how to deal with those feelings. You weren't given many monetary things, because we couldn't afford them. But we gave you wings and encouraged you to spread them and fly." Frank walked up to his daughter and grasped her hands to ensure he had her full attention. He wanted his daughter to understand this was not a quick fix. It would take months, if not years. She had to determine if it was worth it.

"I assume, from what Ryder shared with me, he didn't have the same advantages. I don't know his whole history, but I do know he didn't have it easy. Sweetheart, if you've never had love before, it's difficult to understand. Those are life-long lessons, and you aren't going to teach a grown man those lessons overnight. He has his perceptions and walls he has built to protect himself. You have an insurmountable task ahead of you. If you love him and want to help him, then you must take it slowly. Don't think sex or affection will change him. It might help, but it won't heal him. Teach him each lesson slowly and give him a chance to feel it, absorb it. Bambolina, teach him to love himself first. Otherwise, he'll never be able to love fully."

"How do I do it, Papa? How did you and Mom get through the

hard times? Tell me. I don't want to make a mistake. Why does it have to be so hard?" Francesca was lost. She had never been someone's girlfriend. She didn't know the protocol.

"Every relationship has struggles. Do you think it was easy for your mother and I? I was born and raised a strict Roman Catholic Italian, and she was born a Protestant Irish girl. Her family was taught at a young age to hate Catholics. They moved to Canada to get away from the religious wars of Ireland. The Italians and the Irish hated one another during the times of our immigration.

"Most of our families didn't even attend our wedding. Your mother's parents never forgave us for getting married. They went back to Ireland and never spoke to your mother again. It broke her heart that they never met you kids. I was wrong. I thought I was all she would ever need. When I informed them of her death, they never acknowledged it. I still feel guilty that your mother lost her parents because they couldn't accept me."

"I didn't know. I'm sorry. Mom was such a great person. Her parents missed out on so much because of hatred." Francesca had no idea that had happened. Her mother used to say her parents were gone. She and her brothers had assumed they passed away.

"I made a mistake by not encouraging her to reconcile with her parents. I was selfish and believed I knew what was best. We all make mistakes and have to live with the consequences. Francesca, you're going to make mistakes, and that's okay. Learn and grow from them, and if that doesn't work, then try something else. One step at a time. Figure out what's most important and start there. If you are going to teach patience, you yourself must be patient. Don't rush it. Take the time that he is away and think. Regroup; organize your feelings and thoughts. Pick one task a day and make that your focus."

She smiled for the first time that Christmas morning, thankful her papa was home. He was right; she couldn't charge right in.

That was why he didn't want her to call Ryder. She had to be methodical and supportive. She would be a Trojan horse and work from the inside out without him realizing it. She was going to war with his demons, and it was a battle she would win.

***

Ryder turned his phone back on as he exited the plane. It instantly beeped that he had messages. Disappointment surged through him when he saw none were from Francesca. He had told her not to contact him, and she was respecting his wishes, but it still hurt.

Each of his bandmates had left messages about having an early Christmas dinner together before heading out to Reno tonight.

He grabbed his bag and headed to Evan's place, wishing he could just head to his place and wallow in his misery. However, he had made commitments to the only other people that meant something to him.

Ryder rang the doorbell and waited for Evan to open it.

"What the fuck, Ryder? Since when have you ever knocked?" He grinned. "Merry Christmas, fucker. Glad you could make it. Come on in. Everyone's in the kitchen."

"Thanks, Evan, and Merry Christmas." Ryder followed his friend into the packed kitchen.

Ryder greeted Kevin's parents and sister, wishing them a Merry Christmas. Then he turned to Evan's wife and his family. Lastly, he turned to Pete's mom who wrapped him up in a hug. She felt Ryder tense at her display of affection, but she didn't care. He was one of her boys, and it was Christmas.

Ryder had known the families since before he was eighteen. They were the closest thing to a surrogate family he'd had, though he had never gotten close to any of them. When he had met them, he was still an angry young man and closed off, feeling like they pitied him for having no family of his own. Through the years, he realized he kept them at a distance so they couldn't hurt him like he expected all parents to do. However, they had never given up on him or treated him any differently than the other guys. Whether he liked it or not, he was part of their extended families.

Pete walked up and handed him a beer. "So, how did it go? Are you going to tell us what you flew back to Toronto for?"

Ryder leaned against the counter, beer in hand, and crossed his leg over the other one. "Nope."

"Come on, man. Why so mysterious? I bet my bottom dollar it's a broad."

Ryder lifted an eyebrow at his use of a derogatory term in front of the parents.

Pete, knowing how to needle Ryder, continued, "Hey, Mom, did you know Ryder has been working with mental cases? He must have snagged one for himself." He chuckled at his own comment.

Before anyone could blink an eye, Ryder had his massive hand wrapped around Pete's throat. "Take it back, asshole."

Evan was across the room in a second. "Ryder, he's only joking. Let him go!"

Everyone was shocked into silence. None of the family members had ever seen the slightest bit of violence from Ryder.

"Take. It. Back."

Pete's face was turning red as he struggled to get away.

Evan grabbed Ryder's arm, trying to break the hold. "He can't answer if he can't breathe. Let him go."

The red haze of anger began to clear when he realized what he was doing. He released Pete, who grasped for air, holding his throat and glaring at Ryder.

"What the fuck, man? Have you lost your goddamn mind?" Pete choked out.

Ryder was embarrassed by his actions, but he wouldn't apologize. "Do you have any idea what those kids live through on a daily basis? Some of them struggle for each breath. They can't help how they were born or what people did to them. They are innocent, and they always deal with shit-ass attitudes like yours, asshole. You have no right to judge them."

"I'd rather be dead than live like that," Pete answered. "Promise me someone will pull the plug."

"That's an easy statement to make when you're healthy," Ryder stated. "Their lives are as valuable as yours, so don't demean them by making stupid comments. It takes a lot of courage to fight every day to live in a world that doesn't accept you. They are beautiful and innocent, and their only crime is not living up to societies' standards." Ryder turned to leave. "I'm out of here."

"Ryder, don't go." Pete's guilt quickly ate at him. "You're right; I'm an asshole. I'm sorry, man. Please stay … It's Christmas."

Ryder stopped in his tracks. Pete wasn't the only asshole. Ryder had no right to take his frustration about Francesca out on his friend. Six months ago, he had felt the same way as Pete. Now, he just wanted them to understand what great kids they were.

He slowly turned around. "I apologize to all of you. I overreacted. The kids I work with are special, and they don't deserve to be made fun of. I defend them because they can't defend themselves, and they deserve our respect."

"Impressive," Kevin stated. "I never would have believed you would have become so attached. Gotta say, I'm proud of you."

Ryder had never heard Kevin talk like that. He was proud of himself, but he hadn't expected his friends to understand.

"That means a lot." Ryder gave a chin lift.

"Let's make a toast," Evan's dad broke in. "To Ryder and the kids he works with. Cheers." After they all took a sip of their drinks, he continued, "We all want to hear about these kids who have changed your life. Let's sit down and eat so you can fill us in."

As they headed to the table, each one of the parents expressed their admiration to Ryder.

As he sat down and looked around the table, he realized how selfish he was. No matter how standoffish he had been, this group had always been in his life, encouraging and supporting him. He hadn't noticed it, wallowing in his own self-pity and hatred.

He made a pact to himself to show more gratitude to his extended family. He was blessed far more than he had believed.

"What exactly do you do with these kids and how did you get involved?" Pete's mom started the conversation.

Ryder answered all their questions honestly and without reservation. He told them all about the court hearing to working at the centre, and they shared laughs at some of the antics Ryder told them the kids had gotten into.

"One of the kids knows who I am and our band," Ryder told them. "He always yells out 'Fornication for the nation.' Gives the horn symbol, too. He knows the words to all our songs. I was afraid he was going to blow my cover."

"Do you think he would recognize me?" Evan asked.

"Bro, he would recognize all of you. For Christ's sake, he pegged me, and I never use my real name, and I disguise my appearance." Then he told them how Theo is always trying to stick his tongue down someone's throat or his ear, and the group shared another laugh.

Pete gave Ryder a strange look. "I've only ever heard you laugh, like, three times in twelve years. For that matter, I haven't heard you speak as much as you have today. This job really has changed you." He smiled widely. "And for the better. I like this new Ry Herr."

"Funny, asshole. I think you would fit right in there. Not with the staff, but with the students."

"Ha ha." Pete got a contemplative look on his face. "I would love to meet these kids."

"They don't take kindly to strangers, but it would be cool for you guys to see one of their concerts."

"I want to meet them, too," Evan's sister piped in. "It sounds like such an admirable thing you guys do. Can I come? Please."

Everyone chimed in, saying they would love to go to the centre and see a concert. Ryder was humbled at their sincerity.

They continued to question Ryder about his experiences when the door bell rang. Evan got up to answer it, coming back with their manger Ted.

"Merry Christmas, everyone. Sorry to disturb your dinner. I thought you would be finished by now."

"We should have been, but Ryder has had us in stitches for the last hour," Evan's wife Melissa answered.

Ted was pulling up a chair when he stopped and stared at Ryder.

"Close your mouth. You're catching flies." Pete chuckled.

"Did I hear correctly?" Ted continued to pull up the chair while he rolled his eyes at Pete.

"Yeah, man. Ryder found his personality after thirty years." Pete had always been the joker of the group. Ryder was used to it. He just wouldn't allow it about the people he cared about.

"Ignore the bastard."

"I hung up all the paintings to the specs you gave me. Did you like it?" Ted asked.

Ryder shook his head. "Haven't been home yet. Can't wait to see them, though."

"You're a fucking art connoisseur now, too?" Kevin asked in surprise.

"I have a friend who paints. I bought them all."

"That sounds creepy, dude. You a stalker now?" Kevin asked.

Ryder shrugged. "If she knew it was me buying them, she wouldn't have put them up for sale. She would think I was buying them out of pity, which isn't the case. The girl has talent, yet she doesn't know it."

Evan couldn't let it go. "Come on, bro; there has to be more to it than that."

Ryder stood. The conversation was heading somewhere he didn't intend to go. "I'm calling a cab. Listen, I'm not going on the bus with you guys. I haven't been on my Harley for a while, so I'll take my bike and meet you guys at the hotel."

Ted stood. "I'll take you home and grab your bag. I have a few promotional things I have to take care of before we head to San Diego, so I'm taking my car." He waved at everyone as he walked towards the door. "See you all in Reno."

Ryder said good-bye to the guys, and to the surprise of everyone, he hugged each of the women, leaving them speechless. Then he thanked Melissa and Evan's mom for a great dinner and headed out.

When he walked into his house, it was the first time it felt like a home. Francesca's paintings were everywhere, the names he had given them placed beautifully under each one. He tilted the light above the third one, the person from the gallery having missed the proper angle.

Just before he left, he walked up to the painting of Civita di Bagnoregio in Italy and stared at it for minute. Ryder remembered how Francesca had talked nonstop of the beautiful place and how it was a dream of hers to see it. He wished he could be at her side when she did. He knew that wasn't possible because Taya was going with her. One day, though, he would love to see it with her. Then he remembered what he had done to her. Some dreams never came true.

He needed to get on his bike and let the wind take his sorrow away.

He jumped onto his customized softail, revved the engine, and engaged the suicide shifter. He took off like a shot, absorbed in the music coming from the stereo, until he reached the highway.

Memories of Francesca assaulted him. Her carefree attitude at school. The way everyone watched her interacting with the kids.

It would drive him crazy, watching men drool over her as she completed the simplest of tasks, like getting gas. He wanted to punch every fucker in the face who stared.

She had the perfect body. Her tits were the perfect size—not too small, but also enough to fill his large hands. Her hips were rounded, but her ass was her best asset. It was meant to be worshiped. And if he took both hands, he bet he could wrap them around her waist.

She was so touchy about her weight and refused to ever wear shorts, saying her thighs were too big. He would love to hold those delectable thighs while he tasted her, something he had never done to a woman before because that would have implied intimacy. Still, his mouth watered just thinking about how she would taste.

Just as that thought disappeared, Ryder's phone vibrated to the specific vibration he had assigned to Francesca's number. He slowed the bike down and pulled over to the side of the road.

She had sent him a text with no content; simply a link. He didn't bother to read the link, just pressed on it, wanting to hear what she had sent.

YouTube popped up, and the song, "More Than Words" by Extreme, started to play. The name didn't sound familiar until the melody started up. He had heard the song before, but he didn't remember the words.

His heart ached as he listened. The lyrics spoke volumes. Francesca was still in love with him even after what he had done. She had given him a gift to lessen his remorse. It didn't take away all his pain, but it helped.

Ryder listened three more times before he stowed his phone away and headed back out onto the road.

He spent the next few nights playing for thousands. After each concert, he would saddle up on his bike and head to the next destination. Each night, before he would leave, he listened to Francesca's song. After the goodness seeped in, he would turn on his own playlist and listen to Bob Seger's "Turn the Page." He loved that song. In some ways, it paralleled his life at this moment in time.

He drove for hours, thinking about all the advice Frank had given him. He had been right; Ryder didn't give Francesca enough credit for the feelings she had. He was terrified he would continue to hurt her, but he was already hurting her by denying her feelings. He loved her, so why was it so hard for him to accept she could love him?

In his mind's eye, he wasn't a good person. However, over the last four months, he had grown and developed real attachments.

On the last night of his travels, he popped into a restaurant for a coffee. While he sat there, lost in thought, a song played over the radio that caught his attention. Not his type of music, but it represented how he felt.

He downloaded "Believe" by Mumford & Sons, then wrote Francesca a text.

Coming home tomorrow. Can we talk?

He added the link to the song and hit "send."

A reply came five minutes later.

Can I pick you up?

4:30. American Airlines, he replied.

Beast, I believe.

Chapter 15

"Secret Song" By Staind

Ryder's stomach was tied up in knots. He wasn't familiar with nervousness. If this feeling continued, he would have ulcers within six months.

He was on edge, trying to figure out what he had to say to Francesca. How was he going to look her in the eyes and see the revulsion staring back at him? Maybe he was making a mistake. He shouldn't have been so impulsive in telling her he wanted to talk. He wasn't ready.

Ryder walked off the plane with his small duffle bag swung over his shoulder. The airport was jammed, being the last Saturday of the holidays. He waited patiently while he passed through customs and headed towards the exit, his guilt sitting like a heavy stone in his stomach, and his palms were sweaty. It seemed all of his courage remained in California.

The doors opened, and Ryder scanned the large crowd, trying to find Francesca. She was nowhere in sight. He looked left to right again to make sure he hadn't missed her. Devastated she wasn't there, he turned towards the exit to grab a taxi.

Francesca wrung her hands, leaning against a pole as she waited for Ryder. She had arrived an hour early so she wouldn't miss him, watching hundreds of people walk through the doors, meeting up with loved ones. Some carried flowers, others ran up and threw themselves at the person they were meeting. She wondered how Ryder would greet her?

The flight information board said his plane had landed forty minutes ago, yet she hadn't seen him.

When a large family moved in front of her, she couldn't see the door. She shuffled around, trying to move around the hoards of people. *Really, did that many people need to come to the airport to pick up one person?*

Just as she turned, she saw Ryder's back as he headed out the exit.

"Ryder!"

Ryder froze and realization hit him. She had come.

He didn't think; he just reacted. He turned, stomped towards her without a word, and hugged her to him. He had one hand against her head and another around her upper back, smashing her head against his chest.

He hugged her so tightly that Francesca was having trouble breathing. She could hear the rapid beating of his heart and realized he had thought she wouldn't be there.

"I will always be here," she whispered.

He tightened his grip, emotions clogging his throat.

"Ryder, I can't breathe!" she gasped out.

He instantly relaxed his grip but didn't let her go.

"Dammit, baby, you feel so good. Don't let go. Not yet."

She immediately relaxed. "I won't."

She felt herself getting emotional but refused to cry. She needed to be strong for him.

After being jostled a few times by fellow travellers, Ryder decided it was time to leave. He pulled back and looked at her sweet face, seeing no apprehension or resentment.

"I missed you." He grabbed her little hand with his large one and indicated for her to lead the way. "Come on; let's grab some food and head to my place."

"I missed you, too," she told him as she tightened her grip.

When they got into Francesca's car, she tried to start it a couple of times, but the motor wouldn't turn over. Ryder got out of the car, fiddled with something under the hood, and then motioned for her to try again. It took two tries before it started.

"What was it?" she asked when Ryder got back in the car.

"The battery connectors were loose. This car is a piece of shit, Francesca. You need a new one." Ryder wasn't happy the car had been acting up and he hadn't been there to take care of it for her.

She looked appalled, rubbing the dashboard as she said, "My baby is perfectly fine. She's gotten me through thick and thin, and I love her."

He drew his eyebrows together and scowled at her. "Not funny, Beauty. You have the money to replace this piece of junk. It isn't safe."

"Most of that money went to pay my family's debt. The rest is in case of an emergency. I'll call Joey or Paul at All Pro Auto Service, and they will take care of it. My dad and their dad are good friends, so I trust them."

Ryder wasn't going to argue with her right now. He would save that discussion for another day. "We can stay at my place tonight. Tomorrow, I'll follow you to the garage to drop it off. We'll take mine to work on Monday."

"Okay, thanks." she said, relieved he wasn't pushing the issue. Then she changed the subject as she turned towards Ryder. "I cooked for my papa and brothers, and I cooked extra for us so we'll have time for our conversation at your place. I want you to know, Ryder, I wasn't kidding when I said I believe."

"Thank you," was all Ryder could say at that moment.

How many times would this tiny woman make him feel so humbled?

When they arrived at his condo, he directed her to the visitors' parking. He insisted on carrying all the stuff, and after a small struggle, she relented.

They entered his condo and dropped everything off in the kitchen. Francesca then grabbed his hand and led him into the living room.

"I can't believe you did this." She pointed at the painting and all the photos surrounding it. "It looks amazing."

"I consider it my most prized possession."

"You made it look really good with the frame and the lighting. It almost looks like it belongs in a gallery. But why all the photos?"

"When I brought it home, I stared at it for a while. There are so many things to look at, and it didn't seem right that some of the details weren't getting all the attention they deserved. So, I called a photographer I had worked with before."

Francesca's heart and soul had been filled with such turmoil when her papa had first been incarcerated. She had poured all those feelings into the Stonehenge painting. Ryder was the only one who seemed to understand the depth of emotion she had put into it.

"It's beautiful. Thank you."

Francesca headed into the kitchen. She had made all his favourites, hoping the comfort food would put him at ease. She brought wine and beer, but Ryder insisted on having wine with her.

"Tell me how you spent the holiday. Did you have Christmas dinner with your friends?" Francesca started the conversation.

"Yeah, my friend Evan and his wife hosted the whole gang of

us. Although, I did nearly choke one of my buddies to death when he made a comment about our kids. I was so mad I nearly walked out."

"What did he say?"

He shook his head. "It's not important. Five months ago, I would have said the same thing."

Francesca put her fork down and rubbed the top of Ryder's hand, understanding what he was feeling. "I can appreciate that. You see the kids in a different light now. But you can't attack everyone who makes a rude comment, or you'll find yourself in jail. And really, I don't want to visit you there. I've had enough pat downs to last a lifetime."

Ryder tensed when he envisioned that prick of a guard running his hands along Francesca's body.

Seeing his reaction and realizing what she had said, she quickly apologized then told him, "We need to talk about what happened."

Ryder wiped his mouth with a napkin, panic setting in. His hands curled into fists.

"Ryder, I'm not going anywhere, so relax."

"I can't! How can you even stand to be in the same room as me? I stole your virginity."

She unfurled his fist then led him into the living room and onto the couch. She sat facing him. Meanwhile, he couldn't look at her, so he looked out the window.

"Ryder, you can't steal something that is given freely."

He snapped his head around to look at her. "I had no right! I treated you horribly. You'll never know how sorry I am."

"You have to stop punishing yourself. I'm a big girl. I could have stopped you, but I didn't. I should have told you so that makes me as responsible as you."

That comment ticked him off. His expression changed from guilt to anger as he moved closer until their noses were almost touching. Then, in a low, menacing voice, he said, "Don't you dare put that on your shoulders. *I* fucked up. *I'm* the loser who can't be touched. I never had a real kiss until you kissed me. I'm as new at this as you are."

Francesca recoiled in shock. "What? That's not possible. You couldn't have been a virgin. If so, then I stole your virginity."

Ryder threw his head back and bellowed out a rare laugh that released some of the anger that had been lining his face. He loved how naive she was when it came to all things sexual.

"No, Beauty, I wasn't a virgin. But I am a virgin when it comes to intimacy. I like to fuck, plain and simple. I want release, not hugging or cuddling and all the other bullshit that goes along with it."

He saw her face drop. She went to get up so she could leave.

"Francesca!" He grabbed her wrist, trying to pull her into his lap as he realized his mistake.

She was having no part of it, struggling for all she was worth.

"Stop. Hear me out. It was different with you, and you know it."

She heaved a breath and stopped fighting, telling herself not to cry. She did know it was different, but it still hurt.

"I didn't say that to hurt you. I promised myself to be totally honest. For the first time in my life, I want someone to know what I think and feel. I'm not good at that … expressing myself. So, if I come across as harsh, it's because I'm not used to it."

She deflated with his honesty. "You're right; I can't take everything personally. But if I don't understand, I need you to explain it so there are no misunderstandings."

"Fair enough." He smoothed her hair back and looked right into her eyes. "I've been with other women, but I could never tolerate anyone's touch."

"Why?" This was a concept Francesca wasn't familiar with. In her world, everyone touched, kissed, and hugged. It was as basic as breathing.

Ryder's heart sped up, and he glanced out the window so she couldn't see the shame in his eyes. This was the moment he had dreaded. How did he explain to her that he was less human than most animals?

"I've never been loved, and was never taught how. I was a huge disappointment and embarrassment to the incubator and sperm donor. All their hopes and dreams died with me."

She wanted to look into his eyes and prove to him that he had love now, but he wouldn't look at her. The thought of the life he must have endured hacked away a little piece of her heart. Everyone deserved to be loved.

"Why did they have a child if they didn't want you? Why not give you up for adoption?"

"I wish they had. They wanted a son, but not me." He ran his thumb and forefinger along his goatee while he pondered her question further, lost in a memory.

"I don't understand," she muttered.

He finally turned towards her. "My parents wanted a whole son, not a gimp."

Her confusion turned to rage. "But you're not a gimp. Disgusting word," she spat.

"My father called me gimp or 'boy' most of my life. It was meant to be derogatory and filthy, and the meaning wasn't lost on me." He repetitively stroked his goatee.

"Ryder?"

He glanced back at her like he had forgotten she was there. "I'll tell you, but I need to find the right words." He took a minute to gather his thoughts.

"My father was a famous soccer player in Brazil. He met my mother while she was visiting her grandparents. Her grandfather was very influential, and was one of the sponsors of the Brazilian soccer team. They met at a sponsorship party.

"She was exotic, being from Canada, and a lot of the team tried to win her attention. Not only that, her grandfather was loaded. The star of the team pursued her, and my father—being my father—wanted her because of the other man's interest.

"Anyway, he married her, and she got knocked up in the first year. Three months after my mother gave birth to me, he had an accident. He was in the Euro Cup, and had slid for the ball at the exact moment an opposing player slid. They collided, and the other player's cleat slipped under my father's jock and nailed him in the nuts. He was rendered sterile from the accident, but not impotent. He openly fucked other women to prove he was still a man, but I would be his only child.

"My father was a hard-ass who wanted Brazil's next soccer superstar, so he put all his efforts into me. He had everything: a great career and a beautiful wife and a son. However, he was still an angry, bitter man. Nothing mattered to him. Not his family, not my schoolwork, not church—nothing. I wasn't his son. I was his pawn.

"He worked me day and night from the time I could walk. He smacked me when I made mistakes and would berate me in front of my teammates for the smallest infractions. He beat the shit out of me for missing goals and blamed my coaches for my failures. Eventually, he was banned from being at the field during practices and games.

"During one of my practices, I ran into one of my teammates

272

and cut my leg. I didn't tell anyone, too afraid my father would beat me senseless. I had the chicken pox virus two weeks earlier, and my immune system was weakened. The wound got infected, and I contracted necrotizing-fasciitis, more widely known as flesh eating disease. I hid it until it was too late." Ryder took a deep breath. This was where he was afraid of what she would think.

"By the time I was taken to the hospital, the only way to save me was surgery. My dad was so pissed at the doctors. He didn't want the surgery, and he did his damnedest to stop them. The doctors cornered my mother when they knew he wasn't around to gain her consent. Otherwise, I would have died … They amputated my leg."

Ryder saw the shock, and then the sorrow at his declaration in Francesca's eyes. Her gaze didn't drift to his legs, though, and he was relieved that he didn't see any pity when a single tear escaped.

"How old were you?"

"Eleven. From that moment on, I was his gimp, his punching bag. I never knew when the next punch would come. They came at any time and for no reason at all."

Francesca was beside herself with anger. "I know you don't want me interrupting, but where was your mother through all this?"

"She was there, but she's a weak woman who is terrified of him. I think she blamed herself for me being weak … or he convinced her of that.

"Anyway, they amputated below the knee. After a few months,

they brought me home, and that's when my father became even more hostile.

"One morning, he caught me putting on the prosthetic. He stood and watched with disgust all over his face. He waited for me to stand, and when I did, he kicked my leg out from under me. Then he screamed at me to get up. I did, and then he did it again. He did it until my stump was bleeding, and I was covered in sweat.

"It hurt like hell, but I wouldn't give him the satisfaction of thinking he won. After I got up dozens of times, he realized he wasn't going to win. Therefore, the last time I stood up, he punched me in the head and said if I got up again, he would kill me. I looked straight into his eyes and stood up. He knocked me out cold with the next hit. That's how the nanny found me the next morning, lying on my bedroom floor, surrounded in blood.

"I was rushed back to the hospital, but because of my injuries, I developed another infection. The doctors suggested flying me to Toronto's Sick Children Hospital because they were renowned for treatments and rehabilitation with amputees. They paid to have a nurse accompany me."

Francesca was devastated by his story. Her chest physically hurt, the pressure on her heart gnawing at her.

"Wait, you mean to tell me, they didn't even bring you to Toronto themselves? You've got to be kidding me. They sent their only child across the world with a stranger to have major surgery?

What kind of monsters are they?" Francesca couldn't sit another minute. She got up and started to pace, mumbling about keeping her cool and wanting to beat the shit out of his parents. How could some people be allowed to procreate?

He couldn't argue with her; she was right. He knew Francesca was protective of those she cared about, and he was sure she cared about him. Nevertheless, he didn't want her upset.

"Francesca, I was thankful they didn't come … I can stop if you need me to."

She whipped around, facing him with murder written across her face. "Don't you dare. I want to hear all of it."

Francesca realized she was being insensitive to him, so she tried to rein in her bitterness. She took two deep breaths and counted to ten. Then she moved to sit back down.

He gave her a couple of minutes to get past the anger, then started again, "I had the second operation, where they amputated to mid-thigh. I spent the next five months healing and going to rehabilitation. My parents visited at Christmas, because the incubator's family lives in Toronto. I left the hospital for two weeks and stayed with them at their house. The abuse continued.

"I was never allowed at family functions, or parties, or Christmas dinner, because they were embarrassed by me. They told everyone I wasn't well enough. They had celebrated Christmas early because my father's team played soccer on Boxing Day.

"The day before I returned to the hospital, the sperm donor caught me in a pair of shorts, doing exercises. He ripped them from my body, telling me he never wanted to see my prosthetic again. Since that day, I was forbidden to wear shorts or a bathing suit.

"When I was younger, I never made any friends with my teammates, because my father didn't want me associating with my competition. I never made friends in grade school, because I was so focused on soccer and keeping my father happy. Therefore, by the time I was living in the hospital, I was withdrawn and not very trusting. I just wanted to be left alone. Actually, I just wanted to die. I hated who and what I was.

"I learned to take my frustration out in the gym as part of my rehabilitation. I was so obsessed with my workouts that the doctors thought I would injure my muscles, so they made me try something new.

"A music teacher taught me how to play the guitar and drums. I practiced whenever I wasn't in the gym." He stopped, trying to figure out where to go from there.

"I'm glad you didn't die. I can't imagine my life without you," Francesca whispered, looking so sad and broken.

"Thank you, Beauty." That was enough for one night. "I'm emotionally exhausted, Francesca. Do you mind if we end it here for now? I'll sleep on the couch. You take my bed."

"No," she refused.

He stopped dead in his tracks. Was she done with him now?

His father was right. No one would ever want him.

"I'll take you home," he said in a defeated voice.

She grabbed his hair. "No, Ryder, I just want to lie with you in your bed."

She saw his eyes fill with fear. She wasn't ready for a physical relationship yet, either. They were both too raw.

"I don't want anything else yet. I just want to be close to you," she promised. "I want to feel you beside me. I need your comfort tonight." She also wanted to comfort him, but she couldn't tell him that.

He relaxed. "I would love to try to hold you and comfort you." He grabbed her hand and dragged her to his bedroom. He had never held anyone in his bed, and he wasn't sure what that entailed, but he was curious to find out.

He went to his dresser, and pulled out a T-shirt, making sure it wasn't one of his band's. "Wear this. You can change in the bathroom."

She turned and walked into the bathroom, nervous, but all Ryder had endured as a child dominated her thoughts the most. She put the T-shirt on. It went down to her knees, making her look like a three-year-old.

Francesca looked at Ryder when she walked out of the bathroom with one shoulder exposed. He was in a T-shirt, jogging pants, and running shoes.

"Do you sleep in running shoes every night?"

Ryder gazed down like a child being reprimanded by their parent. "No."

She put her hands on her hips. "Then you need to show me your leg. Get over all this crap. I don't care that you have a prosthetic any more than you care that Veeta is disfigured. Do you care that her legs are mangled and she walks with canes?"

His head flew up, looking annoyed. "No, and don't you ever ask me that question again. Got me?" he snapped.

"I got you. Now you get me. I'm not shallow, so don't insult me like I am. I would like to see you—all of you—and your prosthetic is part of that."

He walked towards her, knowing he had fucked up, ashamed that she thought he believed she was shallow. "It's not you who is shallow. It's me."

She knew that wasn't the case. He was just beaten down to believe that.

She would help change the insecurities he had about himself, even if it killed them both.

"I know, Beast. Now lose the pants, and then the leg." She knew she was being bold and the opposite of her usual shy demeanour, but she was fighting his demons, and her courage required a bold, new attitude.

He quirked an eyebrow and smirked, getting hard from her aggressiveness, something that would change the minute he lowered his pants.

He looked her right in the eyes as he bent to lower his jogging pants. His hard-on fell equally as fast as his pants.

He waited for her to move her eyes down, and when she did, he was stunned by the smile that lit up her face.

"It's beautiful ..." she sighed out. "May I take a closer look?"

Not waiting for his permission, she dropped down to her knees, running her hand along it. It looked like a black wire sculpture of a human leg, and you could even see the definition in the sculpted calf muscle. She had never seen such a cool prosthetic before.

"What's it made from?"

"It's a new technology called 3-D printed titanium. They used my other leg to imprint this one so they are dimensionally correct. They wanted to paint it the colour of skin, but I saw no reason since no one would ever see it. Well, that's a lie. I showed Mason."

Her eyes sprang up. "When did you show Mason?"

"Get up," he growled, bending down to help her up. He couldn't shake the fact that she was right in front of him, on her knees, looking up at him in wonderment. The twitch in his boxers indicated she would get an eye full in less than thirty seconds.

"What?"

"Beauty, you're killing me, seeing you on your knees in front of me with your eyes looking up at me. You've got me harder than a rock."

Francesca blushed from the tip of her toes to the top of her scalp. Then she glanced down at his impressive package and wetness pooled in her panties.

"Oh ... Uh ... Sorry?"

Ryder shook his head at her. "Get in bed, Beauty."

She jumped into bed so quickly she bounced, while he walked to the other side and crawled under the covers. She wanted to snuggle right into him and hold him close. However, her father's advice about taking it slow kept her in check.

"Do you sleep with it on?" Francesca asked, knowing the answer.

"No. And I'm not ready to take it off yet, so don't push it." He blew out a breath then covered his eyes with one arm. The other he moved behind his head while he laid nervously on his back.

She was pushing too hard, and she knew it. Then again, she wanted him to know that his leg was the least of his problems.

She rolled over and hugged him, resting her head on his chest. She felt him tense up, but she would be damned if he thought she was moving.

After a minute or so, he took his arm off his forehead and turned off the light. They laid in silence for a few minutes while he gradually relaxed. Eventually, she closed her eyes and let his scent surround her.

He moved the arm that was behind his head and cradled her body with it, landing softly on her ass. His shirt had ridden up her body as she rolled over, so his hand was laying on the silky-smooth skin of her best asset. He was amazed that his right hand covered almost the entire left cheek.

He figured out she had a thong on when he rubbed higher and hit the lace. Ryder couldn't help himself from rubbing side to side. He loved the feel of her skin, but the part that was driving him insane was the crease where the curve of the cheek met her thigh. He would love to bend over and lick that spot. It was enticing.

Even though his dick was as hard as granite, he was more relaxed than he had ever been in his life.

Chapter 16

"Let It Go" By James Bay

Ryder awoke to feel Francesca curled into him like a kitten tucked into its mother. She was facing his side, in the fetal position, her breath on his ribs. He always threw the covers off in the night because he got hot. She must have been cold, curling herself tightly against him to stay warm.

He reached for the blanket and covered them, turning her gently so her back was spooned against his front, loving the feel of her tiny body tucked against his. He tightened his hold, completing encasing her.

He moved his mouth to her neck and nudged the surrounding hair out of the way as he kissed her sweetly. She made a little mewing sound and wiggled her ass against his groin. Fuck, she was going to make him come all over her ass. When she settled down, he drifted back to sleep for another hour.

He awoke again in the same position, relishing how peaceful he still felt. He had never expected to feel this kind of emotional and physical connection to anyone. What was it about Francesca that drew him to her like an addict to crack? He couldn't get close enough. He wanted to be with her every second of every day. She soothed the raging beast inside of him. She was his muse, and he wasn't sure he could ever let that go.

"I can hear the wheels turning. What are you thinking about so hard?" she whispered in a low, raspy voice.

"How did you know?"

"I felt you tense up. Don't start questioning what's happening between us without talking to me first." She didn't roll over. She wanted to keep him close.

"Feels good to have you in my arms, but I'm afraid it won't last. You're going to see the part of me that's destroyed everyone I touch."

"Ryder, I want you to ignore that inner voice for a while. I know you've been taught to trust that voice to protect you from people who would hurt you, but I want you to trust me for a little while to prove to you that I'm not going to hurt you."

In a strangled voice, he replied, "I don't know how."

She hated hearing the distress in his voice, sounding so scared and unsure.

"You just have to trust me, the same way I trusted you when that guard took advantage of me."

"I've only ever relied on myself."

"All I ask is that you try. Can I ask a few questions now?"

"Go for it."

"Did you move back to Brazil, or stay here with your grandparents after you were released from the hospital?"

"I moved into my parents' house in Toronto with a nanny. I was of no more use to my parents. I don't know what they told my grandparents or the rest of the family. I don't remember ever seeing them again."

Silent tears leaked from her eyes, and her voice cracked when she asked, "You were all alone?"

"Yeah. The nanny wasn't like the ones you see on TV. She was there for the paycheck, plain and simple. She made sure I was fed, went to doctors' appointments, and that I attended school. I'm positive her standoffish attitude was the reason my father hired her."

"So you were all alone until you were eighteen?" Francesca croaked out.

He tightened his hold on her. "No, baby, I met the three guys I work with in high school. We became friends when we realized we had some things in common, and I went to their houses a lot. They never judged; they just accepted who I was and didn't push for more. Eventually, we decided to move to California to start a business together, and the rest is history."

"I am thankful for your friends."

"Me, too."

"Ryder, can we try something?"

He tensed again, not sure he would be able to give her what she wanted. "I'll try."

She rolled over to face him, placing one hand on the mattress and the other hand against his chest, propping herself up. "I want to look at your body and touch you. And I want you to do the same to me. And trust me; this will be as hard on me as you. No one has ever seen me naked. I hate my body, but if you can do it, then so can I."

"Every inch of you is perfect. How can you possibly hate your body?" he answered quickly and without much thought.

She huffed out a breath. "I'm not like my Caesar buddies. They all have amazing figures—slim, trim, and toned. And they are stunning on the inside, as well."

Ignoring her self-hatred, Ryder hesitantly asked, "Will you teach me how to touch you first? I need time to get comfortable."

"Of course. But if I struggle with it, it isn't anything you are doing; it's because I am insecure. This is not about sex, and we won't have sex until we are both comfortable with intimacy. Understand that I'm not trying to frustrate you, or that I'm afraid because of the last time. I think we need to take this slowly and learn to trust each other, making us both less vulnerable. Are you okay with that?"

"I screwed up last time, so I want you to take the lead. Teach me to be the kind of man you could care for."

She took his palms and kissed each one tenderly. Her soft lips against his rough hands had a shiver move up his spine. Then she took both of his hands and guided it towards her neck, wanting him to feel the pulse of her body.

She kept her hands on his as he circled her neck, rubbing the hollow of her throat with his thumbs. She removed her hands when she thought he was ready, and he slowly raised both hands to her face, caressing her forehead, cheekbones, over each closed eye, and completing his exploration by dragging his thumbs across her lips.

She reopened her eyes, spellbound by the gentleness and warmth of his touch. Then she tensed as his hands moved to the bottom of the T-shirt. He waited until she nodded, then slowly lifted the shirt, giving her a chance to stop him. Finally, he pulled it up and off. He didn't put his hands back on her until he got his fill of looking at her beautiful body.

The first thing that captured his eyes was her collarbone. It was prominent, and the skin hollowed out at the apex of her throat. He couldn't resist as he ran the tip of his finger across it, moaning quietly at the feel of the soft skin that covered the bone.

He then glanced down to the valley of her breasts, and farther over to her tightened, pink nipples. His dick was no longer twitching; it was thumping along with his heartbeat.

He ran his hands to her breasts and gently cupped each one. They felt perfect in his hands.

He didn't linger as he heard the catch in her breath. He had to keep this as non-sexual as he could. He wanted to prove he was worthy of touching this glorious woman.

Francesca could feel the quiver travel from her breasts to her core. She was excited and wet, and would die of embarrassment when he discovered it.

He left her breasts and traveled to her waist, circling it with both hands. He looked up for a second before his eyes travelled back down to her waist, saying, "I knew my hands would look massive again your little waist."

She made a *harrumph* sound. "Don't get too excited; you won't be able to do that with one of my thighs." She blushed with embarrassment.

Ryder echoed the sound back at her. "See your body through my eyes, not through the distorted mirror in your head. You have the perfect hourglass figure. I have appreciated it since the first day I saw you. These hips and your ass are hypnotizing. When you dance, you bring men to their knees. Me being the first one to fall."

She thought that was very poetic for a man who speaks so little.

"When have you seen me dance?"

He looked bewildered. "Do you have any idea how many times you dance in class when you're absorbed in something and the radio is playing?" He stuttered over his next words. "I, uh, also followed you and your Caesar buddies to that club downtown. Don't look at me like that, or pull back. I was worried after how you had been acting. It was before I found out about the guard. I won't apologize after hearing he was there watching you, too. I needed to be there in case anything happened."

After she pondered his honesty, she came to the decision he was right. "I can live with that, knowing you were looking out for us. Thank you."

"You never have to thank me for watching out for you. I'll always protect you. Now, can you turn over? I want to touch your back."

She gulped, not expecting that. "Okay."

She cautiously turned over then tensed at his intake of breath.

"I learned something about myself I didn't know until I met you."

She cringed, closing her eyes tightly at what he was seeing. She had a big, fat Italian ass, and she hated it. Maybe she should have Taya create an exercise routine so she could trim down the excess fat.

She was so lost in thoughts that he startled her when he asked, "Do you want to know what I learned about myself?"

"Sorry. Of course. What did you learn?"

"I learned I'm an ass man, and yours is the best I've ever fucking laid eyes on."

She laughed with an unconvinced tone. "You haven't been

exposed to very many women, have you?"

He smirked at her back. *If she only knew.*

"You might not believe me, but I've had more than a few women try to entice me with their bodies. None compare to your perfection."

He didn't want her questioning his comment, so he dropped his hands to her back. They covered from her shoulders to the bottom of her rib cage. He started to massage her gently, feeling the bunched-up muscles begging for relaxation.

When she released a moan, his dick jumped.

"Can I kiss you? I promise it won't go any further. If I don't satisfy my curiosity, it will drive me bat shit crazy."

She tried to get up, but he held her down. Then he placed his hands on either side of her body, lowering his lips to the crease between her ass and her thigh. She jerked in surprised.

He slipped his tongue out and ran it along the seam. He could smell her excitement. It was intoxicating, and that was his undoing. He was losing the battle. If he didn't stop, he was going to lose control and thrust into her, ruining everything.

He kissed the spot one more time before rising.

She turned her head as she lifted herself up, saying, "My turn."

His dick deflated as the discomfort settled in.

"Are you sure you want to do this?"

"Trust me. I promise, if it becomes too much, I'll stop." The sincerity on her face, combined with the words, convinced him it was worth a shot.

He laid on his stomach with his head resting on his folded arms, hoping by pinning them, he wouldn't be tempted to physically stop her wandering hands.

The first thing she did was pull out his hair that was trapped between the muscle of his shoulder and head. Then she ran her fingers through it, massaging his scalp. She dug her nails in and dragged them around, releasing his stress. It felt amazing.

Ryder didn't expect that. He constantly ran his fingers through his hair when he was frustrated. He hadn't known why until now. He realized his body had been craving this.

He closed his eyes, enjoying the feeling seeping through him.

After ten minutes, she moved her hands to his massive shoulders. She didn't massage them, but instead rubbed her fingertips lightly over the muscles, feeling the bulge of tissue that held so much strength. She then moved her hands down his large bicep, following the pattern of the skulls.

As an artist, she was amazed at the 3-D effect. At a quick glance, you would assume it was real. If she ever got a tattoo, she wanted the artist who did this one to do hers. There were other tattoos, but those were for another day.

She returned to his back and traced the muscles around his ribs. He shifted one way then the other.

"Are you okay? Do you need me to stop?" she asked with concern.

"No, I just didn't know I was ticklish."

That discovery made Francesca's heart clench. No one had ever tickled the little boy or the man.

She dug her fingers in deep and tickled away. He started thrashing from side to side, begging her to stop.

When he turned his body to grab her hands, the look on her face stopped him. She was laughing and smiling from ear-to-ear, and her body, especially her tits, were shaking with her laughter. It was the best sound he had ever heard. The simple act of touching him brought her as much pleasure as he was receiving.

It occurred to him this was just the beginning of many firsts he would have with Francesca. Instead of freaking him out, it relaxed him and made him want more.

She looked at the wonderment on his face, pleased with his first experience at being tickled.

He laid back down so she could finish her explorations.

Francesca sensed his surrender and continued to move down his body. She placed her hands on his underwear clad buttocks and squeezed. The man's ass was like steel. She had to remember never to smack his ass, because it would likely hurt. Forget asking Taya to help her firm her butt up, she wanted Ryder to teach her.

She was unconsciously massaging his butt, lost in thought, when

Ryder said, "Starting to feel objectified here, Beauty."

"Sorry but, my God, your ass is amazing. I want one like this."

He chuckled. "Yours is perfection. When you walk, it moves to its own beat."

Francesca quickly forgot her newfound insight and slapped his ass.

"Ouch! That hurt." She flicked her hand, trying to alleviate the sting.

His body was shaking with mirth as he heard her blowing on her hand.

"I think you should move on," he commented, enjoying everything about this exercise in discovery. It wasn't at all what he had expected.

Francesca moved her hand to his leg, feeling him strain, but she continued to push on.

"Is there even one ounce of fat anywhere on your body?" Her light touch was moving the coarse hair on his leg, tickling him and making him shift again. Then she moved down to his calf muscle and foot. "Jesus Christ, what size are your feet?"

"Fifteen," he cockily replied. Then he quickly flipped over and sat up so he was facing her. "Francesca, I need to apologize again about Christmas Eve. I should have prepared you better. My only defence is, I was so lost in passion that I totally lost my mind. I would never purposely hurt you. You know that, right?"

Her features softened. "Of course I know that. You need to get past that night. I have no regrets because it brought us to this place. Our next encounter will be great for both of us."

Ryder grabbed the back of Francesca's head and pulled her forwards to meet his mouth. He captured her lips and pulled on her bottom lip with his teeth until she opened with a groan. His tongue surged inside, and he tasted her in slow laps.

Just by the gentleness of this kiss, Francesca knew she was one hundred percent right. The next time they made love, it would be amazing.

When she ran her hand down his amputated leg, he grabbed her hand, stilling her.

He pulled back from the kiss and looked into her eyes. "We do this together." He removed her hand and detached the prosthetic. Then he picked up her hand and ran it along his stump.

The thigh muscle had been severed in half, and a scar ran across the bottom of the stump. Scar tissue surrounded the base.

She was so proud of him. It took courage to lay yourself open and reveal your most vulnerable imperfection with the fear of rejection as his only guide.

"Does it still hurt sometimes?"

"Yeah, I still get phantom pains. It still disgusts me to look at it."

"Ryder, I don't know how that feels, but it's far from

disgusting." To prove her point, she leaned down and kissed his stump.

He held back his dark retort of revulsion the act instilled. Instead, bellowing out in pain, "Enough. I can't do this anymore,"

Francesca jumped, realizing she had gone too far.

He was breathing in and out deeply, trying to rein in his temper.

"I'm sorry. I just want you to know that it doesn't bother me. It doesn't turn me off. Ryder, I love absolutely everything about you. Your leg doesn't make you less of a man. It makes you more because you have overcome aversion and all alone. But you aren't alone anymore." She rose to her knees and grabbed his hair, yanking him down to her. She kissed him thoroughly as she leaned into him, wrapping her arms around him.

As he mellowed out, he slowly absorbed her kiss as he cradled her to his chest. He ran his hands through her long, thick hair before pulling back to nuzzle her neck, whispering against her collarbone, "I love you, baby ... more than words can ever say. I didn't mean to scare you. I just panicked."

She smiled up at him. "Say it again."

"I didn't mean to scare you. I panicked."

"Not that. What you said about how you feel about me."

"I love you. I have from the minute I saw you. You solidified it when you copped that fiery attitude at me."

"You were ogling and deciding whether to tap me."

"I won't lie. I was. I had never seen such a classy broad before. Let's get dressed, and go out and grab some breakfast. I'm starving."

Chapter 17

"Leather and Lace"

By Stevie Nicks and Don Henley

Francesca and Ryder spent the next few weeks exploring one another and becoming comfortable with their own skin. They had fallen into a routine they both loved. During the week, they stayed at her apartment, which Ryder loved. She would cook and look after the boys for a few hours while he worked out at the gym. Fridays, he would drop her off at wherever Caesar Fridays was hosted. He would work out then pick her up to go out to dinner. After dinner, they headed to his apartment, spending the weekend enjoying downtown Toronto. Sunday morning, they would return to Francesca's for Sunday dinner with the family.

The centre kept them busy, trying to get the kids back in routine. Taz surprisingly had the hardest time adjusting. His grandparents had visited over the holidays and did everything for him, undoing four months' worth of their work. He screamed nonstop the first week back, and Ryder was ready to wring his neck. It was a toss up whether Mason or Ryder would get to him first.

"Ryder, will you grab me the large folding table out of the garage? I have to set the table for two extra people; Maurizio and Paula are joining us today," Francesca asked, putting the final touches on the veal parmigiana.

"Sure. What's the occasion?" He grabbed his coat and put his boots on.

She couldn't look him in the face, because he would know she was lying, so she kept her head down while she worked. "Nothing special. I just love having everyone here."

No sooner had they finished setting the table, they heard the idiots fighting to get up the stairs. Sal won this week's race and came barreling in the door.

"Ciao, Frank the Tank. Come stai? Ryder, how's it hanging?"

Francesca received a kiss on both cheeks while Ryder answered.

"I'd be hanging a lot better if you called your sister by her proper name, asshole."

Sal walked over to him and shook his hand. "Rome wasn't built in a day, bro."

"It wouldn't have fallen, either, if you damn Italians would listen." He squeezed his hand hard to make his point.

Sal winced. "Francesca, your boyfriend's being mean."

"Quit pushing Ryder's buttons."

Ryder smirked with pride at the fact that Francesca took his side over her brothers.

He was still grinning when he turned to greet her father and Lucky.

"Frank, good to see you. How are you?"

Smiling as he had watched the encounter, Frank replied, "Good, son. You?" Frank pulled Ryder into a hug and slapped his back. Frank was the only man Ryder allowed to hug him. For the first time, he didn't tense, but absorbed the fatherly gesture.

Maurizio and Paula joined the group after Lucky let them in. They conversed, and then enjoyed a wonderful meal. Francesca made espresso, and then went to get the dessert Maurizio brought.

Just as she walked into the room, Sal turned the lights off, and everyone started singing "Happy Birthday." When they said Ryder's name, he just about fell off his chair.

Francesca set the cake in front of him then kissed him. "Happy birthday, Ryder."

Stunned, he asked, "How did you know?"

"She's creepy like that," Lucky answered.

"Careful, Lucky, or she's gonna give you malocchio," Sal interjected, lifting his hands up to ward off the superstitious evil eye.

Francesca rolled her eyes as she looked back at Ryder. She told him that the day he asked her to grab his wallet off the counter, it had fallen out, and when she picked it up, his licence was visible and she noticed the date.

"You wouldn't have told me, would you?"

Embarrassed, he mumbled, "I don't remember ever celebrating my birthday."

Lucky and Sal had excused themselves during Francesca and Ryder's conversation. Ryder assumed they were going for a smoke. Instead, they walked back in with half a dozen gifts. Ryder didn't know what to do with himself.

"The cake was more than I ever expected."

"That's too damn bad, figlio," Frank replied. "Family celebrates the birth of one of their own. Now open my present first." Frank handed him a small box that wasn't wrapped.

He took it and opened it. Inside was a gold Italian coin.

"It's an Italian lira. They don't make them anymore since they went to the euro," Frank explained. "It's dated nineteen thirty-seven, the year my papa was born. My nonno gave this coin to my papa when he became a man, and he passed it on to me. It's been passed down three generations, and now I am passing it on to you."

"Frank, thank you, but I can't accept it. The coin belongs to one of your sons." He looked contritely around the table at Frank's sons.

The brothers were smiling, not appearing angry.

"When I call you figlio, I don't use the term lightly. There are only four people in this world who were given that honour. My three biological sons and you. You have earned that title, and with it comes respect and heritage. I can't give you my name, but I can give you my heritage, and you will accept it."

"I will treasure it for the rest of my life. Thank you, Frank. I am honoured." Ryder got up and kissed the man on both cheeks as a sign of respect and acceptance.

"Holy shit, Frankie. I need another napkin. My tears ruined this one." Lucky laughed, wiping away fake tears. Then he got serious. "You earned it, bro. Now open my gift." Lucky handed him a box wrapped in newspaper. "No sense on wasting money on shit you throw out. Besides, it has your birthdate printed on it."

Ryder opened the box and pulled out a black, Harley Davidson, long-sleeved shirt that had a skull with wings that said, "*Bad to the Bone.*" On the back, it said, "*Ride Hard and Live Free,*" with a motorcycle on it.

Ryder reached across the table and bumped knuckles with Lucky. "Thanks, man."

Next, Maurizio handed him a bag. "This is from Paula and I."

Ryder pulled out a bottle of Amarone wine.

"If you're gonna drink with the family, it might as well be the best."

Ryder shook Maurizio's hand and kissed Paula in thanks.

"Okay, bro, now mine." Sal handed him another box.

Ryder opened it and laughed as he lifted the shirt for all of them to read. On the front, it said, "*Pray for me, my girlfriend is Italian,*" and on the back, it read, "*And her brothers just measured me for cement shoes.*" Everyone laughed as Ryder bumped fists with Sal.

"Thanks."

"Last, but not least … mine." Francesca handed him a small box that was beautifully wrapped with a bow.

He carefully opened the package, knowing exactly what it was when he opened it. Two gremlin bells laid in the box. Both had hearts engraved with the initials R&F.

"I got one for the bike here, and one for the other. Do you like them?"

He couldn't answer as his eyes moistened.

"God, Frankie, they're ugly. What are they?" Sal asked.

"They're fucking unbelievable. I can't believe you knew about these?" Ryder looked over at her in awe.

"Will someone tell us what they are?" Lucky was losing his patience.

"They're called gremlin bells," Francesca responded. "You put them on motorcycles to protect the rider from gremlins, also known as evil road spirits. Gremlins love to ride and cause the rider all kinds of trouble, making other drivers not see you, or they put hazards in your way. The bell lures the gremlins in and the noise drives them crazy till they fall off. Other gremlins won't jump on because of the sound. I want Ryder protected when he rides."

Ryder grabbed Francesca and placed her on his lap. He kissed her deeply, lasting long enough that it made everyone uncomfortable.

"Boys, get the cement ready. He's pushing his luck," Sal proclaimed.

They all laughed as the couple broke apart.

"I love them, baby. Thank you."

"You don't have to thank me. They are for me, too, because I expect to ride a lot with you."

Nothing she could have said would have meant more.

After everyone left, Francesca walked into the bedroom to find Ryder running his fingers over the bells. She wrapped her arms around him, resting her head against his back.

He grabbed her arm, pulling her around to his front. He placed a hand on each side of her face, his thumbs resting on her cheeks. "I'm glad my first birthday celebration was with you and the family. Nothing will ever be able to compare to this. I love you, Beauty." He bent so he could capture her mouth in a sensual kiss.

***

Francesca and Ryder decided to spend the rest of the day watching movies. She had already packed for her trip to Scotland. She and all her sistas would be leaving for Gabriella's wedding in a week.

Gabriella's friend, Edward, had sent her a picture of a beach on the Isle of Skye where Gabriella and Liam had their first kiss. After painting the picture, she was thrilled with how it had turned out. Two silhouettes kissing on a beautiful white sandy beach. She couldn't wait to give it to her friend.

Francesca was excited to see Scotland. She had only ever crossed the ocean once, ten years ago when the whole family had gone to Italy for Zio Antonio's ninetieth birthday. This summer, Taya and Francesca were going to surprise Zio for his one hundredth birthday.

After the last movie ended, Francesca excused herself, telling Ryder she was going to have a bath. She had one more surprise for Ryder's birthday.

She had a bath and soaked in vanilla scented water. Afterwards, she took special care to put on lots of vanilla skin cream. The lady at the body and bath place had said vanilla was a scent that drove men crazy, and Francesca was testing that theory. Then she touched up her makeup and made her eyes look smoky and alluring. Lastly, she put on the white lace nightgown she had bought a week ago for Ryder's birthday surprise.

Francesca walked into her bedroom, trying to figure out how best to place herself so Ryder would think she looked provocative. She laid on the bed with one arm placed up against the headboard and her legs angled one on top of the other. Then she got a glimpse of herself in the mirror and thought she looked ridiculous. Francesca jumped off the bed and tried to place herself on the bench in front of her makeup table. Her reflection again showed how silly she looked.

Back to the bed.

Ryder heard Francesca pacing the bedroom and wondered what she was worrying about now. He got up and peeked through the bedroom door. God damn, she looked hot. He stood and watched as she changed positions around the room three separate times. Every position had him adjusting himself with a devilish grin on his face.

Francesca's next attempt had her sitting on the corner of the bed and crossing her legs with both arms leaning back. She looked into the mirror then blew out a huge breath that had her hair blowing off her forehead as she fell back to the bed.

In exasperation, she said, "I'm never going to look sexy."

"Baby, you'd look sexy in a brown paper bag, sitting on the kitchen table."

Francesca screamed, jumping up. A blush quickly ran up her chest to her face.

"Ryder, you scared me half to death!"

Ryder was leaning against the doorframe, smiling from ear-to-ear. "What are you doing?"

She looked down at her feet while she pretended to move a piece of fluff around. "I wanted to give you the second part of your birthday present. But I'm afraid, no matter what I do, I won't be able to seduce you. I'm not that kind of woman. Sorry," she whispered the last part.

Ryder walked over to her and lifted her chin so she would look at him. Then he grabbed her hand and placed it on his erection. Her eyes opened wide at the realization that she had turned him on.

In a deep, rough voice, he said, "Beauty, there is no other woman in the world who is more erotic or sexy than you. Do I get to open my present?"

Francesca coyly smiled with lowered lashes. "Not yet. This is my gift to you, so I'm in charge ... Okay?"

He couldn't believe she was doing this. He was so ready to take the next step, but he was also a little apprehensive. Therefore, he would gladly hand over the reins to Francesca.

"You're the boss, just like at the centre."

Her smile broadened. Tapping her forefinger to her lips, she contemplated.

"Perfect. If I'm the boss, then lose the shirt, Beast."

Ryder stepped back and yanked his T-shirt from the back, whipping it off and throwing it on the floor.

"Now the jeans."

He stood there, looking at her.

"Now!" She snapped her fingers with an impish smirk.

He made a sound deep in his chest as he did as she requested.

She hummed when she saw the perfection of his sculpted, muscular body.

When Ryder moved to take his boxers off, Francesca stopped him.

"I didn't tell you to touch those. That's my job." She stepped over to him and dropped to her knees.

Ryder's phallus jumped at her sassy command as he groaned out, "You're killing me, Beauty."

"You'll survive, Beast. If not, I'll breathe life back into you."

His cock jumped again at the innuendo.

He ran his fingers through his hair, trying to keep his hands away from her.

Keeping her eyes locked on his, she grabbed the waistband of his boxer briefs and slowly pulled them down. In her peripheral vision, she saw his cock spring out of his boxers.

Unsure but determined to make this good for him, Francesca closed her eyes and opened her mouth, guiding him in and hoping she got this right. She wrapped her tongue under the head and, in the blink of an eye, she spat him back out.

"Holy moly, you have a piercing." Curiosity overrode her embarrassment as she examined him even closer.

Chuckling, he moved closer. "I know. I was there. It's a Frenum piercing."

"I just don't understand … Why did you do that? Didn't it hurt?"

"Yeah, hurt like a bitch, but I heard that it feels amazing, adds to the sensation. I love how it feels, and you will, too. All my buddies got one after I raved about it."

"Jesus, Ryder, now I'll never be able to look your friends in the eyes, knowing what I know."

Perturbed, he said, "When you meet them, that better not be the place you look."

She loved when he got jealous.

She blew out a frustrated breath. "This isn't going quite how I planned. Is there anything else I should know before I start again?"

He winked at her. "Nope, have nothing left. All of my secrets have now been exposed."

She wrapped her hands along his length and stroked up and down. She was pleased when she glanced over and saw his dick seeping. Francesca lapped up the fluid with her tongue.

Ryder buckled. "Son of a bitch!"

She gained courage from his reaction and proceeded to give him the best blowjob he had ever received. Francesca wasn't experienced, but she put her whole heart and soul into trying, and that was his undoing. When he felt the tingle at the base of his spine start to crawl up, he pulled away.

"Hey, I wasn't finished." She pouted, looking affronted. "I wanted to please you. I wasn't very good, was I?"

He needed to reassure her that, what she lacked in knowledge, she made up for in enthusiasm.

"Francesca, you're a natural with that seductive, little mouth of yours. Now I want my turn. Let me know what you like and what you don't because this is a first for me, too. Okay, babe?"

He grabbed her biceps and pulled her to her feet, kissing her with such passion that her thong was soaked. She was embarrassed by the wetness and thought she should warn him. He kissed her so thoroughly that Francesca totally forgot about her warning.

During the kiss, he managed to pull both straps of her nightgown down her arms until it fell and pooled at her feet, revealing the spectacular body he had gotten to know over the last few weeks. She was perfection.

Her pink nipples were always puckered in his presence. Only once had he seen them relaxed when she had been sleeping on her side and one of her breasts had slipped out of her nightgown. They weren't as pink as they were when they tightened for him. The instant he had run his finger down the nipple, it had hardened and peaked.

His eyes continued to travel down her body to her belly button ring. She had a fake diamond for the stud, and it looked adorable on her. He watched as she slowly pulled away the wisp of lace covering her pussy. His eyes travelled down with her thong, and then back up to her junction. His eyebrows popped up at the wax job that left a landing strip, heading directly towards the path he was going to take.

He smiled and looked up at Francesca. She was so red with embarrassment, if he didn't know better, he would have thought she was sunburned.

"Do you like it?" she whispered.

"No, Francesca. I love it."

Her face broke out in a glorious smile. "Good, then it was worth the worst humiliation of my life. I think the waxing girl has seen and touched more of me than you have."

He was blown away by the lengths she had gone to make this night special for him. He promised himself that he would shower her with all the things she deserved: flowers, flattering words, affection.

A year ago, he would have said he wasn't capable of such things, but his beauty deserved to feel as loved and cherished as he did at this moment. Francesca was the first person to love him ... All of him.

He placed his hands on her hips and looked at her, gathering the words he needed to say.

"Thank you, Beauty. I can never express what this day has meant to me, and what you mean to me. You taught me that, somehow, I deserve this. I look at you, and you are so damn beautiful inside and out, and if this is my reward for my shit childhood, I would do it all again if I could have this night one more time." He kissed her belly button then gently guided her to the bed and lay her down.

Ryder could smell the unique fragrance of Francesca's excitement. He had smelled it so often over the last month as they had learned each other's bodies. It had driven him crazy with want.

He took in a deep breath. It was intoxicating and lured him closer to her apex.

He grabbed each thigh and pulled them gently apart. Then he swiped his tongue from her bottom to the top of her slit, her taste tingling in his mouth, sweet and sassy, just like her.

One taste, and he was hooked. He went from tasting to devouring within seconds. He knew if he lived to be a thousand, he would never get enough of her.

Francesca was tense from being exposed so intimately until Ryder began his assault. Then she gave over to the amazing feelings he was dragging out of her with each swipe of his tongue or gentle bite to her clit.

Something incredible was building in her. She hadn't felt it before. It was consuming her and had her begging Ryder for something she wasn't certain of. She had climaxed when he used his fingers weeks ago, but this was different, almost painful.

God help her, maybe she was getting sick. She felt fevered and out of control. Her head was thrashing from side to side, and every muscle in her body was tense and tight as she clutched the sheets tightly in her fists.

Ryder gently pushed two fingers into her core while he sucked hard on her clit, trying to stretch her before he invaded. The pulsing of her internal walls was sucking at his fingers until he felt the little piece of flesh inside of her that skyrocketed Francesca into another universe.

She screamed and closed her eyes tightly, flashes of lights exploding behind her eyes lids.

"Oh … My … God … Don't stop. I need more. Please don't let this feeling end. Ryder, I need you."

He fumbled quickly off his knees, finding a condom in his discarded jeans, and then sheathing himself. Ryder lined up his erection to her soaking wet core and pushed in, slowly at first, afraid to hurt her like last time. But she was having no part of the slow assault.

She threw her legs around his hips and pushed up, impaling herself on his length.

Ryder felt strained as he pumped in and out, stretching her muscles to accommodate his girth. As overwhelming as it felt, there were so many things going through his mind. He had never felt so much emotion and love, yet he was concerned whether she was enjoying it as much as he was.

"Ah … Nothing has ever felt this good. Are you okay? Am I hurting you? Please tell me it feels as good for you as me." He needed to know as a lifetime of insecurities gnawed at his subconscious.

Francesca looked at his fractured expression. "Better than good," she panted out. "Your piercing is rubbing that spot. Let loose. I can take it. I want it."

He lifted her upper body as he stabilized his bum leg and drove relentlessly into her body. The tingles started at the base of his spine, and the hair stood up on the back of his neck. Ryder wasn't going to last, but he wanted to finish with her.

He latched on to one of her breasts and bit gently, sending her into another orgasm as Ryder bellowed his release.

They collapsed onto the bed, sweating and exhausted, but both had never felt better. Then Ryder got up and went to the washroom to remove the condom and wash up. When he was done, he sat down on the bed to release his prosthetic, still dumbfounded that his stump wasn't an issue for her. There was a certain amount of peace that came with that thought.

When he was done, he rolled over and dragged her to his side of the bed. He encased her in his big arms as he kissed the back of her shoulder, making his way to her neck.

"Thank you, sweetheart. That was incredible. I had no idea sex could be like this. I love you so much."

Francesca laughed as she turned in his arms. She tucked one hand against his chest and ran her other hand down the side of his face, relishing in the love in his eyes. "I should be thanking you. I got off two times, and you only got off once." Pondering for a second, she decided to confess, "Do you want to know how stupid I am?"

He scowled. "Don't say that about yourself. You're the smartest person I know."

"You won't think so when I tell you that I didn't know I could have different types of orgasms. When you went down on me, you brought me to a point where I thought I was sick. I couldn't catch my breath, and I was so hot, and then my world exploded into a million pieces of wonderment. What if I had never met you? I would have gone through life thinking there was only one type of orgasm."

Ryder's fragile ego strengthened. This deeper connection was awe-inspiring and made him feel like a virgin who had just had his first real sexual experience. He knew he was in love because, for the first time, he cared more about Francesca's pleasure than his own.

He cupped her face, looking directly into her soulful eyes, and confessed, "We said we would be totally honest, so here I go. I didn't know a woman could have different types of orgasms, either, and I never cared enough before tonight. We are going to explore that theory. I have found my drug of choice, and after just one taste, I know it will never be enough."

This was going to sound nuts, but he said it, anyway. "I sometimes watch documentaries, and I saw one once that said certain animals and insects find their lifelong mate by smell. I'm not sure why that always stuck with me. Now I know. It's like your smell and taste were created solely for me. Sounds weird, I know, but it really does me in when I smell you." Ryder was relieved when he didn't see any hesitancy or fear at his freaky disclosure.

Francesca smiled that impish smile that he adored. "I do the exact same thing. Before I fall asleep each night, since you started staying over, I take a few deep breathes of your scent and close my eyes. Then I have the most peaceful sleep. Honestly, sometimes I still can't believe you want me."

"Want you? I never want to let you go. How am I going to survive when you go to Scotland? What if you meet someone else?" Ryder repositioned them again so she was resting her head on his chest. He had a hand on his favourite spot where her ass met her thigh and the other one squishing her chest to his body.

"I waited for you all my life. No one could ever take your place in my heart. You *are* my heart." Something had been bothering Francesca, and she wanted to get it off her chest. "What happens to us when your sentence is over and you go home?"

"I don't know what's going to happen, but I do know I can't live without you. You are my home, no matter where I am. I'm not willing to give you up. We'll work out the logistics."

Francesca kissed his abs then rested her cheek against his chest. "I love you."

"Love you, too, Beauty. Get some sleep. Guarantee I'm going to wake you again before this night is over." He kissed the top of her head as he heard Francesca take three deep breaths, and then her breathing evened out and he knew she had fallen asleep.

How was he going to make this work? Fornication had a tour

starting in August and a month of practices in July. She was off to Italy at the end of June. The quandary kept him awake for another hour until exhaustion finally took over.

Chapter 18

"In Your Eyes" By Peter Gabriel

Aweek had blown away so quickly, and before they knew it, they were standing at the airport, saying good-bye. They had picked up Dakota and Taya on the way to the airport, and the friends stood there in shock as Ryder consumed Francesca in the hottest kiss they had ever witnessed. The girls melted when Ryder disclosed his love for their friend in front of them.

He turned to Taya and Dakota and asked them if they would watch over his beauty and make sure no guys came within ten feet of her. They giggled like school girls and assured him they would do what he asked. Then he stole one more kiss before walking away, feeling as lost as ever.

Dakota slapped Francesca on the shoulder. "When the hell did that happen? You've been holding out on us, you little witch."

Francesca laughed at her friends' looks, hooking arms with them both as they headed through the door to security. "I have so much to tell you girls. I don't think our seven-hour flight is going to be enough. Girls, I'm in love."

Both friends stopped dead in their tracks.

"Love? Holy shit! As soon as we pass security, we are sitting at the bar with a Caesar and you are spilling your guts. You hear me?" Taya said, giving Francesca a little shove.

Francesca's phoned beeped, and she saw Ryder's name.

Miss you already. Do you really have to go? I'm still here. I could come back and get you.

She responded with a devilish smile.

Yes! I do have to go. Miss you, too! Love you!

Love you, heart and soul. Be safe, Beauty.

Francesca smiled at his term of endearment.

Back at you, heart and soul. ;)

"Oh, get that sappy look off your face right now and get ready to spill," Taya scoffed.

Francesca couldn't stop smiling all the way through security and as she sat at the bar, recanting her story over the last few months to her girls.

Dakota's mouth was hanging open with tears in her eyes. "Why didn't you tell us about your father, honey?"

Embarrassed, now thinking she had surely offended her friends, she said, "All you girls had been so supportive when Tommy died. I didn't think I would be able to get through it, but you guys kept me going. Then Gabriella lost the boys and Marco, and the stuff with my dad just didn't compare in the big picture. Gabriella needed all our attention, and I know how it is to lose someone you love, so I knew we all had to focus on keeping Gabriella above water. Then she went missing, and we were all consumed trying to find her and supporting Manny and Elia, so I dealt with my family stuff and did what I had to. I hope you guys understand?"

"I totally understand," Taya said. "Sometimes we need to deal with things on our own. It doesn't diminish our friendships. It just makes us stronger, so when we really need to support each other, we are strong and capable."

Francesca's gut told her Taya's words had a double meaning.

She grabbed Taya's hand and squeezed it. "Is everything okay? You know I'm here if you need me."

Taya looked her straight in the eye. "I'm good, Frankie. I know if I need you, all I need to do is call. Enjoy some of the happiness you have finally found. Don't worry about me; I'm good."

Francesca knew there was more, but she let it go for now. Besides, Dakota wasn't letting her off the hook so easily.

"Keep going. I have a feeling we are nowhere close to how the giant of a man ended up falling for his 'beauty'."

Francesca blushed. "Don't call me that. I can't stop Ryder from doing it, but I can you, Pocahontas."

Dakota threw her hands up in surrender. "Okay, no name

calling. I'll stop. But, Frankie, you are beautiful; don't ever doubt that."

Francesca scrunched up her face. "Compared to you two, I have always been D.U.F.F—the Designated Ugly Fat Friend. Dakota, you are so gorgeous you look like you stepped out of a fairy tale. And, Taya, you are so striking with that whimsical jet black hair and crystal blue eyes. I pale in comparison, and I'm okay with that. Ryder loves me how I am."

"Girlfriend, I hope you're talking shit, because I am getting ready to knock you out." Taya glared at her. "I know you're the innocent one of the group, but you can't be that naive. I would kill to be as beautiful as you, and I wish I could see as much good in the world as you do. I want to be just like you when I grow up."

Francesca was aghast. How could Taya believe that?

"This is getting out of hand. Thank you for the compliment, but really, I'm okay with being D.U.F.F." She finished her second Caesar and motioned the waiter for another round.

"Wow, Frankie, you really are blind. Ryder has a lot of work ahead of him. Now cut the shit and continue with your story. I thought you guys sold your house because of the memories it held, not because you needed the money."

Francesca continued to relay everything that had happened to her and her family while they were on the plane, and how she met Ryder. The girls asked a lot of questions, and when everything was said and done, the trio fell asleep for the last four hours of the flight.

When they arrived in Scotland, they retrieved their bags and were met by a chauffeur holding a card with their names. The driver opened the door to the limo, and there sat Prince Edward of England.

"Welcome, Caesar sistas, get your arses in here and let's start this party. The little she-devil, better known as Gabriella, is anxiously awaiting your arrival. I'm Edward, by the way, and I know we are going to be fast mates."

Francesca was star struck and couldn't speak. Dakota had made friends with Edward on Skype after the newspaper article came out that Edward was Gabriella's boyfriend. As usual, the media was way off, and Gabriella was really dating Edward's personal bodyguard, Liam.

After hugging Dakota and pulling a reserved Taya into a hug, Edward turned to Francesca.

"You, my little beauty, must be Frankie the Eye-talian."

Francesca blushed at the nickname the girls called her, extending her hand, knowing Ryder would have a cow if she hugged another man, especially the Prince of England. "Nice to meet you, Prince Edward."

"Rubbish, don't give me that cock and bull. I am simply Edward, and if Gabriella hears you call me that, I'll never hear the end of it. Give me a hug, love." Edward reached forwards and hugged Francesca. Then he placed her back in her seat and turned to

320

pull four Caesars out of the fridge. "Bottoms up, sistas. This is just the beginning of a brilliant friendship."

Edward entertained the girls until Zara and Jocelyn's flight arrived two hours later. They got the same treatment as the trio did.

While Edward was acquainting himself with the two new friends, Francesca texted Ryder to let him know she had arrived.

Beast, arrived safe & sound. Love you!

Beauty, come home now! I didn't sleep a wink. Love you, heart & soul.

She warmed while she smiled at his response. She was so torn. She wanted to be here with her closest friends and celebrate Gabriella's happiness. After all Gabriella had been through, she deserved it and more. However, she missed Ryder so much it physically hurt.

Be home soon. Keep the bed warm. ;) XO

Staying at your place. I feel better here. XO

Good. Love you, heart & soul.

Heart & soul, Beauty. Text me before you go to bed.

She didn't reply; otherwise, they would continue to go back and forth. She would text him before she went to sleep.

Her thoughts were interrupted by laughing, and she looked up to see everyone was laughing at her.

"What?"

"I told you she was head-over-heels in love. She didn't hear a word you said, Zara," Dakota answered.

Francesca blushed, something Edward delighted in doing every chance he got over the two weeks they were in Scotland.

***

The friends had gotten wasted at Gabriella's bachelorette party, and one of the girls sent pictures of Francesca putting a few pounds in the stripper's G-string, and him giving Gabriella a lap dance. Ryder was not amused when he got it, and phoned Francesca to find out what the hell was up.

"What the hell is going on, Francesca?"

"Oh, my God, Beast, I waz jus thinkin' of you," Francesca slurred.

"Are you drunk?"

"I waz drunk, but I'm path that now."

"Put Liam on the phone."

"He's ... not here ... right now."

"I'll call you back." Ryder hung up before Francesca said okay. He took the number Francesca had left him in case of an emergency and sent the two pictures to Liam's cell before calling him.

"Who is this?" Liam bellowed with a thick Scottish brogue after receiving pictures of his future wife and a stripper from the number.

Ryder's response was said with the same venom. "Ryder Vaughn, Francesca Moratti's boyfriend. What the fuck is going on? Why aren't you watching the girls? I'm not impressed with those pictures. I thought I could trust you guys to watch over her."

"Sorry, Ryder, I will git over there right now. The lasses thought it would be bad luck if I was there, so I sent Edward to monitor everything. I should have ken better. Someone is goin' to pay for this. I promise ye, I will call ye the minute I git there."

" 'Preciate it. Take care of my girl."

"Ye have me word. I will not let those hellions out of my sight the rest of their trip."

Ryder hung up and waited fifteen minutes before Liam called him back and assured him that Francesca was okay and they were taking her to the hotel with the other girls to sleep it off.

Ryder's nerves were frayed when he sent his last text.

Sleep well, Beauty, because I'm gonna spank your ass when you get home. Heart & soul.

***

Ryder anxiously waited for Francesca in arrivals with a bouquet of lily of the valley. He had discovered they were her favourite flowers when he had gone out to dinner with her father earlier in the week. Frank had suggested he order them through Islington Nurseries because it wasn't an easy feat to acquire them in February. Frank was friends with the owners and said the family would do everything in their power to fill his special order. Ryder was learning Italian families had connections in every business. Frank and his sons were often a better resource than Google.

The doors opened from the baggage claim area, and he saw Francesca searching frantically for him. He took two large steps towards her before she located him, and the instant she spotted him, she started running, dropping her suitcase as she jumped into his arms.

"I missed you so much!" she managed to get out before he lowered his head and kissed her like they had been separated for years instead of two weeks.

Ryder had never experienced this rollercoaster of emotions before. He had physically ached while she was away, and now he was thinking this was one of the best moments of his life.

"Okay, you two seriously need to get a room. This terminal is rated PG," Taya said as she waited for the two love birds to break apart. "Hey, Ryder, thanks for picking us up."

Francesca was beet red when she turned. "Sorry. Let's go."

Dakota turned to her friend as she nodded at Ryder. "Frankie don't apologize for being in love. Hey, Ryder, yeah, thanks for the lift. I feel bad. I could have had someone in my family come."

Ryder nodded back with a half-smirk. "Keep calling her Frankie, and you'll be phoning them from the side of the road."

"Ryder! Sorry, Dakota, he doesn't mean it." Francesca pinched his side.

Ryder jumped at the cruel punishment. "Ouch."

"Don't push it, Beast, or I'm boarding a plane back to

Scotland." She laughed as she moved to gather her abandoned suitcase. Ryder took it from her after a small scuffle. "I am quite capable of carrying my own suitcase."

"I know you are, but I'm doing it. I missed doing things for you." He gently kissed her forehead then pulled the flowers from behind his back, handing them to her.

Francesca squealed. "They're gorgeous! Thank you so much." She yanked his head down for another kiss.

Taya'd had enough. "I'm all for romance, but you two are sickening. I'm going to grab a cab."

The two lovers broke apart, and Francesca turned towards her. "No, you're not. And mark my words, Taya, you are going to be in the exact same position one day, and I'm going to remind you of this conversation."

"Not in this lifetime, Frankie. Love isn't for everyone," Taya fired back while laughing at Ryder's scowl. She was irritating him on purpose.

Taya adored Francesca and was thrilled she had fallen in love, but love wasn't in the cards for her.

Taya had things she needed to deal with today, so she continued to herd them out the door.

Ryder placed his arm around Francesca's shoulder as they started to walk towards the parking lot. When he glanced down, she was grinning from ear-to-ear. He snaked his arm around her neck and put her in a headlock. It felt amazing to have her back.

She giggled as she fought him off. This was one of the things he had missed—the playfulness of the girl attached to him

The couple had just dropped off their last passenger and were stopped at a light when Ryder reached over and slipped his hand into her jacket and down the front of Francesca's top to cop a feel of her breasts. He moved the cups of her bra down and squeezed first one breast then the other.

"Damn, I missed these babies," he said as he tweaked a nipple.

Francesca yelped and tried to push his hand away. "Ry … der …" she exaggerated his name. "Someone will see."

"Don't give a shit. Relax; the windows are tinted. These babies are only for my viewing pleasure. You have no idea how much I missed you."

"I missed you, too, but can't you wait until we get home?" she begged, even though her thong was already damp.

"No." He continued to massage the fleshly breasts he had been dreaming about since the minute she had boarded the plane to Scotland.

"Fine," she huffed, trying to cross her arms over her chest with no luck. "I got you some presents while I was away." She looked over at his profile.

"Thank you. But if you think presents are going to get you out of trouble after I received those pictures, you have another thing coming. You have some serious grovelling to do."

She felt heat rising towards her face. "I swear, all I did was put money in his G-string and, as it turned out, it was Edward pulling a prank. Like, seriously, let's be honest here; do you really think the Prince of England would be interested in the likes of me? Besides, he has a stunning girlfriend, Gillian. I'm afraid you are stuck with me."

"It doesn't make it any better that it was Edward. What, you don't think someone famous could fall for you?"

"No. Definitely not. The pool is vast for someone with his kind of fame and fortune. He could have movie stars, lingerie models, playboy bunnies … He wouldn't be attracted to some little nobody. Besides, I found the man of my dreams." Her smiled lit up with her declaration.

He turned to look at her and winked. "Oh, you're good, babe. But I'm still smacking that ass for touching another man. You are mine, heart, soul, and body." He emphasized that by tweaking her nipple again.

She yelped again and tried to remove his hand to no avail.

Ryder didn't remove his hand for the rest of the way to her apartment. When they arrived, she fixed her bra and adjusted her jacket before she got out and turned towards the trunk where he already had her suitcase in his hand.

Moving towards her, he bent, braced his legs, and scooped her under her ass as he lifted her up with one arm. She squealed, wiggling yet placing her legs around his hips so she didn't fall.

"Ryder, I'm too heavy. Put me down."

Ryder was beginning to believe that spending two weeks with a group of gorgeous women had put a dent back in her self-confidence. He didn't understand it because she was as attractive, if not more, than her friends. Nobody could compare to the woman in his arms. He wanted her to feel as beautiful as she was.

"I bench press three times your weight, and I haven't held you in two weeks. Stop moving around; you need to conserve your energy. I intend on giving you a thorough workout."

"God, I love you so much!" She kissed the side of his head as he placed the suitcase down to open the door.

Once inside, he placed her down, facing the door. She turned and gasped.

Francesca couldn't believe the transformation of her apartment. All her old furniture was gone, and in its place were exquisite pieces and thick, lush rugs.

"Holy crap! What have you done?"

Ryder was so proud of himself that he puffed up his chest as she turned towards him. "Happy Valentine's Day, babe."

Her mouth hung open as she shook her head like he was freaking nuts. "No, no, no. You can't go out and buy me expensive gifts like this. It's crazy and way over the top. Boyfriends buy flowers and chocolates, maybe some lingerie, but not a house full of furniture!"

Ryder nonchalantly took off his jacket and hung it up, knowing this was how she would react. "Bullshit. I can, and I did. Now stop talking and let's go christen the couch, and then the chair, the coffee table, the kitchen table—"

"Stop!" Her temper was rising. She threw up her hands. "Questo uomo è pazzo e ha più soldi di cervello!"

He only understood one word, pazzo, which meant crazy. After that, he didn't want to know the rest.

He ignored her continuous rant and started to unbutton her jacket. She slapped his hands away and grabbed the front of his T-shirt, yanking him down so they were nose-to-nose. Damn, this little sprite was strong when she was pissed.

"You will take it all back tomorrow and put my old stuff back." She was panting heavily, and not in a good way. "I thank you for the beautiful flowers you bought me for Valentine's Day." Francesca kissed him hard, not giving him a chance to retort.

Ryder would let it go for now, knowing this wasn't over by a long shot. Wait until she walked into her bedroom. He had better get some action before that happened.

He picked her up again while they kissed and walked towards the couch. Even though she was mad at him, he still felt calm for the first time in over two weeks.

He had her so worked up that he had stripped them both, sheathed himself, and entered her before she realized they were making out on the couch that he was supposed to be returning tomorrow.

"This first round is going to be quick, Beauty. I've been thinking constantly about getting inside you for the last two weeks. Damn, am I imagining it, or are you tighter than the last time? You feel amazing." Ryder didn't ask if she was okay. Just by watching her clenched eyes and her head thrashing side to side as she called for God, he knew she was good.

Upon completion, Ryder fell to his side. "I love you, heart and soul." He kissed her lips as he rose to dispose of the condom and wash up.

"Love you, too, heart and soul."

She was exhausted and needed to shower before bed.

Francesca dragged her suitcase to her bedroom, opened the door, looked around, and screamed, "BEAST!"

***

The alarm went off at five fifteen a.m. Francesca reached over the gorgeous new nightstand and slammed the snooze button. Then she rolled over, facing Ryder. Damn, she wished she could keep the bed because she'd had the best sleep of her life. The sheets were luxurious and already had their scent on them. Maybe she would keep the sheets. They were close to lingerie, *weren't they?*

Ryder must have slept great, too, because he didn't awake or move a muscle when the alarm had gone off.

After fooling around twice last night, they had talked in bed for hours. Francesca had told him all about her trip and Gabriella's wedding, and he had filled her in on all the things she had missed at the centre.

Francesca stared at the man that had become the centre of her universe. He looked so peaceful while he slept. She marvelled at how she had felt about him when they had first met. Ryder had been reserved and intimidating, his stature frightening; but it had been the scowl on his face and his bluntness that had generally freaked her out.

He wasn't an easy man to read until he let you in. Once you got to know him, you realized he was just a six and half foot cuddly teddy bear. Her sistas couldn't believe the stories she had shared with them.

She was so happy he was all hers, but in the back of her mind, she knew time was running out for them. Two weeks had been torturous; how would she survive when he moved back to California?

She jumped at the pounding on her front door.

"Frankie, you up? Rise and shine, sis!" Lucky yelled out, startling Ryder awake.

"You've got to be fucking kidding me. What are those idiots

doing here at five thirty in the morning?"

"Calm down. They probably just came for breakfast," Francesca said as she kissed his lips before climbing out of the tall bed. She grabbed her robe quickly before her pazzo brothers woke up the whole neighbourhood. Then she closed the bedroom door, hoping Ryder would go back to sleep for a while.

Opening her entry door, in bounced Sal and Lucky.

"Morning, Frankie. How was the trip?" Lucky asked as he kissed both her cheeks.

"Holy shit, this place looks amazing. You're really loosening the purse strings these days, eh?" Sal exclaimed as he kissed his little sister.

"Don't sit on any of it, because it's all going back today." Francesca's reply got their attention.

"Like hell it is!" Ryder remarked, coming out of the bedroom and doing up his jeans with no shirt on. "I'm not returning it, and you have no idea where I bought it, so live with it." Looking first at one brother and then the other, he asked, "Is there a reason you two showed up at five thirty in the morning? Was it something imperative that couldn't wait until after work?"

"Is there a reason you're coming out of our baby sister's bedroom at five thirty in the morning?" Sal's displeasure and sarcasm radiated.

Ryder smirked. "Yeah, because I sleep here Sunday through

332

Thursday, and then Francesca stays at my place Friday and Saturday."

The idiots were speechless. First time since he met them, too. *Good on them.*

His smile broadened as he walked towards the coffee pot.

Francesca was on fire with the blush that was riding up her chest and face. Stomping her foot, she exclaimed, "Ryder!"

He turned at her tone, looking innocent. "Am I lying?" he asked as he settled his ass against the counter, arms folded over his bare chest, his smirk still firmly in place. "You're a grown woman, and your brothers have to start accepting that."

"There are rules to dating our sister, and apparently, we have to educate you on them," Lucky jumped in first.

"Yeah, that's right, rules," Sal sputtered out after reining in his temper.

"Oh, this should be good," Ryder muttered to himself before responding to them on a drawl, "Go ahead. I'm dying to hear."

Francesca had had enough of this testosterone-filled discussion.

"Apparently, although I am standing right here, nobody feels the need to ask my opinion on my life, so I'm going to shower. This conversation had better be over before I return, or you are all out." She muttered to herself as she walked away in a snit about men comparing penis sizes. Then, answering herself out loud, she said, "Ryder would probably win that competition, as well." She laughed, entering her bedroom.

Not finding her remark funny, Lucky started, "Rule one, treat our sister with the utmost respect."

"Check," Ryder responded smugly.

Sal, not liking his smirk, threw in the next rule. "Two, understand we'll never like you dating her."

"Check, and really don't give a shit."

"Three, she is not your conquest. She is our baby sister," Lucky rambled off quickly.

"Check. She might be your baby sister, but she is my world."

"Humph. Four, you never ever stop her from feeding us," Sal added.

"Not checking on that one because you guys take advantage of her. Do either one of you have any clue how much of her own money she spends on food to keep your bellies full?"

Lucky had the good sense to look contrite. "Non-negotiable. We'll start pitching in with the food bill. And I will apologize to her for that."

"Check, then."

"Five, you never discourage her from spending time with us," Lucky said.

Ryder rolled his eyes. "Check. I know how she feels about you two idiots. I would never get between the three of you."

Sal was getting serious now. "Six, you hurt her, and we hurt you twice as bad."

"Respect that. But I would like to see you try. Check." He stood up straighter to prove his point.

"Seven, you never look, touch, or talk to another woman without her knowledge." Lucky stared him down.

"Check, but you have to also add that to *her* list," he cockily replied, lifting one corner of his mouth.

Sal looked at him in confusion. "What the hell does that mean? Frankie would never cheat on you, asshole."

Ryder chuckled again. "I have pics of Francesca putting money into the G-string of a stripper at Gabriella's bachelorette party."

"Well, damn. Are you sure those photos weren't doctored? That doesn't sound like our shy, innocent little sister," Lucky asked, truly shocked.

"Yup. There were huge amounts of alcohol involved, and her Caesar buddies encouraged her. Trust me; that will never happen again, sober or drunk. Otherwise, she'll have a red ass to match her face."

"Fuck you! Eight, you never ever lay a hand on her!" Sal stated, veins popping out of his neck.

"Can't agree to that one. I love to see those pure white cheeks carrying my handprint. She loves it, too. Ask her."

Now it was Lucky who was pissed. "Sal, get the fuckin' cement ready. Really, bro, did you have to say that? I like you, and I don't appreciate you pushing our buttons."

"Totally out of line; I apologize. Don't tell me neither one of you have never played that way. If you do, I call bullshit."

"Rule nine; the most important rule of all," Sal stated. "You never ever, not ever, acknowledge anything about her participating in any sexual activity. It's our God given right as Italian brothers to believe our sister is a virgin until the day we hand her off to the man who has passed all our tests. Get me?"

"Yeah, Virgin Francesca Mary."

"Maria," Lucky corrected.

Ryder drew his eyebrows together in confusion. "Maria?"

"Francesca Maria Moratti. Maria, Italian for Mary. There is a reason my father named her that. She is pure and good," Sal explained.

"Agreed. But—and this is a big but—if you two want to continue believing your sister is a virgin, then stop coming here uninvited. You never know what you're going to walk in on … like the couch we christened last night." Ryder lifted his chin towards the new couch.

The brothers both started to gag as they looked at the couch.

"You had better be joking, asshole. Frankie! Hurry up in the bathroom! I think I just threw up in my mouth!" Lucky gagged out.

Ryder bellowed a boisterous laugh. "On that note, I should probably start the coffee. Francesca tends to get cranky without caffeine."

"That's why we usually bring coffee with us, but we were too excited to see her and hear about her trip today. We forgot."

That comment softened Ryder up.

"And, guys, let me reassure you. I love that woman more than my own life. She will never question my respect or my loyalty. She is my heart and soul."

The brothers exchanged a look Ryder couldn't decipher. Then they approached him. He stuck out his fists, expecting fist bumps. Instead, the brothers leaned in on both side of him and kissed his cheeks in unison. Ryder pushed them away.

"Fuck off, you freaks! There is—"

"Now *that's* what I like to see. The men who mean the most to me getting along." Francesca smiled, arriving just after her brothers' latest antics.

Lucky and Sal had won this round.

Ryder moved in front of her, bending down to look her straight in the eyes as he lifted his arms out wide. "There is something seriously wrong with your brothers." He tapped his head with both hands. "They're not right in the head. You need to make them appointments at the centre. Not funny. I'm serious."

She pecked him on the lips as she giggled.

Chapter 19

"Just Breathe" By Pearl Jam

The week was finally almost over. It was two hours before the weekend started. As a reward, the class was walking over to the coffee shop for donuts. It had been impossible to separate Mason from Francesca after her absence the weeks before, so instead of fighting it, the staff all agreed to let Francesca be his primary caregiver.

Ryder had spent most of the week with Katrina. The bond they had formed after her first meltdown had stayed intact. People in general, and often some of the staff, forgot that kids with special needs still had the same psychological responses as their peers.

All the female staff were absolutely convinced that Katrina was head-over-heels in love with Ryder. She flirted nonstop and did everything he asked of her. The same could be said for Mason regarding Francesca.

There was a chilly breeze in the air. Francesca locked arms with Mason as they walked.

"What are you doing this weekend, Mason?"

"Frankie—" Mason realized his mistake and looked back to see if Ryder had heard him calling her that, but Ryder was way back, walking slowly with Katrina. "I've been talking about it all week. I'm going to Playdium tomorrow. I can't wait. I heard they have amazing interactive video games. Scott got us a deal, and we can play unlimited for three hours. It's going to be the best day of my life. I've wanted to go since I was five."

Francesca was elated at his enthusiasm. It bugged her that, what most kids took for granted, Mason had to fight tooth and nail for.

"You're right; I do remember you telling me a thousand times … or more. It must be the jet lag. Sorry, bud."

Mason adored the woman and often said he wished that Frankie could become his mother. She would be the best mother in the world. She always laughed, was kind, and when he got mad, she never held it against him like everyone else did.

"I love you, Frankie," he whispered into her ear.

She smiled and told him she loved him, too, as she ruffled his hair. "You're a good boy, Mason, and I'm so proud of you."

Ryder watched the interaction between Francesca and the teenage boy beside her. She drew people to her like bees to honey. She never turned anyone away, unless they proved themselves unworthy, and then nine times out of ten, she would try again, strongly believing there was goodness in everyone. She had definitely proved that with him.

He liked who he was becoming after spending so much time with her. He was comfortable with his whole body, and she had also strengthened his soul. He had started seeing the good in people, instead of looking for the bad.

He was struggling more and more about moving back to California. He had made a commitment to the band for this tour, but after that, he wasn't sure he wanted to continue. Life would be perfect if he could just stay at Reach Within and live with Francesca for the rest of his life. Nothing would make him happier.

Fame was something he never wanted. He just wanted to play music and write lyrics. Now he wished he could do all those things and continue giving back to the community. It made him think of all the nurses and therapists who worked tirelessly to make sure he had recovered and walked again. He should have been more grateful. That would change.

The class, except Ryder and Katrina, approached the door. Veeta, in her excitement, pushed her way through a group of teenagers at the door, knocking into one of them.

"Watch what you're doing, you half-baked defect."

Veeta jumped backwards from shock by his demeanour and straight into the people behind her, falling and knocking Amanda, Taz, and Layla down.

Before Francesca could stop it, Mason lost his shit.

"Who the fuck do you think you are?"

Ryder was half a block away, watching the interaction. He picked Katrina up and started to run towards the altercation, yelling, "Mason, stand down!"

The belligerent teenager turned his venom on Mason. "Whatcha going to do about it, retard?"

Francesca was trapped behind the fallen members of their group. She turned to tell Mason to calm down when all hell broke loose.

Mason shoved the kid into his friends. One of the other teenagers then pushed Mason to the ground as the group started to run away, laughing and taunting him.

Mason was up in a flash and running after them, yelling that he was going to kill them.

Francesca got around everyone and took off after Mason. Julianna grabbed her phone to call the centre, requesting backup. Layla and Amanda were up and tending to Veeta, Taz, and Theo. And Ryder dropped Katrina off with the group before he ran after Francesca and Mason.

Francesca reached Mason just as he was raising his fist to hit the kid who had knocked him down. She grabbed the back of his jacket, and with all her strength, whipped him around. The motion of his fist was already in full-swing as he nailed Francesca in the head, sending her headfirst into a concrete lamppost with a powerful thud.

Ryder watched in slow motion as it all unfolded, hearing her scream, and then hearing the blow of her head hitting the concrete post.

"No! *Francesca!*"

Mason screamed, "Frankie!" as he bent down to see blood pouring from the side of her forehead. "Fuck, Frankie, I'm sorry ... So sorry." He was crying uncontrollably as he grabbed the front of her jacket, trying to force her up.

As Ryder reached them, he screamed at Mason, "Don't touch her!" Knowing with head and neck injuries you weren't supposed to move them.

Ryder scared the shit out of Mason. He released Francesca's jacket and stumbled back, landing on his butt. He looked frantically at the ferocious man beside him as Ryder pulled out his cell phone and called 911.

"I didn't mean to hurt her, Ryder, I swear. Please don't be mad at me. I wouldn't hurt her on purpose. They just made me so mad."

The sorrow in the kid's voice was heartbreaking, but before Ryder could deal with Mason, he had to get Francesca an ambulance.

"I have a woman with a serious head injury on the corner of Autumn Breeze and Tamarack," he barked into the phone. "Send an ambulance as soon as possible." Panic was seeping into his bones.

"Please, stay on the line—"

"No, I can't stay on the line. Send the goddamn ambulance!" he seethed out before Julianna snatched the phone from him and walked away to talk to the dispatcher.

He knelt beside Francesca. "You're okay, baby. I'm here. It's going to be okay. An ambulance is on its way." Fear like he had never felt before washed over him. He couldn't lose her. She was the best thing that had ever happened to him. He leaned in closer. "You stay with me; you hear me? I love you."

Julianna came back and moved to Francesca's other side as they heard the sirens of an ambulance approaching. She checked Francesca's pulse then checked her eyes, reciting everything she observed to the dispatcher.

Ryder held her hand, mumbling for her to be okay, as the paramedics rushed to her side, asking Ryder to stand back so they could work.

"Be gentle with her please!" he begged, full of fear.

One paramedic was taking her vitals while the other started to ask questions.

"What's her name?"

"Francesca Moratti," Ryder answered.

"Age?"

"Twenty-five."

"Allergies?"

"None that I know of."

"Has she ever suffered from a head injury before?"

"I don't know." The panic was rising. Ryder ran his fingers through his hair. *Fuck! Fuck! Fuck!*

"Can you reach her family?"

"I'm her boyfriend. I live with her. I'll call her father and brothers."

"Okay, good. They can meet us at the hospital. We're going to need her medical history."

Julianna's mouth dropped open at Ryder's answers. No one at the school had known they were dating. She would have to think later about what needed to be done about his disclosure. Right now, they needed to make sure Frankie was all right.

Mariana arrived at the scene with three other staff members, whom she directed to get the other kids back to the centre. Then she quickly moved to Julianna and started to question her about the incident.

"Where is Mason?" she asked, looking around.

Julianna looked left then right, and then behind herself. "He was here a minute ago. Is it possible he went with the other staff?"

Mariana got on her phone and called Layla's cell, and then called the centre. Meanwhile, the two paramedics had braced Francesca's neck before rolling her onto a backboard. They lifted her onto the stretcher and loaded her up in the vehicle.

Ryder looked at Julianna. "I'm riding with her. I'll call you from the hospital as soon as I know something."

"Mason is missing," Mariana informed them as she got off the phone.

Ryder remembered Mason begging him to listen about being sorry. "He was really freaked out—blaming himself," Ryder responded as he jumped into the ambulance. "Find him, so I can reassure Francesca that he's okay when she wakes up. Make sure those punks don't get him. There were at least nine of them. Keep me up to date."

The door closed on the ambulance, and the siren wailed as they sped off.

***

Ryder was lost in a fog of despair. He had silently watched her all the way to the hospital, making sure she was breathing. Up and down her chest rose, confirming she was listening to his silent pleas. The gash on her head was still bleeding, and her right eye was swelling and distorting her face. So much blood. He was getting concerned about the amount, and how much more she could afford to lose.

"Just keep breathing, Beauty," he whispered.

They unloaded her and were met by the emergency doctor and nurses, who directed the paramedics to examination room three.

Ryder was following the stretcher when one the nurses grabbed his arm and directed him to the waiting room.

"You don't understand. I need to be with her. Please just let me stay with her. I don't want her to wake up alone," Ryder pleaded with the nurse.

"Sir, I can't let you go in there. Let the doctors take care of her. As soon as they assess her, one of us will come and get you, and then you can sit with her."

Ryder gently laid his hand on top of the one she used to pull him back. "Please, ma'am, don't leave her alone. She has spent her life caring for people who can't look after themselves. She deserves to have someone look after her."

The depth of pain on his face and his words struck a chord with the compassion-fatigued nurse. She realized what she saw every day was terrifying the giant in front of her.

"Is she a nurse? And what are your names?"

"Francesca, and I'm Ryder. No, she isn't a nurse, but she works with special needs kids; that's how she got hurt."

"Okay, Ryder, I'm Caroline," she said soothingly. "I'll look after your Francesca and stay with her. I'll come and get you when I can't be there. Don't worry; she's in good hands." She patted his hand before he released his grip.

Even with the reassurance, he was still frantic.

Pushing his hands through his hair, he blew out a breath. "Thank you, Caroline. Please, just make sure she continues to breathe, and come and get me as soon as you can."

346

"Will do. Go get a coffee. We will be at least a half an hour to an hour." She smiled before turning and leaving.

Ryder walked out to the front of the building to the sidewalk. He pulled out his phone and looked up Frank's number, pushing the button.

"Hello?"

"Frank ..." Ryder couldn't continue. He had a lump in his throat that wouldn't let the words pass.

During his months in the hospital as a child, he had seen many kids come in with head injuries, and not all of them had survived. He knew there could be internal bleeding, swelling of the brain ... If her skull was fractured, it could have punctured her brain. Her brain stem could have been damaged. Her spinal cord affected.

The pain in his chest clenched.

"Ryder, is that you?"

The sound of Frank's voice crippled him. He wanted to sob and beg Frank to tell him everything would be okay.

He took a big gulp of air, a strangled sound coming from his closed-up throat.

Upon hearing this, Frank became concerned, knowing something was terribly wrong.

"Son, take another deep breath and talk to me. Is Francesca okay? Are you okay?"

Ryder felt the man's panic deep in his bones. He had to do this.

He swallowed three times before he could speak. "Francesca's hurt. We're at the hospital. We need you," Ryder finally said. Never in his life had he felt so helpless.

"Ryder, where are you?" Frank was beyond himself with fear.

Ryder swallowed again, trying to dislodge the lump. "Trillium Health Centre."

"I'm on my way. You need me to stay on the line with you?"

"No, just please hurry." He hung up and instantly felt a little better. Frank would know what to do.

Ryder saw a man smoking and approached him. "Could I buy a few? I'll give you ten dollars."

The man looked shocked and a little scared of the huge man in front of him. "Here, take five."

Ryder pulled ten bucks out and handed it to the man. "Thanks. Can I get a light?"

The man lit Ryder's cigarette then quickly walked away.

Ryder took his first drag in eight years. He felt the smoke fill his lungs. It was a horrible feeling to be powerless.

"Just breathe, Beauty," he whispered as the memory of what had happened replayed in his mind.

He would never forget the look on Mason's face as he swung around, fist cocked back before he pummelled Francesca's head. The horrible sound of her head smacking into the pole at the exact place a metal plate hung, indicating the voltage in the pole. Some of her

348

hair and blood had been left on the corner of the sign. He shivered at the sound he had heard and took another deep drag of the cigarette.

Ryder looked up at the sky and started to talk as he paced the sidewalk. "You don't know me, but Francesca believes in you. If you really do exist, then you know my beauty. You have to make sure she's okay, for her sake and for Mason's. I don't expect it for me, because I've never done anything worth that kind of compassion, but she has. Francesca has spent her life nurturing and caring for everyone around her." He took another drag as he contemplated his next words.

"Do it for Frank, because he's a good man and has lost so much already." Knowing how he felt about Francesca, he couldn't imagine losing his wife, and then his son. "Don't take his daughter." Taking another drag, he thought quietly for a while then looked up again. "There has to be some divine law about how much people should endure in their lives. These are good people and have dealt with enough. Please, I'm begging you; don't take her." His breath caught on his last sentence.

He lit the next cigarette before butting out the first one. Then he sat down on the third step and leaned his forearms on his legs, staring down. He sat that way for fifteen minutes, smoking cigarette after cigarette, before he felt a hand on his shoulder.

He jumped, standing up, startled out of the thoughts that were consuming him.

"Frank, I'm so glad you're here." Ryder's shoulders slumped with relief.

Frank grabbed the big man and hugged him. "Have the doctors told you anything?"

"No. They said it would be at least a half an hour to an hour before we would know anything." He started to pace again.

"Mrs. Ramara from the centre called and briefly told me what happened while we were driving here. Son, she's going to be all right. I can feel it in my bones." Staring up, he looked at Ryder's glistening eyes. "Lucky and Sal went straight to the waiting room. Let's go join them, and you can tell us what happened." Frank guided Ryder up the steps towards the entrance.

Lucky and Sal went to them as soon as they saw the two men enter.

"What the hell happened?" Lucky asked, full of concern.

"Let's take a seat first," Frank told them, leading the group to a set of chairs.

When they were all seated, Ryder told them the events leading up to where they were now.

Sal was angry and spoke without thinking. "I don't understand why she has to work with that psycho. He is twice her size. He should be locked away in the looney bin."

Ryder jumped to his feet, temper ignited. "Shut your goddamn mouth. How dare you judge Francesca's abilities, or Mason.

350

Francesca is great at her job, and she loves that kid. She would never forgive you if she heard you talk like that. It's not the kid's fault his mother shook him and scrambled his fucking brains."

Frank got up and stopped Ryder's pacing. "Sal didn't mean it. He's a hot head. He's just scared for Francesca. Relax, son." Frank turned. "Salvador, if you can't keep your temper under control, go back to the shop. We'll call you when we hear something."

"Sorry, that was me talking shit. I'm just worried." Sal had known as soon as it came out of his mouth that he was wrong. "It scares me all the time that she has to deal with that kind of stuff. She's just so tiny. I can't lose ..." Sal dropped his head into his hands and shook with the tears that overwhelmed him.

The lump was back in Ryder's throat as he sat in Frank's empty seat and squeezed Sal's shoulder, managing to croak out, "I know, man, I know."

"Ryder?"

Ryder lifted his head and saw Caroline. He stood quickly and walked towards her.

"How is she?"

The rest of the men gathered around to hear what the nurse had to say.

"She just opened her eyes. We're sending her for an MRI, and then the doctor will talk to you. I thought you might want to see her for five minutes before we take her up. She was calling for her mom.

351

Is she here?"

The first crack in Frank's armour could be heard as he gasped out loud.

Ryder's heart sunk. "Caroline, this is Francesca's father, Frank, and her brothers, Lucky and Sal. Her mom died years ago."

Looking at the four men's faces, she could see their fear. Caroline responded, "Okay, listen, don't panic. It's common for someone with a head injury to be disorientated. Let's get you and her dad in there. I want you to describe exactly what happened to the doctor before her MRI."

Guilt resided in Ryder's chest as he looked over at her brothers, expecting them to tell him he had no right to see Francesca before they did. Instead, Lucky asked if he could relay their love. Sal agreed, telling him to tell her that they were in the waiting room and would see her soon. Relieved, he turned back to the nurse.

Caroline indicated they should follow her, and soon they stepped into the curtained area where Francesca laid in a bed. She was hooked up to an IV, blood pressure machine, and heart monitor.

Caroline saw the men falter. Francesca's face had swelled even more in the hour Ryder had been separated from her. The gash had been stitched up, but there was still dried blood surrounding the area and where it had flowed down her neck. The neck brace was still firmly in place, and Francesca was lying on the back brace they had placed her on at the scene. She also had a dark bruise forming on her jaw.

Ryder went to one side and Frank went to the other. Her eyes were closed, but her unaffected one opened as soon as each man grabbed one of her hands.

"Bambolina?"

"Papa, what happened? Where am I?"

"You're in the hospital. You had an accident at work," Ryder answered before Frank could say anything.

She tried to move her head and winced in pain. Closing her eye, a tear escaped.

"Francesca?" Ryder's panicked voice filled the room.

When she opened her eye again, she saw Ryder leaning over her.

"You're here," she whispered as the pain started to subside.

Relief filled him. "I wouldn't be anywhere else. How are you feeling?" He raised her hand with the IV in it and kissed her fingertips.

"Really sore, and my head is pounding. I can't stand that beeping. Please make it stop." She grimaced.

Ryder instantly turned towards Caroline, raising his eyebrows in a questioning look.

Caroline moved to the machine and placed it on silent.

Francesca weakly smiled at Ryder in thanks.

"Better?" he asked.

"Uh-huh." She licked her dry lips. "Ryder, what happened?"

Ryder lifted his head and looked at Frank, relaying that he didn't want to tell her yet. Then he looked back down at Francesca and said, "You hit your head, but we can talk about it later. Lucky and Sal are in the waiting room and send their love."

It took her a minute to process what he had said. "Papa, tell them to go back to work. You all shouldn't be away from the shop. I'm fine, really."

"Bambolina, would you be anywhere else if one of your brothers was lying in this bed? They want to be here. They love you."

When Francesca smiled and closed her eyes, Ryder immediately started to panic.

Caroline, seeing his fear, spoke up, "This is normal. She will fade in and out of consciousness. It's her body's way of dealing with the head trauma. They are going to take Francesca for an MRI now, and then they will transfer her to a room. The attendant will be here in a minute. If I could ask you to wait a minute, the doctor wants the details about what happened and her medical history."

As Caroline started to disconnect the blood pressure machine and the heart monitor, the men said their good-byes.

Frank bent over and kissed his daughter on the cheek. "Rest, my angel. Ti amo la mia dolce, bambolina." He turned and moved outside the curtained area, giving Ryder a minute alone.

Ryder walked over to her good side. He brushed her hair back and held her hand. "I love you, Francesca. Promise me you will just keep breathing. Heart and soul, Beauty." He leaned down, and as gently as he could, kissed her lips.

When the attendant took Francesca up for the MRI, Frank and Ryder moved back into the room and waited for the doctor. Ryder sat in a chair, so overcome with emotion he couldn't look at Frank, his eyes swimming with tears.

Ryder hadn't cried in over eighteen years. The last time had been just before his father had given him his last beating. He hadn't shed a tear during the final beating, thinking he was going to die and wanting to go with dignity.

Tears were a sign of weakness. His father had drilled that into his head. Now, though, he couldn't stop them.

She had been awake, and surely that was a good sign. But what if some complication arose and he lost her?

He rubbed the palms of his hands against his eyes, trying to keep his heartache contained.

Frank walked over to him and placed his hand on Ryder's back. Ryder felt the man's comfort and lost his struggle, quietly releasing a gut-wrenching sob.

Frank didn't say a word, just kept his hand on Ryder's back until the sobs stopped. He knew Ryder would truly be one of his own sons soon. He was terrified for his only daughter, but he had faith in

God that this was not her time. She had much to do still. The man in front of him needed his daughter.

***

It was twelve-thirty a.m. when Ryder startled awake from a sound outside of Francesca's room. He had arranged for a private room, leaving his credit card open for any extra charges.

The doctor had talked to the family after the MRI and told them that she had a hairline fracture in her skull and a serious concussion. Thankfully, there was no swelling or bleeding in or around her brain. The doctor was optimistic, but he had said they would keep her for a few days to monitor her.

No amount of reassurance made Ryder feel any better. He wasn't leaving her side until she was released.

Ryder had been sitting there for hours alone after convincing Frank and the boys to go home, assuring them he would call if anything changed.

He had asked the nurse earlier for a paper and wrote the lyrics to Pearl Jam's song, "Just Breathe." The song had been playing in his head nonstop, so he wrote the lyrics down to help clear his mind. He had folded the paper and placed it on Francesca's nightstand. He must have fallen asleep after that.

The door opened and a nurse walked in. "Sir, the police are here and would like to speak to you for a minute."

He stepped out into the hallway and shut Francesca's door, his mind was racing with questions, unsure of what they wanted.

"Mr. Vaughn, I am Officer Fitzpatrick, and this Officer Chang. We need to speak to you about Mason Wilson."

Ryder's heart sped up. He felt guilty that he hadn't thought of Mason since arriving at the hospital. "Is he okay? Did those boys hurt him?"

"Sir, we issued an Amber Alert at four p.m. yesterday, but no one has seen or heard from Mason. We understand that you and Miss Moratti are very close to him. Is there anywhere you can think of that he would go?"

"No, he's always with his caregivers. Did you try that sad excuse of a mother?"

Fitzpatrick stared at Ryder. It was making him uncomfortable.

Fitzpatrick finally asked, "Do I know you?"

"No, I've only been living here since September." Ryder knew he wasn't one of the cops who had arrested him twice before, so he must have been a fan of Fornication and seen something through the disguise Ryder used.

"I can't shake this feeling that we've met before." The officer shook his head. "Anyway, yes, we checked with his mother. She is screaming bloody murder over the fact that the centre lost her kid. She's looking to sue the centre and have custody returned to her."

"She caused his disability, and now he can't control his actions or temper because of it, and she wants him back? Unbelievable."

Ryder shook his head in disbelief. "I wish I could give you some places to look, but I have no idea where he could have gone."

"How is Miss Moratti?" Chang asked.

"She has a hairline fracture on her skull and a bad concussion. She should be released in a few days. This is going to kill her. She loves that kid. Did you find the punks who started all this?"

"Yes. We spoke to each of them, and their parents. They are basically good kids from good families. It's that mob mentality; they think they are so tough in a group. Get them alone, and they cry like babies. Their parents agreed to enroll them in a community-based sensitivity training program."

The hair on the back of Ryder's neck stood up. "Mob mentality or not, they shouldn't be picking on kids less fortunate than themselves. Mason is a great kid. He was protecting one of his own."

"Mr. Vaughn, I'm going to be blunt here. We issued an Amber Alert, but because of Mason's history with violence, we are going to have to warn the public. There will be a news conference at seven a.m. We don't want the public to approach Mason. We are concerned about not knowing his state of mind. He didn't have his meds last night, so we are considering him dangerous and unpredictable."

"Are you kidding me? That kid has a development delay. He's like a four-year-old in most aspects. He still plays with toy cars." Ryder was having a hard time reining in his own temper.

"Sir, with all due respect, he could have killed Miss Moratti," Fitzpatrick responded. "We can't risk him hurting someone else. We read through all the incident reports from the centre and at his group home. He might act like a four-year-old sometimes, but he also acts like an out of control teenager, and he has the strength of three men when he is enraged. We also know of his attraction to Miss Moratti, and we know he is very sexually aware. We don't want him attacking a young girl."

"This is bullshit! Mason would never attack anyone for sex," Ryder said, full of confidence. "The kid doesn't know how to get a meal. He doesn't have money for food, or the knowledge to find shelter. He could freeze to death out there all alone. Right now, that should be your main focus."

"We understand your concerns, but he is a loose cannon, and that puts him and the public at risk," Chang answered. "We set up a police command post at the centre to use for the search. If you think of anything, please contact us as soon as possible. Some officers will be back to talk to Miss Moratti later this morning."

"She doesn't remember what happened, and I want to tell her before you guys discuss it with her. Don't come too early. I want to talk to her doctors to assure this won't set back her recovery. If the officers upset her, I will throw them out. End of." If she knew what they were planning, she would be frantic and insist on going to look for Mason herself.

"Mr. Vaughn, we aren't the bad guys here. We don't want to upset Miss Moratti. We just want to find Mason. I'll make sure the officers are sensitive to her condition. Here is my card." Fitzpatrick handed Ryder his card and extended his hand.

Ryder shook it, knowing that he was being a dick, but someone needed to stand up for Mason and Francesca.

He turned and walked back into Francesca's room where he quietly eased his large frame into the chair beside her. It was going to break her heart when he told her Mason was missing and that they considered him a danger to society.

She had shifted in her sleep, and he couldn't see the rise and fall of her chest, so he gently moved the covers from her chest. Up and down, he watched her chest rise and fall.

"Just breathe, Beauty," Ryder whispered. Then he fell asleep after watching her breathe for an hour.

***

"Ryder," Francesca said with a hoarse voice, startling him awake.

He opened his eyes and smiled at his beautiful girl. "Hey, sweetheart. How you feeling?"

"Sore and so thirsty. Can I have a drink of water?"

"Absolutely." He poured the cold water from a thermos, placed a straw in the cup, and sat on her bed as he assisted her to sit up and take a drink.

Francesca tried to mask the pain of moving, but it was too much. Her head felt like it was splitting in two. She grabbed her head, trying to contain the throbbing as she groaned. This was worse than her hangover after Gabriella's bachelorette party, and that day she had thought she was dying.

She felt the lump on her head. "Ouch, that hurts. What happened?"

"I want to talk to the doctor before we have that conversation. You have a fractured skull and a serious concussion. I don't want you upset. You need to heal; that's your number one priority."

That sounded very ominous and piqued her curiosity even more.

"Ryder, please, it hurts too much to think. If you don't tell me, I'll drive myself crazy trying to remember. Just tell me and save me a world of pain."

Ryder was torn. If he didn't tell her, trying to remember was going to cause her undue pain; but if he told her, she was going to be stressed out. It was a no-win situation.

Where was the damn doctor?

Right on cue, the doctor pushed through the door. "Good morning, Miss Moratti. I am Dr. Talbot. How are you feeling this morning?"

"My head is killing me. Ryder just explained that I have a fractured skull and a concussion, but he won't tell me how it happened. Care to shed some light?"

Dr. Talbot approached Francesca and took out his stethoscope to listen to her heart. "Give me a minute to check you over, and then we will discuss your accident." He listened to her heart, checked her ears for blood, looked at her wound, and then pried her swollen eye open. After checking her pupils for dilation, he gently prodded her head, knowing he was causing her pain but needing to confirm there was no fluid collecting. When she flinched for the fourth time, he apologized. "Sorry, Miss Moratti." Then the doctor slung his stethoscope around his neck and looked at her. "Okay, everything looks good. I have no problem with your friend telling you what happened—"

"Boyfriend," Ryder butted in, and Francesca rolled her eyes.

Dr. Talbot chuckled. "I have no problem with your boyfriend telling you what happened, but if you become upset and I have to sedate you, it will prolong your recovery. I will be forced to keep you in the hospital longer. I can't express enough the seriousness of your situation. Head injuries can go one of two ways. If you follow all my instructions to the letter, you will heal, given time. If you choose to ignore my warnings, you could cause permanent damage, and you most certainly will be plagued with severe headaches for the rest of your life.

"When I release you, I will be revoking your driver's license for a period of two weeks. No TV, no reading, no computer or tablets, and I want you to stay out of direct sunlight. I don't want your brain

362

stimulated. I want it to rest and heal. Now, with the information I have given, you can make an educated decision whether you need to know how the accident happened."

Francesca absorbed his warnings, but her curiosity would not let her rest until she knew. She had to cope with whatever caused her accident and not freak out.

"I understand, Doctor, thank you very much"

"Don't worry, Doc; I'll make damn sure she does."

The doctor chuckled again. He was sure that was a battle she wasn't winning, no matter how tough she was.

"Good to hear. I will check on you tomorrow. Have a nice day." He walked out of the room.

Chapter 20

"Lost Boys" By Ruth B

Francesca turned gingerly towards Ryder, who was still sitting on her bed. "Okay, spill."

Ryder ran his hands over his face. He wasn't known for his subtlety, and he didn't want to upset her more than she already was going to be.

Just as he was about to start, one of the hospital employees entered with her breakfast tray.

"Moratti?"

"Yes, thank you. Will you just put it on the side table?"

The attendant placed the breakfast tray down and left.

"Okay, now tell me what happened."

He frowned as he looked at her. She was pale and bruised, and he could hear the weakness in her voice. "I want you to eat first. Then we'll talk." Ryder stood up and lifted the lid off her food, pushing the rolling table so it rested over her legs.

Francesca scrunched her nose. "Ew, I'm not eating that. I don't even know what it is."

"Francesca!" he hollered out.

Indignant, she said, "What? I'm not eating that stuff. You eat some first, and if you like it, then I'll try it."

Francesca was testing his patience. She needed to regain her strength.

Ryder stood up and went around the bed. He lifted the spoon and put the food in his mouth. Then he quickly grabbed a napkin and spit it out. Without saying a word, he took his phone out of his pocket and dialed.

"Hey, Frank."

"Son," he greeted. "Is Francesca awake?"

"Yeah, she is, and she's much better than yesterday. The doctor just left. She looks good. I'll tell you everything when you get here. Listen, I have a favour to ask. Will you stop at Tim Horton's and grab some bagels and coffee? The stuff here is disgusting. I wouldn't feed it to a dog."

Frank chuckled. "Not a problem."

"Thanks." He hung up and turned towards Francesca. "Your dad is bringing us breakfast. Rest until he gets here." He bent down to kiss her, and as he leaned in, she grabbed his hair.

Yanking him closer and straining her sore muscles, she inhaled a ragged breath. "You will tell me what happened now, or I'm kicking you out of here, and I will tell security you aren't allowed back in. Then I'm calling the centre. Julianna will tell me what's going on."

He looked at her angry face. "Seven fucking feet tall, Beauty. Only you have the guts to threaten me." He shook his head as much as he could in her grip. "You get stressed out, I stop. And I swear to you"— he pushed his face closer—"I will disconnect that phone and throw it out the goddamn window. Get me?"

She leaned forwards and kissed his lips. "Thank you."

With her look of satisfaction, Ryder knew she had worked him over.

He sat back down beside her on the bed and held her hand. "Do you remember anything about yesterday?"

Francesca leaned back against the pillows, getting comfortable. "No. The last thing I remember was Thursday night. Ryder, I can see that you're trying to figure out how to tell me, so please don't sugar coat it. I need to know the truth."

As nervous as he was, he told her the whole story. By the end, tears were leaking from her eyes.

"Please tell me Mason is okay. Have you talked to him? Can I call him and let him know I'm okay?"

He was apprehensive. "Beauty, Mason disappeared while I was looking after you."

Francesca's good eye popped open. "What do you mean, *he disappeared*?"

"Nobody's seen him since he hit you. It's my fault." Ryder was ashamed at how he had treated Mason. Francesca was going to be disappointed in him.

He played with her fingers, trying to think of how he could explain himself.

"Ryder, I know how much you love Mason. I'm sure it's not your fault."

Ryder didn't lift his head as he continued with the story. He was looking at his thumb rubbing circles on the top of her hand. "I couldn't think straight. I thought I was losing you. I couldn't comfort him. I failed him. The poor kid thinks this is all his fault. He thinks I blame him and hate him. I'm sorry."

Francesca was crushed for Mason, but she had to convince Ryder he wasn't responsible so he could focus on Mason.

"Ryder." He didn't lift his head, so she tried again. "Ryder, look at me."

He lifted his eyes to hers, expecting to see revulsion. What he saw reminded him of why this woman was the centre of his universe.

"Don't blame yourself. I don't blame you." She turned her hand so she could lace her fingers with his. "It's awful to see someone you love hurt. I know that. I experienced it with my mom and Tommy. I know that, when you're scared, you don't think clearly. Mason will forgive you; he doesn't hold grudges. Mason loves you. But you must go find him and talk to him. Don't let the police find him. They don't understand him like you do. This needs to come from someone who loves him. I would go myself if I could, but I know there's not a chance in hell you or my family are going to let me."

"You're damn right about that. Francesca, you could have died. I couldn't breathe until I knew you would be okay." That damn lump was back. Ryder swallowed twice, trying to get out his next words. "I can't lose you, Francesca. There's no going back for me. I wouldn't want to live without you. My whole damn world is wrapped up in a tiny, little package with a seven-foot personality. I didn't start living until I met you. I love you, heart and soul." He bent over and kissed her gently, trying not to add anymore pain when all he wanted to do was consume her. He wanted to crawl into her bed, wrap her in his arms, and never let go.

"Oh, for Christ's sake, do we need to chisel the dating rules in stone or tattoo it to your forehead?" Lucky chuckled as her family walked into the room.

Ryder snarled at the interruption.

"Ah, man, not again." Sal smacked his own forehead.

"Good morning, bambolina. How's my baby girl today?" Frank asked, putting the coffee and food on the rolling table. "Ryder, did you sleep last night?"

Astonished, Francesca looked at Ryder. "Did you sleep here?"

"Yes, and I'll stay here every night until you come home." Turning to Francesca's father, he addressed the man, "So damn

368

relieved she's going to be okay."

Ryder moved out of the way so her father and brothers could kiss Francesca. Then he carried the hospital tray to the windowsill before removing a bagel from the bag and moving the rolling table back in front of Francesca.

"Eat now," he commanded.

She looked at him, seeing the determination in his scowl. "I'll eat if you do. After you eat, you can go look for Mason."

"Francesca," he growled. "I'm not leaving you. They have a search party looking for him."

"What if Mason is hurt somewhere or scared? The nurses will take care of me." She was ready to do anything she needed to get him to agree to find her boy.

Ryder wasn't budging. "I could have lost you yesterday. I'm terrified to let you out of my sight."

Francesca understood his fear. It had scared her, too. She was on the mend now, though, something she couldn't say the same about Mason.

"Ryder, I'm not asking; I'm telling. Neither one of us will rest until he's found. I'm fine here by myself. He needs you. It's so cold out there, and he is all alone." She started to cry. "Please, please, Ryder. You heard the doctor; no TV, reading, or stress. If you go, I can relax and sleep, knowing we are doing everything in our power to find Mason."

Francesca's tears were like a knife to Ryder's heart. He was torn, wanting to do whatever she asked, but not wanting to leave her. The dilemma was ripping him apart.

"I'll stay with Francesca," Frank promised. "If he's not found today, I'll come every day until he is. Go look for Mason. If you don't find him by six tonight, go home, shower and change. When you're done, come back here with some dinner for my daughter and yourself. You can stay the night with her and search again tomorrow. Sal will bring us lunch. I want Francesca to get better, and she isn't going to do that if she's worried."

Ryder looked at Frank. The man truly was a saint. "How many times am I going to be indebted to you?"

"Papa, you don't need to stay. Really, I'm fine," Francesca cut in.

"I know you are, but Ryder isn't. I'm doing this for him, and for myself. Nothing would make me happier than spending time with my only daughter. Now compromise and give Ryder some peace of mind while he searches for Mason."

Lucky, Sal, and Ryder all made noises at the same time to indicate they didn't think Francesca capable of compromising on anything when she set her mind to something.

"I heard that!" Francesca leered at them with her one good eye.

Sal broke out in laughter. "Bro, she has you wrapped around her little finger, and she plays you like a fiddle."

370

Ryder headed out to the command post. As soon as he arrived, he saw at least a hundred volunteers, plus an army of police.

Dakota, Jocelyn, Zara, and Taya spotted him and ran up to him.

"How is Francesca?" Taya asked.

"She's in a lot of pain, but she kicked me out of the hospital until Mason is found."

Dakota smiled. "That sounds like our Frankie. After she didn't show up at Caesar Friday, and she didn't answer her cell phone, we tried you. You didn't answer, so we called Frank. He told us what happened and assured us that you were staying at the hospital with her, and that she would be sleeping until morning. So instead of sitting around, watching her sleep, we did the only thing we knew would help her and started searching for Mason."

Ryder knew how close the girls were, but he was astounded at how intuitive the group was when it came to their friend.

"You chicks are amazing. That's exactly what she would have wanted." The lump was back in his throat as he said, "she scared the shit out of me yesterday. She has a hairline skull fracture and a bad concussion. Her dad is with her. I apologize I didn't call you girls. I guess I'm not very good in these situations."

Taya, who very rarely touched anyone, placed her hand on the sleeve of his jacket. "Don't apologize, Ryder. We understand. It's hard to watch the ones we love suffer. We'll visit her as soon as we find Mason."

"Thank you." Misty-eyed, he looked away, thankful he had his sunglasses.

Jocelyn redirected his thoughts. "We searched until eleven last night, but no sign of Mason. The police are going door to door, while the volunteers search everywhere else. We've been broken up into groups, and grid patterns have been set up for the area. Some are searching the plazas, and others are searching the parks and fields in the area."

Ryder ran his hands through his hair. "Did you know the police had a news conference about an hour ago?"

"Yeah, the centre called and prepared us," Zara answered. "I know you care for him, but Ryder, it's for the best. That way, if someone spots him, they can alert one of us who knows him to help bring him in. It sounds harsh, but it's safer for everyone, especially Mason."

Even though he knew she was right, it still irritated him. "Then what happens to him once we find him?"

"They will take him to the hospital, and if his health is good, they will admit him for a two-week psych evaluation," Mariana answered. The group had been so engrossed in their conversation, they had neglected to see Mariana and Julianna joining their conversation. "Then Children's Aid, the police, his group home, case worker, and the centre will formulate a plan. This is a very serious situation. The Ministry of Labour is involved, and the centre could be charged."

Ryder was infuriated. "Francesca didn't do anything wrong!"

Mariana held her ground. "Not charges against Francesca. Charges against Reach Within. We have to prove we did everything in our power to protect our employee."

Hearing Francesca was not being charged didn't ease his anger.

"That's bullshit, and you know it, Mariana. Nobody could have predicted that Mason would go off like that. If I had any indication, I would have been right by his side. Do they want to go back to the nineteen-fifties when we locked people up with special needs and pretended they didn't exist?"

Mariana smiled from ear-to-ear. "Mr. Vaughn, if we could convert you, then maybe there is hope. Now, let's go find our boy."

***

The four girls and Ryder had been walking for four hours through the park they had been assigned to search. They stood arm's length apart from each other, yelling out Mason's name every few minutes. They talked endlessly about Mason's habits and conversations Ryder had with him, trying to think of any place he might hide out. The fact that there were no sightings of him was daunting, but they also hadn't found a body, and that was encouraging.

Zara was freezing, even with two pairs of mittens on. Jocelyn had reported it was minus four degrees Celsius, which they had to convert to twenty-five degrees Fahrenheit for Ryder.

He was starting to lose hope. How could a boy with no street smarts survive in these temperatures with no shelter, food, or water?

They looked along the banks of a creek, behind and around trees in the park, sheds the maintenance crews used to store equipment. They searched the community centre from top to bottom, in changing rooms, the boiler room, offices, sports equipment rooms, the gym, and of course the bottom of the pool, praying he hadn't fallen in and drowned.

They stopped to have lunch after they confirmed he wasn't in the park or the community centre. They all knew the same area would have to be checked again in a few hours in case Mason was evading them, and then dodging back in. Ryder continued to hope that Mason was that clever, and that he was one step ahead of them.

When they started out to the next location, Ryder confessed his crime in Mason's disappearance.

Dakota stopped with her mouth hanging open. "Ryder, this burden isn't yours to carry. It's the nature of the beast. You haven't been educated on developmentally delayed children enough to understand that, most likely, whether you yelled at him or not, he would have run."

"That's right, Ryder. Fight or flight is instinctual with these children," Taya added. "It's a basic animal instinct. The centre is full of kids and adults who are considered runners. That's why we let the kids have a safe environment to have meltdowns, because nine times out of ten, they would run if we couldn't provide that."

"Francesca told us on our trip that the first thing she taught you was not to take things personally. This isn't about you. This is about Mason, and how his undeveloped mind sees things. He's been doing really well lately, but those milestones will never lead to changing who he is. You know better than anyone that the smallest thing can set him off. You've made a difference in his life, and that is huge to a kid like him; but Ryder, you will never cure him. This is the existence he will lead for the rest of his life." Zara hoped she hadn't offended him, but she knew he needed a reality check.

They continued to walk for a while as Ryder mulled over everything they had said. Each one of them had a specialty in their field they offered to the clients at the centre. Yet they were more than that. They were like parents, friends, teachers, social workers, psychologists, therapists, and nurses all wrapped into one person. It was not a job for them; it was a calling.

Ryder stopped, and each of the girls did, too.

"I want you girls to know that I have the utmost respect for you. All of you are kind, compassionate, and extremely intelligent. The world is a better place because of you. Thank you for helping me get through this."

"Dieu, Ryder, I think I'm falling in love with you. Somebody better warn Francesca. I just might have to fight her for you." Dakota smiled as she hugged him.

He chuckled with embarrassment. "As much as I respect you, there is only one woman for me. And I love her."

Taya pretended to put two fingers down her throat. "Gag me." After everyone laughed, she said, "Let's get going. We have a lot of ground to cover."

***

It was Sunday afternoon, and the search was now in its forty-eighth hour. They were all getting discouraged when Dakota said what they all knew.

"We've checked this school a dozen times. I liked it better when we used to bring the kids here for drama classes."

Ryder was instantly interested. "What do you mean, you used to bring them here?"

"I thought it would be a good experience for the kids to have interactive play therapy," Dakota answered. "We didn't have the resources for drama equipment, like costumes and sets, so I contacted the principal at this school, and he said we could use their drama room in one of those portables for an hour and a half, twice a week. Unfortunately, their enrollment went down this year and their drama program was cut. Such a waste. I'm sure that portable is still full of all that great stuff."

"Yeah, remember Frankie talked nonstop about acting out

Pirates of the Caribbean and *Peter Pan* at every Caesar Friday for a month," Zara commented. "I think she liked it more than the kids."

Ryder smiled, envisioning Francesca playing Tinker Bell and Mason being *Peter Pan*. That triggered a memory of a conversation Ryder had with Mason on Christmas Eve.

"One day, I'm going to run away, and no one will be able to find me. I'm going to find somewhere to fit in, like the lost boys in Peter Pan."

"Ryder, what are you thinking?" Jocelyn asked, seeing the wheels turning in his mind.

"I might know where he is. It's just a hunch, but it's worth a try."

"Where?" Taya asked.

He didn't answer. Instead, he turned to Dakota, urgency flooding through his veins. "Which portable was it? Show me."

Dakota pointed to the end portable, and Ryder very quietly walked the perimeter. The portable sat on blocks of cement with metal skirting around the whole base. Ryder bent down and saw the skirting was broken in one corner. He pulled back on it and saw that someone could easily crawl underneath.

Just as he rose from the structure, he saw the custodian come out of the main building.

Ryder jogged over to him. "Excuse me. I'm with the search party for the missing kid. Do you have a key for the end portable?"

"Yeah, but he can't be in there," the custodian answered. "We check to make sure they are locked every morning and evening. I checked myself this morning, and every volunteer has tried the doors and windows. There's no way that kid got in there."

"Can I just look?"

"Sure." The guy shrugged, handing him the keys.

Ryder walked back to the women and encouraged the custodian to stand aside. When he was ready, he wanted them to cover each side of the structure in case Mason slipped through.

Ever so quietly, he went up the three steps to the door. He gently inserted the key and turned the handle. He couldn't cover up the sound the door made when he opened it, or the rush of cold air.

Ryder walked in and closed the door. It was dark with the curtains closed.

Quietly, he listened, and then called out, "Mason, it's Ryder."

Nothing.

"Mason, I'm so sorry, buddy. What I did to you was wrong, and I want to explain. You should never move a person with a head injury; that's why I yelled at you not to touch Francesca. I don't blame you. I just didn't want her moved.

"Buddy, Francesca's in the hospital, but the doctors say she's going to be okay. She misses you, and she told me to tell you she loves you. Remember when you told me Francesca would forgive me at Christmas? You were right; she did. And, buddy, she forgave you the minute she woke up."

When he still didn't get a response, he tried a new tactic.

"Mason, Frankie will never forgive me if I don't bring you back."

Mason instantly started to cry as he blubbered out, "Her name is Francesca!"

Ryder smiled with relief as he pushed the send button on his cell phone. "You're right, buddy. Mason, I'm really sorry. Can I sit with you awhile and talk?"

Ryder waited so long he was afraid Mason had either escaped, or wasn't intending to answer.

"Turn the light on, on your phone. I threw stuff all over the floor to let me know if someone came in. I don't want you breaking your transformer leg."

Ryder laughed. "Aw, Mason, I've missed you so much." He turned the light on, but still couldn't see Mason. "Where are you?"

"In the closet where they keep the costumes."

Ryder carefully manoeuvred around all types of things. As he moved a heavy cape off the door, he saw Mason sitting on the floor with tears and anger in his eyes. There was also junk food wrappers all around him, and he was using a desk lamp for a light.

"Hey, you mind if I sit? My leg is killing me. I walked for two days looking for you."

Mason waved his hand, indicating he could sit across from him, not beside him. It was obvious Mason wasn't letting him off the hook.

Ryder looked around. "So, is this what Neverland looks like? No fruit and vegetables, only junk food and no adults to piss you off?"

"Yeah, pretty cool, eh?" Mason's mask dropped as he wiped his tears away and smiled.

"Yeah, cool, but where did you get the junk food?" Ryder started counting the bags.

Mason was visibly proud as he answered, "On Friday, I saw the chip truck come to fill the machines in the high school. He dumped boxes of old chips in the dumpster. So, after everyone left, I crawled in there and grabbed a whole box. I also found half-finished bottles of water."

"Wow, you must be Peter Pan. No lost boy could have done that. You're very resourceful. How did you get in here?"

"You're right; I am Peter Pan, and I can't tell you how I got in. It's magic. You'll never guess in a million years, so don't even try. And if I'm Peter Pan, then I should give you some food. Do you want cheesies or chips?"

This kid was so smart. He had found food, water, and shelter, and he had also eluded the entire city for two and half days.

"I'm a cheesies man. I like when my fingers turn orange."

Mason's smile grew. "Me, too! That, and it pisses off the

workers at the group home when I wipe them on the couch."

Ryder smiled back. "Mason, we need to talk about what happened."

"I know." He lowered his eyes. "I fucked up, and I hurt Francesca. I didn't mean to. I was just so mad at those guys for scaring Veeta and calling me a retard."

"Mason, look at me. Everyone knows you made a mistake, and that you're sorry. But there are always consequences for our actions. The police have been looking for you, along with all the staff and lots of other people."

"Are they going to take me to jail for hurting Frank— Francesca?"

"No, buddy, but they do have to take you to the hospital, because you've been off your medication for three days, and they want to make sure you aren't hurt."

"I only scraped my side on the grate under the room when I crawled through the escape doo—Damn, I just told you my magic trick."

"Easy, buddy, your secret is safe with me." Ryder made an X sign over his heart. "Besides, if I do, you can tell everyone my secret about being a transformer. Deal?" Ryder leaned forwards and stuck out his fist to bump with Mason's.

"Bud, the police are outside. We should go out and meet them. I want you to know I'm here for you. Mrs. Ramara is going to the hospital with you, and Scott will meet you there. I want you to know I'm a phone call away, and you can call me any time. Officer Fitzpatrick and Officer Chang promised to take good care of you."

"You don't want to come with me?" There was pain written all over his face.

"You know I would if they allowed it, but you also know I'm not a real employee at the centre. I'll be at the centre when you come back. And I mean it, if you need me, you let Mrs. Ramara or Scott know, and they will contact me. Okay?"

"Okay." As he got up to stand, Ryder motioned him over. "What?"

"I need a favour first. Come and sit beside me. I want to take a selfie of us and send it to Francesca so she knows you're safe."

"Can I talk to her before they take me?" He looked so innocent when he asked.

"Sure, let's text her first." Mason moved beside Ryder, and they smiled with orange teeth. Ryder snapped the picture and showed Mason. "What do you want to say?"

"Tell her I'm sorry, and that I love her more than my video games."

Ryder chuckled as he wrote what Mason requested. Two minutes later, the response came.

Thank God, and yes please. :)

Ryder dialed the number and handed the phone to Mason.

"Frankie—I mean, Francesca, hi! ... Yes, I'm okay. How are you?" Mason's voice broke with a sob. "I'm so sorry. Frankie, don't cry, too. I'm okay." He rolled his eyes. "Yes, I'll see you soon ... I love you, too, Frankie." He hung up and handed the phone to Ryder. "I'm sorry I made her cry." Mason stood up, scared again.

Ryder beamed at Mason. "They are tears of joy. She's just relieved you are okay. Love you, bud."

Mason threw himself into Ryder's arms and hugged him tightly. "I love you, transformer man."

Ryder bellowed out a laugh as he walked Mason towards the group waiting outside.

Chapter 21

"With Arms Wide Open"

By Creed

The days turned into weeks, and weeks into months. The beginning of June was the beginning of the end of the school year and Ryder's sentence.

Life had proven to be more than Francesca could handle at times when Dakota had a life threatening accident in March, proving to all of them that life was fragile and often unpredictable.

When Francesca had come home from the hospital, Ryder was like a mother hen, smothering her to the point where she had threatened to stay with her father and brothers if he didn't let up.

Francesca had been more than ready to return to the centre after recuperating for three weeks. She had been switched to a medically dependent room that didn't have any behavioural students. The doctor and Ryder had both been adamant that she remain out of harm's way.

Francesca missed the kids in her classroom, but she had gotten

Mariana's assurance she could return in September if the doctor gave his okay. Mariana had also explained that, because she had knowledge of her and Ryder's relationship, they could no longer work together. After contacting Judge Belmore, Mariana took responsibility for writing the reports, as well as submitting them bi-weekly to the judge.

Mariana had suggested it would also be good for Mason to forge relationships with the other female staff in the room. Mason had not adjusted well to the switch or his new behaviour plan. He was angry and convinced they had moved Francesca because he had hurt her. It took Ryder bringing in the x-ray of Francesca's skull to convince Mason the hairline fracture caused her pain when things were too loud. He accepted the explanation after Ryder placed a blindfold over his eyes and made him listen to the noise in the room for fifteen minutes.

Edward came to town to support the girls during Dakota's crisis, furious no one thought to tell him about Francesca's accident.

Edward thought he recognized Ryder, and it took him less than forty-eight hours to figure it out. He had met Ryder's band when they had once played in England. Ryder asked Edward not to disclose his identity to the girls until his sentence was almost over, and Edward reluctantly agreed, knowing what it felt like to be judged for his lot in life, and not the man he was.

It had been a long week at the centre. Francesca and the girls were going to Pulcinella for Caesars, and Ryder was going to meet her later for dinner. Jocelyn had called to say she had a last-minute client and if they could wait until six. They decided to have a couple of drinks before Jocelyn arrived and to uber to the restaurant.

Francesca was the first to walk into the restaurant, and she nearly jumped out of her skin when everyone she loved yelled, "Surprise."

Ryder was standing in front with a bouquet of lilies of the valley and a huge-ass grin. "Happy birthday, Beauty."

Francesca was beet red as she walked into his arms. "I am going to kill you for this. My birthday isn't for another week!"

"It wouldn't have been a surprise if I waited. I know you hate to be the centre of attention, but everyone here is close to you. Nothing you can't handle." Ryder kissed her forehead, then released her so everyone else could greet her.

Francesca's father and brothers were the first to hug her. Then Maurizio, Paula, and then all the girls. Next was her friends from school. Surprisingly, Judge Belmore was there, too.

Francesca was floored when Ryder introduced her to four people she didn't know.

"Francesca, I want to you to meet my friends; Evan, his wife Melissa, Pete, and Kevin."

"So, you are the beauty we've heard so much about. How did a dirt bag like Ryder end up with such a gem?" Pete inquired.

"Don't start, or I will finish it." Ryder slugged him on the shoulder.

Melissa stepped forward and hugged Francesca. "Happy birthday, and welcome to our little family."

Francesca instantly fell in love with the beautiful blonde in front of her. "Thank you. I am honoured. Ryder talks so much about all of you. I'm happy to finally put faces to names."

Evan and Kevin were next to hug Francesca and thank her for making Ryder so happy. She was so touched by their words that she welled up.

Ryder hugged and kissed her. "No tears tonight, Beauty. Go and mingle with your guests while I talk to my friends."

"So, is it all set?" Ryder asked as Francesca moved out of ear shot.

Evan moved in closer. "Ted arranged everything. Our first pre-concert before the official tour kicks off in Italy. Rome being our first of five stops over three weeks' time. August, the U.S."

"You guys have no idea how much this means to me. Thank you." Ryder was so thrilled the guys had changed the timeline and added the Italy tour dates to accommodate when Francesca was scheduled to be in Italy.

"Oh, yeah," Melissa responded with sarcasm. "It was *so* hard to convince me to go with Evan to Italy for three weeks." She smiled brightly as she cuddled into her husband. "I should be thanking you."

"If Francesca represents the female population in Italy, I can't wait to see if I can find an Italian girl of my own," Kevin said.

"Anything for my brother," Pete said with sincerity, shocking the friends around him. "What? Don't look so shocked. Ryder means as much to me as you fuckers."

"You guys have always had my back. I haven't said it before, but I want you all to know, we may not be brothers by blood, but we are brothers." He pulled each man in for a hug and back slap, shocking them speechless.

Everyone was drinking and laughing and chatting away when suddenly the room became deathly quiet. Francesca moved around Judge Belmore and, to her absolute surprise, there stood Gabriella, Liam, Edward, and Gillian.

She squealed as Edward started to speak.

"Bugger, all you tramps didn't start without us, did you?"

Half the crowd couldn't believe their eyes. Gillian Wainwright and the Prince of England. Many were already questioning if Evan was famous, because Layla's boyfriend swore he was the lead singer of a band.

Francesca ran first into Gabriella's arms, and then Liam's, Gillian's, and lastly, Edward's.

Edward held her in his arms as he whispered, "Happy birthday, love. I thought I would take some of the attention away from you so you can relax and have a good time."

"You're the best, Edward. Love you!" she whispered, tucked into his embrace as he kissed her head.

The brothers broke out in laughter as a scowling Ryder wrestled Francesca away from Edward, telling Liam he had better watch his charge better. Then, once Francesca was tucked neatly under his arm, he greeted the group and thanked them all for coming.

Maurizio announced dinner was about to be served, and everyone found a seat. Once the glasses of champagne had been given to each person, Ryder stood.

"First, I want to thank all of you for coming and being a part of Francesca's birthday celebration. Maurizio, thank you for allowing me to host it here and for the amazing food. I'm not a man of many words. I just want to say"—he turned towards Francesca—"I love you, Francesca, and everyone is here because they also love you. So, raise your glass. To you, my beauty." He raised his glass and took a sip as people clapped. Then he kissed his girl quickly on the lips.

After the meal, a large cake was rolled out into the dining room. When Francesca saw it, she jumped up in panic, looking all over the restaurant.

"Not again. Where the heck is Edward?"

Gillian was in hysterics, knowing exactly why she was freaking out. "Relax, Francesca. I swear he just went to the bathroom."

"I'll go check. I don't trust the wee bastard, either." Liam got up and headed towards the bathroom.

When the two men came walking back into the room, Ryder decided it was safe, so he grabbed Francesca's hand and walked her towards the cake. After everyone sang "Happy Birthday," a music box with the figurines of Beauty and Beast dancing to the song, "Beauty and the Beast," rose out of the cake.

Francesca started to cry as she hugged Ryder. She would never have guessed the man was capable of such a romantic gesture.

"Thank you," she whispered into his chest.

Ryder clearly understood the words she couldn't say.

He cleared his throat as he spoke loudly. "I knew you would be uncomfortable with gifts, so I asked everyone to donate drama equipment for a room at the centre in your honour."

Maurizio came into the room, followed by three waiters, each pushing trolleys with boxes full of costumes and props.

Francesca placed her hands on her face and cried harder. It was the perfect gift. She was surrounded by the people she loved and blown away by their generosity.

When someone handed her a tissue, she wiped her eyes and looked at all the stuff people had brought. She kept looking at Ryder, thinking her man couldn't get any better.

Maurizio came in and whistled with two fingers, getting everyone's attention. "We forgot one." He placed a big, wrapped box on the table with a thud.

With shaky hands, Francesca opened the box to find a bunch of twisted metal. She quirked her head to the side and looked at Maurizio.

He pointed towards the dark window.

Ten seconds later, bright lights went on, and Francesca gasped, holding her shaking hands over her open mouth and shaking her head from side to side.

Ryder was beside her, pointing at the box. "That's your old one, so I can't return this one."

Francesca started to fall as her legs gave out, so Ryder scooped her up and started walking towards the door.

Once outside, Frank opened the door of a shiny red 2000 Z3 convertible with black interior. The car of her dreams had a big white bow on the top and plates that read, "*Beauty*."

When she could finally speak after he placed her in the driver's seat, she turned towards Ryder. "You didn't?"

"I did, and there's nothing you can do about it. I had your old car smashed—those are the pieces inside. This one is registered in your name, insured in your name, and plated in your name." He radiated with pride and love.

She looked at him and *whooped* to his absolute delight. "I *love* my damn car!"

***

Ryder lifted his head from between her legs, his mouth

glistening with her essences. "Let it ring, Beauty." Then he smiled as he realized he didn't need to say that because she was unaware of the world around her.

While she was coming down from her euphoric high, Ryder moved up the bed and leaned against the headboard, grabbing Francesca and turning her limp body as he lifted her over his lap. This had become their favourite position after realizing missionary was too difficult with the unevenness between his leg and stump.

She came back to the world of the living as he placed her knees on either side of his hips. She rose up, taking him into her hand and stroking his length a few times, spreading his pre-come. Ryder hissed at her touch and bucked his hips up.

Francesca looked into his lust-filled eyes as she positioned him at her core. They both groaned as she lowered herself with excruciating slowness, feeling every inch of his cock rubbing against every tight, textured muscles within her walls.

Ryder closed his eyes, relishing in the feel of her hips rotating while his erection was tightly sheathed.

The phone rang, and they ignored it. This moment in time was meant strictly for the two of them.

Francesca's head lulled to the side as his piercing dragged across her G-spot. She was covered in a sheen of sweat, a result of her last two orgasms.

Her back was softly arching and her breasts were calling out to him. Ryder licked his thumbs and circled the tight raspberry-coloured buds then blew lightly across the wet tips as she hissed out his name.

Ryder's fingers went back to circling and pinching her nipples, bringing her to newer heights. She bent forwards, placing her hands on his shoulders and preparing for the ride of her life. Once settled, she started to move with abandonment while Ryder moved his hands to her hips to help.

"No, Beast, I'm in control here." She squeezed the muscles in his shoulders to back up her statement.

He smirked. "You're the boss." He loosened his grip but held on, knowing she was going to get wild.

Over the last six months, Francesca had found her sexual prowess. She was such a lady until she crossed the threshold of the bedroom door. Then she transformed from Mary to Magdalene within mere steps.

Without dislodging from him, she pulled her legs out from under her so her feet rested on the mattress, then she rode him like an expert bull rider. She moved up while rotating her luscious hips, and then slammed down with enough force to make a slapping sound.

As much as he tried, he couldn't stay still, and raised his hips to buck right up to the entrance of her womb. She repeated up and down motions until he was ready to burst.

Feeling the sign that his body was getting ready for release, Francesca slowed down, not ready for the moment to end. She brought her hands to his jaw and leaned over, bringing her mouth to his and swallowing his groan of frustration. She licked his lips, tasting the sweat of his exertion. Then she dipped back in to attack his tongue and show dominance, all while lifting her hips up and slowly down, taunting and teasing his heightened state.

She had pushed too far and released the devil within him.

Ryder grabbed her hips as tightly as he could and repeatedly thrust for all he was worth. She screamed in ecstasy as she reached her pinnacle, and he jarred her forwards until her forehead fell into the crux of his neck, roaring with his completion.

She could feel the hot jets of his release bathe her inner core. When his body heaved with relief, she collapsed completely on top of him. They breathed heavily, trying to regain some air into their spent lungs.

The phone rang again.

"I swear, if that's your brothers, I'm going to wring their necks." Ryder huffed as he reached over to snatch the phone off the nightstand.

Francesca just giggled softly as he yelled into his phone, "What!"

His demeanour changed as he listened, and his body sprang to attention.

"When did it get released? Has Ted started damage control? Okay, let me get online; see what's been said. I'll get right back to you."

She lifted her head and looked at his stormy face. "Is everything okay?"

He could see she was nervous after picking up on his vibes. "That was Evan. I need to deal with an issue, and then we need to talk. I was hoping it could wait another week or two, but the decision has been taken out of my hands."

"Ryder, you're scaring me. Just tell me now."

Ryder cupped her warm face. "Do you trust me?" He stroked her face with his thumbs, willing her to say yes. He needed to know that she would accept this part of him.

She could read the uncertainty on his face, which freaked her out, but she did trust him.

"Of course. You know I do." She placed her hands on top of his. "Ryder, I want you to know … I can handle anything if you are by my side."

He sincerely hoped that would be the case.

They showered, got dressed, and then went into the kitchen, each lost in their own thoughts. The whole time she made breakfast, her stomach was in knots. Ryder was on his phone, sending and receiving texts and emails. As they sat down to eat, she prepared herself for the worst.

"I can't wait anymore. Spill now."

Ryder gathered her hands. "Francesca, I told you that I worked in California in the music industry with my friends, but I never told you what I did specifically. I wasn't trying to hide it ... What I do for a living is not who I am."

"O ... kay. So, what do you do?" She couldn't help feeling that this was the strangest conversation they had ever had. When Francesca's mind started to wander to bad things, she started to tremble.

Someone knocked at the door just as Ryder opened his mouth.

"Fuck, who the hell is that?"

Francesca got up from the table, equally as mad as Ryder. "I'll get rid of whoever it is."

When Francesca opened the door, a man and woman she had never met stood there.

"Um ... yes?"

"We are here to see Rolando. Is he here?" the man answered.

"I'm afraid you have the wrong address. There's no one here by that name." Francesca started to close the door, but the man placed his hand on the door to stop her.

Ryder walked up behind Francesca, and with a deep, threatening voice, asked, "What the hell are you two doing here?"

The older man's spine stiffened at Ryder's tone. "We need to talk." He pushed his way into Francesca's house, with the woman following in his wake, closing the door behind her.

"Are you fucked in the head? I said all I'm ever going to say to you two. Now get your sick, hate-filled asses away from my girl and out of our home. You're never to come here again." Ryder was beyond furious.

Francesca was scared, feeling the hatred pour off Ryder. Who could he hate this much?

The man's face scrunched up with uncontrollable rage. "Listen, boy, this can go one of two ways. You can hear us out and make a better offer, or we'll sell your story to the media who have been hounding us all morning for your history. You decide, gimp."

That answered Francesca's question.

She could feel Ryder's body shaking with unleashed fury.

Before Ryder could control his temper enough to move Francesca away from the two creatures without hurting her, Francesca exploded.

"How dare you force your way into our home and speak to your son like that! You don't have the right to breathe the same air as this man." She gestured towards Ryder, who was shocked silent by her explosion of rage.

Ryder had never in his life had someone stand up for him. The lump that seemed to appear every time he was surrounded by her unequivocal love stifled his response as he watched his tiny warrior go to battle with his past.

His father looked around the little hobble they called a home and, with hands fanned out, ignoring Francesca completely, he said to Ryder, "You are rich and famous beyond words, yet you call this a home?"

"You arrogant bastard!" Francesca spewed. "Things you purchase and own don't make a home. The people who love each other inside of it does. But you wouldn't know that, would you? You had the greatest gift of all … a child, and you tried to beat him down, but he was stronger than you. Ryder has a family now who respects and loves him unconditionally."

Francesca turned to the weak woman standing slightly behind her husband. "And you!" She pointed at the woman. "You I hate almost more than this bully. You gave birth to an innocent, little boy, and then stood by all those years and watched him get beaten physically and mentally. How did you feel when your son laid in a pool of his own blood at the hands of your husband? You are no mother. A mother protects her child and loves him; nurtures him through his childhood. She puts her own life in front of her flesh and blood. You are a sick and twisted bitch!"

Ryder's mother began to cry, yet Francesca couldn't muster a bit of sympathy for her.

Mr. Vargas, having no use for women, turned back to a silent Ryder. "What kind of man stands there and lets a woman talk for him? Where are your balls, boy?"

Shocking everyone, a lethal voice came from the entrance. "The type of man I am proud to call son."

They all turned to find the doorway filled by three very agitated men.

"Ryder is a man of strength and honour who doesn't need to raise a fist and beat those who are weaker to prove how much of a man he is," Frank continued. "Now, I suggest you remove yourselves from this home and get the hell out of here before I physically remove you."

Mr. Vargas stood his ground. "So, you decide to call him son after you learn he is famous and rich? How much does he pay you for that title?"

Frank's face relaxed as he guffawed his response, realizing the type of person he was dealing with. "You will never understand, and I won't waste my energy explaining it to you more than once. Ryder doesn't have to buy that title; he earned it. He gained my respect by being loving, kind, and standing up and protecting those he loves. He gives it freely and without conditions. He fights with integrity and courage for all of us he calls family. He learned to trust and is trustworthy; and that is why I am proud to call him my son.

"Be a real man for once in your life and walk away without a word. Go back to your pathetic, lonely existence and reap what you have sown." With a quick breath, he turned. "Lucky, Sal, remove the trash before I choke from the stench."

Mr. Vargas, stunned by his declaration, sneered back at Ryder, "You'll regret this, boy."

The two brothers quickly herded the dumbfounded couple out the door and down the steps. They waited until the Mercedes drove away before they ascended the stairs.

Frank approached Ryder. "Are you okay, son?"

Ryder was still tongue tied after listening to the love of his life and the man whom he respected more than anyone in the world defend him. He wanted to say something profound like they had just done, but his mind couldn't catch up with his heart.

Clearing his throat, he started, "Neither one of you will ever know what you did for me today. Nothing has ever struck a chord so deeply inside of me. I feel claimed and worthy, like I have truly found my place in the world. Thank you."

Francesca was bawling at his confession and threw herself into his arms.

Frank wiped away a stray tear. "I'm sorry you had to endure those people as long as you did. We'll make sure you always have us to support and love you like you deserve. You belong to us."

Chapter 22

"Everything I Do" By Bryan Adams

Francesca was right. One simple phone call had changed their lives.

Ryder waited for the brothers to come back up, and then he explained to all the Moratti's what had just transpired and why.

Lucky was giddy and star struck. "So, does this mean we get front row seats at your next concert?"

Before Ryder could answer, Sal sneered, "Don't think because you're famous that things have changed. She is your one and only. We are going to be even more vigilant with you now."

Ryder wasn't the least bit ticked off about Sal's threat or attitude. In fact, his respect for the man grew. Putting Francesca's happiness and well-being above all else was admirable in Ryder's book.

"I love your sister; that's never going to change. She is the only one for me. And, Lucky, you won't be in the front row. You'll be back stage with the rest of the families." He winked at Francesca.

She smiled, but it wasn't her usual smile that lit up the room, and Ryder's heart cramped up with fear that she might not accept this side of him.

"It doesn't matter to us what you do for a living, if you like what you do," Frank told Ryder.

Ryder didn't look at Frank, he kept his focus on Francesca. "I do like what I do, but I love you more. I would give it up in a second if you're the least bit uncomfortable with it. Francesca, say the word, and I'm done. I won't lose you over my job."

"I would never ask you to give up something you love so you can be with me." Francesca was overwhelmed with all she had heard, and his words had struck so deeply it took her breath away. "It's how you make a living. It's not just a job; it's your life. I'm just not sure how I fit into it anymore."

Ryder bent down in front of her as quickly as he could with his prosthetic leg, clasping her tiny hands in his. "You don't fit into my life. You *are* my life. We'll work this out, I promise. Just give me time to work out the logistics." He released her hands and pulled her mouth to his lips for a gentle, reassuring kiss.

She kissed him back, but not with the same confidence she had before, and he felt it deep in his soul. He knew he had to get it all out so she knew everything.

He awkwardly stood, pulling his chair in front of hers and

placing his hands on her thighs. "I don't need to work anymore. When the band first started making good money, Evan's father insisted we didn't blow it all. He made us go to a financial advisor to invest some of our money. That way, if the success ever ended, we would be financially set.

"The guys and I invested in different things, but we got lucky with a little company that was just starting out, like us—some social media thing with pictures. Anyway, the company took off and grew to a billion-dollar company. We sold our shares after they went public, and along with the income we make performing, we never have to work again. So, don't think it will hurt me financially. I meant what I said. Say the word, Beauty, and I walk with no regrets. I don't want to lose this life we have created together."

Francesca was tied up in knots. His confession did nothing to alleviate her fears. Why couldn't he just be a normal person, with a normal job? She knew she wasn't girlfriend material for a rich superstar. She would embarrass him. She was too shy and self-conscious. The media would eat her alive. Ryder was going to figure that out when he returned to the band in a few weeks.

She was having trouble breathing. It felt like she had a two-ton weight on her chest. She wasn't sure how she would survive watching groupies crawl all over the love of her life. She knew it would kill her if Ryder left her for someone else.

"I guess I'm just overwhelmed. I need some time to think

alone." She saw the defeat on his face as she broke the hold he had on her. "I'm going for a drive. I'll be back in a while."

Ryder panicked. "No, you're not leaving me. Talk to me, please. We can work this out, I swear."

Francesca turned away from him, lost and confused. She didn't want to hurt Ryder any more than he had been, but she was suffocating from fear and worry, desperate to get away from everyone.

"I'm so sorry, but I have to go." She grabbed her coat and purse, and ran out the door.

"No, Francesca, please—"

The door slammed, and Ryder moved to go after her, but Frank grabbed his arm.

Ryder turned with a look of betrayal written all over his face.

"Son, let her go. Give her some time. She'll come back to you; I'm sure of it. If you don't, she will withdraw and do something rash. Francesca is a smart girl, but she has never felt or seen her own strength or beauty. That's one of the things that makes her who she is. She's just afraid she won't measure up to your life. Give her time to find her inner strength to fight for what she believes in. Let her remember what you mean to each other and the support you gain from one another. Have faith in her and your love."

Ryder rubbed his chest, convinced the pain was a heart attack from his fractured soul. "What if I lose her?"

"Then you never really had her. And you don't believe that, do you, Ryder?" Frank said sadly.

He hung his head. "No, I know she loves me, heart and soul."

"Then put your trust in that, and give her space and time to come back to you, and accept all that you are."

***

Francesca drove for four and half hours, listening to Ryder's band Fornication. She wasn't a fan of heavy metal music, and sweet Jesus, there was so much swearing. Songs about women's body parts and having sex. She wondered if Ryder wrote any of them and about who? There were a few slow songs, and she was sure Ryder was singing with his deep raspy voice. It didn't sound like Evan. Those songs made her cry.

How could she date a famous rock star and not even like most of his music? What kind of loser was she that she couldn't appreciate something that made thousands of people worship him?

Francesca remembered all the conversations they had about music. She felt like a fool for telling him that rock bands didn't care about lyrics, and that they were more interested in the instrumental rifts.

The next song was about tying a girl up and having sex. Was that what Ryder wanted? Did he want to tie her up but was afraid to ask for fear of her reaction? Had he been stifled sexually because of her? He must have been so frustrated being with a virgin. Ryder could have any woman in the world; why would he want her? Even if he wanted her now, how long would it last before he became bored and moved on to more exciting women? She asked herself a million questions with no answers.

She surprised herself when she ended up in Windsor, Ontario, at the American border. Luckily, she didn't have her passport on her; otherwise, she wasn't sure where she would have driven to.

The sun was low in the sky when she realized she hadn't eaten all day, so she pulled into a nice restaurant attached to a motel. She was seated by the hostess, her stomach still in knots yet grumbling. She knew if she didn't eat, she would get a pounding headache, so she quickly looked at the menu and ordered the first thing she saw with a glass of wine.

While she waited for her food, her mind wandered again. Francesca couldn't believe it was just yesterday when she had been celebrating her birthday and Ryder had given her a car. And not just any car, but the car of her dreams. All those months she had made him drive in her old junker. She knew he hated it. He was used to the lap of luxury. No wonder he had replaced all of her outdated furniture.

She cringed when she thought of the stupid gremlin bells she had bought him. They had cost her a few hundred dollars compared to the thousands he had spent on her. He praised her food, but she would bet her last dollar that he had eaten at restaurants all over the world with famous chefs. She could cook, but not to the caliber he was used to. Francesca was driving herself crazy. She had to stop.

While she took a sip of her wine, she glanced at all the couples laughing and talking, holding hands and enjoying each other's company. She wondered why her life couldn't be that simple.

Now that Ryder's identity was splashed all over the newspapers, they could never come to a place like this and have a simple date. He would be recognized, and they would never have a minute of peace.

Francesca's phoned beeped. She took it out of her purse and saw that Ryder had texted her once and her papa four times. Edward and Dakota had also texted, but she would deal with them tomorrow.

Opening the texts, she saw that both men were worried, wanting to know if she was okay. She couldn't deal with Ryder yet, so she texted her papa, telling him she was fine, and that she was spending the night at a motel. She also asked if he would contact Ryder and let him know she was safe and that she loved him. Then Francesca slowly ate her dinner, mulling over all her fears.

After her third glass of wine, she decided to check into the motel.

Once she settled in the room, she took her phone out and found a list of songs she had compiled. It was created from pages of lyrics Ryder was always leaving for her. She started to listen to each song, word for word. They spoke of deep feelings of love and some of fear associated with love.

Francesca didn't know what to do or how to feel. She loved Ryder more than she believed she was capable, but she was uncertain if their love was strong enough.

She eventually fell asleep atop the bedspread, a tissue box within reach. Then she was startled awake by a knock at the door.

At first, she couldn't figure out where she was, and then it all came rushing back. Another knock at the door, she figured it must be the maids, having no idea what time it was.

Francesca moved with apprehension towards the door, surprised when she opened it and saw who it was.

"Edward, what are you doing here? How did you find me?"

"Hello to you, too, love. I'm fine, thank you for asking." Edward walked right in and removed his coat.

"Sorry, how rude. Hello. How are you? Now what are you doing here?"

"Why else would I come to a motel? To get starkers with you, of course." He laughed.

She furrowed her eyebrows. "What's starkers?"

"It means to get naked." He laughed at his own joke. "Sorry, love, just some bad British humour. I came because I think my friend needs a shoulder and some advice from a wise man. And I am just the bloke to give it to her."

Francesca deflated, realizing he knew the truth about Ryder's identity. "I'm so confused. Did you see the news reports? They have a video of you and Gillian from my birthday party. I'm so sorry. I know how you covet your privacy."

Edward took her hand and led her to the bed to sit. Then he pulled out a chair from the desk and faced her. "Frankie, I don't give a rat's ass about me. I'm worried about you, and how you are handling all this. I have known about Ryder since March. He asked me to keep his confidence with good reason, and I respected that. I didn't mean to keep you in the dark, but it wasn't my secret to reveal. And to tell you the truth, I totally understand why he did it."

Frustrated with his comment, she began to pace, wringing her hands and trying to find the right words.

"Edward, I love Ryder, but I don't understand why he kept it from me. For God's sake, we share a bed; why did he lie?"

Edward stood up. "He didn't really lie, did he?"

"No, not really, but he didn't tell me the whole truth, either. In my book, that's just the same." Her eyes filled with tears.

"Darling, he did that to protect himself. You have no idea what it's like when people assume they know you because of what they read. That is an illusion of who they want us to be. He wanted you to know the real Ryder, not his image." Edward pointed at himself. "People assume they know me all the time. They don't. They know the illusion of Edward, the Prince of Arlington. They have no idea about the man I truly am—my fears, my failures, what makes me happy or sad, or that I fluff and blame it on other people."

She giggled through her tears. "I assume that fluff means fart?"

He grinned, and then became serious. "My point is, nobody has a right to be judged for their persona. You are going to learn that soon enough, because the press is digging into your life. They want to know all about the mysterious woman who captured the heart of the elusive Ry Herr. Francesca, Ry is a character Ryder created to do what he loves without giving away who he is. Does that make any sense to you?"

"I think so, but Edward, it changes everything. I'm not some model. I am plain Jane. I'm not super smart, and I'm beyond broke. I have nothing to offer a man like Ryder. I can't compete. How will I ever be able to keep him interested in me with all those gorgeous women throwing themselves at him?"

Aggravated beyond words, Edward lashed out. "You're right; you're not that smart if that's what you believe. I can't believe you just said that. It's one thing to be insecure—we are all insecure about ourselves, famous or not—but it's another to assume that, because he is famous, he would consider cheating on you, or that you aren't enough woman for him. Maybe you shouldn't be with him if you think he would jeopardize the love you both have for a quick shag."

Francesca normally spoke with her hands, moving as fast as her mouth. Now, though, she was even more exaggerated, getting frustrated that Edward didn't understand.

She slapped her chest with an open hand as she cried out, "I can't be something that I'm not! He must realize that I'm a simple girl. I don't want to live like the rich and famous, and never will. I won't fit into his world.

"I want to support his career, but honestly, I don't even like his music. I freeze up when I meet someone new—how long did it take me to get comfortable with you? Can you imagine how embarrassing it will be for him when he introduces me to other famous people?" Francesca threw her arms in the air. "I was never interested in famous people. I didn't have time like other girls my age. I was cooking and cleaning, and looking after my dying family members. If he introduced me to Mick Jagger, I wouldn't know that he wasn't Justin Timberlake. I was a sheltered, little virgin when I met Ry—" Her hand flew over her mouth at her disclosure.

She started to sob harder, breaking Edward's heart as she blubbered through her next sentence. "You see? I don't think before I speak! I embarrass myself." She finished on a gut-wrenching sob.

Edward started yelling at her, beyond angry. "For all the king's men, has he ever not made you feel like you were the most important person in the world? Has he ever not supported you? Has he ever made you feel ugly or unworthy? Francesca, the man is and always will be absolutely head-over-heels in love with you!"

They both jumped when someone started pounding on the door.

"Francesca!" Ryder roared. "Edward, open the fucking door."

Edward calmly walked to the door and opened it, coming face-to-face with an enraged Ryder and a very pissed off Liam.

How did these people find her?

Ryder charged in, grabbing Edward by the scruff of his shirt and pinning the prince to the wall. Liam was on Ryder like white on rice, but to no avail. Meanwhile, Francesca was beside herself with terror.

In a deadly lethal voice, Ryder growled out, "I don't give a shit if there are three or thirty guards out there, if I hear you speak to Francesca like that again, I'm going to rearrange that pretty fucking face of yours. You get me, *Prince* Edward?" He thumped the prince against the wall once last time.

Ignoring Ryder's threat, Edward turned towards Francesca with a huge-ass grin on his face. "Point in case. The Neanderthal would risk his life for you. It's a gift to be loved like that. Don't throw it away because of your insecurities. I love you, Frankie, but you need to be the woman he is defending."

Ryder released an amused Edward and gave him a murderous glare as Edward walked away from him like he didn't have a care in the world. Then Ryder stomped towards Francesca and yanked her up into his arms, placing a protective hand against her head and holding her close to his pounding chest.

"I don't care if he has the whole British army behind him, nobody talks to you like that," he said ever so softly.

Francesca softly cried against his chest. "It's my fault. Don't be mad at Edward. He's right; I am a fool. Now I've caused even more problems." She pulled herself back from Ryder, wiping her nose on her sleeve. "Edward, I'm sorry. I didn't want you to get caught up in the middle of my drama. Liam, please don't be mad at Ryder. It's my fault. I apologize. Please don't hold it against him."

"Don't worry about it, lass. The wee bastard has a way of pissing people off." Liam instantly abolished any guilt she felt. "Usually, it's me trying to throttle him, and Gabriella holding me back."

Francesca regained her composure. "How did you find me?"

Edward smirked. "There are some advantages to being rich and famous." He winked at her before heading towards the door. "Well, mates, there is never a dull moment around my gaggle of girls. I'll see you both at six p.m. for Caesars at Zara's before our flight leaves tonight. Cheerio. And, Francesca, heed my words."

Edward and Liam left the room and closed the door behind them. Then it was so quiet in the room you could have heard a pin drop.

Francesca wrapped her arms around her waist in a protective stance, trying to keep herself isolated for their conversation. She knew if she let Ryder touch her, it would be game over. She would crumble and do anything he asked. Meanwhile, Ryder was devastated, thinking she was terrified he would physically hurt her after his attack on Edward.

"Francesca ... Please, Beauty, tell me you aren't afraid me, and that you know I would never hurt you."

She lowered her head, ashamed she had made him feel that way after all the physical abuse he had endured as a child. "No, Ryder, I know you would never lay a hand on me. I just need to think clearly, and I can't do that wrapped up in your arms."

"Why? Do you think I don't care what you say or how you feel? That I only care about my own perspective?" Ryder was crushed Francesca felt like he would try to manipulate her.

She stomped her foot in frustration. "God, no! Ryder, I love you, and you have always made me feel important. I don't trust myself. I'm so weak, and I need to do what is right for both of us." She took a deep breath then let it out. "Ryder, I have to let you go."

"Baby, you can't leave me. I have … I didn't think I was capable of loving someone or being loved, or worthy enough for it. Please don't take away the best thing that's ever happened to me. I would rather be dead."

"Please don't say that. I can't imagine a world without you. I just don't want to change your life, or for you to change who you are because of me."

He desperately wanted to reach out to her. His desperation was off the charts, and he was losing control, knowing if he couldn't convince her, she would leave him for good. He choked out his convictions with one last desperate plea.

"I had no life before I met you. I just existed. I hated the man I was. I had no real relationships, no family. My life changed when I met you. It did, Francesca. It changed for the better. I am proud of the man I have become. I was reborn when we met. Beauty, you opened my eyes and brought colour into the world. I don't just exist anymore. I make a difference in people's lives. I learned to accept my disability. And I can finally look in the mirror and not cringe at the sight of myself. You taught me how to be compassionate, and that gave me strength to help the kids at the centre.

"Before I met you, I didn't dream about having a happy life. I had no clue it existed. You gave me that. Now I have a real father and two dumbass brothers who drive me to the brink of insanity. But I love them, and I learn from them every day how to be a better man.

"You think you don't measure up to my life. You're wrong. Trust me; I know because I have never measured up to anyone until I met you. Now I believe I am finally worthy and have everything I could possibly want. I finally realized I have a heart ... just to have it ripped out." Ryder pounded his chest over his heart. "Fuck! I'm about to lose everything I love, and I can't do a damn thing to stop it!"

The giant man fell to his knees with his hands covering his face as he cried. He hadn't even cried when his father had nearly beaten him to death. Then he got deathly quiet. Ryder was done. There was nothing left to say.

God help her, Francesca broke the strongest man she had ever met. She was worse than his parents. He had offered her everything, and she had rejected him. She had been so selfish.

"What have I done!" She ran towards him and cradled the shattered beast in her arms, kissing the top of his head while she rocked him. "I am so sorry, Ryder. Please forgive me." She was crying so hard, while he wasn't responding. She drove the beast back into his protective mode where no one could hurt him. "I was blindsided; afraid I would hold you back. I was convinced I wasn't good enough for you; afraid you would leave me. I hurt you before you could hurt me." Francesca crumbled, unable to face what she had done. "I am the one not worthy of your love. I don't deserve it. I'm sorry."

After ten minutes of silence, Francesca realized he wasn't coming back to her, so she stood and gathered her things while quietly sobbing.

"I will never love anyone the way I love you. I hope one day you can forgive me." She opened the door, tears cascading down her cheeks, and walked out into the cold.

She was desperately trying to get her key into the car lock, crying and frustrated as she dropped them. She bent down to retrieve them when she slipped and fell, landing on the ground where she convulsed with tears and a broken heart. Her strength was gone; her will shattered.

When Ryder snapped out of it, he didn't know how much time

had passed. He had cracked when he thought he had lost her, going into the dark place inside his mind that he hadn't visited in over eighteen years. However, as her words continued to replay in his mind, they slowly coaxed him back into the light. He couldn't remember everything she had said, but he did remember her pleading for forgiveness and saying she loved him. That was enough for now.

He should have been patient like Frank had asked, instead of backing her into a corner. She could run, but he would track her down to the ends of the earth. He needed to fight for the purest soul he had encountered.

When he rushed out the door, his heart dropped at finding his beauty curled up in ball on the cold ground, silently crying.

He cautiously walked up to her and bent over to pick up his other half. He cradled her gently in his arms, as if she were a small child as he walked back into the room.

Holding her in one arm, he pulled the sheets back and placed her on the bed. She didn't say a word as he ever so gently removed all her clothing.

She was shivering and her teeth were chattering as he quickly shed all his clothing. He didn't take the time to remove his prosthetic leg as he crawled in beside her. Turning, he then enveloped her into his warmth, nuzzling her neck as he made his way to her mouth.

As he consumed her mouth, all the gentleness seeped away,

replaced by the frenzied passion of two souls banding together as one. No words were needed. No words were spoken. They let the hunger and rawness of the act speak volumes. Forgiveness was given and accepted without a word exchanged. Both knew home was in each other's arms. The rest would work itself out.

Chapter 23

"Time of My Life" By David Cook

The staff at the centre threw Ryder a going away party two days before school ended. His kids surprised him when they got up on stage and sang one of his band's tamer songs. Mason played the drums, one of the male teachers played the guitar, Taz played the bells, and the girls shook tambourines, while Theo belted out the lyrics, to the amusement of everyone standing there. Ryder was so proud of all his kids.

Then Ryder was blown away when Julianna told him the kids had gifts for him. She explained to everyone that they had let each of his kids decide what they wanted to give him. The results were awe-inspiring.

Veeta limped slowly up to Ryder without her canes, refusing anyone's help. She smiled at him with pride at her accomplishment and handed him a frame she had bedazzled to the max—she couldn't have fit another gem on it if she tried. Inside the frame was a picture of all her favourite princesses.

"Sos you aw-ways remem-ber alls of th-the mo...vies we watch-ched togetha," she struggled and stuttered to enunciate each word, which was as much a gift as the frame.

Ryder was elated, kissing her on the cheek as she blushed.

Next was Taz, who didn't speak, so Julianna explained that, when she had asked Taz what he wanted to give, he had gone to the desk drawer and grabbed a box of ear plugs.

Ryder laughed out loud when he opened it, waiting for Taz to pull his fingers away from his ears to give him a high-five.

Theo gave him a box full of paper lips and tongues he had coloured.

"Theo loves Ryder and wants to give him lots of kisses. Give me some tongue!"

Ryder laughed as he backed up when the little shit threw out his arms, opened his mouth, and closed his eyes. Ryder was a lot wiser since the first day, but Theo still managed to get his tongue in Ryder's ear. Ryder grabbed a paper tongue and put it Theo's mouth, which Theo thought was hilarious.

"Ryder's funny, funny! Thanks for the tongue. Fornication for the Nation!" He lifted his hands with the horn symbol.

Mason was so excited when he handed Ryder a long box. Ryder opened it, finding a plastic sword. Mason pulled another one from behind his back, just as Ryder took his out.

They raised their swords together as Mason said, "From Pan to his lost boy. We will never be alone again."

Emotional, Ryder grabbed the kid and hugged him tightly. Mason had to hit Ryder on the head with his sword to let him go.

"I promise, buddy, you will never be alone again," Ryder whispered.

Katrina had been struggling the most with her good-bye and refused to move when Julianna called her forwards. She shook her head and hid her face in the corner of the wall.

Ryder stopped Julianna when she went to the girl. He walked over to her and crouched down beside the little girl, placing a hand on her shoulder.

Katrina turned and threw herself into Ryder's arms as she started to cry, "I don't want to say good-bye. Please don't go."

Ryder's heart split in two as he held the shaking girl in his arms, unable to answer her right away. There were no words he could think of that would ever express the love he had for her and the rest of the kids.

When he regained his composure, he lifted her tiny face. "Katrina, this isn't good-bye. I may not work here every day next year, but Mrs. Ramara and I talked, and I'm going to volunteer here whenever I'm in town. Sweetheart, that's going to be so much that I'm sure you will get sick me.

"How about this? I promise I will be here to get you off the bus the first day of school in September. Trust me, Katrina; I'm not walking away from you."

The little girl looked up at him. "You promise? Will you play with me and my animals?"

"Of course. And on my travels, I'll find different animals from different places to add to your collection. Are we good?" He winked at the adorable girl.

"Only if you promise I can do your hair during spa."

Ryder roared with laughter as he grabbed her chin. "You sneaky little thing. You're blackmailing me, aren't you?"

She giggled as she cuddled up to him, batting her eyelashes. "I made you a stupid card, but can you wait a sec?" She ran to her bag on the floor and sat down as everyone watched. She dumped all her animals on the floor, searching. When Katrina found what she was looking for, she ran back to Ryder and handed him her lion. "Now you have to come back, 'cause that's my favourite."

"I am honoured. I'll give it back to you in September. Thank you for trusting me and for teaching me about unconditional love." He wrapped the girl in his arms.

Mrs. Ramara stepped forwards. "We have one more gift for you, Mr. Vaughn. But first, I would like to say a few words. I want to tell you that I honestly had my doubts about you when you first came here—appearances aside." All the staff laughed, Theo's laugh heard above everyone else's. "You really learned a lot, opened yourself up, and embraced all that we are. You are an asset, and you have apparently made an impact on these students. For that, I say thank you. And if your day job doesn't work out, you always have a place with us. So, without further delay, this is from all of us."

Ryder opened the package she handed him, and inside was a scrapbook filled with pictures and words from every student and staff member at the centre. Ryder smiled as he briefly scanned the pages.

When he closed the book, he took a deep breath and said, "Thank you. I will treasure everything, always." He turned to Mrs. Ramara. "If you think you had doubts, it was nothing compared to mine. This has turned into the best year of my life. I learned a lot about human perseverance, strength, and courage. Before I came here, it was a miracle to get me to talk, and now—"

"That's true, so stop getting mushy. Blah, blah, blah … The end!" Mason yelled out.

"Mason, that's rude. Apologize!" Francesca reprimanded the boy.

Ryder smiled at her. "Thank you, but honestly, that's one of the best things about this place. The kids have a voice, and they're not afraid to use it. Mason's right; I should wrap it up. The last thing I want to say is, I set up a foundation. The first day of school every year, there'll be a donation of two hundred and fifty thousand dollars deposited in the centre's account. A committee will oversee how the money is spent to benefit all the students' needs. Thank you."

There was a loud gasp from the crowd who were all shocked into silence. Then Dakota stood up and started to clap. One by one, everyone joined in.

Francesca ran to Ryder to hug him and everyone followed suit. It was one of the happiest and saddest days of Ryder's life.

***

Now Ryder had completed his full sentence, and Judge Belmore had released him with absolute discharge, meaning it would not appear on his record.

Ryder sat with the judge and talked all about his experiences at the centre, and how grateful he was for the judgement she had given him.

When he rose to leave, Judge Belmore shook his hand and said, "I want you to understand, the centre didn't change who you are. *You* did that. You opened your heart and mind, and now understand the value of your life. I am very proud of you. Look after Frankie for me."

He smirked at her final jab, calling Francesca, Frankie. "Judge, you just love to push my buttons. I'll take care of her, and remember your promise." He winked at the older woman before walking away.

***

"Francesca, your phone is ringing again. You want me to grab it?" Ryder asked. The phone had been ringing off the hook for the last five minutes.

"Yes please. Tell whoever it is I'll call them back," she yelled back through the cascading water.

Ryder grabbed her phone and saw it was Taya.

"Sorry, Taya, but she's in the shower. You want to leave a message?"

"I really needed to speak to her, but I don't have time to wait," she responded with urgency. "Will you just tell her that I'm sorry, but I have to back out on our Italy trip? I have a family emergency. In fact, I'm walking onto a plane, heading to Croatia, right now."

Ryder heard the apprehension in her voice, which was out of character for her.

"Sounds serious. Anything we can do to help?"

"I wish you could, but no, this is something I have to handle myself. I'm just sick about leaving Francesca high and dry. She's been looking forward to this trip, and I feel horrible. I wouldn't do this to her if it wasn't important."

Ryder walked out the balcony door and quietly shut it behind him. "I need to tell you something in confidence. Promise to keep it to yourself?"

Even though she was in a huge rush, Taya was curious. "Talk quickly. I just went through my last checkpoint."

"My band is flying to Italy for impromptu concerts."

"I hope you know, I would have been really pissed if you tagged along, but I can forgive you." He could practically hear her rolling her eyes. "One more thing, let everyone know I won't have phone or internet service. On second thought, I'll text you an emergency phone number, but please don't give it to anyone, and don't let them know you have it."

Ryder didn't like the sound of that. In this day and age, it was impossible not to be connected to the world somehow ... unless you didn't want to be.

"Are you sure I can't help? I have lots of connections and resources. All you have to do is say the word, and I won't ask questions."

She was silent for a minute, and Ryder thought maybe they had lost connection. Then she spoke in a soft voice, so unlike the tough chick he had gotten to know.

"You know, for an ass, you really are amazing. I gotta run. Tell Francesca I love her. Remember, please don't give anyone the number. Bye."

The line went dead, and Ryder was even more concerned that her family emergency was more than she was leading him to believe. At the same time, Ryder understood wanting privacy.

He went inside and heard his phone beep. The phone number she had sent was unlike any number he had ever seen, and the text had obviously not been sent from Taya's phone. No name, just random numbers.

Before his mind could wander any further, the bathroom door

opened and Francesca came out, professionally dressed and with a towel wrapped around her hair. He wasn't looking forward to breaking the news that Taya wouldn't be joining her on her trip.

"Who called?" she asked as she unraveled the towel from her long, burgundy hair.

"Come and sit down for a minute," Ryder suggested as he grabbed her hand and led her to the couch.

"What's going on?" Francesca looked at him for answers.

"Taya called. She has a family emergency in Croatia ... She won't be able to go to Italy."

"Oh, no. What happened? Did she say? Is she okay?"

"She just said you wouldn't be able to reach her. Don't panic. You know your friend is capable of looking after herself. I'm just sorry about your trip." He saw the underlying disappointment all over her face, but Francesca's worry overrode the disappointment.

"I hope she's okay. I know she has a few relatives in Croatia, but I didn't think they were that close. If she's okay, that's all that matters. I still have to go see my family, but now I'll just come home a couple of weeks sooner than I expected." Sadness filled her eyes. She couldn't go alone on the rest of her trip, and now she would have to go to her mother's grave again without fulfilling her wish. "One day I'll walk the steps of my mother's dreams."

"We'll go together some day. If I didn't have to prepare for our upcoming tour, I would go with you. Sorry, sweetheart."

Francesca smiled, knowing he would make her dream come true one day. "Thank you. I love you and really am going to miss you. Maybe I could rearrange my flights and visit you in California, seeing as I'll be coming home two weeks early."

Ryder knew she wouldn't be coming home early, but decided to play along.

"Sounds great. I was struggling with not knowing how I was going to survive without you for a whole month. Now you can come and see my place." He smiled as he ran his thumb down the delicate curve of her jaw. Moving his hand to the back of her head, he pulled her forwards for a kiss.

"I'm going to have to cancel all of my reservations for the tour Taya and I were taking and change my flight. I hope I can still get my money back."

"Let me handle all that. You have that Autism conference today. And now that school is done, I don't have much to do before you leave."

"Thanks. I appreciate it. I'll leave my itinerary on the kitchen table with phone numbers. I better get going, or I'm going to be late."

***

Francesca was excited but nervous when she walked onto the plane and showed the flight attendant her ticket.

"Miss Moratti, you have been upgraded to first-class. Follow me."

Francesca stopped in her tracks. "How did that happen?"

The flight attendant stopped and turned to her with a smile. "Sometimes, when the first-class section isn't full, the airline randomly picks passengers to upgrade, free of charge. Seeing as you are travelling alone, and we have one seat left, today is your lucky day."

Francesca wasn't buying it. "So it's random? Are you sure? Or did someone change my ticket?"

Surprised, the flight attendant said, "I don't know about you, but I don't know many people who upgrade other folks. No, this is pure luck." The flight attendant then directed her to her new seat.

Francesca immediately pulled her phone out and texted Ryder.

Beast, if you did this, I'm going to kill you! :(

Don't know what you're talking about. Love you.

REALLY? Love you, too! XO

Really. Enjoy your flight. Sleep well. Text when you land.

Francesca struggled to settle in, not feeling like she belonged. She was absolutely amazed at how people got treated in first-class. She thought the people who paid for this luxury would be upset that she got upgraded, but they paid her no mind.

She didn't take off her shoes, waiting for them to tell her it was all a huge mistake and drag her back to the economy section. Once she realized they weren't going to move her, Francesca finally relaxed, but she didn't sleep, afraid to miss a minute of this luxury.

Francesca texted Ryder as soon as the plane touched ground. Then she gathered her luggage and went to find the shuttle to the train station.

Rome's airport was a zoo and very intimidating for a woman travelling alone. She looked around to get her bearings and saw a man holding a sign with her name on it, which made her wonder if the train provided the service.

She approached him, and after establishing she was the one he was looking for, the young man retrieved her bags and asked that she follow him. He walked to a large limousine and opened the door for her.

She instantly stopped, realizing the train station wouldn't send a limo.

"There must be some mistake. I didn't order a car." There was no way Francesca was getting in a dark, assuming car with a stranger.

With a thick Italian accent, the man asked, "Are you Signorina Francesca Moratti?"

"Sì, but I didn't order a car, and I am traveling very far. I can't afford this. Thank you, anyway." She tried to pick up her luggage, but he stopped her.

"Please, Signorina, I have been given my instructions. I take you to Giffoni Sei Casali in the province of Salerno, no?" The driver was getting nervous.

"Sì, that's where I'm going, but I didn't order a car. I can't pay for this."

"It has already been paid for, signorina. Please, let us go."

That's when it hit her like a ton of bricks.

She ignored the young man as she pulled her phone out of her purse and dialed.

"Good morning, Beauty," Ryder answered.

"Did you order me a car?" she asked in a clipped tone.

Ryder knew this was coming, but he hadn't been prepared for her attitude.

"Yes, I did. If you think I'm going to let you travel alone on a train, in a country you haven't visited since you were a child, you are dead wrong."

Francesca growled in frustration. "Ryder, I am a grown woman. I can pay for my own transportation. Stop making decisions for me without consulting me first."

He knew if he continued pushing her, she would walk away, and there wouldn't be a damn thing he could do to stop it. Therefore, he took a different approach.

"Babe, please give me this. I know you can take care of yourself, but when you originally made your plans, Taya was supposed to be with you. And if you had family meeting you there, I wouldn't have interfered. I'm already out of my mind with worry about you being alone. It's ripping my heart out that I couldn't go with you. Please, Beauty, do this for me."

Now Francesca felt like an absolute heel. She relented with a sigh. "I'm sorry, Ryder. I didn't sleep on the plane, and I guess I'm a little cranky. Thank you for thinking about me. But I am paying you back."

"Sure, whatever you say," he placated her. He wouldn't let her pay him back. "Can I talk to the driver?"

Francesca looked at the phone like it had grown horns as she passed her phone to the driver. "Here, he wants to talk to you."

"Hallo? Sì—I mean, yes. Yes, sir." The driver was starting to sweat. "Sì, I understand. Ciao." His face was pale as he handed the phone back.

"What did he say?" Francesca was beyond curious.

"Please, signorina, I need this job. I am begging you, for the love of God, just let me take you to your famiglia."

Francesca put her hands on her hips. "I'm not going anywhere until you tell me what that overgrown ape said to you."

He gestured, shaking both his hands through the air, as he cursed his luck in Italian. "Che palle!"

She squinted her eyes at him. "I do not literally have balls, and figuratively, I'm not a pain in the ass!"

The driver slapped his hand over his mouth. "Oh, Dio mio, you understand Italiano?"

She smiled evilly. "Sì, I understand."

Throwing his hands up, he said, "I will tell you after you get in the car, and we drive." He opened the back door to let her in the limo.

She shook her head. "Nope. I'm not some rich girl. I'll sit in the front with you, grazie"

"Lei sta per farmi uccisi o licenziato," he mumbled as he shut the door.

Francesca giggled, and when he slid into the driver's seat, told him, "I heard that. I'm not going to get you fired or killed, so relax."

He smirked. "If this is what driving Americans around is like, I should get myself a new job."

She fastened her seatbelt, telling him, "I'm Canadian. My name is Francesca. Now tell me what he said."

Now that he had her in the car and was travelling at a fast rate, he got cocky. "I am Bruno. Pleased to meet you. You are from the continent of America, are you not?"

"Yes, but—"

"Then you are American. My cousins are from Canada, too, and they are touchy about being called American. It means no disrespect any more than when you call me European."

She snickered. "My apologies. Now tell me what Ryder said."

"Che cosa, I give you ride, no?"

Francesca laughed out loud. "No, no, my boyfriend's name is

Ryder. R-Y-D-E-R. What did he say?"

Bruno glanced over. "First promise me I am not gonna meet this Ryder. Something tell me, even outside of dark alley, he would be a little pazzo, eh?"

"Promise. He is in North America and is staying there. Now tell me," she begged.

"Okay, he said—his words not mine—'She is the most stubborn female in the world, but she is the love of my life. If you don't take care of her, I will track you down and make you suffer, slow and painfully. Understand?' Of course I say, 'Yes, sir!' "

Grabbing her purse and rummaging through it, she said, "I'm so sorry, Bruno. He tends to be a little overprotective. Even though he is six and half feet tall and built like Michelangelo's David, that still doesn't give him the right to talk to people like that. I'll phone him now and make him apologize."

Taking his hands off the steering wheel, he started waving them around. "No, no, please. Oh, Dio, I need this job."

She chuckled at hearing the panic in his voice. "Relax. He is all bark and no bite. Truly, he is just a big marshmallow at heart. He would never hurt you. I'll make sure of it."

"He's right; you are stubborn."

That was the beginning of the three-and-a-half-hour drive to her family's farm.

The party was in full-swing when they arrived. It seemed every person from three towns had come for the birthday celebration. They were all surprised when the limousine pulled up, and Francesca's uncles and cousins approached with curiosity.

She squealed as she jumped out of the car and yelled, "Sorprese!"

No one recognized the long burgundy-haired girl since they had only met her once ten years ago. Then Lena Moratti pushed her way through the crowd and yelled, "Francesca, my grandchild, how is this possible?"

Francesca ran to her grandmother and hugged her.

Lena was so happy, she ignored everyone's questions until she convinced herself her granddaughter was truly in her arms. Then she turned Francesca around and announced her granddaughter's arrival from Canada.

Francesca understood the old language, but they all started speaking so fast and in perfect Italian, so she missed ninety percent of what people were saying. She was passed around from one relative to the next, hugging and kissing her, and pinching her cheeks, repeating, "Che bella."

Suddenly, out of the house came a scream, and Francesca watched as Zia Concettina came flying out the door, yelling her name. Concettina had visited Canada a lot when Francesca was young before she got married. She had also come for two weeks to support Francesca's papa when his wife had passed away.

"Francesca, oh, Dio mio, my bambina! Let me look at you." Concettina pulled her in for a hug. "I knew you would look exactly like me when you grew up."

Francesca laughed. They looked nothing alike. Her zia had dark eyes, dark olive skin, and was tall and slender.

"Really, Concettina, I am day, and you are night."

She scoffed, throwing her head back. "Psh, we look exactly alike, right, Mamma?"

Lena, possessing the same dark humour, replied, "Eh, Francesca is right. She is pure goodness; and you, my daughter, are pure evil."

Everyone laughed as Concettina replied, "Well, not hard to see where I inherit my evilness from, eh, Mamma?" She squeezed her mamma's cheek then gently patted it twice.

Francesca lost track of time as she visited her family. At one in the morning, her cousin Piero came running out with a portable phone. "Cugina Francesca, telefono. America!"

"Grazie, Piero." Francesca took the phone, assuming it would be her papa. "Hello?"

"Goddammit, Beauty! I've been worried sick, trying to call you for seven hours."

Francesca held the phone back as he yelled, and Zia Concettina raised an eyebrow.

"Relax, Beast. I'm with my family." She got up and walked away for some privacy. Her not so subtle zia followed her, not happy that a man was yelling at her niece.

Ryder released a breath, calming himself. "Sorry, Francesca. I thought you were going to call me when you arrived. I didn't sleep a wink, worried that stupid driver crashed. I left thirteen messages. What was I supposed to think? I finally phoned Frank for this number. I had to listen to your idiot brothers tease me about being pussy-whipped."

She smiled up at the quarter moon, listening to him rant. When he was done, she told him, "I love you. I'm sorry I worried you. I should have called. Bruno and I ended up talking all the way here, and then, when I arrived, I got caught up in the birthday celebration. Again, I'm sorry. I'll carry my phone with me from now on, I promise."

With a lethal voice, he questioned, "Who the hell is Bruno?"

"The driver you hired." Francesca laughed. "I felt bad after all the trouble we gave him. He was really sweet and thought we were both crazy." Now trying to sooth the beast, she said, "Ryder, you don't need to be jealous. You are my heart and soul." She yawned loudly, her lack of sleep catching up to her.

"Don't count on it," he grumbled. "Love you, too. Are you having a good time? You sound exhausted."

"It's everything I dreamed about. But I am beyond exhausted. Can I call you later?"

"Of course."

"Good night." Francesca ended the call and cradled the phone to her chest.

"Well, ooo la la, somebody is in love."

Francesca screamed, not knowing her aunt had been listening behind her. She smacked her zia's shoulder, and then locked arms with her as they walked towards the classic, old farmhouse.

"Yes, I met the man of my dreams. I'll tell you everything tomorrow. I am beyond exhausted and need a bed."

"You ruined all my fun, mia bella. I give you till sunrise. Then I am coming to your room. I want the whole story."

Chapter 24

"Angel Eyes" By Jeff Healey

Francesca looked around, amazed at the beauty that surrounded her as she helped her cousin Rosa set the table outside for Sunday dinner. It was right out of the movie *Under the Tuscan Sun.*

In Francesca's mind, the farmhouse should have been called a villa. A stone wall surrounded the courtyard and an arched entrance allowed access to the courtyard and house. Opposite the arch was a large gate that took you to the livestock and fields. Right beside the gate was a large stone oven that was over a hundred years old. Then, beside the stairs to the farmhouse was a large covered area that had three walls and opened to the courtyard. The family used the area to store supplies and to lay out the tomatoes, nuts, and grapes at harvest time.

The large courtyard could easily hold a hundred people. A trellis covered three quarters of it, with hanging grapes that provided shade for the four large tables that were placed together for thirty-four family members coming for the two o'clock meal.

The farm was large and used to house four large families. Now it held two smaller ones, plus Francesca's grandmother and uncle. Francesca thought that people back home would flock to this spectacular place if it was converted into a bed and breakfast.

She wished Ryder could see it … On second thought, he would probably be overwhelmed by all her family. He had enough trouble with just her two brothers.

There was a flurry of activity going on around her. A few of her aunts and cousins were making pizza in the outdoor oven. Some of her male cousins were starting a fire in a pit that they used to cook the meat. Her nonna Lena was in the kitchen, making the sauce for the pasta. And a few relatives were in the room beside the cantina, cutting the cured salami, prosciutto, and cheeses for the antipasto platters. Once the antipasto and bread were on the table, the large pot of sauce would be brought down and placed on the grill to keep warm, with a huge pot of water for the pasta.

Zio Antonio had one job at the ripe old age of one hundred, and that was to ring the bell, signaling to everyone that dinner better be on the table in ten minutes. When the bell sounded, the pace picked up.

Rosa and Francesca were placing bottles of white and red wine every few feet on the table when all conversations suddenly halted. Looking up, Francesca saw a frazzled Bruno jump out of the limousine, sweating from head to toe.

"Bruno, what's wrong? What's happened to you?" Francesca ran to him and grabbed his arms, concerned something had happened.

Bruno instantly jerked out of her hold and paled considerably. "Oh, Dio mio, now I am dead for sure!"

"Hello, Beauty."

Francesca snapped her head towards the rear passenger door, and there stood her man.

"Ryder!" she screeched as she ran around the back of the car, Bruno long forgotten.

Ryder braced himself as she launched into his arms, wrapping her legs around his hips. He was thrilled by her reaction, holding her tightly under her ass while kissing her deeply, unconcerned that there were thirty-three family members watching.

They were entirely lost in each other when he was whacked in the back by a broom.

"What the hell?" Ryder yelped, gently placing Francesca down before turning to face his attacker.

A little old woman stood no more than four and half feet tall with her broom cocked and ready to take another swing.

Ryder backed up, bumping into Francesca at the fierceness on the old woman's face.

"Che cazzo, get your hands off my granddaughter, disgraziato!"

Nonna Lena moved in closer, trying to intimidate the giant.

"You go, signora! Show him who's boss," Bruno bravely stated from the other side of the car.

Francesca turned and gave Bruno a dirty look, knowing they didn't need anyone to fuel the fire, before she stepped between her grandmother and boyfriend.

"No, Nonna, he is boyfriend from Canada."

With wide eyes, her nonna's scowling, wrinkled face broke into a huge grin. "Your boyfriend? You have a boyfriend, Francesca!" Then her smile disappeared in an instant as Nonna squinted. "He doesn't look Italian. Let me get a closer look. Come here and give Nonna a kiss." Lifting her hands up to a still nervous Ryder, the incredibly strong woman grabbed his hair and yanked him down. She kissed both of his cheeks then whispered, "We no call polizia. We call the famiglia. You treat her good, or else ..."

Ryder chuckled. He was going to like this feisty old broad. "Understood."

"Nonna, this is Ryder Vaughn. Ryder, this is my grandmother, Lena Moratti."

"Che cosa? Writer? What kind of a name is that? I don't understand you younger generation."

Francesca giggled. "R-Y-D-E-R."

Nonna attempted to say the name three times before declaring, "This name is no going to work for me. We call you Rafael, va bene?" Bringing her hands together, she swiped them across one another like it was final.

"Nonna, you can't just change his name!" Francesca cried out.

"Whatever she wants. Apparently, she's the female version of the godfather that Maurizio is always warning me about. Let it go, Beauty."

"Va bene. See? Smarter than he looks." Lena winked at Ryder.

"Nonna! That's not nice." Francesca was mortified.

"I don't know, Mamma. He looks pretty good to me. Although, I could probably teach him a thing or two," Concettina said as she strolled over, swishing her hips from side to side.

"Oh, my God, have you all gone pazzo?" Francesca was blushing from head to toe. "I am so sorry, Ryder. They aren't usually this unruly. No, that's a lie; they are. But I apologize for their rudeness."

Nonna flicked her head up towards Ryder. "Eh, Francesca? Your papa better know about Rafael. Does my son approve?"

"His name is Ryder and—"

"Yes, I approve," Frank said as he got out of the car, with Lucky and Sal in tow.

"Francesco, praise the Holy Mary." After doing the sign of the cross and bringing her fingers to her lips, Lena ran to her son as fast as her little legs would take her. She was immediately enveloped in her prodigal son's arms.

Frank moved to his daughter and kissed her as Nonna Lena moved to her grandsons.

"Papa, what are you doing here? What about parole? And if all of you are here, who is working at the shop?"

"We decided to come after Ryder had Mr. Quinn obtain special permission with the Parole Board. Some things are more important than money, and our family deserves a much-needed break."

Francesca walked over to Ryder and grabbed his hand. "Thank you. You'll never know how much this means to me. But what about the tour?"

Ryder quickly kissed her again. "Anything for you. Actually, the guys and Melissa are here. We scheduled a few small concerts in Italy so I could take you to see all the places your mother wished to see. We leave next week."

Francesca gasped, covering her mouth with her hand as tears filled her eyes.

"No tears, Beauty." Ryder gestured towards her grandmother. "Or that little spitfire over there is going to take me out at the knees with her broom."

As she introduced him to everyone, she heard comments in Italian, like *huge, enormous, giant,* and of course, *monster.* Her family was not tall in stature.

Her hundred-year-old zio shocked everyone when he stood on a chair, claiming he had to look Rafael in the eyes to determine if he was good enough for his great-niece. Everyone held their breaths, waiting for his blessing.

"Va bene, tutti a tavola a mangiare!" he said as he pulled Ryder in for a double cheek kiss.

Everyone cheered as Francesca breathed a sign of relief. Then the cousins added more place settings as Ryder assisted Zio Antonio down from the chair. The old man made him sit beside him for the meal.

"What did he say?" Ryder questioned Frank as he approached.

"He said, 'Okay, now everyone to the table to eat.' If he breaks bread with you, that means he accepts you. You're good, son, even though you already had the only blessing you ever needed. Thank you for indulging an old man."

Francesca saw Bruno was still standing there. "Bruno, please join us for dinner before you leave."

"Grazie, Francesca, I will need my strength. Your boyfriend hired mio company and requested I be your personal driver for the next three weeks. No offence, but not my dream job!"

She laughed at the man still covered in sweat. "Trust me; I will protect you." She laughed harder as she approached the table to seat Bruno, who adamantly shook his head and pointed to the other end of the table ... away from Ryder.

They sat down and enjoyed course after course of one of the finest Italian dinners Ryder had ever had.

Frank explained to Ryder that all the food was produced at the farm. Ryder was amazed, but had trouble hearing Frank from across the table. Everyone was yelling and flailing their hands. The winner of the discussion seemed to be the one who yelled the loudest.

Ryder turned to Francesca. "What are they all angry about?"

She chuckled. "No one is angry; that's how we talk." At the disbelieving look on his face, she said, "You'll get used to it, I promise." She rubbed his thigh, her gentle touch giving him a hard-on.

He gently removed her hand and placed it back on her leg, then bent down and whispered, "If you continue, I'm going to sling you over my shoulder and take you upstairs."

She blushed as her temperature rose.

"Nonna, those two are up to no good. Look, Francesca is blushing," Sal ratted her out.

"Mind your own business, Salvatore. They are in love, capisce?" She cuffed him playfully on the side of the head. It seemed distance and time hadn't changed Nonna Lena in the least.

After four hours at the dinner table, the women got up to clear it, while the men broke out the cigars, espresso, and hazelnut liquor, which was also a specialty made on the farm. When they finished, Concettina, Frank, and at least ten of the cousins took Ryder on a tour.

There was a hundred-year-old cantina under the farmhouse that

446

stored all the wine, vinegar, cured meats, and cheeses, as well as six hundred jars of tomatoes. Then they took him into the fields to show him the livestock. Next, they walked through acres upon acres of hazelnut trees. Frank explained that the hazelnuts were used to make Nutella and liquor. Now Ryder understood where Francesca's obsession with the chocolate nutty spread came from. God forbid she go one day without fresh bread and Nutella. Zia Concettina confessed she loved it, too, and was the one responsible for Francesca's obsession.

Next, they traveled up the hill to the barn where they had forty heads of water buffalo. Ryder was impressed they made and exported fresh buffalo mozzarella made from the milk. He had tried the caprese salad at dinner with the fresh buffalo mozzarella, just-picked tomatoes, basil, and extra virgin olive oil. He promised himself he was having a caprese salad and some type of pasta every day that he was in Italy. It was that damn good.

The sun was beginning to set when Frank said they should get back, seeing as Ryder had made Bruno stop and buy fireworks on the way to the farm to celebrate his first night in Italy with Francesca.

Everyone gathered around the fire pit they still had burning with liquors and espresso. Francesca had saved a seat for Ryder and greeted him with a quick kiss.

"What do you think of the farm?" she asked.

"I can see why you couldn't wait to come here. Your family, they aren't all related to you, right?"

She smiled. "Yes, all of them are related to me."

Sal got everyone's attention. "Ryder wanted to contribute to the day's celebration so, without further delay …"

The sky erupted in a glorious ball of exploding lights as the first firework detonated. Francesca expressed her appreciation for the beauty as she laid her head against Ryder's shoulder and squeezed his hand.

Frank stood and stopped their cousin Michele and Sal after the first one. "Please, can I have a minute?"

Francesca sat up, curious as to why her father stopped the firework display. She noticed everyone turning to look at her. When she turned to Ryder, he was down on one knee.

She threw her hand over her mouth, shaking from head to toe.

Ryder grasped her shaking hand and brought it to his mouth for a kiss. "Beauty, I love you with my whole heart and soul. You changed my life. You would think, with my job, I could express how much I love you, but words just can't do justice to my feelings. Instead, I will simply ask you … Will you do me the honour of being my wife forever?" Ryder reached into his pocket and pulled out a white box. Inside sat the most beautiful ring Francesca had ever seen.

She was sobbing as Ryder tried to put the ring on her unsteady finger.

"I need an answer, Beauty."

"Yes, a hundred times, yes." She grabbed his face as she fell to her knees to plant a kiss that had the whole group catcalling and whistling.

"Break it up, you two," Frank interrupted. "You have your whole lives ahead of you."

After they broke apart, Ryder settled Francesca in his lap, wrapping his arms around her.

Frank continued, first in English then Italian so everyone understood. "It is my great honour to welcome Ryder into our family. For those of you who have just met him, he is a man of integrity, and I am proud to call him my friend, as well as my son. My daughter has chosen exceptionally well." He looked at his daughter. "Francesca, you are a gift from the angels and deserve to be happy. Ryder will make you very happy.

"I want to thank Ryder for the respect he showed me by coming to me over a month ago to ask for my daughter's hand in marriage. He asked if he could fly us here to share in their private moment, and I selfishly accepted. I asked one thing of him, and he honoured my request.

"Francesca, that gorgeous ring on your finger was your mother's engagement ring. We went together to our friend Patrick from Cullinan Jewellers and redesigned your momma's ring to make it yours. It will always link your momma and my love to yours. I wish you both a lifetime of happiness together. Congratulations."

Francesca sobbed as she looked at her stunning ring while Ryder comforted her. Then she looked up at him, full-on sobbing and cried out, "Oh, my God, I am actually going to marry the man of my dreams."

"I love you, babe," Ryder said as he finished wiping her face with his shirt.

He kissed her as the spectacular display of fireworks were set off to celebrate their engagement.

***

Francesca quietly snuck through the farmhouse barefoot when she was sure everyone was sleeping. She very softly opened the door to Ryder's room, and then gently closed it behind her before she made her way to her sleeping giant.

She stood for a moment, simply taking in his sleeping form. He was lying on his back with the sheet covering the lower half of his body. His prosthetic was propped up against the nightstand. She was surprised to see it looked like a real leg and had to touch it. She smiled at the feel and implications of having a realistic looking prosthetic. She then turned back, full of warmth, to see his face was at rest. He looked younger, more at ease.

Ryder thought she had changed his life, when in fact, it was the other way around. He was the kindest man she had ever encountered, and she was lucky enough to be chosen as his wife. Francesca vowed to herself to be the best wife in the world for this gentle soul of a man.

She ever so slowly pulled the sheet down from his body and saw his large penis laying against his thigh. It was so impressive, even at rest.

Francesca gently ran the tip of her finger along his velvety soft cock, watching it twitch at her familiar touch and start to grow.

Ryder moaned and rolled over, causing her to jump back.

She giggled softly as she bent down and rubbed her fingernail gently across the hair on his leg. When his stump quivered, she did it again.

His hand came down and brushed across his leg like he was swatting a fly. He huffed as he rolled over again onto his back. His cock must have known she was close because it continued to become engorged.

She removed her robe and crawled onto the bed between his legs and licked his cock from base to tip. It jumped at the warm then cool sensation of her tongue dragging slowly up then back down.

Ryder moaned again in sleep.

When she was satisfied he was hard enough, she engulfed his erection with her mouth.

Ryder, dreaming Francesca was giving him head, reached down to grab her hair, trapped between reality and a dream world. Then reality knocked at his subconscious. This couldn't be a dream.

He quickly opened his eyes, and with the light of the moon, he saw her leaning on her elbows with her back's gentle slope leading up to her ass. The vision was as intoxicating as the feel of her mouth gliding up and down.

"Francesca," he whisper-moaned as he finally captured all her thick, long hair in his hand.

His heart sped up at the whiskey-coloured eyes filled with lust staring back at him. She smiled as best she could with her full mouth.

Then he caught the sparkle of the ring where she held the base of his cock while she plunged down as far as she could with a slight gag. The vibration of the gag had him raising his hips as her mouth ascended, not wanting to lose the connection.

She repositioned herself, climbing over his leg while never breaking the rhythm of her up and down motion. Once she balanced her upper body on his side, she used both hands, stroking whatever part of his cock that was not blanketed by her mouth. She felt the shiver of his body as it prepared for ejaculation.

"My turn," he rasped out as he jackknifed his upper body and grabbed her shoulders. He wanted to go down on her before he came, or got caught by the patriarch of the family.

She squealed, taken by surprise as he flipped her onto her back and spread her legs. He tried to mute her squeal with his mouth, frantically lapping at her tongue and driving his passion to new heights.

He pulled away, kissing a path down her body, not leaving a spot untouched. When he reached his destination, he inhaled deeply, loving her musky vanilla scent. He parted her lower lips with the fingers of one hand as the other curled around her hip, pinning her.

Ryder dragged his tongue through her moisture, moaning at her taste. He circled her clit as he dipped one finger into her wet core, and she had to throw her hand over her mouth to keep from yelling out.

Ryder added a second finger, curling them slightly, searching blindly for the little spot he had discovered set her on fire. When he found it, he rubbed it mercifully.

Ryder latched his mouth onto her clit and sucked hard. She went off like the fireworks they had watched earlier. Even with all his strength, he had trouble holding her down.

He removed his mouth and turned to see she had moved his pillow over her head to contain her screams. He moved his mouth back to suck some more while her walls were still contracting around his fingers. He kept it going until he felt the spasms slow down.

Francesca's body melted into the bed as Ryder moved behind her and placed his arm around her body to hold her securely to him. He nudged her leg up and entered her while covering her mouth with his other hand. He couldn't be soft and gentle, because he was too far gone.

He pulled her tighter to his body as he relentlessly pounded into her from behind, the bed shifting with the relentless movement. In the back of his mind, he was scolding himself for being so rough. However, his dream turned fantasy had snapped his control.

Francesca was in a sexual fog, not thinking, only feeling, and it felt amazing. At this angle, the curve of his cock was rubbing her G-spot without slowing down. This orgasm was going to be different than any she had ever felt.

Her leg muscle cramped at the awkwardness of trying to keep it up. The pain should have driven her to distraction, but it only intensified the frantic feelings building in her core. Then it happened.

She exploded, detonating like a bomb, all sense and time ceasing to exist. She screamed into Ryder's hand then clamped down on the meat on the underside of his palm.

The pain and the passion drove his climax up from the tips of his toes, traveling upwards through his legs, into his balls, shot through his cock, and into the warm, pulsating womb of the woman he loved. He shook as he pumped his seed into Francesca, releasing all the tension coiled tightly in his muscles.

They collapsed together, sweating, desperately seeking air to replace all that was lost with their exertion. When Ryder's senses came back, he moved away the hair plastered to her face. Her eyes were closed, and her breathing was returning to normal.

"You okay, Beauty? I was really rough."

Francesca opened her eyes, turning her head to face him. "Do I look broken? Um, we do have one serious problem, though."

Uncertainty at what she was going to say had him rising and allowing her space to get up and say whatever was troubling her.

"Talk to me. What's the problem?"

She looked down at the sheets, and his heart plummeted, thinking it was serious enough she couldn't face him.

"That was the most amazing orgasm I have ever had. How are you possibly ever going to beat it?"

Relief swept through him. He threw his arm around her neck and put Francesca into a head lock. "You scared the shit out of me. I thought I really hurt you, or that you were having second thoughts."

Francesca was giggling, trying to break out of his hold. "Let go, Beast." Ryder immediately released her, and she looked at him adoringly. "I can't wait to spend the rest of my life with you."

Ryder petted her hair, loving the feeling of her draped across his chest. "I hate to do this, but you have to get back to your room and get some sleep before anyone catches you in here."

Francesca rose to her knees and cupped his face. "This is why I love you so much." She brought her lips to his and kissed him thoroughly. Then she got up, put on her robe, and blew him a kiss as she snuck back out, pulling the door gently closed.

"Well, I hope it was as good as it sounded, bella."

Francesca squeaked as she jumped, caught by Concettina. "Holy crap. You scared the life out of me." Francesca held the top of her robe closed.

Concettina laughed. "Then you shouldn't be sneaking out of your fiancé's room at four a.m." She tapped her lips with a finger, looking contemplative, before a sly smile appeared. "To tell you the truth, if I had a man like that, I would do the exact same thing."

Francesca blushed. "Please tell me you didn't hear us. I would be mortified."

"Aw, Francesca, you are so carina. You aren't the first Moratti woman, or the last, to sneak around this farm at all hours of the night. Relax, bella, your secret is safe with me ... as long as I get details."

Francesca slapped her aunt as they walked back to her room. "Not in a million years, Zia. Go make your own noises with your husband."

"You insist on ruining all my fun. Go. I hear someone. I will cover for you!"

Francesca took off like a shot, loving the thrill of dreaming up tonight's adventure.

Chapter 25

"Heart & Soul" By Fornication

Bruno loaded the car, while the couple said their good-byes. Francesca left the important good-bye for last.

"Zio Antonio, I am going to miss you. I expect an invitation to your hundred and tenth birthday. Promise me you will do everything Zia Concettina tells you." Francesca hugged him tightly, knowing it could be the last time.

"I am surprised your zia hasn't killed me yet. I live now simply to torment her." He grinned with a bit of evilness, almost making Francesca believe him. "I am an old man. I have lived a good life, but I miss my wife, your zia, and I am ready to go.

"You, my sweet child, made my birthday celebration a dream come true. I can now die a happy man. I always had a soft spot for your mother, and I see so much of her in you. Go and live your life. Be happy. I will not make it to your wedding, but I made it to the engagement. For this, I am thankful. May God bless your union, and may you have a dozen children."

Francesca was getting teary-eyed. "Zio, really, do you see that man over there dealing with twelve children?"

Zio grabbed her hand and placed it over his heart. "Child, it is the mother that is the root of the family, the one who holds it together and teaches it to flourish. You, my sweet girl, will teach the giant how to be an exceptional papa. If he hasn't already learned, he will, that the woman holds all the power. Use that power wisely.

"I love you, Francesca. Go before you make an old man cry." He turned to Frank and Ryder. "Rafael, come. We need to talk … And bring my nephew to translate."

Francesca went to say good-bye to her nonna as Frank led Ryder to Antonio, explaining he wanted to talk.

Zio linked arms with Ryder and Frank, leading them through the gate. "Francesco, you translate, and do not change my words, understand?"

"Si, Zio."

"Rafael, you have been given a gift from God, and I want you to treat her well."

Frank interpreted, changing Rafael to Ryder.

Zio pinched his forearm hard. "I said exactly, capisce?"

Frank chuckled, rubbing the area that was surely going to bruise.

"What did he say?" Ryder asked.

"He told me to translate exactly."

Ryder cracked up. He had grown to love Zio over the last week. They'd had many conservations just like this one.

"When you live to one hundred, you see many things. You experience good and bad. You witness pain and sorrow, as well as happiness and love. You, my giant, show much love for my niece. I watched you closely this week, and I understand why Francesco freely gave his blessing. I know you will protect and love her sensitive heart.

"Francesca has known a lot of pain in her young life, and it is your responsibility to bring her happiness. That little girl gives all of herself to everyone. She is an angel. Marrying her is a gift of honour and will reap many rewards.

"I have also asked many questions this week, because it is my right as the patriarch. I know you have no family worthy of that title. But that all changed last week when you placed that ring on my sweet child's finger. It linked, not only you and Francesca, but you to all of us. With that link comes the responsibility to respect the heritage and tradition of our family. And most importantly, to harbour the next generation. Before I die, I want to see a child. Do not make me wait. I am old and very tired of waiting."

Ryder felt so overwhelmed to hear and receive Antonio's words that a stray tear escaped the corner of his eyes. Embarrassed, he quickly wiped it away.

Zio stopped and turned directly towards Ryder, grasping his

hand and looking at the single tear clinging to his finger. "Do not hide your emotions. Wear them proudly, for it means your heart is open. It took me too many years to learn that lesson. I was a hard-headed, stubborn young man who sadly missed much. I do not want that for you."

Ryder grabbed both of Zio's weathered, frail old hands and clasped them in his larger ones. "It will be my honour to grant all your wishes. I was reborn when I met Francesca, and I'm now proud of the man standing in front of you. I will get right on making babies, and I will treat them with the love and affection I've learned from this family. I will model myself after Frank and be the best father I can be. If I'm lucky enough to live to see my grandchildren, I will try to be like the man standing in front of me. I will guide and impart wisdom like you. I was introduced to you as uncle, but I will leave here calling you grandfather." Ryder didn't need his next words translated. "Ti amo, Nonno. Vi vedrò prima di sapere che."

The little man broke down in Ryder's arms, overwhelmed by his adopted grandson's words: *I love you, grandfather. I will see you before you know it.*

Sobbing, Antonio spoke against his chest, "My wife and I could never have a child. Therefore, no grandchildren. Today, I am blessed with my first."

Ryder looked down at the little man in his arms. "Nonno, I know in my heart you will make the wedding, I promise." Ryder

460

kissed first one cheek, and then, as he kissed the other one, he held on a minute longer, just to absorb his grandfather's love.

He held the little man close to his side as they walked back to the car.

Francesca saw the three men walking towards her with tears in their eyes. She was curious, but she didn't ask, sensing it had to have been an extremely private moment.

They got into the car and opened the window. Zio reached for Ryder's hand and walked beside the car as it crawled down the road, refusing to let go until the last minute. Then Antonio waved until the car was out of sight.

They drove in silence for a long time, each lost in their own thoughts. Francesca didn't know their first location until five and half hours later when she saw a sign for Gradara. She squealed with excitement.

"Ryder, do you know where we're going?"

Ryder grinned. "It was on the top of the list. I'm guessing the castle is why your mother wanted to visit this place."

Francesca's eyes lit up. "Oh, it's so much more than that. Have you ever heard of *Dante's Divine Comedy*? Or the famous paintings of Francesca and Paolo?"

"Do I look like I know shit like that?"

"It's not shit. My mom told me the story as a child, and I have always remembered it. There are rumours that Shakespeare was inspired by their story and wrote *Romeo and Juliette*. I don't know if it's true, but I chose to believe it."

Ryder got caught up in the enthusiasm in her eyes and body language that showed she was excited to visit the place.

"I would love to hear it."

"The legend says that Francesca da Polenta of Ravenna was given to Giovanni Malatesta of Rimini because the family had been at war. Their union was a way for the families to come together in peace. Giovanni was crippled but still led the Malatesta troops and sent his brother Paolo in proxy to marry Francesca. Paolo and Francesca ended up falling in love and had a love affair that lasted for ten years until Giovanni came home from war and caught the two lovers together in bed and murdered them. The castle belonged to the Malatesta family, and this is where the lovers lived and died. I can't believe I am actually going to visit it!"

Ryder's mouth hung open. "That's a horrible story. The cripple was betrayed by his brother and wife."

"Ryder, no, it wasn't because of his affliction; it was because he was a cruel and heartless man who sent his brother in his place because he didn't want Francesca. Paolo saved her from a loveless life. And ten years of love is better than a lifetime of loneliness. Some paintings depict the couple in the second circle of Hell together."

They discussed Paolo and Francesca all the way to the top of the mountain. There, Francesca got out of the car, captivated by the beautiful stone walls encasing the charming village and castle. It looked magical from what she could see through the grand stoned archway.

Francesca fell in love with the ancient village, the breathtaking castle, and the welcoming people. The main street sloped up to the castle, glorious with all its shops and restaurants. Francesca asked people to take many pictures of the two of them so she would be able to take them to her mother's grave.

They had dinner at a restaurant named Tavernetta Paolo e Francesca and bought three bottles of wine from the owner. The wine was named after the couple, with a label showcasing a renaissance couple embraced.

They stayed at a beautiful bed and breakfast with a view of the castle. Then, the next morning, they explored more of the city.

Ryder hated to end the adventure, but they still had a four-hour drive to Rome for their first concert that evening. They found Bruno at the bed and breakfast and headed to their next destination.

Rome itself was a zoo. People were driving like maniacs and, for once, Ryder was thankful for the driver he had hired. The young Bruno turned into Mario Andretti, cutting people off, lifting his arm and swearing constantly. They arrived at the hotel in one piece, where they met the rest of Ryder's bandmates and families who had accompanied them.

Ted had reserved a private dining room for the band before the concert. After an amazing meal, they headed out to Villa Celimontana, an outdoor venue just behind the Coliseum.

Francesca was beyond herself with excitement. She couldn't believe she was seeing her first Fornication concert in Rome with the Coliseum within view.

Francesca and Melissa sat in the front row. The intimate crowd grew beyond their section, the lawn seats behind them and into the park. The large crowd screamed in excitement.

Fornication had just finished one of their top hits when Evan spoke into the microphone.

"Thank you, Rome. We love you!" The crowd went wild, and then Evan continued, "We have a special treat for you tonight, but I need your help. Ry has written a new song, and you are going to be the first to hear it. So, help me get him off his perch, and get him down here! Ry! Ry! Ry!" Evan encouraged the crowd with a waving motion.

The volume increased as Ryder came down from his elevated spot behind the large drum set and to a stool a roadie had just set out. Then he was handed an acoustic guitar.

Ryder was in costume—as was his persona for concerts—wearing a ripped T-shirt with no sleeves, faded jeans, thick leather bracelets, dark sunglasses, a dreadlocks wig, and a biker bandana across his forehead.

The lights softened and a spotlight shined down on Ryder as he sat. He slung the guitar strap over his shoulder, then raised his eyes and found Francesca in the front row. Looking into her eyes, he said, "This one's for you, Beauty. It's called, 'Heart and Soul'."

Evan started with a haunting melody on the piano, as Ryder joined in with his guitar.

With his raspy voice, he began to sing the song in a slow, luring voice.

My girl's just a tiny little thing with a seven-foot personality.

My beauty saves souls without a second thought.

Minds or bodies, broken and worn, she envelops them wholeheartedly with open arms.

My girl doesn't judge; she couldn't care less what the hell's wrong.

She's the beauty who tames the beast within me.

She's faithful and loyal to a fault. I could kill those who use her without remorse.

I hurt her so bad, convinced I wasn't worth the kindness inside her delicate soul.

But she forgave and taught me to care. To stand proud and comfortable within my skin.

She fought my demons and released the pain buried deep inside me.

My girl's just a tiny little thing with a seven-foot personality.

My beauty saves souls without a second thought.

Minds or bodies, broken and worn, she envelops them
wholeheartedly with open arms.

My girl doesn't judge; she couldn't care less what the hell's wrong.

She's the beauty who tames the beast within me.

The tears she sheds destroy me. She wipes them away to hide her
despair.

Her grace and courage are often her curse.

She dug deep inside me to save the man I didn't know I could be.

A thousand years would never be enough to give her my undying
love.

To begin life at thirty was a gift after the horrors of a childhood no
child should live.

But I would do it again without remorse if, in the end, she was my
reward.

My girl's just a tiny little thing with a seven-foot personality.

My beauty saves souls without a second thought.

Minds or bodies, broken and worn, she envelops them
wholeheartedly with open arms.

My girl doesn't judge; she couldn't care less what the hell's wrong.

She's the beauty who tames the beast within me.

She's a gift the world can't do without.

I love her, heart and soul.

Ryder looked up from his guitar as he struck the last chord to see Francesca smiling from ear-to-ear with tears streaming down her cheeks. She mouthed the words, *"Heart and soul, Beast,"* as she pounded her chest with a fist. Then she blew him a kiss and raised her hands to give him a standing ovation.

Everyone followed suit as Evan yelled out, "I hear a number one hit from that, Ry."

The night flew by. Francesca never took her eyes off Ryder while he pounded the drums. Every few minutes, he would twirl the drumsticks through every finger, then throw them up, catch them, and hit the drums without missing a beat. He was a master at his craft, and her respect increased tenfold.

After the concert, Francesca was led backstage, and the minute she saw Ryder, she flew into his arms. He wasn't prepared for her launch and stumbled backwards into Pete who stopped them from falling.

Oblivious to nearly causing them injury, she grabbed his face and attacked his mouth.

Then Kevin yelled, "Enough Romeo and Juliette. Save the porn for later."

Embarrassed, Francesca pulled away from Ryder to see at least thirty people staring at them.

She tucked her red face into the crook of his neck and whispered, "Sorry."

He lifted her chin. "Don't ever apologize for loving me." He kissed her, turning her quickly in circles, loving the laughter falling from her lips. "Let's get out of here." He turned to the venue coordinator and asked for a secure exit, certain he wouldn't be recognized after removing his costume.

Hand in hand, they walked to the Coliseum and shared in its wonders and the splendor of the entire evening.

It was late when they stumbled into their hotel room where, still on a high, they made soft, passionate love. It was late when Ryder finally tucked his Sleeping Beauty into his arms.

***

Bruno was the couple's tour guide in Rome as he drove them to all the sights Francesca had requested to see. First, they went to Fountain of Trevi, and Bruno told them it was tradition to throw coins over your right shoulder.

"If you throw one coin, it means you will see Roma again. Two coins, you will find a new romance. Maybe a nice Italian boy, eh?" he teased, causing Ryder to growl. "Three coins will lead to marriage. Personally, I think that the politicians created this to get more money from tourists. But, va bene, we need the money."

Francesca scoffed at his suggestion but couldn't get to the

fountain fast enough, dragging Ryder to toss coins.

There were some cute shops around the fountain. They were thrilled when they discovered a glass shop, where they bought each of their students a gift made from hand-blown glass. Ryder was pleased when he found an incredible glass pelican with a little red glass fish in its mouth for Katrina. He knew she would covet this animal above all others.

Next, they went to the Pantheon and marvelled at the structure that's only source of light came from a small, round hole at the top of the building. Then they went to the Vatican and toured St. Peter's Square, marvelling as Bernini's columns lined up in a perfect row when Bruno made them stand on one of two circles.

They saw St. Peter's Basilica, where Ryder had to drag Francesca away from her third visit to stare at Michelangelo's *Pieta*. She was in awe, looking at the beautiful Virgin Mary holding her son Jesus after his crucifixion. She had no idea it was the only statute Michelangelo had ever signed, something Bruno explained. And he only did that because people were saying his work was created by another sculptor.

They toured Sistine Chapel, and when Francesca saw guards walking throughout the room, saying, "Silenzio" and ensuring no photographs were taken, she was so disappointed. She told Ryder nothing meant more to her than seeing the ceiling, especially the *Creation of Adam.*

Francesca wandered for an hour in awe, explaining every individual fresco to Ryder. He was impressed by her knowledge and thrilled by her fascination.

There was a small scuffle, and Francesca watched as guards led Bruno away, but not before he carefully passed a camera to Ryder, undetected by the guards. Ryder had pulled Bruno aside when Francesca had gone into the washroom and offered him five hundred euros if he could get at least twenty photos of the ceiling.

It took twenty minutes for the guards to release poor Bruno. In the end, Francesca was over the moon when Ryder showed her the pictures. Bruno laughed about the experience as they finished their day, having an overpriced meal in Piazza Navona where they listened to musicians play as painters painted in the square surrounded by *The Fountain of Four Rivers*. Ryder recognized the location from the movie "Angels & Demons."

At midnight, Francesca asked Bruno to drop them off at the Villa Celimontana park so they could see the Coliseum one last time. Then they walked back to the hotel, hand in hand, stopping across the street at a cafe and sharing a litre of Ripasso wine as they talked endlessly about all they had seen.

***

"Our next stop is San Marino, isn't it?" Francesca guessed their next location when she realized they were again heading towards the Adriatic Sea. She rubbed her hands together, unable to contain herself.

At first light, they had parted ways with the band. Ryder had explained they would meet up with them before their concert in Florence.

"Yes. We have a four-and-half-hour drive, so you might as well fill me in before we get there."

She smiled. "Remember yesterday when I told you that the Vatican was the smallest independent country in the world? Well, San Marino is the fifth smallest country. Isn't it neat that two out of five of the smallest countries are located within Italy?"

Ryder had been to Italy more than a handful of times for concerts. However, he had never toured the sights. It had been more about partying with celebrities and high-ranking politicians. Being with Francesca and seeing it through her eyes was mind blowing. Her enthusiasm and knowledge was contagious.

"So, we have actually travelled to three countries in a matter of days? And surprisingly, Bruno hasn't killed us yet."

"Francesca, your beast is being mean again. Control him, please."

Ignoring their bantering, she continued. "It's the fifth smallest in the world, but the third smallest in Europe. We are going to walk around the medieval town and visit the two towers. I can't wait! This is so cool." She leaned sideways and kissed Ryder as she picked up her Italy travel guide to reread the information on the country.

Ryder pulled her closer to his side and read over her shoulder, confounded on how much his life had changed in less than a year.

As they drove up Mt. Titano, they started to see the captivating country. Francesca had the window open and was taking pictures. Once they reached the top, they found a flurry of activity and people dressed in medieval costumes.

"Bruno, do you know what's going on?"

"No, but I will find out." Bruno rolled down the window and spoke to a couple of men dressed in leggings, tunics, and cloaks. When he got his information, he turned towards the couple. "It appears we couldn't have come at a better time. They have a festival called Medieval Days."

Francesca was thrilled at the turn of events. "Yay! I can't believe our luck. Quick, let's go. I don't want to miss a thing." She was already out the door, dragging Ryder with her, while Bruno suggested he book them into the hotel, saying he would meet up with them afterwards.

Ryder and Francesca walked up the steep, narrow roads, walking in and out of shops. In one shop, they had all types of liquor, and the couple just about fell over when they found the most unique hand-blown glass bottles of Grappa.

"Do you even realize what you're looking at?" Ryder smirked, knowing damn well she hadn't.

Francesca looked at him like he had lost his mind. "Yes, of

course. It's a glass figurine in the middle of a bottle."

Ryder's smile grew. "Look closer and tell me what they are doing."

She carefully lifted the bottle and examined it. Ryder saw the instant she realized what it was by the blush rushing up her chest.

"Oh, my God, they are in a sexual position!" she whisper-hissed in embarrassment.

Ryder laughed at her reaction, deciding he had to buy one.

Francesca was mortified. She walked out of the store, convinced the merchant thought they were perverts.

Ryder came out five minutes later, still amused.

They then spent the day enjoying the festival and the city, watching a medieval wedding re-enactment and marvelling at the owl show. They watched a crossbow competition in the main square, and then sat in a restaurant, looking over the square.

Just as the sun was setting, a parade went up the main street. They watched a group of men twirl large flags then throw them in the air and catch them.

She turned towards Ryder with enthusiasm. "That reminds me of you with your drumsticks. I never did tell you how impressed I was. I could watch you for hours. I was so proud of your talent at the concert."

"Thank you. For almost a year, I've been fascinated by you and your job. Glad I could impress you with mine." Ryder bent sideways and consumed his fiancée's mouth.

Once they were through with their meal, Ryder ordered another bottle of wine and purchased two wine glasses from the restaurant. Once the bill was paid, he took Francesca's hand and led her up the walkway to the highest point of the city. It was dark, except for the lightning show from a storm over the Adriatic.

Ryder lifted Francesca up onto the ancient wall and pulled the cork from the wine the waiter had kindly opened and re-corked. He poured two glasses then handed one to her.

"Here's to us, and you becoming Mrs. Vaughn very soon. I love you." They clinked glasses.

Francesca smiled as she took a sip of the glorious wine. "Mr. Vaughn, are you trying to get me drunk?"

"If it means Magdalene coming out to play, then you bet your life." Ryder laughed as he cupped her face and muscled his way between her thighs. When he moved in and kissed her senseless, she could feel his erection growing rapidly.

Ryder's breathing increased as he deepened the kiss. He placed his glass on the wall then slid his hand up her sundress, feeling her body heat. She purred into his mouth as he moved her panties to the side and dipped one finger into her moist core.

Francesca pulled back from the kiss. "Ryder, someone is going to see us."

"It's dark. No one will see. Let go, baby." Ryder removed his hand from her core, undid his jeans, then pulled out his cock.

"No, we can't. Let's go back to the room." She tried to bat his hand away.

"Be adventurous. I want to always remember fucking you on this wall, in this medieval town, with a thunderstorm as the background." Ryder reached inside her dress and bra, gently rolling one of her nipples while he devoured her mouth. He moaned as he brought his dick in line with her entrance and gently pushed in.

She moaned out his name as he picked up the pace, thrusting in and out.

Pulling his face away from hers, he looked down, trying to get a glimpse of their joining. Nothing had ever been so erotic.

Francesca also looked, just as a bolt of lightning gave them the view they had both been hoping for. The rumble of the earth shaking as the thunder quickly followed added to the craziness of their intimate encounter.

The sky suddenly opened, and they got drenched. Still, they didn't move until Ryder bucked his final thrust and they wailed together in completion.

Chapter 26

"I Finally Found Someone"
By Barbra Streisand and Bryan Adams

They arrived at Greve in Chianti in three and half hours, and travelled another fifteen minutes to their bed and breakfast, Relais Fattoria Valle. The building was a captivating, old, two-level coach house with large rooms that had antique furniture. Even the key was a skeleton key.

When Francesca opened the windows, the view was spectacular. They were surrounded by mountains, covered in terraces of olive trees and grapes. Looking down, she saw a patio adorned with beautiful wrought iron furniture with steps leading to a dazzling pool surrounded by an orchard of gnarly old olive trees.

"Look at the pool. I hope we get a chance to go swimming."

As Ryder joined her at the window, he saw it did look inviting, but he had never swum before. If they had time, he would watch her from the lounge chairs. Ryder had promised himself, when they travelled to Tropea, he was going to fulfill her dream by standing in the Mediterranean Sea with her. Right now, though, he had other plans.

"Maybe later. We have a lot to see, so let's get going. I told Bruno we would be down in the car in five minutes, and that was ten minutes ago."

Their first stop was the Leaning Tower of Pisa. Once there, Francesca scrambled out of the car.

"Wow, it's so much bigger than I thought. And the marble is stunning. I can see veins of pink. Huh, I assumed it would look so much older and weathered."

"I don't know. It looks exactly like it did in the Loony Toon's cartoon where the man tricks the little dog by telling him the tower was falling, and the little dog holds it up for days."

Bruno was horrified by Ryder's description. He explained the importance of the tower, and that it was built as a bell tower for the Cathedral. The tower started to sink during one of the phases of construction because of unstable ground. He went on to explain, after hundreds of years, engineers managed to stabilize the tower and restored it in 2001.

Bruno laughed at the couple, as they came up with different ways to give the illusion of holding up the tower like the little dog from the cartoon while he took pictures.

After buying a pair of leaning coffee mugs, they proceeded to Florence where Ryder had a concert at the Viper Theatre, a small venue just outside the city. First, though, he had a surprise for Francesca.

"I'm starving. What did you want to show me down this little road?" Francesca asked.

Ryder stopped in front of an unassuming building and handed the attendant the tickets. Then the three of them walked into the museum. She was astonished Ryder had obtained the tickets since they were sold out when Francesca had tried to buy them.

She stopped just around the corner as she spotted the statue of *David*. Ryder couldn't keep up as she took off towards it.

"Jesus! I didn't realize the statue was going to be so big. It's beautiful. Look at his hands and feet; they are so realistic and large."

Francesca circled the statue many times, absorbing every detail and pointing things out that Ryder neither cared about or was interested in. However, this was her dream, and he wanted to fulfill it completely.

Next, they toured the rest of Florence, buying leather purses for her sistas before stopping at a deli, where they indulged in creating their own ginormous panini sandwiches. Full, they then headed to the venue for the concert, and then arrived back at the bed and breakfast at two a.m.

They laid in bed the next morning until eleven then took a walk to a cute, little winery up the street, where they had a tour of their cellars and vineyards. At Francesca's request, they then met the band in the tiny town of Greve in Chianti at two in the afternoon.

"What exactly are we doing in this one blink town?" Pete asked.

Francesca linked arms with Ryder. "Follow me. There is this wine cellar I want you all to experience. It's called Enoteca Falorni. I want you to sample the best wines in Tuscany."

They walked behind the main street and down a flight of stairs into the caverns under the town. Enoteca Florini had been turned into a gorgeous tasting bar, where they could sample over a hundred different regional wines. It was an incredible scene as they walked into an abundance of rooms filled with unique machines, allowing them to sample as many different wines as they wanted.

Ryder purchased prepaid cards, loaded them with euros, and handed one to everyone. The group wandered around, inserting the cards into the machines and sampling as many different types of wine as they could drink.

They laughed, becoming tipsy after the first hour, and decided to order some antipasto. They sat at a large group of tables, eating, drinking, and discussing which wines they liked as they all got up intermittently to sample more vino.

Kevin was loaded when he started reminiscing about their years travelling together. The guys took turns telling different stories about all their misadventures. Francesca was in her glory as she listened to stories of Ryder, but she was also intimidated as they talked about all their famous encounters.

Ryder wasn't paying attention. He had been on his phone all day, sending and receiving texts and emails. When she inquired as to what had him so occupied, he simply replied he was talking with Ted about the tour. It was strange to her that none of the other bandmates were preoccupied.

The next day was a total write off. Everyone was recovering from their hangovers. Then they travelled to Sienna for their third concert, and Ryder was again engrossed with his phone. Something was up, and she was starting to get worried.

The next morning, Francesca left the beautiful bed and breakfast with a heavy heart as they headed farther south to the destination she had been dying to see, Civita di Bagnoregio. She had never seen Ryder so distracted, and he wouldn't tell her what was going on. Her gut feeling told her something was wrong.

She texted her papa and told him she was freaking out because Ryder was acting so strange and she didn't know what to do. Her father told her to relax; that she was now seeing Ryder at work, which was a big part of his life, and something she needed to come to terms with. Francesca knew he was right, but she started to feel neglected.

She knew Ryder hadn't heard one of her descriptions of the cool place they were going to see tomorrow as he typed endlessly away on his phone. This was her once in a lifetime location that she had been dying to see, and now, with him so preoccupied, she felt like she would be seeing it alone.

Ryder had booked them a room in a castle near the town, and it was beyond anything she could have dreamed. The room was out of a fairy tale. A large canopy bed with white organza was the centrepiece of the room, the washroom was as big as her whole apartment and luxurious beyond belief, and it appeared they were the only guests in the entire castle.

That night after the concert, Ryder and Francesca didn't have sex for the first time on their trip. She tried to seduce him, but he claimed he was tired. She panicked, her heart hurting and her mind going into overdrive. Her premonition was coming true. He was already getting bored of her.

The next morning came early. Ryder quickly showered before dragging Francesca out of the bed and hustling her into the shower, insisting she get up before the sun so they could get to Civita di Bagnoregio just after sunrise. He hoped the mist lingered around the city, giving it an even more enchanting feel for what he had planned.

Francesca felt like she hadn't slept a wink, tossing and turning all night with apprehension. Her apprehension only got worse when she overheard Ryder on his phone through the cracked open bathroom door.

"I was afraid you wouldn't get my message and would miss the plane I sent for you. I'm grateful you're here." He laughed at something the person said. "Believe it or not, I think I'm falling for that undeniable charm of yours … No, of course she doesn't know about you being here … Okay, thanks … Love you, too, babe."

Francesca's heart plummeted. It had been a woman. Was it possible he had someone else on the side? Why would he bring another woman to Italy? Why did he ask her to marry him if he was falling in love with someone else?

No, she had to stop this. She was being silly. She had faith in Ryder. She knew he would never hurt her like that. Nevertheless, her insecurities ran rampant after all the stories she had heard the other day from his bandmates.

There had to be an explanation. She had to give him the benefit of the doubt. She would wait and see if he said anything. If not, she would bring it up tonight.

"Francesca, hurry up! Quit dragging your ass. I thought you were excited about seeing Civita di Bagnoregio."

She stepped out of the bathroom. "Who was on the phone?"

Ryder looked guilty, stumbling through his words. "No one important. Let's get going."

For the first time since she had met Ryder, she knew in her heart he had just lied to her.

"I'm actually not feeling well today. Why don't you go without me?"

Ryder moved to her with concern. "What's wrong?" He felt her forehead. She was cool to the touch, but she did look pale.

"Sweetheart, talk to me. Is it your stomach? Does your head hurt?"

She couldn't tell him it was her heart. "No. I don't know. I just don't feel well. Take the day and do whatever you want. I'm staying here."

"No, you've been talking about this place practically since the day I met you, and I want to take you there. Maybe it's just nerves about finally seeing something you have wanted to for so long. Come on; I'm sure you'll feel better once we get there. I'm more excited about seeing this place than any other."

That sounded like the Ryder she knew and loved. But what about what she had heard? He hadn't been out of her sight since he had arrived in Italy. Surely she had misheard him.

She would compartmentalize her distress until later. If they were going to have a successful marriage, then they needed to communicate. She would focus on that for now and put faith in her fiancé.

They travelled the thirty minutes to the location of her dreams where the narrow cobblestone road ended at a cliff. When they got out of the car and walked to the edge, both Ryder and Francesca gasped as they saw the most spectacular sight they would ever see.

A mist-filled gorge surrounded the inner core of a city which was all that was left of a once thriving ancient metropolis. It looked like a castle standing alone above the clouds with the sun just poking above.

"Your mom guessed right, Beauty. This is the most stunning vision on earth. And I am thrilled we got to see it together." He placed each of his arms down on either side of her, leaning on the edge of a stone wall and caging her in. He brought his head down close enough to smell the apples from her shampoo and nuzzled her neck.

She turned in his arms and cupped his jaw, bringing his mouth to hers for a sensual kiss.

They heard click after click, and when they lifted their heads, they saw Bruno taking pictures. It was a beautiful moment captured for years to come.

After standing engrossed for more than a few moments, Ryder received another text, tensing as he read it.

Francesca also tensed, knowing, like the phone call before, this text was going to change her life.

Not letting the allure of the moment deter her any longer, she asked the question that had been driving her crazy. "Ryder, please tell me what's going on. You haven't been yourself, you are always on the phone, and I heard you telling a woman earlier that you love her."

"Frankie, you've had enough trouble; don't go borrowing more," Taya said as she walked up to a stunned Francesca.

"Taya! What are you doing here? I thought you were in Croatia, dealing with a family emergency."

Taya wrestled her friend away from a grumbling Ryder, who was telling her not to call her Frankie. Hugging her tightly, she whispered in her ear, "I was, and I have to go back tomorrow, but I couldn't miss this. I'm the woman he said he loves, because I walked through hell to meet you here today."

"Is this what all the texting and emailing has been about?" Francesca asked, turning to look curiously up at Ryder.

"I asked Taya here to be your maid of honour."

"What are you talking about? You and I talked about this. I wanted to ask her myself." Her faced dropped when she realized the job was done.

Ryder felt an instant bit of fear. "I didn't have a choice. You said you wanted all your family and friends to attend our wedding. This was the only way I could make it happen."

Francesca started to back up as things started adding up in her mind. "What are you talking about?"

Ryder stalked her just as the rest of her friends and family came into view. She was backing up more quickly now, and Ryder had to lunge for her before she tripped.

Smiling, he lifted her up and onto the stone wall, holding her shaking hands as he again got down on one knee. "Francesca, will you do me the honour of becoming my wife in front of all our friends and family today, in this beautiful place?" He pointed towards Civita di Bagnoregio.

Trying to absorb all that was happening, Francesca lifted her tear-filled eyes. "Really?"

"Yes, Beauty, really." He smiled, watching her process and taking longer than he had expected. "I need an answer."

"But what about a dress? I don't want to get married in jeans. And what about flowers, tuxes, rings ...? Ryder, this takes months, if not years, to plan."

Sal stepped forward, carrying his tuxedo. "And what about me being a groomsman?"

Gabriella stepped forward with her daughters who were carrying baskets full of rose petals. "And what about flower girls and bridesmaids?"

Nonna Lena stepped forward with a beautiful embossed handkerchief. "And something old?"

Zia Concettina stepped forward with a garter, twirling it around her finger. "Something blue?"

Frank came forward with a beautiful bouquet of flowers. In the middle, nestled into the flowers, was her grandmother's diamond broach that her mother had worn at her wedding. "How about something borrowed? Bambolina, Ryder has fulfilled all your dreams. Give him the answer he's been waiting so patiently to hear. It's time for the traditional Italian wedding breakfast, and then you need to get ready."

Francesca looked back at Ryder with tears swimming in her

eyes. "Isn't it bad luck to see the bride before the ceremony?"

Ryder laughed as he pulled his girl off the wall and hugged her tiny body close. "My bad luck disappeared the minute I laid eyes on you. As long as I continue to see you, I will only have good luck. Let's go celebrate and savour all the day has to offer."

***

The breakfast was amazing. Then Francesca sat with her closest friends, plus her zia, having their makeup and hair done. The stylist informed Francesca that Ryder had insisted her long hair be curled then pinned up with only a few pins so that, as soon as the ceremony was over, he could release her hair. She was stunned he had looked after even the smallest detail.

Taya came forward in her black gown with a sweetheart neckline and a small gem-encrusted belt under her breasts with a ribbon of blue through the middle that matched perfectly to her crystal blue eyes.

"Wow, you look stunning!" Francesca breathed out.

"I pale in comparison to you, my little eye-talian. Up you get. Your dress awaits," Taya said as a woman walked into the room, carrying the dress of her dreams.

Francesca covered her mouth. How was it possible when nobody had known about this dress?

When she regained her composure, she asked. "How?"

Taya teared up, which was even a surprise to her closest friends.

"Apparently, you have a secret Pinterest file that you left open on your iPad a couple of months ago, and that beast of a man took pictures of everything you ever dreamed of. Look at my dress and the flower girls." Taya gestured at them. "Now look at your dress. Ryder contacted Edward, and he used the same team that made Gabriella's dress. They had your measurements from her wedding, so they recreated everything in that file, right down to your Italian lace vail. The man adores you. He pulled all this off ... with our help, of course, in a matter of three weeks." Taya grabbed Francesca's hand and pulled her crying friend up into a hug.

"Frankie, we all love you and couldn't be happier for you," Dakota said. "This is just the beginning. Ryder will make sure your life is full of love and happiness, and I can't think of anyone more deserving. The only thing he couldn't do was have your mother or Tommy here, but he did arrange to have the wedding in the location of your mother's dream. Somehow, I know she's here, giving her blessing and watching over you."

Francesca cried even harder as she was passed from one friend to the next. The last one to hug her was her zia.

"Ryder asked me to be a bridesmaid. Even though I am older, I can still hold my own with this gorgeous group of women. I was honoured beyond words. He said it was your wish, but he also said he would have asked me even if you didn't. Even though you aren't my daughter by birth, you are still the daughter of my heart, and I feel the need to impart some words of wisdom.

"You have an amazing man. Cherish all that he is. Treat him like you do all these girls." She indicated the women in the room. "Respect is the core of any marriage. He will drive you crazy at times because he is a man but, if you trust in him and the love you have, you will always be happy. Lastly, don't ever be afraid to use the body God gave you to bend him to your will." Concettina laughed as she pulled her sobbing, laughing niece into her arms.

A very irritated makeup girl spoke up in very broken English. "You had better be finished because I am only doing her makeup one more time." With that, she sat Francesca down to rework her magic.

A little while later, Francesca proceeded to the footbridge that led up to the city. Frank was standing with Ryder and Zio Antonio, laughing at something, until they saw Francesca approach. Then all three men were stunned into silence with their mouths gaping open.

Ryder swallowed twice as his heart sped up, trying to get moisture into his suddenly parched mouth. Francesca was a vision surrounded by her bridal party.

Francesca smiled at Ryder as he looked her over from head to toe. Her ears were adorned with the chandelier diamond earrings he had sent to the room as a wedding gift. Her dress fit her curves like a glove. It was Italian lace that had an off-the-shoulder lace jacket with three quarter sleeves that came across her bust and hid the dip of the dress between her breasts. It was formfitting, accentuating her tiny waist, then following the curve of her hip and thighs before billowing gently out like a tulip as only lace will do, leaving a long, stunning trail of lace behind her.

On top of her up-do with tendrils hanging loose was an Italian lace veil with scalloped edges. He hadn't seen the back yet, but he knew it was super low, just above the curve of her ass. He looked forward to catching a glimpse of her tiny back and luscious behind. He licked his lips in anticipation just before he looked up and caught a flash of sparkle from the brooch in her bouquet.

While Ryder was taking in his bride, she was looking at him. He was dressed in a black tux that fit him beautifully, and his long hair wasn't as unruly as it usually was. But it was the adoring smile and the sparkle in his eyes that took her breath away.

"Francesca, you have never looked more beautiful." Ryder told her as she stepped closer to the group.

She suddenly looked shy, glancing down as she replied, "Thank you."

Ryder stepped forwards and placed the tip of his finger under her chin, lifting her face upwards. "Today, we begin our new lives with our heads held high. I love you more and more each day. Now and forever, Beauty." Ryder stepped back, questioning Frank, "Is Nonno sure he can walk that far? I still can have a Vespa take him up."

Frank turned to Zio Antonio and spoke in Italian. Then turned back to Ryder. "He insists that he only gets to walk his grandson once to his wedding. He says he will lean on you for support."

The ever-present lump was back in Ryder's throat as he watched the old man link his arm with Ryder's. The two of them started up the four hundred and three metre steep incline.

Next, Zia Concettina followed the path covered by a red runner, lined on both sides by all their family and friends. Zara, Jocelyn, Gabriella, and Dakota followed, with the two flower girls dropping white rose petals up the walkway. The group moved very slowly as Zio Antonio set the pace.

Frank folded his daughter's hand firmly in the crux of his arm. "Are you ready, bambolina? Your prince awaits." He nodded to Taya to start walking.

"Oh, Papa ..."

Frank waited until she looked at him. "No tears, my baby. This is the happiness day of your life, and I want to remember a smile on your face, not your tears. Va Bene!" he said as the first of many tears rolled slowly down his face.

"Si, Papa. Do as I say, not as I do."

"Si, my daughter." He wiped away the first wave of tears. "One more thing before we start. Francesca, not even I could have picked a more perfect man for you. I am proud of you both and wish you a lifetime of happiness. I love you, bambolina." Frank kissed his daughter then started to walk.

Francesca was so caught up in the moment that she didn't even notice everyone who was standing on the footpath over the gorge. One by one, everyone came into view as she walked passed them. It was all her friends from school, even Mrs. Ramara and her husband, and the parents and the young men she looked after at night, Ryder's friend's families. Every one of her family members from home and from Italy, Maurizio, Paula, and Bruno—they all stood with pride as the couple passed them. Then, right before the top of the path, there stood all their students with their parents or caregivers.

Veeta stood in an ice blue dress, copied from the movie *Frozen*. Katrina wore a dress covered in animals with a lion purse, which she opened and smiled from ear-to-ear as she showed Francesca her glass pelican. She watched as Katrina's grandmother urged the girl to put the delicate trinket back into her purse. Next stood Taz and his parents and sister, looking dapper with his new belt they had purchased from Florence.

Theo jumped away from his parents into Francesca's path, yelling, "Give me some tongue, Francesca!"

His parent embarrassingly corralled their son, dragging him back to his place.

"Maybe later, Theo." Francesca laughed as she heard her future husband bellow with laughter farther ahead.

As they approached Mason, she saw he had a tear travelling down his cheek.

Francesca stopped her father and walked over to the teenager, taking the embossed handkerchief wrapped around her flowers and wiping his tear.

Mason looked down with adoration. "It just fell because you're smoking hot and burning my eyes."

Francesca laughed as she looked up and pulled him down, kissing his cheek. "I love you, too, buddy."

"I love you, too, Frankie," he returned with a soft whimper.

She walked back to her father and proceeded through the gates and into the grand piazza. In front of San Donato church stood Judge Belmore, dressed eloquently beside a priest. To the left stood Ryder and Zio, with Sal, Lucky, Evan, Kevin, and Pete, all looking stunning in their tuxes.

Francesca looked at a glowing Ryder as her father guided her towards her future.

When they reached the front, they turned and watched all their guests follow the same path.

Once everyone had taken their seats, Ryder and Zio moved down two steps as Edward and Liam, in full British dress, removed their swords and raised them above the two men.

Francesca gasped in delight.

Judge Belmore stepped forward with the priest. In English, she asked, "Who gives this man away?" followed by the priest in Italian.

Zio Antonio stood prouder and taller as he claimed, "I, his

grandfather, give him to the woman of his heart, but not away."

Francesca and Ryder both choked up with giggles at his declaration.

Next the priest and the judge asked, "Who gives this woman away?"

Frank tried twice, and on the third attempt, said, "I, and the spirit of her mother, give our daughter to this man." He leaned over and kissed Francesca before leading his beloved daughter towards Ryder and Zio.

Both men joined the couple's hands as Edward and Liam lowered their swords yet remained beside the couple.

As Zio stepped down and moved to sit to the right of the aisle as representation of Ryder's family, Frank moved beside Ryder.

Francesca tilted her head to the side, trying to figure out why Frank hadn't gone with Zio.

"Your father is my best man, Beauty," Ryder answered her look as he squeezed her hand.

Tear number one trailed down her cheek.

The ceremony began in both English and Italian. The sacred vows were given and answered with joy. Finally, the priest announced in Italian, while Judge Belmore followed in English, "I now pronounce you, husband and wife. You may kiss your bride."

Liam and Edward raised their swords as Ryder wrapped his large arms around his delicate wife and kissed her deeply.

"That's it, Ryder! Give Frankie some tongue!" Theo screamed as he stood up and gave them the horn symbols.

The couple giggled but didn't let up, until Mason groaned, "If you don't stop, I'm going to lose my shit."

The English-speaking people broke into laughter, while the Italians were all asking what he had said.

In a fit of laughter, the couple broke apart, but not before Edward said, "Those kids are right up my alley. I'm sitting with them at dinner."

The priest looked out at the crowd and spoke as Judge Belmore repeated, "It is my great honour to introduce you to Mr. and Mrs. Francesca Maria and Ryder Rafael Vaughan."

Zio yelled, "Si, Rafael!"

The couple walked back down the aisle, hand in hand, to the piazza where they were joined by all their well-wishers.

After they greeted everyone, the couple was then whisked away with the bridal party for pictures around the captivating town. The caterers had set up all the tables around the piazza, where guests were served wine and hors d'oeuvres. Shortly after the couple returned, everyone was seated.

Frank was the host for the afternoon and spoke first in Italian, and then in English, "I would like to thank every one of you for being here today to celebrate the union of my daughter Francesca and my son Ryder Vaughn. Ryder has requested that they have their first dance now so he can enjoy his meal. So please, Ryder, Francesca, the floor awaits you."

Ryder reached over and removed the four pins holding back Francesca's hair, watching as all the glorious long curls fell. Then he unhooked the lace jacket from the back and removed it before holding out his hand for hers, walking his beautiful bride off the platform and to the centre of the piazza.

"Lift your hands out and cupped together," Ryder instructed.

She quirked her head to the side, but did as he asked.

Ryder dipped his hands into his pockets then pulled them out with closed fists. He brought his hands out and filled her smaller ones with glitter as the song, "Glitter in the Air," began to play.

She looked up at him just as the second tear fell with the motion of her head lifting, watching as he filled his own hands with glitter.

The sound of chairs scraping the ground drew her attention to those around her. She saw everyone start to slowly spin, releasing the glitter into the air. It was a breathtaking event as the sun captured the sparkling fragments dancing around the whole piazza.

"I wanted Tommy and your mom to be here with us. Now spin, Beauty."

Francesca threw her hands up and released the tiny bit of sorrow inside of her from missing her mom and baby brother. She laughed freely, grabbing more and more glitter from Ryder's pockets as she spun.

At the end of the song, the crowd remained on their feet and cheered for the couple and their tribute.

Ryder grabbed one of Francesca's hands and curled it onto his chest above his heart. Then he wrapped one over her shoulders and the other curled down around her waist. She laid her left hand on his shoulder as her favourite song began to play.

"That was for them. Now this song is for you."

She looked up at him as their hips began to sway to the music. "How did you know 'I Finally Found Someone' was my favourite song ever?"

"I didn't. It was the first song I heard you sing while I sat on that bench outside your classroom. No lyrics were ever more true."

Francesca looked up at Ryder, more in love than ever. She giggled to herself.

"What are you thinking, baby?" he asked.

"Yesterday, I was devastated, thinking your feelings for me had changed. You wouldn't stop texting, and then you turned me down last night—"

"Beauty, that was the hardest thing I've ever done," Ryder cut her off, unconcerned about the two hundred guests watching their every move. "But I remembered you telling me that we had to abstain the night before our wedding. So, as much as it killed me, I respected your wishes. That will be the absolute last time for the rest of our lives, I promise.

"Thankfully, we have the entire castle to ourselves for the next two nights, and I am definitely going to make you pay for having to turn you down. Then, after our last concert in Pompeii, which my nonno insists he is coming, to, we are heading for a week to Tropea for our honeymoon. When I take this dress off tonight and ship it back to Toronto, I want you to ship Mary with it. Magdalene and I have a few very naughty experiences ahead of ourselves."

Francesca giggled, thinking it was the least she could do. He had given her the wedding of her dreams, and now she would give him the honeymoon of his dreams.

They continued to move to the music as they quietly talked like they were the only two people in the world.

"I love you, heart and soul, Beast."

"Heart and soul, Beauty."

Epilogue

Thirty Years Later...

"Home" By Blue October

Hey, Maurizio. Sorry. I got your message, but I couldn't get here any sooner. Francesca needed me to go to the cheese store. The kids and grandkids are coming over for dinner tonight, and you know my beauty; we couldn't serve day-old ricotta. It must be fresh today. I brought some for you, too, and some Calabrese bread."

"Thank you, my friend. No need to rush. It's not like I'm going anywhere." Maurizio rolled his eyes. "My daughter has a meltdown every time I sneak into the restaurant and work for a few hours."

Ryder laughed. Rosalina was a lot like her mother Paula.

"So, what's so important you needed to see me today and couldn't wait for our regular Thursday night poker game?"

"I have something important to give you. I wanted to make sure we had some privacy." Maurizio struggled up from his seat at the kitchen table and went to his briefcase on the counter, retrieving an envelope. He waited until he sat back down before speaking. "I was entrusted with this letter and instructed to give it to you six months to the day of his passing. Today is that day." Maurizio held the envelope out to Ryder.

Ryder stumbled back in his chair, too intimidated to take it.

It had been a hard six months for him. His number one priority had been helping Francesca and the children recover after Frank's death.

A piece of his soul had died that day. He had not only lost his best friend, mentor, protector, and confidant. He had also lost his father. There were times that first month when he wasn't sure he would ever feel happiness again. That was, until his newest little granddaughter, Faith, threw her chubby little arms around him and said, "Nonno, I wuv you!" grabbing his cheeks and planting a big sloppy kiss on his lips. He swore he had heard Frank whispering in his ear, *"Hold on to every bit of happiness God has granted you."*

Maurizio stood up and walked to Ryder, placing a hand on his shoulder and putting the letter on the table. "I understand how you feel. I miss him, too."

It was too much for Ryder. He thanked Maurizio and stuffed the letter into his jacket pocket, quickly leaving the house.

He carried the letter everywhere he went for the next three months. Just like the coin Frank had given him, it was never out of his possession. Every time Ryder was upset, scared, or indecisive, he would reach into his pocket and rub the coin. His first thought as soon as his fingers touched it was, *What would Frank do?* That coin had helped him through many difficult times before he could get to the man himself for advice.

***

His youngest child, Rio, found her father sitting on his beloved Harley with the motor running. He had been quietly sitting there for over fifteen minutes.

"Daddy? Daddy, what's wrong? Why are you driving the neighbours crazy with the sound of your bike rumbling?"

Ryder snapped out of a memory with the weight of the letter resting against his heart. "Hey, princess. Sorry, I was just thinking."

Rio stomped her foot. "Daddy, you can stop the bullshit. I see right through you. Something's been bothering you for months now. I'm getting my helmet, and you are taking me somewhere." She looked so much like Francesca it was scary. And apparently, it wasn't just her looks that were exactly like her mother.

She walked into the garage, retrieved her helmet, and told her father to follow her directions as she jumped on the back of his motorcycle.

Ryder could never say no to his fifth child. He pulled out of the driveway, turning left as she instructed. After fifteen minutes, Ryder tensed when he realized where his princess was taking him—the place he hadn't visited since he laid a final white rose on the coffin.

Rio, feeling her daddy go rigid, wrapped her arms tighter around him, lending all her support as they drove up the hill and parked near the row Frank was buried.

Rio got off first, took her helmet off, and extended her hand. "You need to talk to him, Daddy."

Ryder took off his helmet and simply sat there.

"I can't do it, baby," he choked out, lowering his head as tears filled his eyes.

"You can, Daddy. Come on; he's been waiting for you." Rio took his helmet and placed it on the handlebars. Then she took her father's hand and guided him off the bike. "I'm going to be right there with you, just like he was."

He looked at his beautiful daughter and reached into his pocket to hold the coin for strength. Then he took her hand, and she led him to Frank's grave.

He was shocked to see the picture on the gravestone. It was one taken of Frank at their wedding so many years ago, laughing while throwing glitter. It made him smile, knowing he could never have pulled off the wedding of his wife's dreams without his father-in-law.

A sob escaped from the depths of his heart.

"It's okay, Daddy." Rio started crying. "He's with Grandma and Uncle Tommy now, happy and peacefully at rest. Before he died, he told me he wasn't afraid to go, because he knew he would be reunited with the love of his life. Talk to him. He'll hear you, I promise. His body resides here, but his spirit surrounds us every day."

Ryder looked at Rio, seeing the tears streaming down her face. How had she become so smart for a twenty-year-old? It had to be from Francesca's side. God knew it couldn't have come from his.

He pulled her down with him as he bent to sit, resting comfortably against Frank's gravestone with his baby beside him. When he felt the man's presence, he started to speak.

"Frank, I'm sorry it took me so long to get here. I miss you so much. My life just isn't the same without you. I feel guilty because I haven't been able to read your letter. Somehow, I know when I do, it will become final, and you will really be gone. I wanted to wait forever to hear your last words to me." Ryder removed his hand from his daughter's so he could wipe his eyes and take out the letter.

With shaking hands, he tried to open it, but his grief got the best of him, and he dropped it.

Rio picked it up and opened it, carefully smoothing out all the wrinkles. Then she started to read it:

"To my dearest son, Ryder Rafael ..."

Ryder laughed out loud at the Rafael part, and was now eager to hear Frank's last words to him.

Rio started again:

"To my dearest son, Ryder Rafael,

I may not have been your father by birth, but in every sense of the word, you are my son. And because you are my child, I have tried to guide you as well as learn from you.

As I sat down to write this letter, I started thinking of some of my most cherished memories, and there have been many. Do you remember when you called me from the bathroom of your condo in California? You had locked yourself in there because Francesca was threatening to kill you after finding out you were the one who had purchased all her paintings. It took us both an hour to talk her down. I'm still laughing about that conversation thirty years later.

Ryder, you taught me about the power of giving lyrics, and now I would like to give you that gift. Take a moment and download a song you might remember, although it was over twenty-five years ago. The song is called "Home" by Blue October. Listen to that song, and then finish this letter.

Now that you have heard the lyrics, I am sure you are smiling from ear-to-ear from the memory. You and Francesca had just celebrated your anniversary and, at the time, you only had three children.

We were all sitting in the kitchen after an amazing meal, and you two had exchanged gifts in front of us. As was your tradition, you gave each other lyrics, knowing words with meaning far surpassed anything monetary. You gave her that song, and after she read the lyrics, you cranked the stereo, grabbed my baby's hand, and danced around the kitchen, bellowing out the lyrics.

The children laughed and danced around you, thrilled by your excitement. Her laughter was heard throughout the house, telling all of us, it was the best gift you had ever given her. It was also the best gift you had ever given me.

Every time I heard that song afterwards, my heart was filled with love. It is the best memory I have of the two of you, by far, and that is saying a lot, considering you moved me into your home the minute you built it, not six months after marrying my bambolina. That was a gift I could never repay, because you filled my life with children and joy. You allowed me to be a part of every aspect of their lives.

I will never forget when Cassy was born. Francesca had been in labour for fifteen hours, and the doctors sent you out so she could get an epidural. You walked into the waiting room, white as a ghost, and threw yourself into my arms, bursting into tears, telling me you couldn't survive another minute of Francesca in pain. You claimed Cassy would be your only child.

The minute I saw you holding your pink bundle of joy you named after my wife, I knew there would be more. She was your first, but I told you that day Cassy would not be your last. Was I wrong, son?

Then you promised Zio Antonio that Francesca would have a son next, and that, if he lived long enough, you would name that child Antonio. It still makes me proud that you flew the whole family to Italy so he could witness the baptism of his namesake. You fulfilled his dream, and he died with peace, knowing that his legacy would live on.

I didn't think you could outdo yourself until you insisted your next son be named after my son Tommy. I swear to anyone who listens that my Tommy's happy spirit lives inside that carefree, cheerful boy.

That memory brings us to your fourth child. Sorry, I had to put my pen down because I was laughing so hard ...

I remember your face when Francesca announced, if the baby was a boy, she was naming him Bruno. You were adamant that no son of yours was going to be named after that smart-mouthed limo driver, giving her a choice of ten other acceptable names.

My son, I remember her fourth labour was the most difficult delivery because he was a bruiser, weighing in at nine pounds, eleven ounces. When you again thought she wouldn't survive the birth, she made you promise that, if it was a boy, she could name him Bruno. My little angel got her way, and I would say Bruno's humour is his most wonderful trait. You might disagree, but even in the worst situation, he makes us all laugh. He was named well.

Francesca, taking the advice of her doctor, got her tubes tied, and I believed that was it. Then, to discover Francesca was pregnant again, both thrilled me and scared me to death. Your little Rio came into the world at only two pounds, two ounces, and it broke my heart to bring the priest to the hospital to give her the last rites. But she was her father's daughter and fought for the life she was given.

You asked me every hour to go to the chapel and

help you pray for her little soul. We didn't know for almost a year if she was going to have any medical issues, but you forever had little Rio resting on your bare chest, providing heat and love. I think she thrived because of the love and affection you both gave her.

She is a very special little girl who will offer you much comfort over the years to come. She is also the feistiest and will challenge you even more than Bruno.

Ryder, you have created a beautiful family, and it was my honour to be a part of it. I told you once that angels come in many different forms, and you were the ugliest I had ever seen. Son, that wasn't true. The beauty you have within you far outshines the most dazzling sunsets I have ever seen. Your soul is good and pure.

Son, please listen to my words now. I know you will struggle the most with my death, as I struggle with leaving you. But I have lived a good life, filled with so much happiness and love. I know you will understand when I tell you that I miss my wife and wish to be reunited with my other half. So please, don't be sad for me. Celebrate my reunion.

508

I may not be with you in body, but my soul is always around you. Listen to that song again and know I am standing right beside you, carrying you through this hard time.

Go home and dance with your wife, sing that song aloud, surrounded by your children and grandchildren, and know we are watching.

Continue to make good memories that will make me proud.

I love you, my son, heart and soul."

Ryder laid his arms and head upon his bent knees and cried his heart out. He allowed himself to grieve for the man who had impacted his life the most. When he was done, he promised himself to only smile from now on when he thought of Frank.

When Rio composed herself, she took out her phone and repeatedly played the song from her grandfather's letter until her father's eyes dried up.

Ryder looked over at the child that Francesca had named after his birth place. Francesca had insisted, even though Rio was an accident, that the girl was a gift to Ryder he couldn't live without.

"Thank you for knowing what I needed, princess. I think you inherited Grandpa's wisdom. You are indeed a gift. I love you, baby." He stood up and wiped the grass from his pants. "Now get on your phone and text all the family. Tell them I'm requesting their presence at the house tonight. We are celebrating and honouring your grandfather with the only request he ever made from me. Let's go home."

THE END

Thank you for reading my book!

After the acknowledgements, please read the first chapter to Dakota's story.
Thicker Than Blood, being released 2017!

Acknowledgments

To my heart & soul, my husband, Tony. When I found you, I found my future. I found the lyrics to every love song I have ever heard. You make me laugh until I can't breathe. You pick me up when I can't stand. And you wipe away my tears. I couldn't survive one day without your love and respect.

Your courage, patience, and strength has never diminished over the years; it has only grown stronger. You have stood by and encouraged me to follow all my dreams. You are always my biggest fan and supporter, even though you never read a single page of any of my books. (Wait, don't get mad at him yet) But you listened to every word when I read them aloud to you at least twice. You are my beast who brings out the beauty within me. Heart & Soul!

To my four sons, I love each of you with my whole heart and soul. You all amaze me every day, and I am so proud of you. You drive me to the brink of craziness, and in the next breath, you calm me.

I tried to find words that describe each of you, but the words ended up applying to all of you. You guys are strong, loyal, curious, dependable, generous, loveable, hot-tempered, and hilarious. You make me want to kill you one minute, and then you have me laughing my guts out the next. The only thing I wish for all of you boys is to find the loves of your lives. And my revenge is to wish you have children just like yourselves. Heart and soul!

To Eve and Nawal, you girls are amazing, and I am proud to call you the daughters of my heart. Your sense of family is awe-inspiring, your bubbly personalities radiate, and my boys couldn't have picked more stunning women, inside and out. Heart and soul!

To my beautiful little princess, Isabelle: To have a girl after four boys was a dream come true. You are adorable, precious, and beyond sweet. Being your Grand-Marie is truly one of the greatest honours of my life. And remember, if Mommy and Daddy won't give you something, Grandma always will! Heart and soul, Izzy!

To my parents, you are by far the strongest, most loving people I know. Your relationship with each other has inspired me throughout my life. To be in love after fifty-eight years is a testament to forever! Heart and soul!

To my oldest brother, Joe. Wow, what can I say? You are my biggest non-reading fan, insisting I didn't tell a soul when my first book was released because you wanted the first copy. You bought three and told everyone you knew. You even had a special case made for the book and display it in your sports memorabilia room as if it is your most valuable possession. It humbles me beyond words. Most of my love for music came from you, so this book honours you. If you decide to ever read this book, you will find a lot of yourself in Francesca's brothers. Your sick sense of humour, protectiveness, love, and loyalty go beyond words. All I can say is, heart and soul. Except, you won't read the book, so you won't understand it means I love you.

To all my girlfriends, thank you for your unconditional friendship! I love Caesar nights, girls' nights, drinks on Fridays, coffee nights, spa days, and time at the cottage. You are the strongest, most intelligent women in the world, and I gain strength and courage from your love. You make me laugh, you listen when I'm mad, and wipe my tears when I'm sad. You rock my world, and I couldn't imagine my life without you all. Heart and soul!

To Tina, thank you for help with proofreading my book. Your humour—or what you assume is humour—makes me laugh. Rest assured, I am laughing at you, not with you. Concettina is you through and through—sharp-ass tongue with a big heart. Heart and soul!

To Kendra, you are my daughter, not by birth, but definitely in my heart. I am going to hound you until you follow your dream, one chapter at a time. Heart & soul!

To Kristin at C&D Editing, I could never have released one book, let alone two, without you. You have the patience of a saint, and I know I test them to the limits. When I get my first edits back, it takes my breath away. You work so hard to make me look good. Your professionalism is awe-inspiring, and your kindness is boundless. I love when I pick up on a southern thing, and you question a northern thing. Your knowledge is astounding. I better stop or else everyone is going to want your services, and I won't be able to get in. Know that you mean the world to me! Heart & soul!

To Ravenne at Ravenne Design, thank you for my beautiful cover! You work so hard trying to put my vision into a stunning cover. You are unbelievably sweet and so easy to work with. Thank you for your patience. Heart & Soul!

Last but not least, Diane Zparkki, my writing partner, who shares my love for reading and writing. You write your books, and I write mine. We critique each other's books, chapter by chapter, and offer advice and encouragement. We walked each other through the process of publishing our first books, talking each other down from the ledge more times than I can count. You are an inspiration to me, and I still stand by my words that you are the most interesting woman I have ever met. Some outside force brought us together, and I will always believe it was so we could walk hand in hand to put our mark on the world. Heart & soul!

Thicker Than Blood

Chapter 1

A Little Tied Up

It was a beautiful sunny day, so who knew Dakota's whole world would change in the blink of an eye?

Spring was her favourite season. She could feel the warmth of the sun against her face. It was the first warm day this year. She was so thankful the snow had melted a couple of weeks ago, and she could look forward to spring. Everything seemed to be reborn, and the animals were all awakening after months of slumber.

Dakota loved nothing better than to drive her two-thousand thirteen candy apple red Bug, with the tunes cranked and the sunshine awakening the landscape. Since it was such a gorgeous day and she didn't have to be at her next school for forty-five minutes, she could take the back roads instead of fighting the traffic.

The road she was travelling on had beautiful big trees, and a large ravine that led to the Credit River to the right. The houses that lined the street were mini-mansions, and she often wondered what kinds of jobs people had to live in them.

Out of the corner of her eye, she caught movement. Taking her eyes off the road for a second, she followed it. On more than one occasion, Dakota had been lucky to see a deer coming up from the ravine.

When she fastened her gaze on the movement, she was shocked to see a black bear. No, she couldn't possibly have been seeing a bear. It had to be one of those Newfoundland dogs. They were massive and black. This was the outskirts of the fifth largest city in North America, and bears were never this close to the city. It contradicted everything she knew about black bears' habitats.

She blinked twice, not believing what she could clearly see. The bear, sensing it was being watched, turned towards her, rearing up on its hind legs. It was massive. The creature must have escaped from a zoo, but there weren't any zoos near this location. Dakota stared in awe.

Glancing back at the road, she saw she was approaching a sharp turn and had crossed the line, heading directly towards a large, old blue Cadillac.

Dakota tried to correct her position into the on-coming lane. Her steering wheel felt funny. She tried to pull the wheels to right, but it wasn't responding.

Her heart started to pound with panic, knowing she was not in control. The blood drained from her face as her panic rose. She was jerking the wheel, and her lady bug, as she loved to call it, wasn't doing what it was supposed to.

Everything moved in slow motion. Her instincts told her she was going to crash head-on.

She tightened her hands on the steering wheel, glancing down and seeing her knuckles were white. As she lifted her head, she saw the blue Caddie still coming towards her, hearing its horn blaring.

She saw the old woman in the passenger seat turn her head and scream at her husband. She could see the old man's lips press tight together, knowing, like her, the inevitable was going to happen.

She glanced down at her feet, both were on the brake, pressing down hard. She could hear the screech of the tires and smell the burning rubber.

Somewhere in the recesses of her mind, she waited for her life to flash before her eyes, knowing she was going to die.

She turned her head slightly to the right a faction of a second before impact and saw the bear still standing on its hind legs, almost like he had been trying to warn her.

The cars impacted. The sound of metal screamed as bolts exploded and metal crushed. Paint chips flew in every direction as it popped off the bending metal.

Dakota screamed, closing her eyes as the air bag exploded in her face then instantly deflated after the impact. Her neck snapped back, and then her head and arms jarred forwards and backwards, the seatbelt locking her torso in place.

A piece of metal pierced up through her shoulder and into her neck. The console and dashboard pushed forwards, crushing her body and resting on top of her legs. The music continued to play as the crunch, screech, and banging of the metal continued to contort from its original shape. The windshield shattered, but it didn't fall apart. It was a spider web of shattered glass she couldn't see out of.

Finally, everything stopped. Her body heaved into its final resting place. All she could hear was the hissing of some hose that had been disconnected, and the radio still playing.

Oddly, she never realized that people in crisis sometimes have a lot of time to think, and she had the wildest thoughts going through her head. First, she was pissed that she had turned the radio up so loud, because now it was driving her crazy. Dakota just wanted to turn the damn thing down. Then she realized she was going to be late for her appointment at Fairfield School. She had come up with the neatest game to help Miss Rutherford incorporate little James into her music class. She had just purchased some expensive instruments, and hoped they survived the crash. Dakota wondered about the older couple. How had they fared in this heap of twisted metal?

Suddenly, the music stopped and ringing began. Damn, her phone was on Bluetooth, ringing through the speakers. How had her phone survived all the jostling and smashing?

It continued to ring, and all she could think was, *Sorry, I can't come to the phone right now. I'm a little tied up.* She huffed out a breath that would have been a huge fit of laughter if it didn't hurt so much.

She believed her mind had snapped. She was so totally and officially certifiable that she should be committed. No one should have such bizarre thoughts after being in an accident.

She pulled her thoughts together and tried to move. Oh, no, that was so not happening. Dakota would have to leave that to the professionals. Maybe a cute fireman would untangle her from this mess? It would be just her luck to have a hot firefighter rescue her while she looked like shit and was acting crazy. She was destined to be alone the rest of her life.

With everything else going on inside her head, she had another funny thought. The car didn't even resemble her car anymore, yet the radio still worked, playing, "What Hurts the Most" by Rascal Flatts. The irony wasn't lost on her. If she could, she would have laughed.

It was amazing how life took different turns. Just over a month ago, Dakota had been in Scotland, celebrating one of her closest friends, Gabriella's, wedding. Dakota had the time of her life, and she realized it was because she had the most amazing group of friends.

They referred to one another as The Sistas of The United Nations, because each of the girls' parents were from different parts of the world. Dakota's own heritage was Native American on her mother's side, and French from her père's side. The eclectic group of women were as different personality-wise, as each of their unique cultural backgrounds, and Dakota adored every one of them.

Gabriella's husband Liam was one of the personal bodyguards to one of England's princes. The friends had adopted the king's youngest son, Edward, and his girlfriend Gillian into their sistahood. He was their honorary "chick with a dick." He fit in beautifully with the group because of his amazing sense of humour and his eagerness to get to know each of them.

Edward and Dakota had developed an early friendship through Skype when he solicited her help to organize a bachelorette party for Gabriella.

Dakota's cheeks still hurt when she smiled or laughed because of all the smiling she had done in Scotland. She fondly remembered the humorous antics her friends had gotten caught up in while they were all together. Thanks to Edward, Dakota and her friends got to spend two weeks together of uninterrupted catching up and celebrating.

She caught herself remembering something that had happened and burst out laughing. Now that she was home, though, it all seemed like a dream.

Dakota had never expected to visit Scotland's Balmoral Castle, the vacation home of the King of England, let alone attend Gabriella's wedding there. Edward had hosted and organized the wedding, and it had been a surreal experience.

The memories would be forever ingrained in her mind. Dakota would treasure the peace that settled in her heart from knowing that, after all the tragedy in Gabriella's life, her friend was finally getting her happy ending.

Life had been anything but calm since she had returned. The week after they all returned from the wedding, another one of her friends, Francesca, had been hospitalized after being hurt by one of her students.

The student had panicked after injuring Francesca and ran away. All the girls, plus Francesca's boyfriend, had been part of the search party. They had found the student, and Francesca had just returned to work after spending three weeks recovering.

Dakota often wondered how women who didn't have a group of strong females surrounding and supporting one another survived. *No that wasn't true,* she told herself. She was her sister Koko's only real female friend.

Koko was Dakota's identical twin sister, and although they looked alike, their personalities couldn't have been more different.

People always described Dakota as a free spirit, embracing both of her cultures. But she was drawn to the Native American culture and had spent the last five years learning everything she could about it. She had researched and studied animal totems, the meaning and construction of drumming, shamans, and medicine men, strongly believing in the Great Spirit. And she had adopted the theory that all natural things were a part of the fabric of the universe.

She was open and accepting of things she couldn't explain yet felt in her heart. She took traditional concepts from her French side and mixed it with her spiritual understandings from her Native side, blending both worlds until she was happy with the spirituality she had chosen for herself.

Even her choice of clothing told the story of her beliefs. At work, she wore long, flowing skirts or chino pants; and loose, feminine tops, matched with Native American accents. After work and on dress-down Fridays, she wore jeans with tank tops, draped over with shirts that had Native designs, buffalo skull prints, feathers, or animals. She finished off the look with capes, leather vests, or buckskin jackets.

When Dakota went out clubbing with her girls or on dates, she had sexy dresses with a flare, still staying true to her own style. What pulled this outwardly Native theme together was her beaded jewelry and chokers, along with silver necklaces. She never wore just one piece of jewelry; Dakota liked to layer them, the necklaces in different lengths, and at least three bracelets adorned one wrist, one always being a leather cuff, and then chunky beaded bracelets.

She never wore high heels. They just weren't her thing. If she wasn't in a pair of funky sandals, she loved to wear leather knee-high boots or calf-hugging suede boots, with fringes.

Dakota had more than a dozen satchels made of natural fibres, with long straps that crossed her body. She had never owned a designer purse in her life. She didn't need a lot of compartments because she only ever carried her wallet and bronzed coloured lip gloss.

Like her mother's people, she had long, straight, jet black hair; dark brown, almond-shaped eyes; with softly arched eyebrows. From her French side, Dakota had inherited her delicate fine bone structure and tiny nose. She never wore nail polish and kept her nails short on her dainty hands.

With the mixture of her two cultures, she wasn't brown-skinned like most Native Americans. She had skin that looked like it was kissed by the sun.

Her smile completed the exotic look. Her face lit up when her apple cheeks lifted, softening the crinkles of her large brown eyes. Her spirit and her beauty were as captivating as her outlook on life. People were drawn to her like a moth to a flame.

Koko, on the other hand, was the opposite in her beliefs. She didn't believe in any higher power. She worshipped the money tree. She gravitated to her père's French culture, and unlike Dakota, never admitted to her Native American background, believing it lowered her status.

The twins' names were Native, but if anyone asked about Koko's name, she always said she was named after Coco Chanel.

Koko was all about high fashion, money, influence, and power. She was the head buyer for an exclusive clothing chain, Oh Là Là Très Chic, and was a walking billboard for the store. She had put countless hours and effort into her career to get to her prestigious position. She had climbed over a lot of people to get to the top, and she was ruthless when she wanted something. How the world perceived Koko was very important to her. She wanted people to envy her status in life.

She walked the walk, and talked the talk.

Koko was a fashionista and dressed to the nines every day. Elegant dresses, tight skirts, perfectly pressed blouses, only designer jackets and blazers, stiletto shoes that cost as much as Dakota's rent. Koko owned eighty-six different designer purses in every colour, textile, and animal skin ever made. She referred to them as her babies and carried a special hook that she attached to a table so her babies never had to touch the dirty floor.

Koko's makeup regime was intense, but the results were breathtaking. She had perfected every makeup technique out there. Her flawless face matched whatever ensemble she wore on her body. Men didn't take a double look. No, they stopped dead in their tracks. They followed her every move until she was out of sight, and then wiped the drool off their chin.

Although polar opposites, the twins were close. They were each other's best friend and support system through their whole childhood.

They had gone their separate ways after high school. Koko went to school in the United States at Kent University in Ohio, where she had gotten a BA in fashion and textiles. Dakota had stayed in Canada and got her degree as a Therapeutic Recreation Specialist from Brock University in St. Catharines.

The girls developed friendships within their own chosen

environments, and although their friends didn't mix, they remained a staple in each other's lives.

Dakota had met the sistas when she had done an internship at Reach Within Centre. The centre was a community-based organization, providing services for special needs children and adults, as well as their families in the greater Toronto area.

After graduation, Reach Within had offered her a position to join their team to work in conjunction with the schools some of her clients attended. Dakota set up programs for the special needs students that were integrated into those mainstream schools. She assisted the teachers in programming non-traditional methods using art, sports, music, and drama. Dakota loved her job and the kids, or clients, as she was supposed to refer to them, and couldn't wait to get to work every day.

The cross over between her Native studies and non-conventional teaching strategies blessed her with challenging and rewarding results with the students. Last semester's goal was to teach sequencing and importance of timing, getting the students to make their own drums, and then teaching them rhythm and patterns achieved her goal. The students had fun while learning the importance of waiting to hit their drum in sequence to create better sound.

This semester's goal was the value of music and how it related to colour. She wanted to determine if one of her deaf students could learn to appreciate music through vibrations and visual stimulation of different colours. She would soon find out.

All previous thoughts dissipated. Her thoughts of the wedding changed to her dire situation, knowing she was seriously hurt in her mangled vehicle. The song was now on its fourth rotation. Somehow, the playlist must have switched to repeat instead of shuffling.

She listened quietly to the words of "What Hurts the Most," reminding her of why it was on her playlist. Every time the musician drew his bow down against the strings of the violin, the haunting sound sliced through her heart. When Dakota had first heard the song, she had thought the writer had experienced the same heartbreak as her.

Dakota had been drawn to the song after her breakup with Caden. Every word described how she felt about ending her relationship with him. She could sing every word and often cranked the volume to sing out loud and share the composer's pain. Tears filled her eyes at knowing she would never get over the loss of Caden.

Dakota had recently started dating Brayden. Maybe he would be the one to help her mend her broken heart? If not, she would continue to search. However, she had promised herself she needed to at least give Brayden a chance.

She had to stop comparing all her dates to Caden. Yes, he had been everything she wanted and more … in the beginning. Then he had betrayed her in the worst way.

Trust wasn't something she gave out easily anymore. Most men weren't willing to go the extra mile to earn it.

Uh-oh, now she smelled gasoline. She wondered if her lady bug was going to explode.

Caden had always told her that cars didn't explode like they did on TV. Geez, she hoped he hadn't lied to her about that, like he had everything else.

Be nice, Dakota. You could be dying. Is this how you want to meet the Great Spirit, by trashing the love of your life.

She heard someone talking and pulled herself away from her thoughts.

"Ma'am? Ma'am, are you okay? I'm going to crawl in your back window. Don't be frightened. I am here to help."

That sounded just like Caden. Her mind must be playing tricks on her after thinking about the man.

Dakota heard glass falling, and some grunts and groans as the man tried to manipulate his way through the back window of her lady bug.

"Ma'am? Ma'am, are you okay? I'm an off-duty paramedic. Is it okay that I help you? I know it sounds silly, but I have to ask," her rescuer asked as he crawled into the backseat behind her.

She squeaked out her response, using her voice for the first time since the accident. "Please don't call me ma'am. I'm only twenty-seven. And, yeah, I could use a little help here. I hope you didn't damage my back window getting in here."

She heard him gruffly laugh at her response.

"Nope, definitely think I helped. Now you have unobstructed sunshine. Miss, I'm going to—Holy fuck, Dakota? Aw, baby girl, what the hell happened?"

"Caden?"

Made in the USA
Charleston, SC
14 December 2016